TIGERMAN

Nick Harkaway was born in Cornwall in 1972. He likes deckled edges, wine and breathtaking views. He does not like anchovies or reality television. He lives in London with his wife and two children.

Praise for *Tigerman*

'His great gift as a novelist – one he shares with writers such as China Miéville, Lauren Beukes and even Eleanor Catton – is to merge the pace, wit and clarity of the best "popular" literature with the ambition, complexity and irony of the so-called "literary" novel.'

Stuart Kelly, *Guardian*

'Every sentence is perfect, every idea has weight and force and you can't put the damn thing down. The last chapter shattered me. Nick's last two books were outstanding, but *Tigerman* throws him into completely new territory.'

Joe Hill

'Harkaway occupies that enviable territory where books of a speculative nature intersect with the mainstream . . . *Tigerman*, is his best yet, a funny, moving and thought-provoking tale with very localised apocalyptic overtones . . . it's brilliant.'

Independent on Sunday

'A very traditional, almost Wodehousian English satire . . . Tigerman is about the often unspoken affection between fathers and sons, how the feelings are felt no less keenly for being unsaid and can provoke fathers to perform heroic acts. However, it also serves as a cautionary tale of the dangers of not sharing those feelings sooner . . . A captivating read.'

SciFiNow

'Extraordinary . . . The action sequences in Tigerman are some of Harkaway's best. As ever, the writing is economical but lively, revelling in modern idiom . . . [Has] the cinematic scope and dynamism one has come to expect from Harkaway . . . The ending of Tigerman is pitch-perfect, thrilling and dramatic.'

Literary Review

'Tedious is the last word you could use to describe [Harkaway's] writing . . . He tops his intellect in a ring-master's hat. But for all the entertainment to be had from the reading, the serious stuff is in there . . . Harkaway is a writer who nests big ideas inside bigger ideas.'

Herald

'Harkaway has crafted an engaging story that examines the nature of heroes and the tropes of old-school pulp fiction, mixing sharp characterisation with an energetic portrait of a society heading for apocalypse . . . Often hilarious but with an undercurrent of dark violence, this is an impressive novel that conceals provocative questions inside an old-school tale of ripping adventure.'

SFX

NICK HARKAWAY

TIGERMAN

✺ WINDMILL BOOKS

Published by Windmill Books 2015

2 4 6 8 10 9 7 5 3 1

Copyright © Nick Harkaway 2014

Nick Harkaway has asserted his right under the Copyright, Designs and
Patents Act, 1988, to be identified as the author of this work.

First published in Great Britain in 2014 by William Heinemann

Windmill Books
The Random House Group Limited
20 Vauxhall Bridge Road, London SW1V 2SA

Addresses for companies within The Random House Group Limited can
be found at: www.randomhouse.co.uk/offices.htm

The Random House Group Limited Reg. No. 954009

www.randomhouse.co.uk

A CIP catalogue record for this book
is available from the British Library

ISBN 9780099591757

Typeset in Fournier MT by Palimpsest Book Production Ltd,
Falkirk, Stirlingshire
Printed and bound by CPI Group (UK) Ltd, Croydon, CR0 4YY

For Clemency:
I knew I wanted to be a father.
I didn't know how much
until I was.

'My father had formed one of those
close English friendships with him
(the first adjective is perhaps excessive)
that begin by excluding confidences
and soon eliminate conversation.'

Jorge Luis Borges,
Tlön, Uqbar, Orbis Tertius

1. Pelican

O n the steps of the old mission house, the Sergeant sat with the boy who called himself Robin, and watched a pigeon being swallowed by a pelican.

The whole business had come as a surprise to everyone involved, not least of all it seemed to the pelican herself, who had engaged in the attempt almost absently and now appeared to be wishing it was over and done. She was by nature a placid bird, slow to take wing and hard to rile, but the pigeon had been presuming on her good nature for several months now, scooting between her and the pieces of bread that people tossed in her direction as they wandered by, fluttering down to snatch treats of fish almost from her beak.

This morning, the pelican had had enough, and when the pigeon came between her and a bit of tuna, she had just opened to the fullest extent and engulfed the fish fragment and the pigeon both, to squawks of outrage and alarm from her antagonist. To the Sergeant's eye, her swollen gullet had possessed at that moment the dreamy smugness of a trick well played, but he acknowledged inwardly that the faces of birds were impenetrable, so it could as well have been the foreknowledge of indigestion.

The boy had been very impressed, which is to say that — contrary to established practice — he put down the comic book he was reading on the wall beside him and stared, his attention entirely taken up by the drama unfolding. The Sergeant had never seen him do this before. Even last year, when the volcano had briefly erupted and ash and fire had been falling all around, and the Sergeant had scooped him up under one arm and run like hell for the shelter of a convenient cellar, the boy had retained a desperate grip on *Planetary* no. 7, and clamped his other hand to the elderly Nokia cellphone which he kept in his left hip pocket.

These items were the only evidence that someone else cared for him. The phone kept working and every so often he had a new comic, worn about the edges but with all its pages, and rarely more than three months out of date. Sometimes he carried a knapsack which contained several at once, when the supply had been irregular and he'd been hoarding two or three while waiting for the previous issue, so as not to have things happen out of order. He was very particular about continuity, he had told the Sergeant in so many words. Events should happen in their proper time.

'Otherwise the story will not work,' he said. 'Totally bogus narrative structure. WTF?' He actually spoke the letters 'WTF', and rolled his eyes.

That was just how it was. The boy's English was self-taught and uneven, peppered with guest appearances from movies and TV, from online games whose players were in America, Europe and China. When he spoke he could shift in one moment from the manner of a too-serious Harvard freshman to that of a teenaged Shanghai gold-farmer sweating in a vast warehouse of machines.

On the topic of stories and character, he was particularly donnish and sniffy: 'There must be development-over-time or it is just noise.' And when it appeared that the Sergeant was not entirely following this line of discussion – it was one of their earlier conversations and the older man's education in these matters was not yet properly begun – he had changed tack and demanded whether the Sergeant might have any lightweight twine that would work for a kite string. Which he had, and had happily given up.

The pigeon's head disappeared, and the noises of protest from the pelican's throat began to fade. The boy picked up the comic again and read with his usual intensity. The Sergeant leaned back against the stone in such a way as to suggest that the affair had been nothing special, though in all honesty he'd never seen anything to compare with it.

They were an unlikely twosome. The man was of medium height and craggy. He was still six months shy of forty, but he looked fatigued and even a little lost. His face was leathered by a life of actual soldiering in inclement places, and he had scars, about which he was self-conscious. Scars were supposed to be narrow white lines which looked raffish, not puckered worms slithering forever across your shoulder and itching abominably. They should be discreet, so that a man could boast about them to girls. He was thickset – and some of that was this recent bout of soft living, he had to concede, even if the rest was working heft – but he seemed to move carefully, as if the world was fragile and he didn't want to break it.

The boy meanwhile was androgynous in the way of boys, with no fat on his body at all, and scruffy black hair cut short. He seemed to be interested in everything, had a restless intelligence which might even qualify as genius. The Sergeant guessed his age as between ten and fourteen, but could not narrow the range. There was dust on him always, and often grass stains or splashes of oil. His forearms were corded with child's muscle from whatever work it was that he did – and it seemed he did a bit of everything – when he wasn't reading comic books and spending time with his friend. He wore a long smock which was rather too big on his shoulders, so that on a bad day he looked like a match-stick man in a lampshade. In the late-afternoon light and under the cracked façade of the mission house, he resembled a monk, and the Sergeant expected him at any moment to lift his head and preach from the Book of Superman. Chapter 9, verse 21: *the world shall know thee as a blur and as a sign upon the heavens, as a hope and an earnest of good things.*

3

When the boy had finished reading, he looked up to assure himself that nothing of importance was taking place with the pelican, and then glanced over at the Sergeant. It was the hour of the day when they usually went to Shola's and took tea. The island of Mancreu had very few customs left, but tea had somehow clung on, and of all the cafés and bars – and as far as these two were concerned the remaining living rooms and campsites and samovars as well – Shola's made the best tea. Shola had a proper kettle and he didn't leave the dregs in the pot or the scale in the water. He was a dandy and a gambler, but he knew tea.

The Sergeant had left his car at the fish market, ten minutes away along the seafront. This was also customary. Walking along the front allowed him to say hello to everyone. The afternoon greeting was important for social order. Like tea, a British sergeant taking his ease along the promenade was a solid, familiar thing. It said that there was still sense in the world. In theory, of course, the British presence here had been withdrawn three years ago, claims of sovereignty having been yielded to the NATO and Allied Protection Force on Mancreu, NatProMan. The Sergeant was technically the senior officer (albeit non-commissioned) in the United Kingdom's Mancreu Command, and as a side job he was senior consular staff member, too. 'Just don't issue any bloody passports without checking the rules,' the actual Consul had told him as he left, 'and for Christ's sake don't let anyone talk you into signing any treaties.'

'Could I?' the Sergeant asked.

'No,' the Consul said. 'But you could make a frightful mess, so don't. Take the keys, enjoy the house, and rest up. I understand that's why you're here. Just nod to everyone and don't annoy Kershaw at NatProMan and this'll all be done in a few months. They can't keep the place around much longer. It'll be nice for you.'

'Yes, sir.'

Saying hello, therefore, was the greater part of the Sergeant's official function. He was to keep the consulate open and ensure that assistance was forthcoming to any British citizens who needed it, though this essentially meant calling the British Embassy in Yemen, and in any case had never actually been required. In many ways his real job was simply to occupy Brighton House, the sprawling, haunted old manse on a hill overlooking Beauville – the only town of any size on the island – which had in former times been the seat of colonial power. With its back to the mountains and the jungle, and its pocked face to the sea, Brighton House was almost identical to every British holding in the various candle ends of Empire – even if perhaps the coming destruction of the island did make it dolefully unique.

And so these were his days, week in and week out, and had been for more than two years: walk, take tea, and say hello. As the inheritor of what remained of British authority, he could additionally marry anyone who for some unlikely reason wanted him to officiate rather than a local priest, and he could facilitate adoptions and divorces for EU passport holders. Other than that, he could if he chose investigate local crime at the behest of a relevant person (it was unclear who was relevant so he tended to interpret this according to his lights) and he had the right to sit in on NatProMan Strategic Board meetings as representative of the United Kingdom – which had chosen firmly to abrogate such representation and therefore he was under orders not to.

Seen on the map, the island of Mancreu was a double arc, the shape of a seagull sketched by a child. The central segment, the beak, was thirty miles deep, the wingspan perhaps a hundred. Along the concave edges, mountains reared out of the restive water of the Arabian Sea. Mancreu was a first-and-last isle perched on the lip of the great mid-ocean ridge, midway between Socotra and the Chagos Islands. The people were an unbothered ethnic jumble of Arab and African and Asian, with the inevitable admixture of Europeans. France and Britain had held Mancreu alternately for centuries, with the French coming off considerably better, until late in the Victorian period it fell almost by accident under the Union Flag once more, and British it had remained thereafter, far flung and mentioned mostly in the footnotes.

To the north, the water grew pale green and warm. To the south, it turned blue, the bottom falling away into a frigid darkness which was the site of the indigenous population's hell. The south coast was known to be peopled with demons: fish-finned men and feral women ruled by Jack the Wrecker, Mancreu's resident fairy king. Bad Jack was capricious. If the milk turned, Jack had molested the cow. If you left honey on the doorstep, Jack might trade it for cash or rum or even a hunting rifle. He was known to rescue lost travellers, but also to rob them, and if a ship went down in bad weather, well, no doubt Jack had stood on the cliff with his lantern and seen it onto the rocks for spite. He was, in other words, the warm-water image of every bogeyman up and down the British coast, and likewise an object of knowing derision until the night drew in, after which people were discreetly more circumspect. Bad Jack, *Mauvais Jacques*, Jack Storm-eye – and even, by some strange twist, Jack of the Nine, the bitter memory of a colonial governor's justice.

The name, Mancreu, had been given by mariners grateful for the sandy beaches on the lee side. Those early sailors thought the island was an image of the Grail carved into the face of the Earth. On embroidered pieces of canvas cloth, sometimes crude, sometimes alarmingly intricate and ethereal, they showed Mancreu as the curved palms of the Virgin catching the blood of Christ. In Beauville, this perception was still a matter of known fact. Elsewhere in the world it was less well understood, but from time to time a ship out of North

Africa would put in, crewed by tyro seamen from missionary towns baked dry and starving, and somewhere near the bow would be a benediction in French:

Hail, Madonna of the Gull's Wing. Hail, Madonna. Let your mark be upon us sinners, and your voice upon the deep. Bid the blue water roll softly. Speak to the clouds and hold their thunder. Guard us from men of ill-intent and from plagues and sorrows. Hail, Madonna. Hear us, Madonna. Bring us home.

There was still a scrivener's office on the harbour front, where a holy sign-painter hung his papal warrant. He was an albino – or something like it – named Raoul. He was subject to strange infirmities, either in consequence of his condition or from overuse of magic inks, but was said in person to be magnetic, like a poet or a prophet. He was also said to have been a mercenary, a leader of men, or perhaps a great pirate before the calling found him and the writing of God's word on ships became his life. The Sergeant had never ventured into his lair. It was his experience that one did poorly by involving oneself in matters of local religion. The world looked one way if you believed, and another if you did not, and that was all there was to it.

The scrivener's beautiful daughter was famous around Beauville, and famously out of bounds. White Raoul's girl: what might the father do, should her heart be broken? Or worse: should harm befall her? What might he not do? Take down his sign, for sure, and close his shop – but what else? Might he not write maledictions with the same strength as blessings? Or call upon whatever armies he once commanded to avenge her tears? Might not the papal warrant, conferred in the name of mercy, give equal prominence in God's eyes to a father's rage? Beautiful Sandrine must live a lonely life, uncourted and unkissed, because it was not known where Raoul's disapprovals might begin. The Sergeant had never seen her. He wondered sometimes if she were a myth, a sort of running joke on the big foreigner. More likely he'd walked past her a dozen times and not realised it,

7

and her beauty was more to be found in its own fame than in her face.

'Tea,' the boy said firmly.

They walked together in silence to the dented, oil-stinking old Land Rover which served as the Sergeant's official military conveyance. He unlocked his own door and threw the keys across the roof to the boy – if the car had ever possessed a central locking system it was long defunct – who caught them and let himself in, then ducked into the passenger seat and passed them back without looking. The older man felt the keys land in his palm and inserted the right one into the ignition even as his foot pressed the brake. When the engine spluttered a little unwillingly and the cabin jerked they were neither of them caught off guard, and a mutual puff of air through pursed lips expressed disapproval of this automotive weakness.

The friendship he had with the boy was one of a small number the Sergeant had established on Mancreu. He had not expected to find any, but his tenure had endured far beyond original estimates and an infantryman alone was a profoundly unnatural thing. Infantry was by definition an army, a river of soldiers which washed up and over and could not be stopped. It was your family and your friends and the way you lived and most of all it meant you were never by yourself. Somewhat less so for an NCO, perhaps, whose responsibility it was to get the job done, harry and cajole the lads in the right direction, then haul them home again in one piece, so far as any of these things was possible. Rank made you a little bit a stranger, but also gave you new roles to fill: uncle, nursemaid, gaffer, big brother, pastor, best mate and headmaster – that was a sergeant. One thing you never were was short of conversation.

On Mancreu he had no platoon to look after. Brighton House was vast and empty. There were two ballrooms in the east wing, both dim and sheeted. On his third day he had unwrapped a leather armchair in one of the drawing rooms so that he could sit, and discovered over those early weeks that he rather liked the quiet. In fact, he could spend ages in it. He had found it hard at first to listen without tracking things, without placing them and knowing them for friend or enemy, but gradually that automatic classification had faded away and he was left with rustling leaves and waves and a cowbell somewhere far off, and the idling of a fisherman's outboard in the choppy water beneath the cliff. He walked the endless corridors on the upper floors alone, wondering what the rooms had seen. There was a local bird with a quite infuriating cry like a sneeze, and he amused himself by saying 'bless you' whenever he heard it. Occasionally he thanked himself on behalf of the bird. After a while he found that he could forget the clock and even dismiss memory and awareness almost entirely, fade into the scenery and let his senses be everything that there was of him. It was wonderful.

On other days, though, the lack of amiable chatter drove him mad. The sound of his footsteps bounced around inside his head as if he was Brighton House itself, empty and dry and dismal and waiting for a renewal which would never come. He might, from time to time, visit his French counterpart on the island for a drink. Dirac, representing the absence of Gallic interest in doings on Mancreu, was good company, but quite often he was busy because he had several lovers in Beauville and was always on the lookout for more. The Sergeant supposed that this was in keeping with appropriate French post-colonial behaviour, just as walking the beat and taking tea was for himself. All the same, on those Sargasso days he needed company, and – this being the shape of things and he being who he was – it was inevitable that he should have become involved with the Beauville Boxing Club. A boxing ring was a place where strangers could get to know one another, where awkwardness did not figure. You didn't have to be polite, or funny, or diplomatic. You didn't even have to be a decent boxer, although he was. You just had to show some good heart and sooner or later the club would take you in or it wasn't a proper club. There were always personalities, of course, but they came after the boxing, they happened outside the ring. Those things tended to resolve themselves, especially if you didn't have much to prove.

And it was just as inevitable, given his official position and his advanced age in the eyes of the local champions, that upon his arrival at the cool half-basement which served the Beauville club as its headquarters he should instantly be accorded the status of referee. He had intended to do a little sparring here and there, even arrange some friendly fights to keep himself fresh, but there was almost no one who would get in the ring with him. It was a no-win situation for the younger boxers. If he was a poor fighter, they might lay out the Brevet-Consul, a middle-aged geezer with a dodgy guard and weak ribs. Sure, there'd be no real consequences, but they had no way of knowing that, and in any case it would be a piss-poor sort of victory to carry around. On the other hand it was not impossible – not impossible at all, given the build of the man and the power in his legs – that they might lose, get flattened by a fellow who could just as well be a senior citizen as far as the streets of Mancreu were concerned. Neither option was appealing to the muscular fishermen and farmers who boxed here.

Which left him with Shola the café-owner and Pechorin of NatProMan.

Shola was tall and lean and an outrageous boaster. To hear him tell it he had loved every pretty woman between Bangkok and Tehran and all of them missed him terribly. He dressed like a pirate, or a drug dealer from an old American movie, and he worried a great deal about his hair, but he could hit fast and straight when you weren't expecting it. He was an enjoyable opponent, filled with humour and ready enough to step back before a bout got past the point of good fun. His torso – like all of them he boxed without a shirt – was enviably beautiful, hard lines and ripples. He spoke with a faint French-North African lilt, but he was Mancreu born, his family washed up in the early 1900s, and a century later they were still here.

His manner invited confidences and friendship. 'But when will you go?' the Sergeant had asked, as they soaked in the club's whirlpool after thirty minutes of ducking and jabbing. By the upside-down logic of Mancreu it was the first question between new friends, like a schoolboy's 'what's your favourite team?' and with the same cautious offer of alliance.

Shola rolled his head along his endless shoulders, and sighed. 'No idea. When it is time, you know? When it is good and time. But for me there is nowhere *to* go, now. No other island like this in all the blue oceans of the world. Caribbean is all over hotels. Maldives are sinking and half of the people want women to wear veils. No music, because that might lead to dancing. I will go to El Hierro, maybe. It's in the Atlantic. Very long way. But I think when it's time I'll go and see El Hierro. Maybe me and that island could fall in love a little bit. Always room for the right bar on the right island. There's carnival there. And lizards, man! Big lizards!' He held his hands apart, and grinned.

'But when?'

Shola shrugged. 'Not today. There's still people here today. And not tomorrow, either. I have bookings for lunch. Maybe next week, if I get around to it.' Which he obviously wouldn't.

'Don't wait too long.' The Brit abroad is always the voice of caution. Persons of other cultures are known to be undisciplined, prone to leaning out of car windows and cooking with garlic. The Sergeant had shed the perception as far as he could, but the traces of it occasionally embarrassed him even now. He cringed.

'Lester,' Shola said happily, 'you are an old woman. You know that? But you box like a rhinoceros. They teach you that at sergeant school? I think I have broken my hand on your head.' And then the laugh, a huge laugh which said: *yes, of course, I will be your friend*.

The other man, Pechorin, could not have been more different. He was a squat Ukrainian, and sullen, as if whatever place he went offended him on arrival. He was not so much a boxer as a hitter. After a few tentative engagements he could be guaranteed to lose his temper, and his hallmark combination would come out: double jab, cross, hook hook hook and on and on until the hooks became haymakers, and he could never understand how everyone slipped the last punch and got behind his guard. The Sergeant did not often box with Pechorin, but when it was inevitable he adopted a sort of mirror posture, never letting the man land anything on him, never provoking him, until the referee declared a winner on points. There was no point asking him when he would leave, because he was here on deployment. He would leave when he was ordered to, and he cared nothing one way or the other. In any case, Pechorin was not comfortable in the whirlpool with other men's bodies on display, so he was never there.

Shola's café was where the Sergeant had first encountered the boy. It had been the second week after his official investiture as Brevet-Consul, and his second visit to the place after meeting its owner in the ring. His arrival this time was the intentional sort of accident. He had been ambling along the shady streets on what was either a reconnaissance or a stroll, thinking he just might pop in but then again perhaps he wouldn't, but as he approached to within a few steps of the door and considered walking on by, Mancreu performed one of its seasonal lurches and the rain started: explosive golf balls of water, gentle at first but growing rapidly more weighty and numerous. He glanced up, saw no relief, and dashed inside.

He was greeted by a burst of mirth – a drenched foreigner is always hilarious – and ushered in. Shola himself had been absent that day, but the barman, Pero, had known him for a friend of the boss and bawled for the good kettle. The result had been a pungent caravan tea, bitter and startlingly good. Better, in fact, than any he could remember drinking pretty much anywhere, although some part of him wondered if that might not have more to do with his memory and his recent history than the tea itself.

He lounged and exhaled, and felt some small part of himself relax, like the moment when the elastic band on a child's toy plane, wound and wound until the twisting redoubles upon itself and then let go to power the propeller, spasms once and releases that second layer of knots. He stretched backwards over his chair, and when he looked down again he noticed vaguely a boy, also drinking tea, sitting in the corner with a comic book. Beside the boy was a big, blocky mobile telephone in grey plastic. It was so old it had a visible aerial.

The Sergeant drank his first pot dry very quickly and ordered another, and some bread and butter. These also turned out to be excellent – the butter was a pale vanilla froth which spread onto the sourdough and lifted it to something like the level of the tea.

By the time he had finished the bread, the rain was worse, battering on the corrugated-iron roof; rain in the tropical style, by the gallon, with the force of a fist. It was loud, but not unpleasant because Shola had padded the interior of the roof with bags of sheep's wool. The noise was muffled rather than entirely blocked, but the wool meant sitting in the place during a storm was like listening to a troop of mounted horse on the road rather than being inside a giant metal drum. More customers were coming in, cursing and laughing, water streaming from their faces and sloshing from their shoes.

The Sergeant smiled an occasional greeting when someone made eye contact with him, drank his tea, and listened. Like the boy, he had a mobile telephone, a bulky, simple thing with large buttons and a big battery which went on for days. It was next to his tea. At some point – he wasn't sure when, the action was automatic – he had inserted the battery and switched the device on. He had to do this because except in emergencies he did not travel in-country with a live phone. It was a residual proscription, pointless here, where anyone who was looking for him could just come to the house, but it went against the grain to reveal his location while he was on the move. He restricted the phone's sign-ins to those places he was known to go and otherwise kept it inert, so that an enemy seeking him in transit must identify him by sight and in person, and risk a comparable exposure.

He took another sip of tea and idly, with his left hand, traced the outline of a deep gouge in the tabletop. It had probably been made with the sight of a handgun. An idiotic thing to do, a lousy use for a gun and bad practice for a soldier, but of course any number of people who had sat in this place with handguns had probably not been soldiers, and many of them – soldiers or not – had undoubtedly been idiots. You couldn't look at Mancreu and imagine that the island hadn't seen more than its fair share.

The rain stopped, and a few minutes later the Sergeant came to the end of his tea and of his introspection, and at the same time the boy apparently concluded that he had read and reread his comic book as much as he wanted to. The Sergeant reached for his phone to remove the battery, and was aware of an immediate sharpening of interest and a searchlight intensity in the air.

He kept his hands very much on the table, and softened his shoulders. He didn't want anyone to make any mistakes about how relaxed he was, how calm, and how he did not intend to reach for his side arm. He wondered who had come in, and how they had done it without making any noise, without the light from the door falling across him. Perhaps they had come from inside the bar, from the private rooms.

He looked up and found the boy watching him, eyes shadowed, body almost entirely wrapped in the dark of his corner table. The bodyguard's table, the Sergeant called it in his mind, a table he would not have chosen to sit at because he didn't want to be known as a man who kept his eye on the door. It was enough that he was a soldier. He didn't want the people of Beauville to think of him reckoning each drinker, making sure he could kill them if he had to. Though of course some part of him did all those things, in the back of his mind, registered newcomers and regulars, weighed them and categorised them, so that if it ever came to it – whatever 'it' was – he would know whether to stand or flee, how many could he take down, what would it cost him, and how bad would it get.

Very bad, was the answer, always. One way or another: very bad.

The Sergeant kept his eyes on the boy – not aggressive, just interested – and the boy looked back at him in exactly the same way, reassessing, cataloguing, considering. Why? Where did this stark, sudden appraisal come from? The boy was part of the landscape, a customer. The Sergeant had a vague notion he had glimpsed him before: getting out of a coracle on the waterfront; running errands and bringing messages; sitting and reading. Why was he allowing himself to be visible, exposing himself by this close, intrusive scrutiny? The Sergeant had pegged him as smart and jittery and possibly traumatised. So. What now?

The boy's body was very still, a mirror of his own demonstrative calm, and the Sergeant, changing the focus of his attention without changing the position of his eyes, followed the line of one scrawny shoulder down to the hands. Then after a moment he snorted approvingly. He relaxed, and felt as much as saw the boy doing the same. For all their physical differences, in this moment they were identical: backs straight, heads slightly forward as they prepared to push themselves to their feet. And each of them was holding his phone's battery in preparation for putting it away, in a separate pocket. A twin paranoia. A wise man does not catalogue his road home.

The boy nodded to him. The Sergeant nodded back.

'You are smart,' the boy said.

'You too.'

The boy nodded.

'You like comics?' the Sergeant asked, then heard the echo of the question and saw his own child self shaking his head at the stupidest thing ever said by man.

15

But the boy was gracious, respecting the gambit for what it was. 'Yes.'

'Which ones?'

'All. Some DC, for Batman. Grant Morrison! But mostly Marvel. Warren Ellis. Also Spurrier, and Gail Simone. Bendis is full of win.'

The Sergeant grinned. He had never heard this expression before, but he approved of it. *Full of win*. It had a digital flavour, merry and modern. More things should be full of win.

'I like Green Lantern,' he said.

'Which one?' the boy demanded.

Oh, sod it. Now he remembered: there were so many Lanterns to choose from, and always changing, and the wrong one was like the wrong football team, the wrong church . . . 'Hal Jordan,' he said, dredging up the name.

'That is totally Old School,' the boy approved. 'Jordan is bad ass.' He separated the words: *bad ass*. The Sergeant suspected he had learned them by reading. He wondered which comics allowed that sort of language, and realised: probably all of them, these days.

'You like Captain America, too?' the boy asked.

The Sergeant hesitated. 'Not so much,' he admitted. Bright colours and battlefields didn't mix for him. Steve Rogers was an invincible man, an overman who wore what he damn well liked, and survived. It was the men around him who didn't make it. No. The Sergeant did not like Captain America. Perhaps he had once, when he was younger.

The boy nodded as if this was to be expected. 'Batman?'

'Yes.'

'Batman is best. Bob Kane was a god. Also Bill Finger.' The Sergeant had only the dimmest idea who these people were.

The boy seemed to realise that the conversation had become too technical, because he proffered the comic he had been reading. 'Here,' he said. 'Christian Walker is full of win.'

The Sergeant took it, then hesitated. 'How will I get it back to you?'

'I'm around,' the boy said vaguely. 'But there is n.p. – I do not collect them.' The boy stopped, grinned. 'That is not true! I do collect them. But to read, not like a crazy shut-in dude!'

'I'll get it back to you,' the Sergeant promised.

'*Kswah swah*,' the boy replied with a shrug. *What happens, happens*. Very Mancreu. On the Arabian mainland they said *insh'Allah* – if God wills it. If God willed it, you might arrive punctually for your appointments, but generally He willed that you show up more or less on the same day. Time and matter were flexible; only God was real. On Mancreu, even God had somehow faded away. The universe was what it was, mutable and strange, and God had made it in His image, so He too was probably imponderable. The nature of His will varied from soul to soul, and what actually happened often wasn't what anyone understood by it. Perhaps God, being everywhere and seeing all things from outside time, was incapable of willing anything which men could grasp as a plan.

So *insh'Allah* seemed to suppose too much. On Mancreu, you just said: *what happens, happens*. It was practically the national anthem.

When the Sergeant asked what to call him, the boy had glanced away and said 'Robin.' The Sergeant accepted the lie politely, but never adopted it, and as their acquaintanceship grew he avoided sentences that required him to use a name at all. In his mind, his friend was a unique identity, a presence which had no need of a borrowed label to encapsulate it.

Today, with the image of the pelican and the pigeon still causing occasional head-shaking, they left the Land Rover across the road from the café and bowed each other mirthfully across the threshold. It was not unknown for them to spend twenty minutes doing this, each insisting that the other go first, making more and more out-rageous speeches of diplomatic deference. Today, though, they merely tussled, the boy shouting 'Put up your dukes!' and jabbing inexpertly at the Sergeant's stomach until the man acknowledged himself subdued into accepting the honour and entering ahead of his friend. He paused two steps inside to allow his eyes to adjust.

Physically, the café was a single rectangular room, but it had the appearance of an L-shape because one corner was taken up by a rather grand wooden staircase that Shola had salvaged from a defunct hotel. The bar was topped with a sheet of folded copper, very worn and very much polished, and the tables were a hodge-podge of round and square. The rickety chairs were moved from one place to another by customers as they came and went, so that only when the café was absolutely full did anyone have to sit on the perilous yellow typist's stool which Shola kept folded by the bar. Along the walls of the room were benches made from drift-wood, silvered and polished smooth by years of slithering backsides.

In the crook of the staircase, with a patrician view of the door and the bar, there was the *shtammteh*, the table which was by common understanding Shola's own. It was never reserved. It was simply not somewhere you sat unless you were invited. Even the boy and the Sergeant, upon arrival, made a show of dithering and finding a suitable place, and then Shola came and chided them and moved them to the *shtammteh* to take their tea with him.

The new delivery must just have arrived, because Shola served them a rich gunpowder tea which they had never had before, demanding to know what they thought of it. The Sergeant held a long swallow in his mouth, the perfect tempera-ture baking his gums but not burning them, warming his throat and making his whole body feel cooler. He tasted pepper and smoke and the smell of snow. This was not tea. It was some-thing else, a kind of elixir. It was what tea aspired to be.

'It's good,' he said, and saw Shola's mouth twitch in a smile.

The boy rolled his eyes. 'He means totally awesome. This tea is made from hunnertenpercent secret inside-the-door-teaching *tea fu*! It is the daddy of tea. This tea is the tea of Obi-Wan

Kenobi on Tatooine. Every morning: this tea, then lightsaber practice. Strong in the Force!' He made a lightsaber noise. *Vvmwomm, Vvmwomm, TCHA FWSH!*

Shola obligingly refilled his cup. 'I should order more?'

Such an order was a statement of commitment to remain for another month. The boy nodded gravely. 'I will come and drink it.'

Leaving – Leaving with a capital 'L' as opposed to merely going out of a shop or a house – had become a ritual. You couldn't call it a tradition, because it wasn't, would never be, old enough. It was a sort of shared insanity, like cutting your own flesh to·see if it hurt. If you were Leaving, going away from Mancreu and not coming back – and tacitly everyone was Leaving, of course, no one had suggested the population should stay and die when the hammer fell, but still, Leaving before your neighbours was a form of defeat or desertion – then you threw a party. Above all, you had a bonfire, and you burned what you couldn't take with you and couldn't give away. Not just what no one wanted, but the things you couldn't let go of, things you'd rather destroy with your own hand than see shattered by the impossible, cleansing heat that would burn Mancreu down to the rock, to the waterline and the granite on which the island stood, and past even that, down and down into the mantle of the Earth to scour the place of a genera-tion of stupid human abuse.

In the beginning, Leavers had printed posters, spent money on them, tried to sell themselves on a festive atmosphere somewhere between a wake and a christening. *This chapter is over, this world is over, but there is a new one!* But the falseness of it, of forced departure claimed as opportunity, showed through like a broken bone. Now they wrote in white chalk on the black telegraph poles which connected Mancreu's trembling phone network to the exchange: a wide, shamed L and then a time and a place, always after dark, always outside town. The Leavers came first, and the next to arrive were always other Leavers or those who knew they

19

would be, very soon, and then the celebrants, the ones who had outlasted another crop of the weak. People wept and marriages shattered, truths were uttered which should have been kept deep inside. Family heirlooms, beautiful pieces of wooden furniture, jewellery, even pets and livestock burned. This wasn't a clean break. It was *sati* by proxy, and that only because no one had yet been desperate enough, wild enough, sick enough in the heart to step into the flames. But the Sergeant had privately told Jed Kershaw that it was only a matter of time.

He had begun going along to all of them that he could, a sort of inverted ghost at the feast: the man from a cold, wet island which wasn't going to burn. He stood outside the circle of the bonfire light and watched as first-edition books and prized saucepans joined photo albums and cradles on the pyre, put a stop to fights before they became feuds or murders. After the first few Leavings, the tone had shifted to something bacchanalian, and then fatigue had set in and replaced that with a sort of silent goodbye which was almost wholesome. Recently the mood was becoming one of breathless transgression: who could destroy the most valuable thing? Who could show their self-despite most graphically as they betrayed the only home they had ever known?

But his presence seemed to act as a sort of dampener, as if the uniform called everyone to remember that most British of virtues: the stiff upper lip. Or perhaps it was like being a Health & Safety inspector, and no one could really get crazy knowing he was around. He nodded sadly to grandmothers burning their feather mattresses and fishermen burning their coracles, to crab hunters immolating their traps and postmen burning their bicycles. He shook hands with the Leavers and sometimes that meant everyone else could suddenly stand to look at them and even talk to them after all. He was an undertaker, a cypher.

An army chaplain had once told him that she had spent years trying to find the right form of words for the bereaved, only to realise that the clichés were the best. Widows and orphans didn't want to be comforted. They wanted to be recognised.

'You say "it was very quick, he didn't suffer,"' the chaplain had told him. 'You say "I'm sorry for your loss." If you're in a hospital and there's one of those silences which needs breaking you say "I understand, at the end, he felt no pain" and then you fuck off and let them get on with it. If you want to get punched in the eye you say "he's in a better place."'

So the bonfires proceeded in something approximating an orderly fashion, which was almost worse than if they hadn't, and the Sergeant had become a sort of necessary thing: you couldn't have a real Leaving without him. The Last Consul had to be there to set the official seal on it, though it was clear to no one whether the seal meant excommunication or absolution.

Staying had not been dignified with a capital letter. No one was Staying. Staying meant dying when the island died, and then there'd be nothing left to die for.

In this exchange regarding the buying and the drinking of tea, though, Shola and the boy had just agreed that they would not Leave for another month. In general, neither showed any inclination to Leave at all; Shola at least acknowledged that one day he must, though that day was forever retreating towards the horizon, but the boy did not. He lived in a perpetual now, and his vigorous objection to the island's future cleansing was twinned with a stalwart denial that it would ever come to pass. The Sergeant suspected that would have to be dealt with soon. He had an image of the boy, when the day came, chaining himself to the pilings of the Beauville jetty, and NatProMan soldiers cutting him free with saws. Better to find a soft exit strategy.

Shola seemed to be thinking along similar lines. He glanced at the Sergeant and for a moment the fatigue in him was palpable. This time, the Sergeant understood, he had had to think seriously about going. He couldn't be making money. Couldn't really be breaking even. The more people left, the more farms and fishing boats weren't making food, the more expensive everything was and the fewer customers he had. And when Shola went, something would happen. Beauville would shift in some indefinable way from being a place which could recover to a place which was dying – not because of him alone, but because dozens of other Sholas, good-hearted men and women who had done their best and made it bearable for everyone else, would also go. Because it was finally time.

'What's it called?' the Sergeant asked, pointing at the pot.

'The label says "Heaven's Limitless Canon",' Shola replied. 'I think they mean "cannon", like a gun, but who knows? You reckon it's worth drinking?'

'It is.'

They had another round and the conversation shifted gratefully to the merits of taking various biscuits with this tea of teas. Beneseffe the Portmaster was called to adjudicate between the ginger nut and the plain digestive, a matter which required the gravest of scrutiny, although Beneseffe, more usually a traditionalist in such matters, unexpectedly held out for the chocolate Hobnob.

It was heartening for the Sergeant to find other people talking like this with the boy, as if he were seeing their friendship in a warm, homely mirror. He felt a species of pride, too, on hearing his young friend give as good as he got in the fierce biscuit debate, concocting ever more outrageous arguments in favour of his case. Then he wondered if he should try to talk to the boy like that. Perhaps the boy wondered why he didn't. But they had silence, and not many people had that.

The taking of tea concluded and the boy having departed on night-time business of his own, the Sergeant returned to Brighton House alone.

Three years ago the residence had been a blinding lighthouse white, trimmed with yellow at the corners and along the gutters. Then the first of the Discharge Clouds had washed over Brighton House, and everything died except the tomatoes. On the

22

mountainsides, the red rain had just burned the leaves and run rapidly away towards the sea. The slow-growing hardwoods had survived, albeit bent and scarred, and the underbrush had returned twice as thick. But here, on the flat croquet lawns and manicured terraces, in the planters and window boxes, the concentrated goop sat in great swirling lakes and wrought havoc. The dry season's dust had stuck to the paint and left the building veined and tinted like a giant cheese. The gardeners had packed up and gone with the diplomats, taking their ladders and their shears and their green aprons from Keen & Ryle of Chichester. The veinous Gorgonzola manse was fossilised, standing alone behind the bare earth that had been the rose gardens. The grounds were left to what might come. The sturdy Tumblers and Black Princes and Purple Russians, the Nebraska Weddings, the Soldakis and the Cherokees, the Brandywines and Radiator Charlies – a whole General Assembly of edible nightshades – saw their evolutionary moment and took over. By the time the Sergeant was handed the keys and told he should make himself entirely at home, because there was no prospect of anyone ever returning to Brighton House, the seaward side of the building was swaddled in vast, overripe toma-toes vying for sunlight and moisture. They rustled when the wind blew, and squeaked as taut, glistening skin rubbed against hirsute stems and flopping, musty leaves. When it rained, it sounded like men on the march, and when the sun came out you could hear them growing, whimpering and shuddering upwards, expanding, bursting, and starting again.

He parked the Land Rover at the back as he always did, and went in by the staff entrance. The rear hall was dark, and rather than turning on the lights he chose to walk along it in the gloom. After a moment, his right hand trailed along the wall and caught the door of the little bedroom he had assigned to himself. It was just behind the staff kitchen, so he didn't have to bother with the central heating. He just kept the old Rayburn stove alight and used it for water, cooking and warmth. It gave him a pleasant sense of familiarity, a translucent memory of hundreds of evenings spent here and thousands more in his mother's kitchen long ago – when, like the boy, he had been a reader of comic books. Although back then comics were printed in two or three colours on grainy paper, and superheroes fought bank robbers rather than aliens.

Where the boy lived, and with whom, was one of the intimacies to which the Sergeant was not privy, and the boy became politely deaf when quizzed. It was agreed between them that such issues were not necessarily any of the Sergeant's business, and he did not press. All the same, in the back of his mind there was a need to know. It was something he had absorbed in Afghanistan: on deployment you are always in combat. Even when no one is attacking you, the battle goes on. Things happen behind the horizon and beneath your feet; the whole landscape is your enemy and the people can change their minds about anything minute to minute. In the high valleys they don't believe in September 11th, not because they don't credit human wickedness but because they don't honestly believe in skyscrapers. Half of them think the soldiers they're fighting now are just Soviets who never left, and a few of those believe the Russians are just a cat's paw for the Brits – those who aren't waiting for the Queen to come in fullest glory and give them whatever their grandfathers' grandfathers were promised by Victoria, and as far as they're concerned you could walk to Buckingham Palace in a couple of weeks and HRH would happily roast you a goat for dinner. It's not ignorance and it's not stupidity, it's another planet and you live there as much as they live here. Spend a while on that planet, and you get so that you don't like gaps in your knowledge, even if trying to fill them in is rude.

He sighed, and peered at his face in the mirror: a young face, really, if slightly foxed. And yet, at the same time, the face of a too-old man. He had slipped from one generation to another without feeling the change, and this was abruptly the face of a father, not a son. A childless father, to be sure, but all the same he was exhausted and the fatigue never quite seemed to go away however much he slept. He wondered if this was what it was like at forty, if you just never quite felt yourself again, slowed down and down and down.

He rolled into bed and closed his eyes, hoping that tonight would be a peaceful one, and knowing he would dream of something, because you always did.

Unless, he growled into the pillow an hour later, you didn't sleep at all. Then you didn't dream, you just got heavier and more uncomfortable, and finally you got up again. He was too tired to read, too bored to stay awake, and yet here he was. Excessive tea-drinking, most likely, or maybe just Mancreu. There was a wind they said made you wakeful – it had a name he could never remember. Mancreu had dozens of winds, each with a different supposed effect. Wind to turn the milk and wind to drive the fish away, wind to sigh in the trees and wind to provoke infidelity. There were spirits which went with them. He wondered what these old ghosts thought about the state of things now. Probably, they took a dim view.

He got out of bed and put on his dressing gown. It was a light brown fleece, ordered online with a pair of Haflinger slippers. The slippers were more comfortable, coarse yet cosy wool. Haflinger should make dressing gowns. This one was too warm and overly clinging, like too much ketchup on your chips.

He got a torch from his bedside and wandered the hallways, looking for something, not knowing what it was. A place to sit. Almost, he went to the cypher room to read the incoming messages, but caught himself. He'd lose his grip on sleep entirely sitting in front of that glowing screen, watching the British establishment's own news ticker sharing celebrations and horrors from all across the globe. Instead he wandered into the glass conservatory on the ocean side and peered out at the night. It was cold, but that suited him. He sat down and stared out over the garden to the water and the curve of the waves.

Around about the time White Raoul the scrivener was born, Mancreu entered the modern age. A Franco-Dutch chemical company built a plant in the rough, dry backlands on the unsheltered south side. The people thought it a good deal: useless, grim country exchanged for enough hard cash to build a cinema, dredge the harbour every ten years, and lift the weight of living in an isolated, hopeless Eden. The chemical men found caverns of fresh water deep down, filtered by rock from the ocean, and that was even better: they pumped it out to quench the thirst of the workers, and up to the north Beauville grew and prospered and became a proper waystation for shipping in the Arabian Sea. When the time came to worry about waste, the solution was obvious: into the empty spaces the clear water left behind they pressed the by-products of their industrial toil, until one day in early 2004 the ground shook and the tectonics changed, and magma rose under the caverns.

In retrospect: a hoarding from White Raoul's spidery hands would have been the very thing. The devil was at play. The brimstone oven deep beneath Mancreu cooked and boiled, and in its fiery heart new, strange compounds were birthed and recombined. Dismal substances unknown and unimagined steamed in the deep, and seeped and stained through cracks towards the surface, ever upward into a huge chasm. There they made a balloon of weirdest muck, the fine membrane of earth stretched tighter and tighter until a farmer, ploughing, penetrated the upper crust and was fired some thousands of feet into the air and fully two miles sideways, falling like a burning angel in the middle of the Beauville shanty. Behind him came a warm mist which itched, but nothing more.

That first Discharge Cloud stripped half the island of its pines and shrubs, and rippled the white stones of Beauville like waxworks too close to a flame.

Seven months later came the second Cloud: harmless to humans, but death to rodents, and the Beauville high valleys were filled with the stench of dead marmots. Seagulls and spiders grew fat on the corpses.

The third Cloud caused fish to change sex and provoked a wave of lust and licence across Mancreu. It was remembered for months as a very good party, but the children born of passionate couplings in the Cloud could not speak. A German specialist, flown in to study the matter, pronounced that the entire section of the brain dealing with language – Broca's Area, he said – was missing. A grown woman, caught on the mountainside in the first exhalation of the Cloud, was thought to have lost all function in that region as well, but he could not find her to verify it. It was sad and frightening, he said, if true. All the same, his parent company was greatly interested by the Cloud as a treatment for sexual dysfunction, and filed patents.

The geologists said that the cauldron beneath Mancreu was still boiling, and showed no signs of emptying. The strange murk within was protean, they said. No telling what it would do next. Best to seal it up, if possible – but they had no suggestions as to how this might be achieved. One bold fellow also calculated that the amount of chemical released already exceeded what had been pumped in. He plumbed the depths with an improvised dipstick seven hundred yards long, and said he thought the solution was probably organic, even biological.

And so it proved. A team of Japanese xenobiologists – more used to guessing about the nature of life on other planets and studying strange fissures on the ocean floor – ascertained that the whole process had created a colony of bugs in the deep strata. These protozoa were transforming plain minerals into fuel for the ongoing chemical reaction, and other varieties of microbe then converted waste and water into food for the first. A perfect example of the magnificent adaptability of life, the scientists said. They were extremely impressed, almost to the point of being joyful. A worthy foe. Learned papers were written, but answers – solutions – came there none.

Indeed, the team was still here, a colony of perky boffins who lived apart in a village of seismographs and mobile centrifuges housed in a village of old-style Quonset huts and modern geodesic domes. Of all of them, the Sergeant only really knew the project chief, Kaiko Inoue, who came into Beauville by jeep every other Thursday and bought food and a few small bottles of imported whisky. The Japanese team loved whisky, had fetishised it beyond anything any Scot would ever think of, could name its lineages and recite the ideal chemical make-up of the peat and the perfect conditions for the casking, and had actually developed a special and very grave formal ceremony for its distribution. They had invited the Sergeant once, and he had sat on his heels for three hours and watched, at first with amusement and then impatience and then with a sort of awe as they moved through precise, elegant motions and the scent of the Talisker drifted up and entranced him. By the time he took his first sip it was like heaven and his aching muscles were absolutely forgotten, and that one glass without ice or water was the best he had ever had. Inoue had begun to make whisky here herself. She called it *Island End Uisge Beathe*, and it would only be drunk when Mancreu was in ashes. She would sit in Osaka with her team in ten years, or twenty, in the home of her father who was also a xenobiologist, and together they would break the seal on one of the casks and they would drink, and only then would she know whether she had wasted her time.

'You must come, Lester,' Inoue had said. 'You must come! We will cry for this place, but also we will dance the Funky Chicken.' And she had actually demonstrated, to his delight and the absolute bewilderment of her interns. The Sergeant was not always at ease with scientists, but Inoue was different. She was graceful and she made him feel at home in his skin. She was joyful, and from time to time she painted her fingernails in bright bubblegum colours.

Twenty-two weeks after she delivered her initial report, a new Cloud was belched up by the island and a freak of weather carried it over the sea to the east. Two thousand in the Maldives were stricken with a blight which caused temporary blindness and tinted the skin green with chlorophyll. Governments convened. The chasm must be cleansed. Quite obviously, they told the avid press room, it was dangerous. Should the symbiotic bugs spread into the oceans, the world might rapidly become unfit for human life. Or something might emerge from Mancreu's gullet which ate plastic, or silicon, or devoured crude oil, and the bases of industrial civilisation might perish. If the mountain went quiet for a few months, that just meant it was biding its time.

A new classification for the crisis was formulated. Mancreu was made the first ever UNO-WHO Interventional Sacrifice Zone, a place so wretchedly polluted that it must be sterilised by fire. In acknowledgement of the people of the island and their proud heritage and culture, the execution was deferred pending a final assessment. In the meantime, Mancreu became a kind of Casablanca, possessed of an uncertain legal status by virtue of the sentence of death, expropriated from its notional sovereign by the international will, gladly yielded up to its doom, yet still there and officially claimed by no one.

Then the Black Fleet gathered, and the process of sterilisation remained on hold.

On hold, like the Sergeant himself, who had arrived some time later and should by now have gone home. Well, he was in no hurry. In the night of Brighton House, he listened to the sound of the tomatoes beyond the glass. In amongst them somewhere there was a creature, probably a feral cat. He watched the moon trace its path across the sky and realised that the chill was seeping into him. His feet and lower legs were cold, and so was his nose. He felt a brief, tiny rumble in the ground, as if the island were a dog dreaming of rabbits. The windows rattled, and then it was over. A three-pointer, if that.

Abruptly, he wanted to be back in bed, and when he lay down the mattress was somehow a perfect fit.

2. Dreams

There was white chalk on the telegraph poles the next morning, times and places scrawled one under another. The Sergeant winced as he peered through his window. He wondered who it would be. Beauville families, for sure. A few farmers giving up the ghost. People he knew to nod at. People he had helped, or got drunk with. Children he had lifted up from scuffed knees. Probably a few adults he had arrested and would be glad to see go, but mostly the inevitable winnowing was taking the honest middle, leaving the listless and the feckless, the very good and the very bad. He wondered if he would need to be more and more of a policeman as time went by, if his time on Mancreu would grow more busy and more unpleasant as things gathered pace. Although when would that happen? He had already been here longer than anyone had thought possible. If Mancreu was a potential extinction event – and that was what they had called it in the Security Council – then humanity was being very relaxed about fighting it.

Well. There were things he could do. From the beach to the mountains, at least, he could be the small, necessary face of the law. He was even somewhat equipped for his investigative duties by a six-day course in public order and detection from the Metropolitan Police Service, attended in preparation for his stint in Basra. The course had been intense and rather depressing because the instructors knew and the students knew that the entire job was moribund from the outset, a token gesture towards a civil society the occupying powers could not and would not impose. But on Mancreu, it was enough. Most cases he had come across were simple enough that – if they could not be solved purely by turning up – a little thought and some legwork yielded results. He had discovered a small affinity for asking the right questions. He leaned heavily on the parting advice of his instructor, Detective Inspector Burroughs:

'You grind the facts as best you can, but after that it's about putting yourself in the way of people,' Burroughs had told him, in a brief, quiet moment. 'If you just get out in the river and stand there long enough, you end up with fish in your trousers and everyone thinks you're a genius.'

Since arriving on the island he had dealt with some thefts and some basic assaults, one killing – in self-defence, though that had been far from clear at the outset – and a host of odd, minor disputes which technically were more the province of a magistrate than a policeman. The only really intractable puzzle had been a break-in at the Xenobiology Centre in which nothing was stolen except some of Dr Inoue's notes and a selection of inexpensive desktop toys from Japan. He had initially assumed a journalistic motive, but since there had been no great splash of scientific scandal he had come to the conclusion that it had been the work of a vagrant looking for food. The notes were a draft which had been sitting on Inoue's desk, she said, and eminently replaceable. The Sergeant pictured pages of graphs stuffed into a tattered coat to keep out the south wind. The toys . . . he couldn't find a use for. A crime of opportunity, then, which was copper-speak for no bloody idea. Burroughs would have shaken his head: 'Lester, when you find yourself blaming a tramp because the crime makes no sense and tramps are known to be mad, you're nowhere.'

The Sergeant's neck twinged. He had woken with a stiffness in his shoulders and his head was full of the night's dreams, which had been bitter. Someone had told him once that the act of moving is what erases our memory of dreams: if you wish to remember, you must make a conscious effort to consider each image with the waking mind before so much as sitting up.

He, evidently, was wired differently, or perhaps he had brooded an instant too long before swinging his legs down onto the mat at his bedside, because the recollection was easy and even insistent.

He had dreamed that he held his wife in his arms. The sweetness of it was painful. She was tallish and strong and she smelled of London in the summer rain, of cream teas in Cornwall and of oil paint in his uncle's studio. Her hair was in front of her face and somehow whatever he did he never quite spoke her name, although he knew it, he was sure.

They danced. He had never been comfortable with modern dancing, had told her so early in their marriage, and she had agreed to learn ballroom. They had discovered they liked it and now they were very good, floating across the pale wood of a mirrored salon over a French restaurant in King's Cross. Waltzing, the way a soldier and his missus should.

It went wrong before the song ended. It was abruptly his sad duty to inform her of his own death. He was a ghost, his body cooling far away, his spirit embodied just for this, either a blessing or a vile cruelty.

'I've crossed over,' he said, 'that's what I'm here to tell you. You'll be all right. You will. Take care of the kids and promise me you won't hang about when you're ready, not on my account. You do what you do and I'll be smiling, and remember I'm waiting for you.' He couldn't believe he was saying these things. Euphemisms and platitudes he had always despised. *Crossed over. Gone on. Passed away.* All crap. The word was 'dead' and it didn't mean any kind of good, not ever, not for anyone.

Her face bunched and crumpled and she wept horribly, great racking sobs of utter despair he could not make right, because even the sovereign remedy of the embrace, the kiss on the top of her head, the gentle rocking which had always served before, even these made the whole thing worse because it was the last time ever, and he was dead, and in a moment he would fade away and she would be alone. He had never felt any great sorrow at the prospect of his own death before. Dread, certainly. But her horror awoke his own, and he reproached himself for making her cry and was powerless to mend his fault.

'You can't,' she kept saying. 'Please don't,' and then she was gone, or he was, and all he had was the memory of her crying.

When he woke, he remembered he had never married. His relief was immense, but on its heels came a ghastly aloneness which made the world black around him.

He let the curtain drop back and dressed automatically, looking at his bed and wondering how they had both fitted into it.

He walked around the house. In the communications room there were faxes on the machine. The first few were not addressed to him, but he was copied in. He picked them up and put them in the file without reading so much as a word of the main text. Almost all these memos were about things he didn't need to know, and the ones which occasionally featured relevant information were about the ships in the bay of the Cupped Hands. In theory he did need to know about these, but in practice he had been given to understand that he would be better off not. They were legalistic and indirect, but they dealt with the arguments and instruments by which various interests, including NatProMan and its allies, were making use of the lawless nature of the Mancreu waters for things they might not otherwise be able to do, and the maintenance of that convenient situation against dangerous judicial drifts towards answerability and competence.

'How's your stomach for totally mendacious bilge?' the Consul had asked him.

'Limited, sir.'

'Mine too. File these in the bin, then. Or file them properly, but don't read them. You'll get the urge, otherwise, to send back some clever reply and there'll be no end of shit.'

34

Greatly daring, the Sergeant had ventured to ask if his teacher had himself ever done such a thing. The Consul sighed and looked away.

'No,' he said.

This morning's incoming included a plaintive request from Sana'a.

ATTN: Brevet-Consul Ferris
x: FCO Yemen (Simon, Area Supply)
re: logistics
Lester – can you please check in the arms locker and see whether there's a small consignment of coffee in there? We're doing accounts and it seems we've taken delivery and can't find it anywhere. Hoping it got muddled up with your new-issue gas masks.

The coffee was not, in fact, in Brighton House's armoury. The Sergeant went in through the hi-tech door which ticked and rustled all night long as if talking to itself and checked. He poked around, marvelling as ever at the dangerous and insane toys he had been left to play with. He could have started a minor war with just the contents of one wall, but of course, the island was an anomalous sort of place and it paid, he supposed, to be prepared. Finally he located the coffee in the empty gardener's hut, listed as fertiliser. He replied to the memo in the negative, leaving out, after a moment of soul-searching, the actual fate of the parcel. He had not been asked about the gardener's hut, only about the arms locker. He put the coffee in the larder: the boy drank it sometimes, in the early morning when he had slept on the couch. It made him intolerable for hours, but he was worse without it.

Also in the in-tray, a string of requests forwarded by Beneseffe the Portmaster for the Sergeant's attention on local police matters.

– A lost dog; he felt that one would probably take care of itself, but the lady to whom the animal belonged was very insistent that he must come, Beneseffe said, and very sad. Well, perhaps it wouldn't hurt.

– A ghost woman running half-naked through the shanty, swimming in a watertank and frightening children; she was becoming a fixture, but she seemed to be harmless and she even had a few fans. It helped that she was evidently a pretty ghost, and sometimes left unlikely gifts. An ongoing investigation he wasn't sure he ought to solve.

– A mugging outside the Bonne Viveuse bar and cinema in Beauville. Well, he'd ask around. Not much had been taken, and the statement was sketchy. In all likelihood if he pursued it the man would ultimately have to confess that he'd been conned by a tart. All the same, on the outside chance that it was what it seemed, it might bear looking into.

And, from Beneseffe on his own account:

– Someone stealing fish off the docks. It sounded trivial, but fish was worth a lot, and if the business was between crews it could get nasty.

Well, he had his agenda for the day. Find the fish. Keep an eye out for an unhappy, misplaced dog and a scantily clad phantom. Give the mugging victim time to decide whether he'd been assaulted or just billed for services rendered. And he would do his proper job, walk his beat and be seen, drop in on Jed Kershaw to hear the gossip and be sure nothing serious was happening, nothing he actually needed to know. He would bump into the boy, of course, but before that happened he might drop in on the Witch.

She was not a witch, he reminded himself. She was a doctor. But he had met her as 'the Witch', and his mind held on to the word.

During the Sergeant's first summer at Brighton House, the tomatoes had become unruly. When he realised that enemy forces had taken the conservatory, he had stripped off his shirt and tied cloth around his hands so they wouldn't blister, and he'd gone in with shears and a sickle. The enemy troops were soft and unprepared: he surged and they folded. Superior weaponry was an excellent force multiplier, and he had a plan and an objective and they really didn't know a lot about warfare. He cleared the room without difficulty and sat amid the corpses of the fallen. He put his feet on a great pile of tomatoes and photographed them, and sent the picture to his sister in the next post. She sent him a message back by fax saying that he should make jelly with the Brandywines. The fax came out of the machine hugely elongated, each letter over an inch high but only a few millimetres across, so that the whole thing was impossible to read. It looked like something reflected in a fairground mirror.

The conservatory was won, but that only revealed the extent of the problem. Through the cracked glass, though, he could see out into the jungle beyond, beneath the canopy of splitting fruit. He realised had been expecting a miniature Amazon rippled with green, but everything was black. When he shone a torch through the glass, he saw that the whole mass was almost solid, thick trunks wrapped around one another like intestine. The garden was one vast coil of nested tomato plants.

He went to the conservatory door and opened it, brought his sickle down on the nearest plant. The rubbery stuff resisted, and he had to saw at it, nearly cut his own leg with the point of the blade. With some effort, he hollowed out a space to stand, and began to work, and then suddenly he was hacking wildly, screaming at this repulsive snare of organic stuff. He was a whirlwind, a living saw. He struck and struck and struck and he felt it fall around him, and he worked beyond fatigue with an energy he hadn't felt in years. He toiled and swore and grinned and wept, and he fought. He never once stopped moving, throwing aside pieces of roped plant until he felt the anger in him subside and wondered abruptly and somewhat awkwardly where it had come from. He wasn't one of those men who went off. He'd never been a bar brawler or – something in him cringed back, it was the worst thing he could imagine being – a wife-beater. He didn't really have much of a temper. Hadn't, until this moment. But here he was, alone in a garden, declaring a war of extinction on a field of tomatoes. It was so wasteful. That notion made him stop, bewildered, and he wondered at the idea that it was wasteful to chop down plants, but somehow not so much so to do the same with men.

There was a pain in his back and a warning sense of overstretch in his shoulders. He stared down at his hands – raw and bloody and sliced across the knuckles – and then looked up to see how much desolation he had wrought. He hoped it wouldn't be too bad. Then he had to look around twice more to make sure he hadn't lost his way in the fog of soldier's gardening. But it was true.

He was almost five feet from the door. He had worked for nearly a whole day, in a straight line, and come less than his own height into the forest. He stared out at the vast field with a sense of awe. They should send military planners here, he thought, to learn about insurgency.

During the night, his hands had swelled up, red and harsh, and when he tried to wash them the following morning the warm water felt like fire and he screamed. He couldn't use the radio because his fingers were too swollen, so he walked to Beauville and showed his hands to the boy, whose eyes grew very wide. The boy reached out and took his wrists, gently turned the big red slabs this way and that, and then removed from his knapsack a very old Swiss Army knife, and unfolded the magnifying glass. He peered at the scrapes and cuts, and showed them to the Sergeant through the lens. Ragged, as if he had burned them on tiny ropes. A bead of clear plasma rose from one of the little holes, a puff of red cells within. The boy sighed like an older brother.

'Tomatoes,' he said. 'You cut tomatoes. With your hands?'

'Yes.'

'Next time, with grenades!' the boy said, and mimed throwing one. 'Ka-blam! Already cooked.' He sighed again, then removed from the side pocket of his bag a small pot, and, using his little finger, touched a tiny flake of the wax within to the Sergeant's hand. The relief was ecstatic, so sudden it almost hurt. He gasped.

'Good?' the boy asked.

'Yes! Where can I get some?'

The boy administered more salve, but sparingly. He looked concerned. 'You better come with me. See the Witch.'

'What witch?'

'She is American, the good kind. Johns Hopkins. That is a very good school.'

In the Mancreu worldview, Americans were people who got up early and ran five kilometres before breakfast and urged you to improve yourself. They seemed to believe that the right mixture of Nike, granola and hard work would turn anyone, anywhere in the world, into a millionaire. And, of course, there were darkside Americans too, the ones where all that virtue and enthusiasm found its outlet in villainy, whether for personal gain or the security of the state. It was tricky, with Americans, because you never knew which you were getting. But the boy was a brand snob. Johns Hopkins was a good school, so the Witch was at least somewhat acceptable.

'She's a doctor?'

'She is a witch,' the boy said. 'She has warts. It is very traditional.'

In the event, the Witch had no warts. She was actually rather beautiful, in a distracted way. The Sergeant knew it was a beauty the boy would not be able to see because he was young.

'Lester,' the Sergeant said, when she asked his name. 'Lester Ferris.' He listened to it, wondering. 'Lester Ferris.' It suited someone else.

39

The Witch was looking at him, and he realised he had been repeating the words in different tones, trying them out. 'Sorry.'

She nodded. 'Soldier?'

'Yes. Well. Not for much longer. Retiring.'

That apparently concluded the smalltalk. 'Show me,' she said, then winced when he dutifully extended his arms.

He felt the need to apologise. 'I wasn't intending . . .' To go berserk? To see the red mist and fill up with hate for a yard full of fruit? 'I didn't know this could happen,' he amended firmly.

She turned his hands. He half expected her to say they'd have to come off. She wore a pair of loose trousers and a kind of long shirt with pockets at the hip. It smelled of turpentine, and he wondered if she was an oil painter as well as a witch.

'The tomatoes retain some of the chemicals in the Discharge Clouds,' she said. 'Not in the fruit,' as he stared at her aghast, 'but in the leaves and stems. They break down into . . . well. You washed yourself in all kinds of puke.'

He twitched. The word 'puke' sounded wrong from her, like a duchess with only one ear.

'I'll make a salve up for you. Do you want something for the stress, as well?'

He wasn't sure what that meant.

'Right,' she muttered. 'My mistake.' She looked at his right hand more closely, and growled. 'Damn.' She tugged on his right ring finger. 'What's this?'

The finger was crooked, price of a scuffle a million years ago. Was it in the line, or in a barracks somewhere? The Sergeant couldn't remember. He couldn't feel anything in it at all. He explained. She left him there, rummaged, came back. He was expecting the salve, but instead she carried a roll of twine and a wicked little hooked knife, the kind used by fishermen for nets and by farmers for gelding. He devoutly hoped she proposed to fish, but she did not. She reached over, back, and pasted something onto his finger, then cut a short loop of twine and tied it tightly around the base. 'Look away,' she said, and when he didn't she sighed again and said, 'All right.'

Something wriggled in his hand, a muscle in spasm. A tired finger. That finger. Dead, but now it wriggled.

She took the hook knife, and he reached over with his other hand to pass her the string, but suddenly she was cutting open the pad of his red, sausage finger along the line of one of his grazes, a deft, deep aperture welling blood and pus and something else, a grey-blue thing with a leech mouth, and then the grey-blue thing was a vein and the leech mouth belonged to a black worm which she nailed to the table with the point of the hook knife, and she slammed his hand deep into a jar of clear water which smelled wrong and it bubbled – cauldron! – and he recognised the smell, a kind of disinfectant he hadn't seen since Bosnia. The worm writhed on the table, bleeding. Probably bleeding his blood as well as its own.

'Hate those little fuckers,' she said. 'After a few months they can get into your brain. Disgusting way to die. I told you to look away,' she added unsympathetically as he retched. 'Don't you dare spew on my carpet.' But then she relented and agreed that it must be quite a shock, and gave him a dozen tablets, once a day with food, to make sure he didn't get infected.

'Thank you,' he said.

'Breanne,' she replied.

'What?'

'Breanne. My name. Not Brian or Briony. Breanne.'

'Thank you, Breanne.'

'What are you doing in Mancreu, Lester?'

'I honestly have no idea.'

'You're with NatProMan?'

'No, I'm at Brighton House.'

She stared at him for a second, as if he'd claimed to have come from another world, and then blinked. 'Oh,' she said. 'You're him.'

'Yes.' But if that meant anything to her, good or bad, she evidently felt no need to pass it on.

He dawdled, inventing twinges and concerns, until she smiled and very politely kicked him out.

After that, the boy determined his friend needed to spend more time relaxing. 'You come and meet people,' he ordered. 'Learn Moitié!' The word was short for 'moitié-moitié', literally 'half and half', the Swiss name for a fondue made with a mix of cheeses and the Mancreu name for the mishmash French-Arabic they spoke when they couldn't be bothered with English.

The Sergeant had tried to tell him he was tired, or that he couldn't for official reasons, but there was, he discovered, nothing more persistent than a small boy of uncertain parentage and various talents who has decided he wants to show off his expertise in haggling to his big, slow friend. The boy crouched on the passenger seat of the Land Rover and pointed: 'There! Left! No, totally the other left! Hashtag: SATNAVFAIL! Zomg!' And then they would arrive in a side street or at a corner shop with a faded board outside advertising something as unhelpful as 'fish', and the boy would be welcomed, greeted like a prince, and there was a special price, yes, of course.

The Sergeant made a note of the Leavings, the times and places, and took himself for a run, letting the inner sadist ride him until he was sweating and weary. Then he showered and went out to the car.

3. Murder

The Sergeant turned the Land Rover slowly around a narrow bend, using the horn. The tyres complained on the surface of the road. Mancreu high heat was ghastly, made hard by the flatiron rocks and the merciless reflected light from the ocean all around. The salt dried the air and the dust coated the skin and mouth, and you could feel you were dying of thirst even when you were drinking. When the cold came it was carried on sea winds from the south, but the warm heart of the mountains and the shelter of the Cupped Hands broke the force of the gale on the lee side. The south side was stripped and gnarled by storms and then battered by rain which fell in continuous streams from the thunderheads. This day was in between, the tail end of a bread-oven month, white caps on the water to the ocean side a warning that the rainy days were coming.

He worried about the boy as he drove, and about what would happen to the remaining civilians when the island was eventually purged. It had bothered him from the beginning, but more and more as time went by and the inevitable end drew closer. He had seen refugee columns and resettlement camps around the world, and he did not care to imagine what the boy would become by living in one. A warlord, in the end, or a corpse. Such places did not admit of middle ways. The joy would be cut from him, for sure.

The Sergeant had a plan to deal with that crisis if – when – it arrived, but he was still working out the detail. There were preparations he had to make, investigations he had been conducting quietly for some time. But he had not actually put the plan into action, and he had not spoken to the boy about it. There were good reasons. Sound reasons.

He braked again to go around another impossible bend, avoiding his own eyes in the mirror. None of these reasons was a lack of resolve on his part, or a lack of personal courage. He was almost sure.

The town and the port spread out below him, the invisible ships surprisingly close to the land. He felt his eyes flick away. Everyone found ways not to see what was in the bays. The Fleet could have painted itself pink or burned to the waterline, and no one would have remarked upon it. People saw the harbour and the horizon and nothing in between. Even the fishermen who went out and zipped in between the big vessels, selling fresh fish and crab, and the traders on junkboats who bought and sold DVDs and Coca-Cola and fresh meat and anything else they could lay hands on – even they had a strange amnesia about which ships they visited. It wasn't feigned. It was a habit so totally ingrained as to have become part of reality. The enormous ships were a fact of life, and it was a fact that you couldn't see them.

As with everything else, the boy was an exception. He bartered with the ship captains, argued with them loudly and crudely, demanded – and received – favours, tours, T-shirts, and team hats. He had a Delta Force hat, and a Real Madrid jacket, and a signed copy of something called *Transmetropolitan* which the Sergeant understood by the jubilation it had entailed to be a major coup. The boy had won them at dice or paid for them with gossip or simply asked for and received them. It seemed the captains admired his cheek, or maybe they were just desperately grateful for someone who acknowledged their existence. It didn't matter how tough you were, how psychologically motivated. It hurt to be invisible, even if that was the whole point.

Like Diego Garcia, of rendition infamy, Mancreu had been found new uses by democratic governments wishing to avoid the consequences of their own inconvenient liberties, and by corporations seeking relief from the onerous duties of civilisation. The border on the map had been softened and in places entirely cut

44

away, so that a strange zone of legal limbo was created between the breakers and the three-mile limit. In this maritime twilight it was often hard to tell where nations ended and other entities began; where corporate activity shaded into organised crime, spying into a trade in unlawful commodities. Clustered across the Cupped Hands lay a mass of unaffiliated shipping: prisons for deniable detainees and hospitals for unethical procedures; data havens, grey banks, untaxed subsidiaries; floating harems and forced-labour factories, auction houses for contraband goods; torture facilities for hire. So long as it never touched the shore, the business of the Fleet was invisible.

When the storms came in above the southern mountains, the ships drew apart from one another so that covert prows didn't gouge holes in unacknowledged hulls; so that secret masts didn't scythe across false-flag decks. When the weather abated, they huddled, so they could share cable television connections to the land and shout news to one another from deck to deck. American intelligence officers and their corporate-side cousins traded Sara Lee brownies with Poles for vodka and Frenchmen for cigarettes. Brits gave up HumInt and *lapsang souchong* and bought red wine and fresh milk, and sometimes played cricket on a long, lean supertanker moored forever at the northernmost limit of the zone. And all of them traded snippets of information to the Mafia and the Triads in exchange for occasional housekeeping jobs, *ex gratia* hookers and something to read. And the crooks were good for vanishings, when an interrogation grew heated and a subject expired from his own ignorance. On other deployments the Sergeant had occasionally seen that sort of thing written up by contractors as *self-injurious passive psychological attack culminating in asset compromise*. But here, on the ships of the Black Fleet, those terms of art were unnecessary. So long as the Fleet kept its activities to the waters of Mancreu, no reports were ever written. Intelligence was sourceless, all analysis was done on site and only the pure information ever emerged. The Rule of Law within the territory of the western democracies was preserved, and the conscience of ministers was notionally clean. Mancreu was a tapestry of questions unasked, because the answers were obvious. It had been going on for so long now that, at least to a global press whose owners sipped Chardonnay with prime ministers, it was no longer distressing.

The Sergeant turned the wheel and felt the beginnings of a skid; the road surface was covered in scree and shale. He allowed the car to drift a little, enjoying the play of the tyres and the tarmac, then straightened up and let his route take him in amongst the narrower streets.

Kershaw – his first stop, out of politeness – was not available, which meant the American was probably receiving information or instructions. The Sergeant left a message at the desk with a promise to come back later. He went over to the harbour and Beneseffe showed him the scene of the great fish theft, which was predictably stinky but otherwise not terribly helpful. A fully staffed crimes unit could have taken fingerprints and statements, worked out who had used the winches and the hauler. It would still have been almost impossible to learn much from the physical evidence because everyone likely to have committed the crime was allowed to use the equipment. It was remotely possible that someone not from the port had sneaked in, known how to work everything, gone off with the fish. But that person would then have to dispose of the fish, and how precisely would a shepherd explain his sudden good fortune? Had they fallen as rain? (And on Mancreu in particular: if they had, would anyone buy them?)

It seemed unlikely that this crime would remain mysterious for very long. There was a limited number of things you could do with four tons of fresh fish.

Pursuant to his other investigation – the one which related to his long-term solution for the boy's evacuation – the Sergeant asked Beneseffe casually if he knew who his friend's parents were.

'Which boy?' the Portmaster responded.

'The one who's always around. Comic books and a big old cellphone. Slim, dark hair. Smart.'

For a moment he thought Beneseffe might actually be able to tell him. There was a flicker of recognition in his face. Perhaps it was common knowledge. *That boy who was orphaned in the storm of '02, whose parents died of a fever, who survived the car crash back in '09.* Perhaps this would be simple. But Beneseffe shook his head. There were a lot of boys on Mancreu, even now. 'Ask at the schoolhouse,' he suggested.

'He doesn't go to school.'

'If he doesn't and he should then they'll know who he is, won't they?' Beneseffe pointed out, his tone implying that if this was detective work he considered it easier than people believed.

And they might know, at that, the Sergeant thought. Absence might be conspicuous. He would ask – but not today. Tomorrow. If he asked too many questions all at once, people would notice. The boy might find out about it indirectly, and that was not part of the plan.

Standing outside in the sunlight, he considered his idea of dropping in on the Witch as if by accident, but felt now that this would amount to an imposition of his presence. She must recognise it for what it was: a loneliness, and an approach. It would be better instead to make overt what was in his mind. Send her flowers. Ask her out. She was quite capable of refusing him with grace and making the matter relatively painless, he knew that. He wondered if she liked to read, as well as to play music. He had books he could lend her. Perhaps they would swap books. Perhaps reading would become an evening together, and between pages of a novel she would undress, and kiss him.

He sighed. He should have made his proposition months ago. It might have been possible. Now there was a fatigue about his desire, as if they had been lovers for too long and the flame was guttering, leaving them with a comfortable friendship and nothing more. His mind offered him visions of her, and his body was keen enough to accept the notion, but more and more they came with the hollow familiarity of repetition, and faded away without heat.

Seagulls landed all around him in a cloud, shrieking. One of the open boats was coming in, the bait high and vile in the air. The Witch was banished. Well, now he could not go and see her. Her skin was muddled in his mind with the smell of drying mackerel. Hardly good kindling.

At a loose end, he went out onto the seafront and sat with his feet dangling over the edge of the dock like a child. The dog? The mugging?

Mancreu shuddered, and he rolled himself hastily away from the water's edge. He had no desire to take a dip in the diesel-filmed harbour, swallowing seagull shit and oil. He stretched out a hand to steady himself on the cobbles.

The tremor faded.

He settled, resuming his seat, and listened to the sounds behind him in the town. Someone was brushing a broken bottle into a pan, and over on the other side of the Portmaster's office a lobsterman was chasing a stray lobster along the ground. The Sergeant laughed, but then the man turned and he was wearing a cheap surfing T-shirt, and it was – absurdly – one he had seen before, dozens of times, in Afghanistan. Someone must have donated a crate of them, because the kids all wore them when they went to school.

He sighed. Afghanistan had been a mess. The Americans called it a Total Goatfuck, and they laughed and swore and kept their spirits up by firing huge bombs into the cave systems. Several of the local section commanders had taken to wearing stetsons and sheriff's badges when they went out in public, and one actually made a temporary drive-in and screened a bunch of cowboy movies dubbed into Pashtun and Farsi. 'I want them to know where we're coming from,' he said. 'I want them to understand that this is how we do.'

The Afghans watched the movies, some from the makeshift benches in the drive-in and some through field glasses from up in the hills, and there was a great deal of debate over coffee and raisins about whether Rooster Cogburn really did have true grit. Then one morning the projectionist was found with the second reel of *High Noon* pushed into his open chest.

'What the fuck did he expect?' the Sergeant overheard a senior officer say to a visiting member of the general staff. 'He sent his message, and they sent one back. Their message isn't a lot more insane than his, it's just in capital fucking letters!' And then, to everyone's surprise and embarrassment, the man wept.

The Brits didn't talk about Afghanistan being a Total Goatfuck. That didn't come close to expressing how they felt. They had a sense of having been here before, a sense they got from their regimental histories and from the Afghans themselves, who still recognised the flags they flew and the badges on their shoulders from the wars of a hundred years ago. There were soldiers here whose great-grandfathers had fought the Pashtuns in 1918, and the fathers of those men had fought them before that in 1879, and their fathers in 1840. The Brits shared with the locals a tacit understanding that nothing done here would make any difference, that this was just another layer of bloody patina on the cold, hard soil.

Command gave the Sergeant a new second lieutenant to take care of, a boy called Westcott. He was posh as Royal Doulton and thick as a carthorse. He said the war was going to be 'an improvement for everyone in the long run'. He let it be known that he liked his men to read, because he felt it improved their chances of 'getting a good position' when they got home.

The Sergeant, like many men whose jobs involve a great deal of waiting, enjoyed reading. He carried one paperback wherever he went. He had a small library in his locker and selected something different each time he packed his gear. He had *Three Men in a Boat* and *The Passion* and *The Hound of the Baskervilles*, a few old Eric Frank Russell editions, and a copy of *Bleak House* for the winter. Westcott said he should invest in an electronic book tablet. They could store thousands of books, Westcott said, and they lasted for weeks between charges. A couple of the soldiers already had them, Westcott said, and really liked them. Progress was what it was all about. When he was out of the army, he was going into business and then later when he knew a thing or two he might stand for Parliament – that was giving back, which a person in Westcott's position really ought to do.

Two weeks on, Westcott was reading from his gizmo in a ravine when the sky opened white and purple and bullets poured down. The machine had brought the Taliban right to him; it had a cellular connection Westcott had forgotten to switch off, or maybe he couldn't wait for the latest Grisham and had tried to bloody download it. The Sergeant dragged two men through the howling night and hid them in the stripped carcass of a bus, then went back and found that Westcott had been cut in half. The enemy was a gaggle of boys and an older man, and one of the kids had a box with wires poking out which was their uplink detector. They were dancing and celebrating.

Blue Peter, the Sergeant thought. *My Science Project. I'm fighting sticky-backed plastic and cornflakes packets.* He was only dimly aware of being injured.

A day later, the whole valley was made of glass. The daisy-cutters weren't classed as weapons of mass destruction because they weren't nukes, but they worked just as well by being very big. They were so big they had to be pushed out of the back of carrier planes one by one, down the ramp usually used for tanks and trucks. Each of them was a natural disaster in a box. The air for miles in any direction smelled of oil, hot stone, and charred sheep. The Sergeant sat in the back of a truck with his legs hanging down over the road and watched. Someone had thought it might be a good notion for him to know that the men who had killed Westcott weren't getting away with it. Privately, he thought that whoever that person was must be new here. Still, it wouldn't do to be ungrateful. He recited

50

the whole of a poem he knew about a cat. For a while, it seemed to be all he could say. When he found other words, they were jagged and inappropriate, full of a sense of waste.

They sent him to Mancreu. *Take a break, Lester. Not long on active for you now, is it? Nearly forty. Well, serve it out. We'll find something for you.*

He watched the waves in the harbour and thought about Beneseffe's stolen fish. He would be quite content to stay here. Mancreu life – strange and undemanding and disjointed – suited him. He wondered if there were some other abandoned island somewhere without the death warrant hanging over it, a place which needed a sergeant. El Hierro, Shola had said. Maybe El Hierro. Then he felt like a traitor for having the thought, as if he were married to a sick woman and coveted her sister. Well, he would stay as long as he was permitted. But there was nothing wicked in wondering where he would go, after. That was just life. You had to be practical.

There was a presence at his side and the noise of a pocket radio and he recognised, in a brief lull in the breeze, the scent of the boy. His friend smelled of earth today, rather than salt, so the Sergeant guessed he had not been out on his boat. The radio dangled by a lanyard from the boy's hand, and a breathless northern English voice was detailing Real Madrid's latest triumph on the football pitch. A famous victory, the voice said, which seemed rather premature. Time would decide whether it was famous or not, and most likely it would be just another game.

The boy politely switched off the radio and the Sergeant got to his feet. They walked along beside the water until they came to a broad stretch of sea wall that was flat and warm, in a part of Beauville which was now mostly deserted. Both sat. The boy said nothing. The sea washed and swooshed. After a moment, the boy reached into his bag and produced something wrapped in greaseproof paper and foil.

They had an arrangement regarding food which was acceptable to both. The Sergeant had a considerable inventory of baked beans and spaghetti hoops at Brighton House which amounted to more than a single person could consume over the space of some years. The boy had made it clear that he regarded baked beans as the highest form of culinary genius, but had a correspondingly low opinion of the spaghetti hoop. As with the continuity of stories and the football of Real Madrid, the matter was akin to a religious one, and no heresies were tolerated. The barbecued bean, for example, was taboo. Alphabet shapes could not move him to a gentler opinion of pasta in sauce.

The Sergeant, meanwhile, had long ago eaten all the tinned produce, all the syrups and ketchups and brines, that he could stand. He wanted nothing so much as fresh food. He loved the dubious Mancreu cheeses and the dry sesame biscuits which went with them. He loved the oily sardines and goat-knuckle stews, the mashed roots and flatbreads which were the island's staples. He ate whatever was in season and whatever was for sale and thought himself in paradise. Anything so long as he never had to swallow another mouthful from a tin.

They had therefore evolved a practice suited to their likes. The boy would arrive with fruit, cheese, and bread, and the Sergeant would supply baked beans. They would begin by toasting the bread over a pocket gas burner and warming some beans for the boy. Each would make some disparaging face in the direction of his friend's meal, and then they would sit in loud, masticatory silence for a while, and then speak of whatever might be on their minds.

The Sergeant extended the plate of warmed beans, and the boy took them. He ate one mouthful, and then the next. He seemed to be worried that the heating had been uneven, because he was touching each heaped spoon with the tip of his tongue, like a lizard. The Sergeant took a big bite of cheese and bread.

After a while — it was quite in keeping with the moment, he hoped, not an imposition but a natural thing to do — the Sergeant spoke.

'Do you have . . . family?'

The boy shook his head gravely. 'I am too young.'

A lack of precision could take you to some strange places with a child living on Mancreu, where anything was possible.

'I mean parents. Brothers and sisters. Uncles, even.'

'Aunts and cousins and bears, oh my!' He grinned.

'Really?'

'Sure. Of course.' He made an encompassing gesture. Mancreu life: everyone is family. If you live in the same street or on the same farm, you're cousins or brothers. An older man is an uncle if he functions as an uncle.

'Blood family?'

'Someplace.'

'But here?' *Who takes care of you apart from me? Who's missing you, right now? Where are you when you're not with me?* He felt like a jealous husband. Or how he imagined it would be to be one.

The boy shrugged his private shrug, or perhaps it was merely that his mind had wandered, for the next thing he said was that he had heard the British government had captured a flying saucer in the early part of the 1900s, and did the Sergeant know anything about it? Would the Queen know? Or would it be hidden away from everyone, the way the Roswell saucer was at Area 51? The Sergeant answered these questions with the same serious attention he would have given to anything the boy said, as if they were entirely reasonable and not at all preposterous, and after a while longer watching the waves they went back the way they had come – if not together, then two men going in the same direction at the same time.

They ended up, inevitably, at Shola's. The Sergeant recognised by the boy's heavy knapsack and his contemplative quiet that there was reading to be done. He had in his own pocket the paperback of *The Friends of Eddie Coyle*, and was finding it entirely engrossing: 'Jackie Brown, at twenty-six, with no expression on his face, said that he could get some guns.' He therefore made his way to his own familiar seat, and the boy, without a backward glance, went to the bodyguard's table, and spread out a sheaf of the work of the great Bendis, the bard of Cleveland. Shola obliged them both with quiet and what provisions they desired, and the common life of Mancreu came and went around them, until the day became the evening and the Sergeant's left buttock began to ache in a way he could not any longer ignore. Age, he supposed, and bad furniture.

Shola peered at the Sergeant, appearing to read something in his face which was both familiar and a little bit sad. 'Anaesthetic,' he offered. 'Special Mancreu style.' He produced a bottle from beneath the counter and poured himself a single measure in a little red glass.

The rum was brown and thick, and there were veins like treacle in it. Every September, Shola harvested his small marijuana crop – the plant grew well on the island, at least on the sheltered side – and selected some of the best leaves. He dipped them briefly in boiling water to kill anything living, and pushed a handful into each of twelve bottles of sweet white alcohol. Then he buried the bottles in the mud at the back of his house, and the sun baked the mud and the mud coddled the rum, so that when he dug it up again in July the leaves were beaded with resiny sap. He shook the bottles one by one until the rum was the colour of crude oil, then poured it through a fresh linen cloth, and finally stoppered the finished product again and laid the bottles by for special occasions and dire emergencies. It was quite respectable. Mancreu men had brewed fortified rums for as long as anyone could remember. There were pictures of missionaries drinking them and losing their inhibitions, and stories of Knights Templar finding out about them and mistaking them for Christ's Blood. The original indigenes had made theirs with a local hallucinogenic root, but no one used that any more because it was addictive and had the unfortunate property of sending you blind and mad. Marijuana was better, and you could sell it to the Black Fleet for Swiss francs. Shola no longer trusted dollars. The Chinese owned the dollar, Shola said. It was only a matter of time.

The Sergeant declined the drink with thanks, though part of him very much wanted to accept. A strange, Victorian spectre dangled over him: the image of a fat, hirsute colonial administrator taking to the local drugs and losing his mind, running naked through the streets. Children laughed and pointed, women smirked. Men sucked air through their teeth as something terrible and a little bit funny happened to his exposed member. People – undefinable people, but including Kershaw, Beneseffe, the Witch, Pechorin, and of course, Kaiko Inoue and even the boy – would think less of him.

Shola shrugged and poured half the glass carefully back into the bottle, then drank the rest. The Sergeant, feeling embarrassed at this evidence of his own prudishness, accepted a bowl of soup instead, and returned his attention to Eddie Coyle.

The men came in as Shola was shifting the café from one mood to another. He had turned on the neon lights and taken the tea kettle off the hob, but he had not closed the shutters. He had gone up to the private rooms to change his workmanish daytime shirt for the extraordinarily ugly red silk one he wore at night. Every day he looked exactly the same. Perhaps he had several sets of each uniform. The Sergeant imagined a daytime closet upstairs filled with vests and aprons and grubby trousers, and opposite it an old wardrobe filled with a row of Casanova blouses, vintage 1974 from Yeah, Baby! of Brick Lane, bought from eBay and shipped by sea to Qatar and then on to Mancreu, vacuum-sealed by Shola's explicit instruction, lest the damp creep in and they arrive covered in mould.

There were five men, and they arrived as the Sergeant finished his soup. They were local but not familiar, and from his vantage the Sergeant had time to be uncomfortable with their intent faces and their focus. He shifted his weight from the bones of his arse to his feet, and felt the muscles in his stomach tighten as he leaned forward over his empty bowl.

The shooting started.

They weren't systematic but they made up for it with sheer aggression. They had a shotgun and four Chinese AKs. Two fishermen having dinner before going out for the evening went down first, then the dogmeat seller who always smelled of chum. Two good-time girls at the bar – Isobel and Fleur, or so they had claimed – tried to dive behind it and were hit on the way over. Then Shola.

The Sergeant saw Shola very clearly, because they were on opposing trajectories. The Sergeant was heading out, knees protesting as he hurled himself forward, but protesting in a willing way: *fuck, yes, but don't make a habit of it*. He imagined he must look almost horizontal, head forward, muscles straining to keep up with his lunge for the kitchen and the back door. He had a sudden image of the boy's comic books. Men in those stories ran like this all the time. Heroes did. Towards the action, it must be said, but they were often indestructible and in one way or another well armed. They ran like this to answer a ringing phone, sometimes.

Shola was coming down the main stairs with his barman's rag over his shoulder, buttoning the awful shirt, the wide smile of welcome vanishing as he saw the guns, replaced by a look of horror as his early customers – his friends, mostly – started to scream. He shouted 'Stop!' the way people do when something utterly awful is happening and will continue to happen whatever they say. There was no expectation that it would change anything, but it must be said. The human throat could not keep it inside. People said it to bombs and hurricanes and tsunamis and wildfires. The Sergeant had seen video footage, in 2001, of a woman standing on the street bellowing it at the Twin Towers.

It never made any difference, and no one expected it to. It was the soul's voice, in hell.

Shola's soul was inaudible, but between stutters and bangs the men saw him. Perhaps because he was coming forward, all of them reacted. First the AKs punctured him and he jiggled like a hula dancer, arms wide as if snapping his fingers and inviting you to join in. Then the shotgun tore a fistful from his chest and he stopped being Shola and became a dead thing, flying backwards and landing on his own floor.

The Sergeant realised he was kneeling in the kitchen, concealed by the angle of the bar, and staring back into the room. The boy was still sitting where he had been when it all started. His face was spattered with something which must have come from Shola, a strange granular mixture the Sergeant had never seen before. Brain and bile, perhaps. Or Shola's lunch. The comic book in front of the boy was ruined, piled high with dripping anatomy. The boy was staring straight ahead, quite still. The Sergeant could not decide if he had frozen or if he understood instinctively that movement would kill him.

The killers for their part looked rather surprised to have succeeded so well. They had apparently been expecting some manner of resistance. They kept their weapons trained on the boy. The only question among them appeared to be who would kill him. The Sergeant heard one of them say *temoin*, witness. For God's sake, he thought. Leave him alone. Shola's dead. It's over.

He peeped in again and saw the point man's eyes go from alert to cold. The boy would die in a second or two. The decision was made.

He looked down at his hands and found he was holding a metal biscuit tin. He opened it and saw a smattering of yellow grains, smelled Bird's Custard. What was he doing with it? Ludicrously, this was quite a dangerous object: shake a teaspoon of custard powder in a box and add a flame and the whole thing goes off like a bomb. It has to do with burn rates and surface area. 'Explosive yield,' the Sergeant's demolitions tutor had told him, 'is bloody complicated, so don't piss about with it. If you've got to improvise, assume you need to be a long way away.'

And then he hadn't got the tin any more. What had he done with it? He was kneeling in a pile of discarded yellow powder. He heard a gunshot, and almost immediately afterwards he was deaf.

Part of him – the trained-soldier part, a parcel of endlessly drilled responses which required no thought, which often took over in times of crisis – had been expecting a sort of woofing noise. The best he could have hoped for was a loud pop and plenty of light to blind them. He must have got the proportions exactly right, and Shola's tin must have had a tighter lid than advertised. *Expecting? How had he been expecting anything?*

He stepped through the kitchen door brandishing a long-handled copper frying pan.

Three men were on the ground, and the biscuit tin was sticking out of the far wall, blown open like a razor-edged sunflower. The two remaining killers were staring blindly, but neither of them had yet started shooting. The boy was under the heavy wooden tabletop. Adolf Hitler, the Sergeant remembered irrelevantly, had once been preserved from death by a tabletop.

He could see how it had happened quite clearly, even as he drove the pan down hard on the arms and hands of the first armed man and felt them break. The tin had flown in, and the man nearest had opened fire. A bullet, red-hot and trailing burning residues, had penetrated the tin, igniting the powder. The explosion – there was nothing else to call it – blasted the tin to pieces, firing the greater part into the wall and a cone of small fragments of hot metal directly at the hapless marksman. The bang had been deafening, which was why the Sergeant could not hear anything. The men in the fire zone would not die, though the closest probably would lose the sight in his right eye.

The second standing man was bringing up his gun. The Sergeant suspected the killer was mostly seeing fuzzy shapes, but he knew he was under attack and he knew what to do about it. *A soldier or a militiaman who had seen some sort of combat. The initial attack is blunted, but that doesn't mean you stop. You keep fighting,* because the moment you stop you hand the enemy the initiative. That was right and proper.

The Sergeant's technical approval did not stop him from batting the gun to one side and shattering the man's face with the base of the copper pan. The man pulled the trigger as he went down, and one of his friends on the ground shrieked as he lost a toe. *Well, such is combat (you murdering prick)*.

The Sergeant saw movement and turned to find the boy poking another of the men on the floor in the eye with his comic book. Rolled tight, the comic was a stout wooden stick with a series of cookie-cutter edges at each end. The man screamed as his nerves reported the assault, and the boy kicked his gun away. The Sergeant hit the last man in the head, collected a gun and held it on them, counted: yes, five accounted for. His mouth tasted of bile and burning. He glanced out into the street: they had no backup.

Done.

And that was it. Five armed bandits versus a tween and a man having a quiet afternoon, and they'd won.

The boy looked around in wonder.

'We're alive!' he said, and then again, Frankenstein style: 'I am a-liiiive!' The Sergeant wondered if this was shock, and thought it was, filtered through the boy's weird, frenetic brain. 'We pwn!' the boy shouted. 'We are alive and they are teh suxor!'

The Sergeant had only the vaguest idea what this meant. 'Pwn' was familiar, although he didn't think you were supposed to say it out loud. Someone had explained it to him. He realised with a sickly feeling it had been Lieutenant Westcott, browsing his latest ebook in a Panther CLV, somewhere between Farah and Rudbar. Abruptly he was there as well as here. He knew he was remembering but couldn't find the pause button. The playback just rolled on over the top of the men on the floor, the boy's jubilant awareness of survival.

'It's a typo,' Westcott had said. 'They made it into a joke. You start with the simple statement "we won". If you're typing in a hurry, it might become "own". Yes? And if you're really going for it you might hit the wrong button altogether and get "pwn". The lexicon is always growing. A lot of these games have chat channels as well as control keys, so that you can trashtalk the opposition. Like sledging' – because cricket is always the clearest comparison. 'So the kids type in a hurry because they're under fire. Mostly war games, of course. The Americans use them to train the marines in teamwork, actually. Very forward-looking.'

The Sergeant had had a brief image of every sitting room in every town in the world becoming a training ground for marines. A wealth of potential recruits. Even more enemies. But there were always more enemies than allies, in video games. It had been that way since Space Invaders, which some people had actually wanted to ban on the grounds that it was wrong to suggest there were some fights you couldn't win. You can always win, these people insisted, if you just *go for it*. Nike soldiering. Pep-talk strategy, and never mind the logistics, which will land you high and dry without food or body armour or even bullets. Real soldiers – soldiers like the ones in Hollywood films – could improvise a machine gun with a drainpipe and a bunch of clothespegs.

Like a man improvising a bomb with a tin of custard. He swayed, trying to remember what the real world looked like. The café. The café and Shola's blood and bone everywhere and the smell of it. That was what it looked like now.

'We are made from awesome!' the boy said, hands on hips, hero style. Then memory took hold. In belated panic: 'Shola?'

The Sergeant, about to indicate the corpse, remembered what it must look like and shook his head. He caught the boy's arm as he went to see and held him back. The boy's eyes widened and for a moment he grew stubborn, then limp.

'Shola?' he asked again. *You have made a mistake. Someone else is dead. It is not our friend.*

'No,' the Sergeant told him. He had had this conversation before, knew it very well. He looked around. How many corpses?

60

Five? Six? Was anyone still alive? Any of them might be, except Shola. Shola was dead. But the others . . . He should find out, try to stop the bleeding. He had no idea how to do that. In films, everyone knew those things, but he didn't and he might make it worse. In the real world, platoons had medics, and 'don't fucking touch unless I say'. He looked at the gun and wondered why he wasn't tempted to pull the trigger, finish the men on the ground. He wanted to want to. A few moments ago, if he'd had this gun, he would have used it without hesitating. Now it was out of the question. Pointless. And it was important to take prisoners. He wished it wasn't.

'We beat them,' the boy protested. 'We beat them!'

Yes. That much was true. In comics, and in the games the boy played, that meant that the key actors did not die. In the particoloured fantasy world of Superman, winning meant saving your friends. Ergo, Shola could not be dead. Except he was, and that too was bloody obvious and according to convention: when a white soldier goes adventuring, it's somehow his black friend who gets shot.

'We did what we could,' the Sergeant said, hating the words in his mouth. 'Everything we could. There's nothing to feel ashamed about.' This last with great fierceness and certainty because he knew what shame would do later, if not capped now. He reached for something which would make sense. 'We needed Superman, didn't we? Only he's busy. It's just us.'

The boy nodded in reluctant understanding. 'We are good. We are not *leet*. Saving Shola would have been *leet*.'

Leet, the Sergeant thought, from 'elite', often written *l33t* or even *1337*. Meaning: the very best. The most able.

'No,' he said. 'We are not *leet*.'

'Perhaps we should practise,' the boy murmured sadly.

'Yes,' the Sergeant agreed. He was rehearsing his choices in his mind, looking for better ones. *Evade, counter-attack*. There just weren't any. Not once it started.

He heard a breath, looked down and saw the boy's mouth open in a perfect O. He jerked back and around, looking for a sixth assassin, but there was nothing. The men on the ground cowered, begged. No threat. No threat. He looked back, abruptly afraid that the boy had been shot and was just now realising, grabbed him and checked him with his hands, moving aside folds of bloody clothing and patting the boy's arms and legs. 'Are you all right? Are you all right?' His voice was uneven. Unprofessional. He was angry, the way his father had been angry with him when he burned himself on the kettle. 'Tell me!' He stopped shyly, worried that he had crossed a line.

'I am fine,' the boy said. 'I am fine! I promise! Sorry. I did not mean to do that. It is okay. I was just seeing.'

'Seeing what?'

'Everything,' the boy said. The Sergeant waited for him to crumple, but he didn't. Instead he stared back at the room wide-eyed, as if he were visiting a cathedral. Shock looked like that sometimes. Survival became a miracle, the wretched world a heaven. *Well. True enough.*

Outside, someone was arriving. The cavalry. NatProMan, the Sergeant assumed, because explosions and gunfire would definitely attract Kershaw's attention. Or perhaps he had called them. He didn't remember. He looked down and saw the boy looking up, and realised that neither of them would cry unless the other one did first. He wondered what earthly good that was to anybody. Very manly. As much use as pulling the trigger, he supposed, which was to say none at all.

'We should fight crime,' the boy said. 'That is what we should do.'

4. Aftermath

'Jesus, Lester,' Jed Kershaw said, 'Jesus! Are you okay? Shit! What the fuck is going on? Shall I send in the marines? Were they after you? Was this an anti-Brit thing? Did they think you were one of my guys? Was it anti-American? Was it *jihad*?'

Kershaw was glossy in the heat; his skin had a fried-egg slickness. He was short but seemed to have been fitted with an oversize motor so that he talked too fast and moved like a dragonfly, zigging and zagging and pouncing on things. It was exactly how not to feel comfortable in the heat. His family was Norwegian back down the line, and he looked like a stumpy brown-haired Viking who'd taken a job as a golf pro. You could not have found someone less suited to Mancreu's climate if you'd searched the whole world. Kershaw didn't even like Florida. But he had come down to Shola's and personally taken charge because he was basically decent, and he'd sat at the man's table and eaten with him.

'Fuck,' Kershaw said again, seemingly to nobody. He looked at the Sergeant's uniform, with its splatter of Shola's blood along one sleeve and the dust all over his side from his dive to the floor. 'Lester, for Christ's sake, sit down. Stop being a sergeant for a few seconds and just . . . Holy shit, Lester, are you okay?'

The Sergeant allowed that a sit down might be just what he needed. He was aware abruptly that he had scalded his face, probably walking through the cloud of burned custard. The Witch would laugh at him. Her cleavage appeared in his mind's eye, rising and falling, leaning over him: post-combat lust. He struggled to focus on the matter at hand as she straddled him, guiding his hands, his mouth. *God, yes. I want this.*

And then, more truthfully: *I need a hug*.

'I don't know,' he said, in answer to all Kershaw's questions. 'I think it was about Shola, but I don't know. There's no reason anyone would come after me.'

'You're a policeman,' Kershaw said.

For a moment, the Sergeant thought this rather unkind. He interpreted it as a rebuke: you're a policeman! Why don't you know already? But then he realised that as far as Kershaw was concerned it was an explanation in itself. You're a policeman: some people don't like them. It had not really occurred to him that in many places this would be reason enough to shoot someone dead while they were having soup. His perceptions of copperhood were formed by the dream of England, still. A copper was a bloke in a slightly silly hat who walked the beat, talked to shopkeepers about the price of fish, and sorted out young ruffians. You didn't attack him. It was like attacking a field of wheat, and anyway, you'd have to answer to his mum.

The Witch reappeared, came through the door with her medicine bag. He tried not to see her, then realised when she peered into his face with benign professional concern that this time she was real. He had already opened his mouth to receive her kiss. He shut it. She nodded, began to move carefully around him, tut at the mess on his clothes, probe his bruises.

Kershaw was talking about stability, viable stability under abnormal crisis-induced deindividuational stress, from which according to some NatProMan policy document everyone on Mancreu was presently suffering. He punctuated his speech by yelling at his men to 'cover that body, find someone to do some fucking clean-up, where's the fucking undertaker, is there still a fucking undertaker or has the fucker already fucking fucked off?' The words were irrelevant. His presence was the message. He cared enough to be here, to come in person into what must feel like a very dangerous place, and now he was here he was as confused as everyone else.

'You didn't do anything to make this happen, Lester? I'm not going to find out that you and Shola were running coke to kids in Beauville?'

'That is rude,' the Witch said without looking up. 'And ridiculous.'

'Fuck you, lady! Who asked you anything? What the fuck are you even doing here?'

'You called for doctors. I am a doctor. Deal with it.'

'I meant real doctors! My guys!'

'And they are putting blood back into the women who were shot. Who will live, by the way – I'm so glad you asked.'

'Fucking MSF fuckers,' Kershaw muttered. He was embarrassed, the Sergeant could see, by the callousness of his own questions. But it was his role to be callous, to ask the bad questions while others did the repair work, in case there were bad answers.

The Witch sneered and muttered something about inhibited men from Ivy League schools.

'No,' the Sergeant said to Kershaw, before this could escalate, 'nothing like that.'

Kershaw took that at face value and turned to the Witch, asking, by way of amelioration, 'Is he okay?'

'He will be,' the Witch said. 'Which is a miracle. Lester, turn your head.'

He did.

Kershaw, assured that the Sergeant was not seriously hurt and not a drug dealer, seemed to calm somewhat. Then, too, he had probably needed to know this wasn't some sort of insurrection. There were those on the island who objected to NatProMan's presence. Occasionally leaflets surfaced, printed neatly and distributed invisibly, nailed to walls and left on café tables. They denounced Kershaw by name, railed against the destruction of the island, in English, French, and Moitié. It was not what you would call an insurgency. It felt pro forma, or possibly sophomoric: angry young men with a smattering of political history and a sense of betrayal. The Sergeant couldn't blame them, but in his judgement they – whoever they were – had nothing like the steel for something like this. This was horrible, but it was not revolution. It felt too specific for that. But hardly surgical.

The Sergeant looked for the boy, but he was gone, most likely to whatever place he called home. The Sergeant hoped that whoever waited there would look after him. He felt bad that he had not provided some sort of care while he spoke to Kershaw, but the boy had been quite firm, and he was sovereign. 'Speak to the American. It is necessary.' If there was anyone waiting. If he had anyone. The Sergeant hoped that he did, somewhere, and then hoped that he didn't because that would mean he shared his friend with someone he did not know, that the boy was ultimately not his boy, just a boy he knew. It would make his furtive, half-acknowledged Plan B that much more difficult.

The Witch drove him to her surgery without speaking. She gave him leaves and unguents for his scorched face, more for his bruises, and dressed a gash in his shoulder which must have been from a near miss with the shotgun as he fled into the kitchen. Finally she sighed.

'I knew Shola,' she said. 'Marie will be devastated.'

The Sergeant nodded. Marie, Shola's girlfriend. Wife, really, though not on paper. Widow. Christ, someone would have to tell her. Except that by now she already knew. There was nothing he could do about that. He'd have to go and see her, of course.

'Everyone will be,' he said. And the boy: had he witnessed death like this before? Not impossible. Not here. 'If you see,' as ever he baulked at saying 'Robin', 'my friend, tell him to come and find me.'

The Witch shrugged. Exhausted, he accepted that as a yes. He breathed in, hoping to catch her scent to carry it away with him, but the room smelled of the sea, and of disinfectant.

That night the Sergeant dreamed of a woman, in terms he knew were utterly pornographic. They did things he had only read about: desperate things which arched them both and made them cry out until they spasmed and clutched and clawed their way to satisfaction, and then on relentlessly to more and more transgressive journeys in search of some sort of restitution from the world. He called her Breanne, but when finally his lover laid her head upon his chest and slept, her body was slim and pale, and her fingers were tipped in an absurd sherbet pink.

When he woke, the memory was fading and he was aching and grazed and filled with regret – for Shola, for the others who had died so arbitrarily. If he went armed, habitually, as a soldier in a foreign land should, he might have˙ . . . what? Stood off five men with one pistol? Got into a firefight and died? Or should he have marched around Beauville with an SA 80, carrying the weight of it across his chest, the lethal message wherever he went. And what message, exactly, does an armed soldier give out when he is a thousand miles from reinforcements? Fear, perhaps. Foolishness. Thuggishness. It was idiotic. And yet he felt a powerful conviction that he should somehow have prevented what had happened. Should have been prepared for it.

He covered his chest and shoulders with the Witch's medicaments and felt immediate physical relief. He wasn't sure he approved, until he tested and found that beneath the cool there was still a burn, an awareness which promised later discomfort in the abused meat of his back: earned pain, solid and reassuring. In the meantime, his mind was clear, albeit a little tinny, as if he was hearing his own thoughts on a cheap recording. He sent a message to London, tersely worded and laconic, indicating a fatal shooting incident at a local café and the apprehension of those responsible by an armed force. He did not specify the nature of the armed force. That sort of thing would require further discussion.

Shola would be buried today. Mancreu custom was in this regard more Muslim than Christian. The Sergeant dressed accordingly, formal and uncomfortable, squeezing himself into a uniform he

67

had not expected to put on again until he went home and was formally retired from combat duty. He wore his medals. He had a surprising number of them, the real kind, not the ones you got for turning up. Although turning up was no mean thing, some days. He stared at his chest: bright-coloured ribbons, discs and stars.

He couldn't go for a walk like this, not outside. The heat would flatten him. It would be bad enough at the service. So he walked along the cool, dark corridors of Brighton House, going from one end to the other and hearing the sound of his heels and toes tapping on black and white tiles. *Click clack. Click clack.* The house seemed to approve, whatever ghosts it might have peering down from the rafters and out of the shrouded rooms, and nodding to see a British soldier in full rig once again marching here in the aftermath of bloodshed and victory. Or possibly it was mice, or bats. There had been a bat last year, lost and confused. He had shepherded it out into the darkness and it had crapped on him.

He sat in the comms room and waited for the phone call, and when it came it was from someone he didn't know, Marie's brother. Shola was to be buried at eleven. The Sergeant's presence would be appreciated, but would he mind coming as a civilian? Shola had not approved of war.

In theory this required permission from a senior protocol officer. There wasn't one, so the Sergeant petitioned the Brevet-Consul. Sometimes when he did this he actually spoke both parts, making his own voice more gruff and giving the Brevet-Consul a slightly breathy way of speaking which was to his ear suitably posh. This time he just decided that the Brevet-Consul gave his consent. The Sergeant told Marie's brother he entirely understood, and went to change. He wore a pair of light trousers and a white shirt, with a strip of black cloth around the arm. He had to tear the cloth from a blind in the old pantry, and trim it.

The last time he had been to a funeral it had been his mother's, in a funeral house a hundred miles north of London. It had been a pretty cottage with wisteria and roses and a circle of sweet, pink flowers he couldn't name. Someone had taken care with the hedges, too, so that they were neat without being prim. You parked off to one side in a maze of privet which gave everyone a secluded place to arrive and feel sombre. All in all, if somebody had to die and be burned to ash, this was as good a place as any.

The effect was rather spoiled by the industrial metal chimney poking out over the tiled roof, and the column of off-white smoke which rose from it. Mr Willoughby's was doing a too-good business, and while the good man had not double-booked himself, he had grown careless of the time needed to clear one cremation and bring in the next. Even if he hadn't, though, the chimney would have ruined it all. It was bold and silvered and wide, like the gun from which the human cannonball is fired, to the delight of small children and scantily clad assistants. Lester couldn't stop thinking of his mother being expelled straight up and out in her velour dressing gown, her hand still clutched around her wretched, capacious handbag. He wondered where she would land, and hated himself. But it was funny, you couldn't escape that.

And it got worse. The hall was beautiful, with a double row of stone pots filled with flowers around the walls. No one had mentioned this to the attending pastor, who was allergic to something in the arrangements. His eyes swelled as he gave the eulogy, his nose ran and he could barely form the words. When he did, he sounded less like a speaker for the dead and more like the speaker on a bad railway train announcing something you can't understand.

'Fnorbree fnorry to hew hfidawl rebd, ibb de bnabe obb Jebub Hbrised, ouah blord abb fnabior.'

The pastor spoke for twenty minutes, his impenetrable snuffles rising and falling and soaring to the rafters, and while it began as infuriating and grotesque it ended up boring beyond anything anyone had ever experienced. They had come to be moved, or to move themselves, to weep and say some kind of farewell, to

69

whatever extent you can say goodbye to what is already a husk. But it was impossible to feel anything in the funeral house with the bunged-up vicar exhorting you to pray 'add oub fadeb fnord udd' and the burnished cannon of a chimney rearing out of the roof.

On Mancreu, things were different. They gathered by a little plot at a cemetery on the very edge of the Beauville shanty, where the inhabited part of the island began to blend with the deep brown mountains and the jungle interior. It was a fitting spot. The town Shola had lived in made a respectful curve around the churchyard, acknowledging that even the dead need their privacy. This was a transitional place, belonging partly to the human world and partly to the great green mass on the other side. And if Shola had believed in cremation and never told, well, in a few months or weeks, Mancreu would burn, and any remnant of Shola would burn too.

The Sergeant stood next to the Witch, the broad shadow of Dirac the Frenchman a little to one side, and Beneseffe the Portmaster beyond him, all of them staring down into the hole someone had dug. Pechorin, the Ukrainian officer, was at the back in full uniform. The Sergeant guessed he had not been allowed to come in civvies.

The boy was not immediately apparent. Sometimes he would watch things he deeply cared about from a high vantage point, through an old, vastly heavy pair of field glasses he had bought on eBay. It was as if he feared being burned by too much passion, as if the emotions of others might wake in him a response he would then be utterly unable to control. The Sergeant hoped desperately that his friend would come in person to this occasion, because he thought the boy would regret it deeply if he did not, now and for ever.

Shola's coffin was a long basket made of straw, bound with ropes of tomato stem. The only flowers were woven into the coffin itself, wild flowers and sprigs of thorn, and a few wickedly greenish-purple leaves of marijuana from his own crop. The basket was anonymously shaped; it had no head and no foot. The Mancreu men – Shola's cousins and some sturdy dockmen – lowered it in an old piece of fishing net, and Ma Tatin who owned the chandlery sang something old and deep.

Standing at the head of the grave, Marie thanked them all for coming and said Shola had been a good man and that she had loved him even when he was a pain in the arse. For a moment it seemed that she had more to say, a full eulogy, but she just stood there as if at attention and the Sergeant realised that there were tears on her face and that she would stand there until someone took her away. Shola's cousin Tom shepherded her gently back to her mother, and then said straightforwardly that he would be taking over the café but that anyone who felt they had a stake in it should come and see him and he'd cut them in. The Sergeant wondered why he wasn't more cautious. Someone might take advantage. And then he wondered 'of what?' What sort of idiot would come and demand a part of a failing enterprise on an island which would not exist by the end of the year?

Beneseffe heaved a sigh, and Marie threw in the first handful of soil. Tom beckoned to the Sergeant.

'It must be someone else, before me,' the Sergeant said. 'Surely.'

Tom shook his head. 'We agreed. It's you. You were there. Did right.' Tom hesitated, long face sad, then asked, 'Did he say anything?'

The Sergeant thought: *His lung was on the far wall. His spine was on the floor. They exploded him.*

But instead he said: 'It was too quick.'

The congregation nodded, and gentle hands pushed him forward towards the grave. This couldn't be right. What about the rest of Shola's family? But they were over there in a huddle, mourning and brave. They were waiting for him to go ahead of them, had appointed him to show the way. To sergeant for them, and that, at least, was something he understood. He walked to the graveside and looked around for a decent bit of earth. There was too much dust. He wanted loam. He scratched hopelessly, felt his fingernails bend.

There was a small noise, a scuffing of feet on dry ground. From the back of the crowd the boy emerged, head up, chin jutting. He was labouring under the weight of a terracotta pot, which he carried the way Winnie the Pooh carries honey, with both arms wrapped around it in a hug. The people made way for him slowly, as if, in contrast to their decision about the Sergeant, they somehow blamed him for Shola's death. Perhaps he was an orphan after all; some Mancreu folk believed orphans were bad luck. Perhaps he was just alive when Shola was dead.

The boy drew up alongside him, and the Sergeant saw that the pot was full of rich, black earth. The boy's hands were grazed and scratched. He had dug this himself, the Sergeant understood, without tools, and from the look of the soil he had got it from the high mountainsides. He had been up early for his digging, and he had lugged his benediction here all alone for what must be miles and put it in this fine pot, and now he was standing almost at attention, because this was Shola's coffin with Shola's body in it, and it was the right thing.

Gratefully, the Sergeant drove both hands into the pot, and flung a huge load over the coffin, and then another and another. The world flickered and shifted, and he found that he had thrown it all, that his knuckles were raw from rubbing against the clay. He realised he must have stood there for five minutes, heaving soil over the straw coffin, while the family waited patiently and everyone watched.

'I'm sorry,' he said. 'I'm sorry.' He looked down into the grave, wondering if he should scoop some back out for others to give. Sanity prevailed.

The family lined up and threw in the grey dust of the cemetery on top of his rich earth, and then the gravediggers came and filled in the rest very quickly. Finally, Tom spoke. He said that Shola had been a boxer. When a boxer dies, Tom said, they ring the fight bell nine times, and the dead man departs this world when the last whisper of the bell fades away. And then he did it, banging a drumstick against the mushroom-shaped brass bell from the Beauville club. One, two, three, four, five, six, seven, eight, nine. The ninth echoed, and the bell sang on and on, the metal holding the vibration an impossibly long time. And then it was done.

Shola was gone.

The Sergeant's intention, when the funeral was over, had been to take the boy for a quiet walk and discuss with him everything that had happened, as he would have with any young man who had just seen close combat and casualties for the first time. He didn't have the chance, though, because Dirac the Frenchman and Beneseffe the Portmaster scooped them up, and Tom opened the café in his cousin's honour, just for the afternoon, so that they could sit and be there. Someone had cleaned the place, planed the wooden floor where Shola had died so that they would not walk on his blood. Tom stood on the third step so that everyone could see him and thanked them for coming, and he stayed there so that any time anyone looked up, expecting out of habit to see Shola, they caught his eye, and shared a moment with him, and the hole in the world was known and acknowledged.

In a corner the Sergeant saw Dr Inoue, and she raised her glass – whisky, of course – in salute and approbation. Inoue's face was remarkable, he thought. It could convey volumes. *I'm sad that he is dead, and I know that so are you. I am pleased that you are alive, and I know how hard you tried. I know what you would have wished. I am here. So are you. It is all there is*. And of course, in that briefest and softest of twitches at the corner of her mouth: *my whisky is your whisky, if you should need it*. He smiled back, inclined his head as if receiving a medal, and waited until she turned away. When she did, he felt a weight settle on him, as if she had briefly shared with him the burden of the room.

73

As the wake went on, the Sergeant made one attempt to take the boy to one side, only to be blocked by Dirac and to realise, belatedly and with some gratitude, that Dirac was taking the sergeant's role with respect to them both, and that he, Lester Ferris, was himself a man who had just seen combat when he'd been posted out of the line for fear that he wasn't ready for it yet, who had lost a trooper and might need a bit of looking after.

Dirac was his direct equivalent only up to a point. He was a commissioned officer, a major, but one who knew his job. He was a bit older than Lester, and considerably boozier. His notional title was 'envoy', which meant exactly what it said: he had been sent to Mancreu, and there was a strong sense that he was to stay here until he had atoned for his sins. Dirac was an old Legion hand, trained in Guyana in the jungle and seasoned in Mozambique and Algeria. His skin was a weathered tegument the colour of cigars. He had the distinction of having been given three medals and demoted as a consequence of a single incident.

It had been a perfectly simple diplomatic escort job in North Africa, and with an inevitability which spoke to any modern soldier it had gone wrong from the beginning. The political mission was contradictory and insincere, which is fine until you make it the basis for a military deployment. As soon as you involve a professional soldiery, you have to be honest with yourself about your motives. The logic of armed conflict does not read between the lines. In politics, deaths happen incrementally, as a result of bad healthcare and debt. In war, on the other hand, death starts happening when you show up and continues after you leave. Death is not a side effect, and even if you refuse to count the dead they still pile up, and the people who loved them won't forget: not their names nor how they came to die.

So here was Dirac in some crisis camp at the end of some valley, and here were the precious VIPs who were his flock, and the overworked and desperate doctors they were pressing the flesh with, and there was the press pack from around the world. All along the dry riverbed were the refugees in their hundreds of thousands, carrying their entire lives in a few bags. They were running pell-mell from a man called Gervaise and his militia, the Dogs of the Pure Christ, a hard bunch who'd seen what was happening in Rwanda and Congo and decided they liked it. The camp had a lot of French, Swiss and US nationals in it, so it was under the wing of the UN and had a token guard. The UN couldn't get up speed for a full-on peacekeeping force, though, because a land war in Africa against an embedded enemy wasn't anything the big powers wanted any part of. Dirac's job was to escort the VIPs in and bring them back unscathed. He'd been armed accordingly: light weaponry, no big guns and definitely no air support. This was a humanitarian mission, which today meant for God's sake don't do anything humanitarian. The Dogs of the Pure Christ could read a newspaper and they knew the score too: kill who you like as long as you restrict yourself to your own. The camp was out of bounds – but the refugees trying to get to it were fair game.

The Dogs arrived on the third day of Dirac's mission; a few hundred of them, with mobile artillery. They were very careful. They didn't fire on the UN tents. They lined the ridges along the valley and glowered down at the pathetic worm of suffering below. It made great television, really pointed up the issues. And every night, while the VIPs were talking sincerely to the press pack, the Dogs lobbed shells down into the valley floor and cut the refugees to pieces.

Dirac didn't take to it. It was monstrous, and vile, and it offended him on a personal level. He was a son of the Republic, he was a son of the Legion, and as far as he was concerned the Marseillaise didn't fancy this sort of thing either. *Aux armes, citoyens.* 'I want to do something,' he told his regional commander. 'This is shit.'

The regional commander knew his duty to the political apparatus. He was mostly a peacetime soldier, and he accepted what his civilian masters referred to as the wider picture. Permission to engage was not forthcoming.

'This is shit,' Dirac said.

An hour later he had said it quite a lot more and peppered it a few times with '*Je m'en fous*', but he had a plan. He rounded up the few serious lunatics in his command and told them what he proposed to do, and they kicked the tyres of his insanity and pronounced it good, and that evening before word could get out or they could change their minds they made it happen. They sneaked up into the ravines on either side of the valley and moved down the line in near-as-dammit silence, capturing gun emplacements. They used the darkness and they used their bayonets and they took prisoners as they went. By the time morning came they were exhausted and they'd run out of restraint tags, but they'd captured two hundred and thirty-seven members of the Dogs of the Pure Christ and eight light artillery pieces, along with fourteen shoulder-mounted rocket launchers and a pile of automatic rifles and side arms. Dirac marched Gervaise to the nearest cross-roads and stripped him naked, then thrashed him with a local thorn bush across the buttocks and told him to take his men and piss off. By some unhappy chance the press corps got wind of this before it happened, so there was global coverage of the most feared warlord in the region getting spanked until he wept.

It was an utterly inexcusable breach of Dirac's orders and a woeful piece of modern colonialist behaviour. The French government apologised with mountainous sincerity to everyone involved, and even offered to pay for reconstructive plastic surgery on Gervaise's buttocks. This resulted in the details of the humiliation Gervaise had suffered being once again dwelled upon at length by the international press. The UN investigated – 'a little Italian bastard with grey eyes came, you couldn't hide anything from him. It was like hell. He found my girlfriends, my bar tab, everything. I was completely naked in front of an Italian.' Dirac was summoned to headquarters and told he was no longer welcome in post, then handed over to the French senior staff. They lectured him without a whiff of irony on the proud traditions of the French military which he had sullied with this shameful act, and they told him he was to be demoted – yes, and he was lucky to keep his commission at all! Then they gave him a medal, which went very nicely next to the Pan-African Award for Peace and the German People's Medal of Justice. At around the same time the Mancreu posting became available and Dirac was permitted to resume his former rank on the understanding that he see out the island's destruction however long it might take, that he had been a very naughty boy, and that he was really not to do it again.

'Holy Mother of Christ, Lester,' Dirac said, first in French and then in English to emphasise his point. 'Really with custard?'

The Sergeant nodded. Dirac banged his hands on the table, *papapapapow!* and grinned. 'That was some shit. And you got them all?'

'He got one.' Indicating the boy. 'With a comic book.'

Dirac raised his eyebrows briefly, but when the Sergeant nodded that he was entirely serious, raised his glass in Gallic salute. 'Good work! As good as it could have been, okay? As good as it could have been. Both of you, you need to know that.'

The boy shrugged. 'We were not *leet.*'

Dirac fairly obviously did not know what that meant, and equally obviously did not need a translation. 'No. Don't fuck around thinking you could have done it better. There is no better. There's just not being dead.' And hard eyes, commander's eyes fixing them both in turn to be sure they understood. 'I am not blowing smoke up your asses.'

'When we fight crime, we must be better,' the boy said.

The Sergeant had forgotten that, had assumed it was a transient strangeness born of the moment of Shola's death and their survival. He let it fall away without reaction. Dirac, after a moment, did the same.

With some hesitation, the boy unlimbered his knapsack and drew out the dog-eared and curled issue of *The Invisibles* he had used as a weapon, and offered it up for Dirac's inspection. The Frenchman took it gravely and tapped the end. 'Huh. *Pas mal.*' He gave it back, and sighed. 'As good as it could have been, my friend. If the world were perfect there would be no war and I would be sleeping with Lauren Bacall.'

The boy was immediately interested. '1944 Bacall, or Bacall now?'

'Both!' Dirac replied, with absolute certainty.

This was for some reason very funny, and because there was no reason why it should be, it was acceptable that it was funny. Heads turned in the café as they laughed, faces briefly startled and then reassured. *Oh, yes. It's true: life continues. We grieve and we say goodbye because we are alive.*

They drank beer. Then, at Dirac's insistence, they drank their way through some involved Legion funeral song which seemed to the Sergeant's uncertain ear for French to involve a great deal of discussion of veal sausage and the shortcomings of the Belgians. There was to be no sausage for the Belgians, because they were shirkers. At each utterance of this dire sentence, it was necessary to drink. The Sergeant duly did so, knowing that he would regret it, knowing that the regret, too, was part of the wake. After a certain point, he lost track of what he was drinking and became separated from himself. The remaining sober corner was able to think quite clearly and to see through his eyes, but could not direct the action of his limbs. That job was now entirely given over to a mad percussionist who performed 'The Liverpool Girl' and 'How I Met Your Sisters' and found a willing chorusline in the other guests, and then at some point the babble fell away and people departed, and at last Tom brought food and tea and gently eased the remaining mourners out into the deep middle night. The Sergeant wandered homewards through the chill, serenading the endless sky with a pint-glass-and-spoon rendition of 'The Mountains of Mourne'. By a strange grace, the percussionist appeared to have a good sense of direction.

Where the road forked, however, he surprised himself. Instead of going right, which would have brought him directly home to his bed, he went left, up towards the jungle and the shanty. The cool air was seeping into his muscles and driving the disparate parts of him back together. As he went along the line of a low wall and beside a stream, then down and over a hedge, he stopped singing and took stock. He felt empty, and that was good. His balance was returning. He was placid yet full of an inexhaustible energy, caught in the place between wakefulness and sleep. The compulsion to go in the wrong direction was still undeniable.

He realised he was walking through someone's garden. There was laundry hanging out, and he nearly got caught up on an immense pair of bloomers. The frilled legs grasped for him like some hunting sea creature, but he fought them off with doggy digging motions, and passed by. He plunged through a thorny bush and out the other side, down a lane, and finally felt he was nearing his destination. The road gave way to a track, and the blackness of the lower jungle rose ahead of him. His feet touched hard paving, then soil. Dust. Grass. An elegant iron gate. It was familiar, for sure, but he had no idea why he was here. He went through. The moon overhead was vast and silver-white, seeming to fill the sky. He sat down.

When he woke he was cold, and he knew he was in the cemetery where Shola was buried, and that he had come to say another goodbye, to apologise, and that he had lost another friend in this life and hadn't enough to be giving them away. He made a noise, head in hands: wordless sorrow without the stamp of appropriate grieving moulded onto it. He looked for the fresh grave, entertaining a mad fantasy of digging it up, of waking Shola even at this late date, getting him to a proper hospital where they could treat his injuries. No, not a proper hospital: the Fleet! The Fleet could help him. They must have everything there, all the impossible new medicines, machines to pump his blood, machines machines machines. They could give him a new lung, a new heart, a new spine, grow new bones or steal them from someone else. They could do anything, if they wanted. Anything at all.

A scent washed over him, strange and sharp. It was warm and not unpleasant: leaves and bark, yes, and sweat. An animal smell. A neighbourhood dog, he thought, and awaited the wet nose in his ear. Well, that would be nice. Companionship. Dogs were good companions. They had no solid memory, only a sort of endless now. A happy dog was happy almost all the time, and shared that with you, which he could use about now.

The nose did not arrive. The dog butted him gently, quite high on his back. A large dog, or a smaller one on its hind legs. It sighed, and the noise was amazingly loud in the night. He wondered if his own sigh had been quite so massive, if he had woken anyone. He felt that any dog with that much heart should be rewarded with a hug.

He turned around into a completely alien intelligence, a huge soup-plate face with wide, reflective eyes. They were not yellow or green but a scalding platinum. He smelled meat and musk, tasted it in the air.

The tiger blinked. It was enormous. They were supposed to be smaller. They were supposed to be shy, too. Perhaps this one was lonely. The head was on a level with his own as he sat, and bigger. The whole animal must top three hundred kilos. He'd been part of four-man squads which didn't weigh that much.

It peered at him, neither skittish nor aggressive but imponderable. It snuffled, and he smelled that same scent again, stronger: warm saliva and fur. It sneezed. Tiger snot spattered his chest. He did not cry out. The tiger looked almost embarrassed, butted him again.

Well, dog or not, it seemed to want to know him. He reached out very slowly with his left hand (in case it was torn off). The tiger twitched back from it, then sniffed the offered limb and found nothing to object to. It suffered him to stroke it. The fur was thick and dark, heavy with oil. He wondered whether to scratch it. Domestic cats liked to be scratched. His mother's had. The tiger had taken the initiative, though, and was pushing upwards under his palm. He scratched. Its eyes closed, and it made a new noise, like a distant avalanche. Purring, he supposed, though it seemed a ridiculous word to describe this sound which was almost too deep to hear.

Time passed. The Sergeant's left arm grew tired and he substituted his right. Then his right arm grew tired and he slowed and stopped. The tiger whickered reproach. He shrugged. It considered him and accepted the verdict, then wandered away. He was for a moment forcefully reminded of the boy. *Conversation over, see you next time.* He watched the animal make a slow circuit of the graveyard. He thought it might make a special pilgrimage to Shola's plot, a sort of omen, but it didn't and he was obliquely glad. Then, without meaning to, he shut his eyes for a moment and it was gone. He came upright and opened his mouth to call after it, then stopped: he had no idea what he would say. He realised he had been in some way hoping for its approval.

He took two or three steps forward, hoping to catch a glimpse of it by the trees.

5. ZOMG

He struggled through the next morning because there were things to do, things which couldn't wait a day however awful he felt. He got up. It wasn't pleasant. He ate some soup, wished he hadn't. It swilled around in his stomach as if he was a hollow plastic sack. He knew better than to add bread. It would swell and make him feel bloated and leaden.

The weather was stubbornly ordinary. The natural world was remorseless about human death and just rolled on. Some people took solace in that, in the continuance of a greater cycle, but the Sergeant had found that he did not. Death was bad, and that was all. It was not a mercy, not a release, not a victory, and there was no more joy in a man becoming food for worms than in a chicken becoming food for a man.

He waited for the soup to recede, then took himself out for a run. He pushed himself through the blinding headache and on until he felt the jelly in his legs fade and the poisons in his blood bubble out through his skin. He stank. Tainted sweat fell from his body onto the track, and he wondered if it would make any difference to the cocktail of slurry and strangeness under the island. Booze metabolites and skin, salt and water, filtering down through endless layers of sand and rock to a weird melting pot somewhere down below. He showered, and midway through, as the water spiralled away down the plughole, he abruptly found the notion enormously alarming. He was giving up tiny parts of his physical self to be assimilated by what was under the island, would become part of an alien thing so dangerous that only total war could be contemplated, an annihilation so fierce it would take the stone and the sea with it. He retched, but nothing emerged from him. He allowed himself two ibuprofen tablets from supplies, logged them, and chased them with more water and a sachet of electrolyte salts intended for treating severe diarrhoea. Finally he added a multivitamin and a single bit of crispbread from the larder to settle his stomach. The mixture was sickly, but he knew it would work.

Dressed and dry, he took himself out to the car. He had prisoners to talk to: Kershaw was keeping them for him.

Beauville did have a prison – an old red Victorian box with narrow, barred windows and a high wall – but it had been commandeered by NatProMan to house its overspill, and was now full of administrators, soldiers and a considerable stock of weapons. Serious criminals – of which there had not been many – had been transferred to prisons in the Scandinavian countries where the crime rate was actually dropping so fast that the prison infrastructure industry was having trouble staying afloat. Denmark had been a net importer of criminals since 2011.

It had been understood that the island wasn't going to last long enough for the lack of a prison to be a problem. Except that it had, so the Sergeant, five months into his role as Brevet-Consul, had persuaded Jed Kershaw to fix up an empty wooden building at the far end of the waterfront which had once been a fish-packing plant. The jail wasn't secure by any modern standard, but the refrigeration units were big enough to serve as cells and you could lock them. A team of engineers had drilled holes in the sides so that the prisoners did not suffocate, and had turned off the cooling system so they did not freeze. Until yesterday it had housed only a few serial brawlers and an aged flasher.

The boy was sitting on a low wall with his knapsack, waiting. When he slipped down from his perch and walked across the cracked stone to the Sergeant's position, he did so with such an air of formality that the Sergeant briefly saw him dressed in a lawyer's wig and gown: five feet tall and making the case for the prosecution, or even pronouncing sentence. He had gathered the straps of the bag in his left hand and carried it like a briefcase.

The Sergeant had been aware that this was coming, that the boy would inevitably wish to confront Shola's killers or at least to confront the tangible fact of them. He had decided that he would not argue. Perhaps he should, but in his mind it simply would not be fair – not comprehensible, either to himself or, he felt sure, to the boy – to claim now, when it was safe, that the matter was too grown up, too serious for him to handle. It might have been possible before Shola's blood had spattered his face. Not after.

The men had been separated and held incommunicado. They had been given water to drink and basic medical attention and food. Yesterday, the Sergeant judged, would have been the perfect time to talk to them, but today would do. And the boy would be an added oddness, an unbalancing factor. They might believe Shola had been his father.

Which raised the question of whether he had been, but the Sergeant pushed this to one side.

'I'll get you in,' he told the boy, 'but you don't talk and you do what I say, all right?'

The boy nodded. His lips formed words but there was no breath in them. After a moment, the Sergeant turned to him firmly, made him spread his arms in a T-shape, and frisked him. No knife. No razorblade. No bomb, no gun. No vial of some appalling gas or germ sneaked from a Fleet repository in exchange for a particularly impressive bit of local contraband.

'Sorry,' the Sergeant said.

'No,' the boy replied. 'You are so right. I would waste these *badmashes* in two ticks of a lamb's arsehole. For Shola, I totally would.'

The Sergeant nodded. 'I know you would,' he said.

'Whatever,' the boy growled. 'Emote later. Right now: Voight-Kampff FTW.'

With this perplexing battle-cry, he turned and went inside.

A Canadian marine wearing NatProMan tour ribbons shepherded them with casual courtesy. The Sergeant wondered how it must have felt to a crew of Mancreu hardcases to be herded down these antiseptic steps. The whole place smelled tartly of phenols. In his childhood that same odour had meant cough pastilles, sugar-coated and blackcurrant-flavoured. One winter he'd had flu: the real thing, hot and bloody awful, and no one had realised until he collapsed on the doormat at home. He had walked back from school, eaten half a dozen of those pastilles one after another, his mouth turning itself inside out, demanding more and more to cut the nausea and the confusion. The whole city had been coming and going in his eyes, grey with rain and red with brakelights, then dark. He'd had a cassette-player Walkman clipped to his belt: the size of a brick, with flimsy headphones. Music copied from an LP, his mother's, his father's, a friend's. It didn't matter so long as it drowned out the world while he walked, coat soaked through, fever poaching him in his clothes.

The boy shivered. The Sergeant reached out and checked his forehead. It was quite cool.

'Sir?' the marine said.

'I'm a sergeant,' he responded automatically. 'I work for a living.'

'Yes, Sergeant,' the marine said, and whatever query he had been mustering went away. The Sergeant waited. The marine waited, too, politely but not without a measure of confusion.

After they had all stood in front of the door for a while, the Sergeant realised there was nothing to wait for. Always before in his professional life, whenever he had visited prisoners, there had been a form of words. The custodian of any detention facility had given some sort of warning about proper and improper questions, and the limitations of lawful conduct. But not on Mancreu. Not here. You did what you wanted as long as you were in charge. That was the whole point. He could kill these men: Jed Kershaw might be cross with him, but probably wouldn't be. No one would seriously object, and if they did, there was no law to prosecute him. Everyone on the island walked within bounds out of sheer habit, respected property and persons and decency because they knew those things were important. But there was no constraint any more, just what you did. He wondered if the men, knowing that, had drawn fearful conclusions from the abattoir tiles and the drains in the floor.

The boy nodded to him, and they went into the first cell.

The man inside was a hillman with a wide face. He positively strutted in his cuffs.

The Sergeant asked his first question. The man nodded like a celebrity, smiled. He had been paid by the Americans to murder the barman, and the whores. Yes. Paid millions of dollars in a Swiss bank account. Hundreds of millions. He would be out of here soon.

The Sergeant asked who would get him out.

The President, the man said. Of the United States. He would personally order it, but of course the order would be disguised. All the same, that was just how it would be.

And what, the Sergeant asked, would happen then?

The man would buy a helicopter and a skyscraper and he would live in Switzerland. He would have a big house by the sea, he had seen pictures of it. If the Sergeant wanted a job, he could apply. The Sergeant looked like the right sort of man. Dependable, not ambitious.

The boy stepped in, briefly, to observe that Switzerland was not known for its sea coast.

The man jerked back and for a moment he seemed appalled. His mouth stretched wide as if he was going to vomit. Then he shuddered and rolled his head on his neck (things went pop inside him, bones and gristle). He sighed and shook his finger. Children were a trial, he said. They knew nothing of the world. If the Sergeant would take the boy out, it might be better, and they could speak as men, discuss the details of his future employment.

They moved on to the second cell. The occupant was mousy, so the Sergeant asked his questions quietly. That was in the lessons he had had. It was a crude form of something called kinesic interview. You took your cues from the subject. If you were lucky, it helped. Usually — according to the learned DI Burroughs — you were not lucky.

The man said he was a herder. He had driven the car because he was paid to, and then he was told he was coming in. He had come in because he was made to. Yes, he had carried a gun. Everyone had a gun. He had fired high and wide because otherwise he would not be paid and he was afraid he might also be shot. He still was not sure that would not have happened, after. He was sorry for what had been done by the others. Very sorry. For all his life he would be sorry for the barman and the pretty girls.

It was plausible. It could also be so much shit. No way to know, not really. The Sergeant's gut told him it was probably shit.

The next cell was a slightly different shape, a little closer and tighter — which also made it darker — and the prisoner lay on his bed and did not get up. He was not seriously injured. His face expressed a kind of distant uncaring. He looked at them briefly, flinched a little when he saw the boy, then seemed to accept his inevitability and turned away, in dismissal or despair the Sergeant could not say.

'Don't know anything,' the man muttered as he stared at the wall, from which position no inducement short of physical force could move him.

*

In the fourth cell, on the off chance, the Sergeant changed tack and did a certain amount of shouting. The man in the fourth cell had a missing toe and looked to be in pain – not horrible pain but misery pain – so shouting was particularly unpleasant for him. He wept. The boy shouted too, got right down beside him and shouted high and long into his face. The man protested and objected and demanded more of whatever they were giving him for the toe. That and strong drink.

'Why?' the Sergeant repeated. 'You came into my friend's bar and gunned him down. Why?' And then he was shouting quite genuinely, screaming into the prisoner's face over and over: 'WHY? WHY? WHY?'

He pulled himself back sharply, swallowed. He wished for a chain of command, for men in authority above him to hold him back. He wished for laws to make his limits plain. He wanted very much to beat the murder out of all of them, to bruise them and bludgeon them and let out the fury in his chest. Line them up like fucking tomatoes and cut them down, over and over and over, these bastards who had done this bloody, brutal thing on his doorstep, who had come into his special place, his town, his island and killed his friend, made the boy so bleakly and irretrievably unhappy. Made the boy grow up.

He glanced across at his friend, afraid he would see fear or shock, but the boy looked quite impressed, even encouraging. Well, yes. All he had done was shout. Shouting was fair enough. He turned his gaze back to the prisoner.

But his monstering seemed to have achieved nothing at all. The man stared at them and then, after a moment, he suddenly shouted back, screamed that his foot was rotting and burning and hurting and he wanted more, more, MORE MORE MORE. It was like an echo. The man began to wail then, like an infant. More, more, more. Perhaps he was an addict already and this had just sharpened his need. (More, more, MORE!)

Useless.

The last cell was bigger, and the man in the bed was unconscious. His eyes were burned. It was all treatable, but that kind of medical care was expensive and no one cared. The Sergeant shrugged and made a note to request it. Maybe the man would open up when he saw the world again. Or maybe he'd be able to look a jury in the eye and see their verdict. Whatever. On the scale of things here, the ships and the NatProMan deployment, it wasn't that much money. Maybe they'd save this man's vision only for him to be acquitted or just released and that would be Shola's memorial: an almost miraculous gift to one of his murderers. That was the world sometimes, and Mancreu, especially. *Kswah swah*.

He went in again, cell by cell, repeated his lines. Then he had the boy try in Moitié, listened to the ebb and flow and heard the story in cell two expand a little. 'I was on the high road by the river. There were men, they offered me money. They had bags. I thought these bags contained contraband for sale. I thought we would sell it. At the bar we got out. It is a good place to sell, a bar, everyone knows this. Then they took out guns. I also must carry a gun. I fire into the air. I know no names. I know nothing. I am bystander. I wished only to make a little money to take a ship. To go away before the end. I have no family.'

The Sergeant slipped himself into the discussion, made the man tell it in reverse. It's hard to lie in reverse. The story bent a little, acquired details, but did not change. He didn't know if that was because it was a simple lie, or because it was true.

Then he photographed them one by one, and they made this hard or not hard, each according to his lights.

When the interrogators came out into the fresh air, a light mist had settled over the ocean and the fishing boats and even the Black Fleet seemed to be suspended somewhere between the water and the sky. The horizon line had vanished entirely from east to west, and sea and cloud had melded into a purpled canvas so that the

Arlington Bride – a Swiss-owned, Wilmington-registered cargo hauler which had been one of the first to arrive when Mancreu was extralegalised – appeared to be hovering over the automated lighthouse at the end of the pier. The boy sighed deeply.

'I know,' the Sergeant said. 'They didn't give us anything.'

'No,' the boy replied.

'They will. We'll get there.'

'Maybe.' He had dropped directly into the dejected funk which was the flipside of his manic highs. The Sergeant wasn't sure if this was the sort of thing which would be considered an actual sickness or just a part of being however old he was. Probably it depended where you were. In France, he knew, they used a different manual for psychological medicine. They might well say no. In America, everything was diagnosable, probably even positive traits could be treated if you wanted to get rid of them. Then, too, the boy had real things to be sad about. He had lost a friend, and the interrogation which had promised an explanation of sorts had failed to deliver. Instinct told the Sergeant to keep his friend moving forwards, to avoid letting him dwell on the bad things. There was time for that, but you wanted momentum to get you through it, so that you could grieve without ceasing to function. Sorrow was something you did best if you did it while other things were happening, or it could freeze you in place.

'We will get there. But maybe we'll have to poke around a bit. I've got a few things to look into otherwise, too.' He needed it to be true. He had seen the boy's face in the café after the fight, the look which said Lester Ferris was an actual superstar. He didn't need it to be that way all the time, but the more distant it became the more conscious he was of a kind of pain.

'Yes,' the boy said dully, meaning 'no'.

So the Sergeant told him about the tiger.

It was a strange story and he told it haltingly, and he probably oversold the part about being very drunk, because the boy's lips twitched in puritanical disdain. All the same, when he got to the good bit, about scratching the huge head, the boy's eyes were very wide. The Sergeant had to break off and swear, repeatedly, to the truth of it. He swore several different appalling oaths, each bringing doom and despair on him in different ways if he was lying in the smallest particular, but what finally persuaded his audience was how the story ended, without resolution.

'Real life has no understanding of proper structure,' the boy said, 'which is why news stories are always made of little lies.' This pleased the Sergeant very much because it was a brief flicker of the boy's usual self, like a familiar face in a crowd.

He saw a way forward, considered briefly, and then jumped. 'It might speed things up with my other stuff if I had some help,' he said. 'I mean: usually, in a p'lice context,' and bless DI Burroughs for this bit of coppering nonsense, 'usually these sorts of matters would be dealt with by an investigation team, so it's hardly surprising I'm struggling a bit with the caseload all by myself.'

The boy nodded in a worldly, serious way. Of course. Anyone of consequence knew that about policing. There might be less educated persons who would disagree, his manner said, but we need not concern ourselves with them at present.

Deep breath. 'So what I was thinking was that you could come along. Help out. Unofficially deputised into the Mancreu Investigatory Force, as it were. Only if you want. I know you've got things to do, I don't mean to say you haven't. But if you did want to, well, there's always things I can't get to and which you might be ideally placed for, being familiar with the local environment and so on.' He trailed off, looking at the impossible flying ships.

After a moment, he heard the boy say tentatively: 'Fight crime?'

'Well, yes. I mean, any actual fighting – and there won't be any – but if there was, then that would be my part. You'd be my eyes and ears. Make sure I didn't miss anything. Use that brain of yours.'

The boy seemed to expand, the damp rag of his depression becoming a sort of balloon.

'Fight crime!'

'In a strictly auxiliary capacity,' the Sergeant said hastily.

'Taking the law to the mean streets of the city!'

'Well—'

'Yes! You will need me. I am your kid partner. I will crack wise. I will rock it Gangnam Style!'

'I don't want you getting in trouble. You're a minor.'

'Yes! Pretty weird kid partner, otherwise.' The Sergeant saw teeth, and knew he was being teased.

'You wouldn't be my partner. That's—' He choked down *insane* and discarded *against regulations*, wondering what he'd got himself into. 'Not something I'm allowed to do.'

'Of course! I am not with you. We are in the same place at the same time. If anything happens, I shall run away. I am a civilian.'

'Yes.'

'But when danger strikes: I am off the books and off the hook!'

'No!'

'Excellent! Just like that: deny, deny, deny! Sometimes justice must wear a mask!'

'No masks. No adventure. Just police work. It can be boring, I won't lie to you. But . . .' He hesitated. 'You'd be with me. We could talk.' He dried up again. 'About stuff.'

The boy nodded solemnly. 'Go places, talk about stuff. Find a box of matches, get a DNA sample, hairs from victim's pullover. Investigate! Unassuming sergeant for fallen empire by day! Foolhardy boy companion! And it will be hard work. Gather evidence, data, follow leads. Good men fighting to protect and serve in a town where there is no law!' The Sergeant winced. That was a bit on the nose. 'But then, later . . . when the moon is in the sky and the evildoer thinks he is safe . . . Tigerman strikes!'

'Tiger-what what?'

The boy leaned back away from him, waved his hands to indicate the bigness of this idea. 'Tigerman! You are Tigerman!' Huge circles. 'Hero of Mancreu!'

'I am not. I'm just doing a job of work.' *And I'm probably not supposed to do that.*

'For now! But you were chosen by the tiger at Shola's grave! There is no justice, there's just us! When it is necessary . . .' The boy waved his arms again, now in a gesture which was either movie kung fu or the tricky business of changing costumes in a phone box. 'When it is necessary: Tigerman!' He made a *whoomf* noise in his cheeks. 'Famous victory!'

'Well, as long as you understand there will be no actual Tigerman.'

Whoomf. Hand gestures, definitely pulling open a shirt this time. 'Tigerman!'

'My name's Lester. You can't have a hero called Lester.'

'Tigerman,' the boy said fervently. 'Full of win.'

'No.'

'Yes.'

'No.'

'Win. Full of. Also: famous victory.'

'No.'

'Yes!'

'No!'

But the Sergeant was losing his grip on seriousness. It was funny. Joyful. And he wanted, had wanted for so long, to be a hero for this boy. Not a broken-down old fart. A cool person. The sort of person you'd hope would be your dad.

Whoomf. 'Tigerman!'

They stared at one another without blinking.

'No,' the Sergeant said, just as the boy said 'Yes!' with equal vigour. The man scowled, the boy grinned, and that was that. Each had said his piece, the other knew where he stood, and now they would leave the matter to the world. *Kswah swah.*

They shook on it.

The day had been so weighty and the outcome so momentous that the boy decided a special entertainment was now called for, saying only in tones of great import and mystery that it would be 'hunnerten pro cent zed oh em gee'. The Sergeant recognised the over-revved 'one hundred and ten per cent' and the 'oh my god' parts, but the 'z' quite defeated him. 'Zombie' was the only thing he could come up with and it seemed unlikely, unless 'zombie' had now acquired an additional meaning of 'excellent'. Thinking about it, he decided that this was possible, but that he would be quite happy never knowing for sure. He agreed that he would be home at seven to receive his visitor, and they parted.

'What the fuck, Lester? Don't get me wrong, I'm not asking you personally, I'm asking you as a stand-in for God. But that being the case: "what", "the", "fuck"? Shola was like a pillar of the world. Why would anyone just kill the guy? Fucking *assholes!*'

Jed Kershaw had his hands in the air for emphasis. He was a little man, and he used his hands a lot, held them high over his head and waggled his fingers. The Sergeant had initially found this odd. It made Kershaw look like a small, circular wizard casting spells which never worked, or that puppet show his sister had told him about where the puppets took off all their clothes until they finally were just hands again. But you got used to it, and the temptation to talk up into Kershaw's palm faded away until the American was just another bit of life on the island.

Kershaw would have rejected this idea because Mancreu drove him crazy. He was forever shouting at his staff and down the phone, demanding that the place work properly, behave itself with something like sanity, function in some way which made sense, because he was the bridge between the world where things did make sense and the small circle in this blue ocean where they didn't have to. But what really drove Jed Kershaw crazy, he said, what was going to kill him if this whole situation wasn't resolved pretty fucking soon now, any day now, was how *British* Mancreu was, and maybe also at the same time if this was possible – he wasn't sure – how *French*.

Kershaw had long ago realised, apparently, that dealing with Brits was tricky. You had to listen to what a Brit was saying – which was invariably that he thought *XYZ* was a terrific idea and he hoped it went very well for you – while at the same time paying heed to the greasy, nauseous suspicion you had that, although every word and phrase indicated approval, somehow the sum of the whole was that you'd have to be a mental pygmy to come up with this plan and a complete fucking idiot to pursue it. After six years working with the Brits in various theatres he'd come to the conclusion that they didn't do it on purpose. The thing was, Brits actually thought that subtext was plain text. To a Brit, the modern English language was vested with hundreds of years of unbroken history and cultural nuance, so that every single word had a host of implications depending on who said it to whom, when, and how. British soldiers, for example, gave entire reports to their commanders by the way they said 'good morning, sir' and then had to spend half an hour telling them the detail, which was why the Brits always looked bored in briefings. They could sense the trajectory of the conversation, knew the bad news was coming *now* and the good news *now* and that there was a question on the end which needed thinking about. With a bit of work they could deduce the question, too, but they always waited politely for it to be asked so that no one felt rushed.

Originally – when he had believed it was some sort of snobbish post-colonial joke – this all had made Kershaw dislike the

Brits, but now apparently he sort of admired it. His brother Gabe was a literature professor at Brown, and when Kershaw brought this up with him Gabe had nodded and said, yeah, absolutely, but you had to read T. S. Eliot to understand. So Jed Kershaw had bought *The Waste Land* from Amazon dot com and read it here in Mancreu. *The Waste Land* was a fucking terrifying document of gasping psychological trauma, and it was plenty relevant to the island, but the important point about it was that Eliot was trying to make use of something called an 'objective correlative', which was an external reference point everyone would understand in the same way without fear of misapprehension. Kershaw found this revealing, he said, because it was very British. Only a British poet – and, for Kershaw's purposes, Eliot was one – would imagine that the gap between people living in the same street was so fucking enormous that you had to read the entire body of English-language poetry from 1500 to the present day in order to have a background which would allow you to communicate something as simple as 'your dog is pissing on my lawn' and be reliably understood. Only a Brit could be so appalled by the staggering complexities of meaning which could be found in the word 'piss' that he felt it was necessary to read *Paradise Lost* and *The Mayor of Casterbridge* in order to be certain he wasn't getting the wrong end of the stick. And for sure, only a Brit would imagine that adding a huge raft of literary imagery to the sea of human emotion and history which was English would clarify the situation in any fucking way at all. All the same, there was something glorious in that complexity, in the fact that Brit communication took place in the gaps between words and in the various different ways of agreeing which meant 'no'. But none of that made Mancreu any easier for Jed Kershaw to deal with, and he suspected but could not prove that this was because the island was also French. 'And the French are worse, Lester, because they do all this same crap and they fucking improvise, too.'

The Sergeant took his time responding to Jed Kershaw's question. *What the fuck, indeed.* 'Well, apparently, five guys from the hills, Jed. And for no reason at all that I can get them to acknowledge.'

'Assholes!'

'Yes. And amateurs, too.'

'So what are we talking about? Money? Girls? Boys? What?'

'They won't say. Or maybe there isn't anything. Maybe this is next.'

'What "next"? What do you mean, "this is next"?'

'Maybe this is what happens after a certain point, Jed. With an island that doesn't know if it's coming or going. Maybe people just start getting together and killing one another.'

Kershaw stared at him. 'Fuck, Lester.'

'Yes, sir.'

'Fuck, Lester, that is a nihilistic fucking notion.'

'Yes, sir.'

'You're saying maybe they just, what, they got together in the backwoods somewhere and decided to do a murder? Get in the car, go somewhere, spray the place with bullets, because, hey, what the hell, it's the end of the world?'

'It's just a possibility.'

'So, what, we've gone from leaving parties to . . . what? Everybody goes nuts and starts killing everybody like it's the fucking nutbar apocalypse?'

'I don't say it's likely, sir.'

'You're saying "sir" a great deal, Lester. I recognise professional sir-ing when I hear it. Do you have some British psychological-trauma profile which says this is going to happen?'

'No, sir, not that I'm aware of.'

'Then Jesus, Lester! Do not scare me like that. Jesus.' He looked up. 'The next words out of your mouth better not include "sir", Lester.'

'All right, Mr Kershaw, I shall bear that in mind.'

'Jed.'

'Jed. Yes, sir.'

Kershaw glowered, then grinned. 'You are fucking with me just now, Lester, in a manner you no doubt believe is comradely joshing.'

'If you say so, Jed.'

'I do, Lester.'

And after that they talked, but nothing more was actually said. The Sergeant excused himself before Jed Kershaw had to find an excuse to get away, and Kershaw looked gratefully after him as he went downstairs. In the street, the Sergeant glanced around for the boy but could not see him. He felt a little sad, but stiffened his spine and reminded himself that they were doing something hunnerten pro cent ZOMG later, and that this was apparently good. In any case, the boy had other aspects to his life that were his own.

He looked around once more and got into his car.

The town of Beauville was surprisingly beautiful as he drove back to Brighton House, like a strong-jawed choir mistress allowing the day to see her softer side. The hard, industrial region of Mancreu was away on the south coast, the ferroconcrete slab housing of the 70s chemical men who had come to refine and combine and produce plastics.

But here in the north, Beauville looked alive and even bustling. Along the harbour front, a few of the very oldest buildings still remained, low-ceilinged and achingly pretty, smelling of three hundred years of tobacco and drink, and traced with cracks from earthquakes and battering gales. In a ring around them loomed gawky colonial townhouses and stores; wooden crossbeams taken from ships bore witness to the ongoing settlement by mariners and merchants. The outer circle was a kind of loose net of tracks, farms, warehouses and fisher huts, slowly giving way to the back country. Mancreu was a fisher island first, a tenuous farmland second, and everything revolved around the town where produce could be bought and sold. A small number of people lived out on the mountainsides, herders and weavers for the most part, and a very few bandits who were mostly bandits by inheritance rather than vocation. The Sergeant peered out that way now, thinking of the men who had killed Shola, wondering if they were from some such raggedy clan. He had thought those men had been among the first to Leave, taking their twentieth-century bolt-action rifles and their few belongings and heading off for some other place where they could quietly waste away. But then, this crew had carried proper weapons. Militia guns, not shepherd's companions.

A real policeman, he thought, would follow those guns somehow, track them backwards. Or he might draw inferences from their make and model, from their presence at all. How unlikely was it that that gear was in private hands on the island? Not very. North Africa and Yemen both overflowed with Kalashnikovs. So did large parts of South-East Asia. Mancreu was surrounded by a ring of cheap, durable guns. Surrounded, but at a distance, and something of the British ethos regarding firearms had prevailed here for a long while. He had been right a moment ago: Mancreu bandits carried guns which would not have been out of place at Gallipoli or Ypres, and used them largely for shooting glass bottles and sheep belonging to other people, and only very occasionally for a stick-up. Certainly, they did not spree.

Things did not fit. He was keeping count of them in his mind, but they were all so hazy, so very tenuous. He might be being foolish. After all, Shola had been his friend. He very much wanted the death to mean something. And the boy needed it to mean something, needed this bleak introduction to messy, ketchup mortality to be more than just the consequence of a jostling in the marketplace. It dawned on him that he needed to do something else for a few hours. He could knock his head against what had happened until he bled, and he would still not understand it. He would miss the truth if it was offered to him because he was starting to have ideas about what it should look like and he would ignore anything which looked different. He had to step back.

And then, too, the rest of Mancreu's perpetual crisis had not ground to a halt merely because Shola had died. It felt that way, or it felt that it should be that way, but he had lost enough friends to know better. The silence you feel belongs to you. To everyone else, it's just another day.

He went home by way of the hospital. The other survivors of the shooting knew no more than he did, and he found himself apologising. They told him not to, and he returned to Brighton House pensive and took refuge for a while in the coarse yellowy pages of his book.

The boy arrived at a quarter after the hour bearing a huge sack almost as high as himself, and demanded that they go out onto the terrace facing the sea. The sack shortly resolved itself into a paper bag full of further paper bags, white and ribbed with wire. These, being unfurled, became cylinders nearly five feet in height and two across.

'Thai lanterns!' the boy said. 'Hunnerten pro cent! In many places a bit illegal because of fires. But here, not. Also we send them out there.' He pointed to the blue water beyond the terrace wall. The wind was blowing over the house and out to the horizon, and the distinction between sea and sky was indistinct.

'Send them?' the Sergeant said, and then wondered a little nervously why his first question had not been about the fires.

For answer, the boy produced a stretch of grubby cloth and bundled it up into a ball the size of his fist. He stuffed the rag into a cradle beneath the lantern. 'Hold! We must inflate.'

The Sergeant held the lantern at top and bottom, beginning to understand, and the boy ignited the ball. Hot air billowed up, and the paper crinkled and swelled.

'Wait until it really wants to go,' the boy said.

They waited, and presently the lantern rose in their hands until the boy was on tiptoe. 'Now!' he said.

The lantern lifted slowly, turning from the last brush of their fingers and wobbling as a light breeze buffeted it towards the house. The Sergeant winced. Then it went higher and suddenly seemed to get the idea, floating proudly away over the dark, oily sea beneath the cliff. After a moment more its reflection was visible in the water, a twin glow hanging in another sky.

'Quick,' the boy said. 'Another!'

They launched all seven, a flickering procession of lights climbing ever upwards in a small, attenuated flock, the first one dwindling from view but not extinguished as the last took flight. The lanterns were fragile but tenacious, heading off over that vast ocean towards an unknown end, and by their simple, purposeful ascent and their warm yellow light, they turned the mind to the indefinable colour of the evening and the sound of the wind, to the scale of the world.

'How far will they go?' the Sergeant asked.

The boy shrugged. 'Long way. Sometimes they go up and catch a thermal. Hundreds of miles, then. I have seen them burn and fall, and sometimes they are forced down. But I have never seen one come down at the end of its flight. They are always too far.'

The man and the boy watched as the lanterns winked away in the gathering dark, and then, when the last of the lights they were following might or might not have been the running lights of a ship or an aircraft, or a star, they went inside.

The next morning the boy was gone, as usual fading into the air like some sort of sprite, and leaving only a blanket on the spare bed and an unwashed coffee cup in his wake. The Sergeant tossed the blanket over a window ledge to air and scrubbed the cup, enjoying his own exasperation at the chore. As he worked, it occurred to him that he should start small. Shola's murder was too big to understand, too important for him to take on. He should by rights pass it to someone with experience but there was no one like that so it would have to be him, after all, and yet he had no real idea where to go from here. He was baulked.

So he would begin with the lost dog. It was a small problem, but no doubt it mattered to the owner, and that would tell. It would get him started. At the same time, he would uncover what he could about the boy's parentage. Two small things would be done, both needful to someone, and in the simplicity of these distractions his mind might turn up some new avenue by which he could approach Shola's death.

As he made his way to the car, he found himself smiling. The lanterns had indeed been 'zed oh em gee'.

6. Dog

To his alarm, the Matter of the Missing Dog was more complex than it first appeared. After a visit to the very ordinary old lady to whom the animal belonged, it technically became the Matter of the Kidnapped Dog because someone had been seen by two witnesses actually lifting the animal into the back of a flatbed truck, and he was forced to revise his opinion regarding the likely seriousness of the situation. The first witness he was inclined to dismiss – a housebound old geezer who must have been bored and drunk since before the Sergeant was born – but the second was a sensible young woman who was only visiting Mancreu to help her family move to her home in Botswana. It seemed vanishingly unlikely that she would make up such a tale, or that if she did it would tally with that of the old man.

If the dog had been of a combative breed he might have suspected a fighting ring, but Madame Duclos's pet was evidently not of that sort. She showed him a photograph. The animal was fat to the point of shapeless, like a lumpy brown quilt dumped on the sofa. Even its ears were fat. With her permission, he retained the photograph. As he left, she took his hand and said 'please'.

Why on Earth did people keep dogs? He could feel the dryness of her skin. She chopped her own wood, this old woman.

'Please,' she said again.

'I'll do what I can,' he told her. 'I'll try.'

'Of course you will,' she said. 'The English love dogs.'

He nodded assent.

She peered at him and tutted with the unerring instinct of grand-mothers for unspoken reservations, then half-sang, half-muttered something which might have been an island lament or a dinner call for the dog as she ushered him to the door.

The Duclos house was in an old white-stone quarter which seemed entirely inhabited by old people who dedicated their lives to making things pretty. There were window boxes and vines everywhere along the narrow streets, and as he walked he found that it was unusually densely populated for Beauville in these days. Here three wrinkled men played cards at a white iron table; there a bent old lady swept dust from her step. There were empty houses, but not many. He nodded to the card-players and offered them a respectful *bonsalum* in Moitié. It was almost the only local word he could say with confidence, even now. Every speaker seemed to have his or her own version of the dialect, and each believed it was a solemn duty to instruct this uncouth foreigner in the beautiful tongue.

They waved back, *bonsalum avoumem*, so he switched to English and asked them whether there'd been some sort of joint decision to stay as long as possible. They shrugged amiably. No, they said. It was just that when someone here decided to Leave, they invited someone who was staying a little longer and whose home was not as nice to come and live in their house. Someone old, of course, because the young people might ruin it.

'But that will happen anyway, in the end,' the Sergeant observed.

'That's no reason to invite it,' the dealer said. 'Young people,' and this clearly included the Sergeant himself, 'young people never understand. The last days are no less important than the others just because they are near to the end.' He nodded at his friends. 'Should we stop living today just because death is no longer a stranger? Should we go naked because our clothes no longer fit as well as they did?'

'I should say not!' said the woman with the broom. 'No one wants to see your horrible bottom!'

'Then you oughtn't be peering in at my window!' the dealer retorted. The sweeper shook her fist in mock fury and cackled.

The Sergeant realised that there was another Mancreu here which he had not known about, a Mancreu of the very old. It was easy to think of the island as one place with various parts dangling off it, but in truth it was layer upon layer, and each of them as real as the others.

'Will you all Leave together?' he asked.

The card-players shrugged. 'If we live that long,' the dealer said. 'And when we leave, we will leave the houses as they should be. Perhaps houses have souls and we will meet them again one day. Or perhaps they will just go into this burning with dignity. Your man Kershaw, thought so. He came here when he first arrived and he tried to pretend he saw only bricks. But he cried a little when he realised the houses would die. He's a decent man.'

The Sergeant reassessed them all once more. Old and watchful. The whole street was filled with old, watchful men and women. He tried his luck. 'Anyone seen this dog?'

They shook their heads. 'But it can't have gone far,' one of the players muttered, to general agreement.

The dealer dealt a fresh hand, and the Sergeant took the gentle hint and moved away down the perfect, empty street. A moment later, he heard the man's voice raised in his direction once more.

'Hey, Sergeant!' he called.

'No,' the Sergeant shouted back, 'I don't want to see your horrible bottom, either!'

This rated a huge laugh from the card-players, and snorting approval from the sweeper. The dealer shushed them all. 'You didn't ask about the fish!' he complained.

The Sergeant shook his head. For a moment, the statement made no sense. What fish? But yes, it had been on his list the day of Shola's death: Beneseffe's stolen catch. He hadn't asked them about it, primarily because he had completely forgotten, but even had he remembered there was no earthly reason to suppose that they would know anything. Except, he realised, that they knew everything. They were one of the last stations in what had once been the great Mancreu gossip network, and their art had been refined rather than diluted by their proximity to one another, and their loneliness. So they knew – from who could say what messengers – that he was looking for stolen fish. This was no doubt how the boy got some of his uncanny information: he talked to someone who watered plants and sat by the roadside, someone who chatted and watched, and he traded time for knowledge.

Tomorrow, the Sergeant thought, he would come back here and ask about the boy, if he still needed to. He would bring a picture. He might even explain why. He thought they would understand, and surely they would respect his desire to know whether such a thing was possible before he offered it.

In the meantime, he raised his hands in surrender. 'All right,' he said. 'Now I'm asking. Who took the fish?'

'The Ukrainians,' the dealer said, waving him away. 'Pechorin has a brother on a factory ship. They come by every few months and buy whatever he can steal. You can sell a big tuna for hundreds of thousands of dollars in Japan. He's not a bad man, maybe, but that's a lot of money.'

It would turn out to be true, the Sergeant knew. He'd never prove it, and if he did there'd be nothing he could do about it. But it would be true, and that was something. Perhaps the fishermen who had been robbed would go into business with Pechorin. It might be easier all round.

That cheered him, but by the time he reached the Portmaster's office he was frowning again. He had walked and talked, called in at a petrol station, a *tabac* and a greengrocer, and he had made inquiries. For his trouble, he had no more information about Madame Duclos's missing dog – but he had been asked about three more.

Beneseffe politely expressed his pleasure at the Sergeant's presence in his office, and then smiled much more genuinely at the idea that the fish-theft might be a profitable business opportunity.

'I'll put the word out,' he said. 'Good catch, Lester. Good timing.'

'Been a bit twitchy, has it?'

'Twitchy. Exactly. A lot of sharp knives on the docks. A lot of young men with large balls.'

'Balls and knives don't go well together.'

'No. They do not.'

'Speaking of twitchy, what do you hear about missing dogs?' Beneseffe looked completely blank. 'Never mind. Or guns? Imported guns?'

The Portmaster winced. 'Shola.'

'Yes.'

'I have been thinking since it happened. There are many boats which might bring in guns. Fewer now, but still enough. And no Customs authority any more. But who, and when, and why, and how to find out . . . I don't know. I would just ask, but now they would know why. They would be ashamed.'

'Maybe that would help.'

Beneseffe sighed. 'Yes. If it was you, Lester, you would be ashamed and you would tell me. But not everyone is you.'

'Ask anyway. Please.'

'Of course.'

They drank a cup of tea on the wooden veranda in front of the office – the Sergeant, very much against his instinct, with his back to the street. When his spine itched and tingled in this position, he took comfort in the dirty reflective surface of the windows and in the knowledge that Beneseffe's wide smile was being read all the way from the chandler's stall to the harbour gate as a sign and an omen of peace. *The British Sergeant has done his job. Say that much: say he, at least, understands obligation.*

Their tea was interrupted – though it had come, in real terms, to its natural end and was now just a matter of the last of the pot – by the sound of a large engine, and then a gleeful barrage of obnoxious hooting. The Sergeant, glancing in the glass, saw the image of a Toyota Hilux 4x4 stopped at the kerb, the driver's door opening to reveal a dark-haired elegant woman with violently orange fingernails.

'Hey, Beneseffe! Hullo, Lester!' Inoue said, dropping down from the driver's seat. It was a long way for a person of less than average height, but the brief moment of free fall did nothing to ruffle her. Beneseffe waved a greeting.

'Doctor,' the Sergeant replied. She frowned at him.

'We have discussed this, Lester. We have agreed that we will be informal.'

That made him smile. 'I recall you telling me I was going to be informal, certainly.'

'And are you so amazingly rude that you will argue with me?' Perfect fingers spread on her chest – the nails were like spots of sherbet against her shirt – and her face took on an expression of cartoonish shock. 'Me? A senior scientist and de facto diplomatic representative of a major power?'

'No, ma'am.'

'Mmph. Practise! And practise also answering your phone!'

The Sergeant belatedly took out his handset and inserted the battery. A moment later it chirruped and informed him that he had a message. Inoue rolled her eyes.

'Sorry,' he said.

'Meh. I have business here. The Portmaster has impounded my equipment out of malice. Even now the finest Japanese technology is getting covered in fish scales and salt water in his wretched hovel and soon millions of dollars of sophisticated hardware will be nothing more than dust.'

Beneseffe sighed. 'It's not impounded,' he said. 'It's just not unloaded. There's a backlog.'

'Piracy!'

He rummaged, produced a clipboard. 'Sign, please.'

Inoue scribbled on it.

'She writes obscenities in Japanese,' Beneseffe confided woefully to the Sergeant. 'It's worse than dealing with your boy.'

'He's not my boy,' the Sergeant said. *Not yet.* And: *I thought you didn't know him.* But if the Portmaster was silent on that topic it was in obedience to his own obligations, and those were to be respected – at least while there was still time to look elsewhere.

Beneseffe snorted and made a gesture of resignation. The world was insane, and it was particularly vindictive towards Portmasters who were just trying to get along. He took the tea tray and retreated to his office. 'It was nice to see you both,' he said firmly, and shut the door.

Inoue took the Sergeant's arm and clamped it firmly in hers. She was muscular and bony. He felt, to his confused embarrassment, what might be a fraction of one breast against his upper arm. If Inoue was conscious of this proximity, she gave no sign. 'You are very hard to find, Lester.'

'Sorry.'

'Pfah.' She smiled. There were tiny lines around her eyes, and he realised she was older than he had thought: his age, rather than ten years younger. He had assumed she was a prodigy. Well, she was: an academic powerhouse, the boy had affirmed after a sequence of nested Internet searches which apparently told him everything he wanted to know. *A top-banana brain!* But not an alien. Just regular brilliant. He wondered what it must be like to be regular brilliant, if she noticed how slowly everyone else thought.

He looked over at her, saw concern tighten her lips. They were a sort of silvered purple. He didn't think she was wearing any make-up; that was just the colour of her mouth. He had never spotted it before, but he hadn't met all that many Japanese women and didn't generally make a habit of staring at their lips. He didn't generally make a habit of staring at Inoue's, actually. He wondered if she had noticed and decided that she hadn't.

'I would actually be grateful if you would visit with us today,' Inoue said. 'We have a little situation I think maybe it would be good for you to come and see. In confidence.'

'I can come now,' he offered, 'if that would be good.'

'That would be ideal.'

It would take him out of Beauville, and he would see how the world looked to someone who wasn't the boy, which might be a good idea. He felt a flash of guilt, and put it aside. It was sensible, not wicked. He had responsibilities and it was the grown-up thing to do.

'I was sorry about your friend,' Inoue added abruptly. 'Shola. I liked him. He was a rogue.'

'Yes,' the Sergeant said. 'Yes, he was.' It was like a toast. Perhaps it was the accompaniment to that brief exchange at the funeral, long delayed.

Inoue decided that he would drive her to the Xeno Centre. Someone else would drive her car. That was what interns were for. The Sergeant, who hewed to a similar understanding regarding corporals, nodded gravely and opened the door for her.

She climbed into the Land Rover and he was immediately conscious of how crappy it must seem, how messy and battered, and how it stank of fuel. He climbed in and was about to apologise when Inoue amazed him by putting her small feet up on the dashboard, pressing herself into the seatback. 'VROOOM VROOM!' she yelled, and when he looked at her in absolute amazement she cracked up, her feet pat-patting on the plastic, and made urgent gestures with her hands: *let's go!*

He took the Land Rover up out of Beauville and over the Iron Bridge towards the lowest of the passes which would afford them access to the far side of the island and the Xeno Centre. It was a spectacular drive, and the Sergeant reserved it in his off-duty hours for moments of significance. He had no desire to come here one day, between the old volcano and the plunging gorge of Mancreu's white Lucretia River, and feel that he had seen it all before. To be jaded by this view would be an admission of something wretched he could not name. Inoue was appropriately silent, but in a companionable way, and they passed the first half hour in mutual appreciation of the world all around. Finally, as the Land Rover ducked down into the treeline and the view was obscured by pines, she glanced over at him.

'What boy?'

For a moment, the Sergeant did not understand.

'The Portmaster said I was worse than your boy.'

He grunted. 'There's a local kid, he hangs around. We're friends.' He was wary of discussing the friendship with an outsider, a female.

'The one who was at Shola's, when it happened.' There was almost no discernible pause as she decided how to say it. He nodded assent, finding that her inquiry had not felt like an intrusion.

'Smart kid,' Inoue said, sucking air between her teeth. Not *poor kid*, he noticed. It was an expression of respect rather than pity, which was exactly right, and his reservations faded abruptly away. She would get it. She had a perfect ear for the way things were done. The way they had to be done.

'Yes. Very.'

'Do you have children of your own at home?'

'Never found anyone. Or no one ever found me, maybe. I've moved around. Perhaps the right girl was out there and she kept turning up after I'd gone. Married someone else. I'm thinking . . .' Jesus, was he going to say it aloud, to Inoue? When he hadn't even asked the boy? It seemed so. 'I'm thinking I might try to take him with me, when it's time. I can't offer him . . . Well, I don't know what I can offer him. A home. A place. A friend.' It seemed like very little. Probably there were richer people, couples, who would take a prodigy like the boy, get him into Cambridge or Yale, pay his way. And maybe an American passport was a

111

better thing than a British one. You couldn't become president if you weren't US born, of course, but you could be a state governor, like Arnold Schwarzenegger. Or you could found an Internet company and become a billionaire. Or both. Why not? He tumbled down into himself, brooding. 'I suppose it won't work out,' he muttered. 'But you've got to try, haven't you?'

Inoue, staring straight out into the wilderness, nodded once.

'Trouble is, I don't even know if he's got family. I can't find out who he is. I mean, I ask him and he sort of waves it off. He doesn't think he'll ever leave. And I don't want to say, you know, "come with me" and have him run for the hills because he's got a mum on a farm in the shanty. Which he might.'

Still with her eyes towards the horizon, Inoue said: 'Describe him to me.'

The Sergeant shrugged, both hands on the wheel. 'You saw him at the funeral.' But not close up, he realised, and she'd hardly have taken special notice. 'Dark hair, high cheeks, green and brown eyes. Mid-brown skin. Thin. Twelve years old, maybe more. Very bright – I mean, much more than I can really get to grips with.'

'Hands?'

'Long fingers, dirty nails, not too much in the way of calluses.'

'Long fingers, like crazy long? Or just narrow?'

'Narrow.'

'No arachnodactyly. Okay. When he walks, does he look a little like Charlie Chaplin?'

The Sergeant had never thought of it, but there was a particular amble the boy had sometimes, like a sailor's swagger or, yes, like Charlie Chaplin. 'Yes. Why?'

'Hip structure. Keep going. Epicanthic folds?'

'I don't know what that is.'

'This!' She touched the corner of her eye, the line of the skin.

'Yes. A little.'

She nodded. 'When he speaks Moitié he sounds equally happy with French and Arabic words?'

'It all comes out the same. Not French or Arabic or anything. Just Moitié. When he speaks English—'

She tutted. 'Everyone here speaks English like the movies.'

'Yes.'

'Well. For the record, race is a superstition derived from the clinal distribution of characteristics. But Mancreu is not big and it is not homogeneous and if I had to guess I would say one of his parents was from a mountain family – old island people, that's why his Moitié sounds that way, so integrated – and the other maybe a more recent arrival. And almost all of the mountain people – even when they move to Beauville – they christen their children at the Chapelle Sainte Roseline by the river, because Sainte Roseline has governance over evil spirits. And mountain people always have a lot of evil spirits.' She grinned. 'My grandmother is from the mountains. You would not believe how many ghosts you can get in a very small house.'

He stared at her. She raised her eyebrows briefly: *Over to you. Go and make it happen, or don't.* He wondered if she dealt with all problems in the same way, this rapid reduction to a hinge point, and whether she ever found the clarity made things more difficult rather than less.

'Thank you, Kaiko,' he said.

'You're welcome, Lester,' she replied.

She spent the next hour pointing out strange mutations. Twice, she stopped him and plucked a small sample of plant life. Nothing on Mancreu, the Sergeant began to realise, was quite the way it should be any more. They passed through an abandoned farm and she stopped him again to look at wheat, then took some of that, too. She wore stiff gloves made out of something space-aged and shiny. 'Impenetrable to parasites,' she said sternly. 'You should get some.' He sighed – of course, that story would be well known by now – and nodded.

Inoue softened her reproach with a smile, then bent to peer at another growth. He realised that she was talking to herself, proposing and dismissing courses of action, and felt flattered. He was seeing her in her most professional self. It was intimate – this was what made her Inoue – and it was oddly familiar. She saw things which were out of place and gathered them together in her mind to understand what made them so. It was not unlike what he had done in half a dozen bad places, reading the valleys and the weather and the movement of sheep: soothsaying with bullets. He found himself watching her skill with professional appreciation as they made their slow progress across the island. On the fourth and final stop he even started to spot things for her. She smiled again, with approval.

Then they arrived.

The Xenobiology Centre was a cluster of white geodesic domes and extremely engineered circular housing, fast to assemble and durable, but easy to pack up and transport. It bloomed from the rubble and grey sandy soil about three miles from the boundary fence of the old chemical plant, its back against the foothills. The white material was spotless, so that the whole facility looked eerily new and fungal. They had even landscaped it, with small trees and a gravel drive with parking.

Inoue's team parted in front of her without fuss. They did not ask why she was bringing a clumping great sergeant into their hideaway. They didn't ask anything at all, which as always suggested to him that they knew their jobs very well and were very professional people. They nodded to Inoue and to the Sergeant and got on with what they were doing, although in one case that seemed to involve drinking Coke and playing some sort of game involving elves. Inoue tutted. 'Ichiro,' she growled out of the side of her mouth. 'A genius. I cannot come up with enough jobs to keep him busy, so I permitted the other interns to assign him their extra work.'

'But he's not working,' the Sergeant said.

'No,' Inoue sighed. 'He established a trading floor for basic tasks and cornered the market in coffee-making futures, and then the espresso machine very mysteriously broke down. So he is a task billionaire. He has calculated that if the others do all his chores and nothing else for seven thousand years, they will be free of the debt. And now he only works when something scientifically interesting is going on.' She glanced at him. 'Does this happen with soldiers?'

The Sergeant had been thinking of the boy, and wondering if he and Ichiro knew one another, and if they did, which of them acknowledged the other as the master. Or perhaps they were mortal foes. He shrugged. 'Something like it, yes.'

'And what do you do?'

'I let it be known that I do not approve.'

Ichiro grinned at them, overhearing. He tapped the screen, and the elves were replaced by rows upon rows of data. He took his feet off the desk and leaned in, fascinated. Inoue nodded. 'So long as the others have time for their academic work, I just keep him in information,' she said, 'and he is easy to live with. Come.'

Inoue led the way to the central desk, a round mica bench covered in paper and computer terminals which always made the Sergeant think of King Arthur, and leaned down over a keyboard. He kept his eyes to the front, looking over her back at a framed picture of a marmot on the wall so as not to appear interested in her bottom. It was small and well defined.

'Lester,' she said, drawing his gaze downwards to the screen.

On it was something he recognised as a false-colour image, a scan of some sort to which the computer was adding tints to differentiate shapes which otherwise would be indistinct. In his world that usually meant a night-vision camera, and a covert operation. This was different, all branches and fronds, blue and purple at the edges and angry red at the centre. He realised he was looking at the Mancreu Cauldron, a resonance image of the volcanic well from which the Discharge Clouds came, and there was really only one reason why she would show him that.

'There's a plume building, Lester,' she said. 'A very big one. I think they will finish this. I think this will frighten them.'

Around them the room was quiet. He wasn't sure if it was quieter than it had been or if he was imagining it because it ought to be that way. He nodded, and then it occurred to him that he could ask her the big question about that, and she might actually know the answer, might tell him.

'Will it work? Blowing up the island?'

'No,' Inoue replied. 'It will scour the surface and if we are lucky a tectonic shift will seal the vents. But the bacteria will survive. That's what they do. They already live in an extreme environment. They are protean. And it is possible that the vents will not seal and the bacteria will get into the sea. Again. So far they have not done well there, but that can change. If the chambers discharge directly into the ocean floor, for example, over time . . . And the radioactivity will increase the likelihood of mutation. It is a very bad plan.' She sighed. 'Waiting and learning would be much better. But you can't tell governments that, it is not a good soundbite. And they don't like it when science doesn't give them what they have decided it should say. They have a sort of . . . a tame team, here somewhere, who tell them stories they do like. I may . . . I may have to say something anyway, although it will make me not popular.'

She moved her hand through the air. In someone else it would have been a vague motion, but Inoue's most unconsidered gestures were precise, so her fingers traced a sharp little arc, twisting like wingfeathers. 'Lester, when this gets out it will be bad. The island people believe they are ready to hear this, but they are not. And I think they will need you, but I think you are not ready either. Are you?'

He ought to say yes, of course, but he needed to find out about El Hierro. And the boy, the evacuation plan: that wasn't done, either, not halfway done. And there were places on Mancreu he still hadn't seen. He should run the Lucretia River path again in

116

the sun, it was amazing. He'd have to find ways to stay in touch with people. With Beneseffe and even Kershaw. With Inoue.

Outside he heard the sound of a car, high and snarling. It made him think of kids doing handbrake turns in a supermarket car park back home. He'd been one of those kids, actually. Never very good at it, but you had to show willing. If this was nostalgia, he was bad at it. He contemplated the end of Mancreu, newly real, while whoever it was roared around and around outside, mowing the lawn or cutting down a hedge in an endless grinding whine, and then they slowed down and he could speak, but realised that he didn't know what to say.

He didn't have to. Inoue was looking over his shoulder, and when he followed her gaze he saw a line of quad bikes, expensive toys for bored footballers on their estates along the A13 out of London to the coast, and on them a line of grubby men with scarves on their faces. An actual masked gang. When they had his attention – his, in particular – they revved their engines again and roared away, leaving Madame Duclos's dead, fat dog on the bonnet of his car.

The Sergeant ran outside and realised that he was waving his arms and shouting 'Oi!' and that this was not, on the face of it, the best response. An authoritative military bark would be more to the point, a 'Halt or I'll open fire!' though he did not know whether he would. He did have a weapon – since Shola's death he had quietly added a small side arm to his kit, in a discreet holster which sat directly against his leg and could be accessed through the open-ended pocket on his right side – but getting it would require that he stopped running and if he stopped running they would be out of range. He shouted 'Oi!' again and knew that he really had to stop doing that because it made him sound like an old fart waving a newspaper, but at this moment that was probably all he was. The dust choked him, and then the enemy had retreated, tactical objective achieved. 'Fuckers! It's just a bloody dog! And it's not even a proper dog, just an old lady's floor-ornament. It never did anything to you!'

No. No, the dog was not the sinner here. This message was for him, and maybe for Her Majesty's United Kingdom of Great Britain and Northern Ireland. He went back to see.

The dog lay in its own blood in an indentation on the bonnet of the Land Rover. They had opened it like a hog and thrown it, dying. The landing must have been agonising, though briefly. Had they known that he had once carried a man with a wound like this to safety behind the iron frame of a derelict Russian bus? Had they imagined that he would go into some sort of particular shock on seeing the tableau? Or was this just an average bit of brutality, lacking that greater understanding? Vile enough, in any case.

Inoue was standing at the point of a spear composed of irate Japanese geeks, and he was pleased to see that the principal reaction on her face was a fizzing, imperious outrage. She was brandishing a camera and he realised she must have used it to record footage of the gang's departure. He wondered if she could now run it through some sort of computer the way they did on television and tell him who he was looking for, and knew she couldn't. The assembled male and female members of the vulcanology department (they had a smoking mountain printed in white on their maroon hoodies) were carrying fence posts and looking meaningfully at the row of Hilux 4x4s to let him know they were in if he wanted to give chase. He pictured himself leading a posse of affronted eggheads across the wilds, their righteous fury ebbing as they rode to an uncertain reception, and concluded that the list of great British military follies did not need, even in the name of canine justice and international brotherhood, the addition of the Charge of the Mancreu Irregular Xenobiological Infantry and their non-commissioned officer.

Instead, he approached the corpse with a view to removing it. He couldn't work out how. If he just embraced it he could get it off the car, but then he'd have nowhere to put it short of dumping it on the dirt and he'd get covered in blood and viscera into the bargain. He stood there with his arms wide, then stepped back again and grunted.

A moment later the dog was being rolled onto a pallet and whisked away. Of all people, Ichiro the genius, weeping, had emptied a stationery trolley and pressed himself into service as mortician's porter. Inoue shouted something after him in Japanese, by its tone both shocked and approving, then turned.

'Will she want it back? The old lady?' There was anger in her voice, and she was peering at him, seeking the fury he had already controlled. *It's on a chain*, he wanted to tell her. *Because I'm not a proper copper. My real skills aren't about keeping the peace.*

He could feel them waking in him, all the same. Not the battle-field, not yet – if the fight at Shola's place hadn't done that, this wasn't going to. Just that same questing curiosity which saw the land and the people and took a little bit of them away so as to deliver intuitions and warnings. Hypervigilance, that was the word. The curious gift of perception granted to the very abused, the endangered, and the pursued. In war, the soldiers from hard corners – from ganglands and sink estates, from bad families and badly run care homes – they had a touch with traps and decep-tions. They could see a thing out of place, spot a liar even when he was speaking a language they didn't know. They saw through walls. The best of them could hone and grow the skill within themselves, and an NCO who got one of those, or better yet, who was one, he could keep his boys alive when everyone else was going home in boxes. The Sergeant's gift in that regard was limited, found late and small, but he had a sight of a different sort, born of another sort of trouble. It was less immediate and more haunting: a sense of narrative which was part empathy and part strategy, which told him when something was coming down and when it was overdue. His boys said he could hear the enemy whispering to one another from ten miles away, that he could smell the mortars before they were fired. They called him a warlock, but from the inside it was more like flirting than magic. He watched the smoke and the mountainsides, the faces of local people and the way they held their shoulders, knew when they wanted to dance or disappear, knew what that meant even when they didn't. He read the world, and in exchange he got a few hours' grace before the sky fell on him.

He had thought himself fully engaged with that faculty, here on Mancreu. He realised now that it had been idling in him, pooling at his feet, and that he had been ignoring it.

He made a circuit of the horizon with his eyes, but knew he didn't need to, knew that if there was more to this it would already have happened. There would be no second attack. There would not even – though he would assume he was at risk all the same – be a landmine waiting for him along the road. This didn't have that flavour. It was a come-on, a taunt. *Notice me.*

Well, all right. I will. And don't say I didn't warn you.

He was raging inside. It was old anger as well as new, a long way down in a sealed chamber, and on the whole everyone would be better off if it stayed there. At the same time he was in the grip of Mancreu's end, the deep, dark brown taste of doom and gallows celebration. It was in all of them, in Beneseffe and the crab fishers and in the NatProMan troops. It had been in Shola, it was in Dirac and it must be in him, too. They were all a little bit mad and getting more so, and most of all the ones who appeared to be holding it together. Inoue and her friends had it, with their admirable, ridiculous makeshift pikes and their readiness to do battle with thugs. The Witch had it.

The boy had it in spades.

But beyond that there was something else: a watchful something which seemed to squat just out of sight and which plucked at all his old familiar fear. *I am observed* . . . No. More than that: *I am targeted.* His hands twitched, remembering the burning pain of the tomato sap, feeling the thing wriggling under his skin. Something diffuse, yet close, a monster waiting in the closet.

Thugs at Shola's table. Madame Duclos's dog. *Notice me*. It had a stink of bad endings about it, and his every instinct said to get out from under or strike hard, and strike first, but it was so ubiquitous, so faint and yet so present, that he had no idea how to do either. *Devil's footsteps on my spine*.

Inoue touched him on the shoulder and he lurched away from her, hands almost coming up in a fighter's guard, but he restrained the impulse and waved away his own reaction with a sharp 'Sorry'. A moment later he was running to the Xeno Centre to do what he should have done five minutes ago: he called Jed Kershaw and told him he'd been the victim of a direct and possibly politically motivated minor assault on the property of the UN-sanctioned Japanese scientific mission. If Kershaw had any assets which might reasonably be brought to bear on the situation – any American satellites or high-altitude drones doing atmospheric research or weather balloons which just happened to have a camera pointing at the ground – now would be the time for that happy accident to be shared with the mother country in the name of brotherly love and the avoidance of a Total Goatfuck. He saw Inoue watching from the doorway and realised that she was seeing him as he had earlier seen her, doing something that actually came naturally, that was his strength. She smiled in recognition of the same truth, then took her cue from him and went to boss her swots in whatever direction she felt best.

Kershaw told him to stay the fuck where he was. A rapid reaction force arrived twenty minutes later and secured the perimeter while insisting that everyone sit tight and await reinforcements. Privately the Sergeant found this was a little bit funny and a perfect example of what happened when you put a civilian in charge of military personnel.

The full force took four hours to arrive, by which time it was getting dark, so the drive back across the island was a stern, halogen-lit convoy with the Sergeant's bloodied Land Rover occupying a slightly off-centre position in the traffic. The Sergeant wasn't allowed to travel in it in case the vehicle was marked out for follow-up attack. According to NatProMan's standard operating procedure, the possible object of guerrilla activity – there had never actually been any before – was to be protected both by 'direct target obscuration', which meant 'getting in the way', and deception. He told Kershaw's myrmidons that no formal escort was necessary. The officer in charge, who was all the blond, muscular things a Pennsylvania Dutch quarterback should be, told him that he knew that – of course he did – but that Jed Kershaw had been pretty agitated and would the Sergeant consent this one time to being treated like he was made of glass? Because just between the officer and the Sergeant, who was a pro and that's why the officer could lay it out like this and not screw around – it would sure as hell make life that much easier.

Having used a similar form of words himself from time to time, the Sergeant recognised this as soldier-to-VIP speak for 'get your fucking arse in the car and quit pretending you're bulletproof so we can all go home', and so he did, wondering greatly at a universe in which he could be on the receiving end of such polite flannel. They made their way rapidly along the boring coastal route, outriders ahead ushering the few other cars off the road. The searchlights scoured the countryside around, making a small circle of effective daylight two hundred metres across and a penumbra beyond it of mottled day and dark which was almost harder to resolve than ordinary night. Mancreu looked, by this scorching illumination, all the more desolate and sorrowful: the stark actinic glare picked out old farm equipment, crumbling houses and rusted automobiles, jagged trees and lonely, deserted livestock. Nothing happened to justify the extreme caution, and they arrived at Brighton House in an hour with no more serious injury than a foggy motion sickness which came from rounding corners at speed.

The Sergeant politely but firmly declined a NatProMan guard and invoked his status as Brevet-Consul of a friendly nation to make the rejection stick. The cavalcade rolled away, reluctantly extinguishing the big lights as they headed down towards the town.

The Sergeant let himself in, and the first thing he saw was the boy, sitting in livid silence on the bed in which he had slept, with his back to the door.

7. Bruises

There was no way of knowing how long the boy had been sitting there. It was theoretically possible that he had only just arrived, or that he had been, until he heard the key turn in the lock, reading quite cosily in the corner chair – but there was an air of self-mortification about him, a sense that he had selected this posture in the knowledge that it would be uncomfortable, and his long wait with aching muscles was part of the bill which would now come due.

The Sergeant knocked on the doorframe, then cleared his throat. When this elicited no response, he experienced a strange, appalling hallucination or imagining: that the boy had died and was slowly freezing in place owing to rigor mortis. He saw himself realising and leaping up, pounding on the boy's chest like a madman and giving him mouth-to-mouth – much too late – then carrying the tiny corpse in his arms all the way to Beauville, weeping and weeping and weeping and none of it doing any good. And what was the point of that? What was the point of being a soldier, of being a human being in a world which could work wonders with medicine, if affection – he had almost called it love, but that was a presumption, wasn't it, because the boy wasn't his flesh, his son, and while that was something which could be negotiated it hadn't been negotiated, not yet – what was the point of affection, then, if it didn't exert any traction on the universe? If it didn't heal or protect or do anything at all except hurt? In his nightmare he begged the Witch to help him and she did, she duped him and sedated him and while he was asleep she made the dead boy disappear and when he came to himself he thanked her and then they never spoke again.

But when he risked a glance, ridiculously frightened that he would this time turn out to be right, he could see the boy's chest moving, so that much was good. Still, he knew he was the focus of this frigid rage.

It was new ground. They had never fought before. The Sergeant had never fought in that sense with anyone – and if he had, no one had ever before occupied the strange, vexed, desperate space in his life which now belonged to the boy.

So he advanced, slowly, as if probing for mines with his voice.

'Sorry I wasn't around. I had to go over to the Xeno Centre.'

The boy's face remained firmly turned away. If anything, the ramrod back seemed to grow more disdainful. Instinct told the Sergeant that this was not a bad thing; that it amounted, contrary to appearances, to permission to continue.

'Inoue wanted to tell me some things. And when we got there, there was a sort of . . . well, an attack, I suppose. A gang.'

No answer. No shift. Did that mean rejection, or interest? Was it possible that the boy himself did not know? The silence stretched.

'And I suppose technically I solved the dog thing. I mean, they killed him. Threw him on my car. It's a mess – you should see.'

No, that was a mistake. Too much, too soon. A hiss of affront. He hurried on.

'But I've got a new case now: the masked men. On quad bikes, if you please. Bloody expensive for Mancreu. Can't be too many, so I expect I can find them.' *A case you can be part of. A real gang case, pow pow pow.* And: *I'm sure we talked about this. I'm sure I was allowed.*

The boy shrugged, not his usual lazy lift of the shoulders but a hunching dismissal. 'So you have solved a dead dog. Very good! Very excellent! When it is dropped on you, you do so very good work!' The voice was shrill, quavering. 'And in all this where is your friend? Where is my friend? He is still dead! And there are men in jail and you still know nothing! And when you should

125

be looking, where are you? When I am looking, where are you? You are nowhere, except you are not nowhere you are somewhere, but Shola is really nowhere because *he is dead* and you don't do anything about it. Which is fine. It is all fine. It is only Mancreu. We understand. Not important for the Brevet-Consul.' He turned, face in shadow, eyes glaring. 'Fine. But I thought maybe for your friends. I was wrong.'

'You weren't.'

'I was. Totally. Funny me, ha ha. Ai can haz stupidz.'

'I just have other things too. The only way I can do what I do is if people let me. I don't have anything to back me up. And they let me because I don't just do what suits me. I try to do what needs doing. And Shola . . . that does need doing. But it's not the only thing. I'm sorry. I'll keep after it, you know I will. He was my friend. And so are you.'

'Yes! There are so many other things. So I have been helping, while you were so importantly somewhere not here. I have solved your fish case for you. Your thief is Pechorin, from NatProMan.'

The Sergeant sighed. Too late, then, to tell the boy not to go near the Ukrainians. 'Yes,' he said. 'I heard that, too. The card-players told me, in the old town.'

'Good. So now you find out about Shola.'

'Yes. Of course. I'll . . .' But he still did not know what he would do. 'I'll chase the weapons. Get names on the men, see if I can find out who hired them. If someone did. I'll get there, in time.' And now's not the time to explain that we may not have very much. *Your island is dying, we may never know who murdered your friend: come and be my son.* He pushed on. 'I can interrogate them again. I won't stop, I promise. Even if you weren't asking. If you didn't talk to me any more. I wouldn't stop. But I'd be . . .' *a little part of the full truth, now* '. . . less. I'd be less than I am. And I want to be more.'

The boy seemed to find this funny, somehow darkly amusing, and shook his head. They sat together in silence for a while, and the wind blew around the edges of the house and in through an open window in the other room. It grew noticeably cold. The Sergeant found himself speaking again. He hoped he knew what he was doing, and suspected he didn't.

'I don't know how to be what you need. I want to. But that sort of thing I always . . . well, I asked Shola. He was good with people. He was a good man. Me, I've . . . got no practice. I'm used to having instructions. I'm not like you. I don't . . . I don't have the habit of it yet, the natural way of doing it without orders. But I'll get there. I'll learn' – and here inspiration struck – 'I'll learn to be a bit like him. Shola didn't work for anyone.'

The boy jerked away, and his face reflected absolute horror. It must be a flashback, the Sergeant thought, full Dolby surround sound with all the trimmings, and yes, oh, yes, he knew about those. He moved forward, hands out to receive a faint or fend off an attack. The boy opened his mouth and made a high keening sound like the first flurry of bagpipes when the piper settles them under his arm. He stopped, eyes wide, and then made the noise again and again until it tailed away into a gasping cough, then flung himself on the Sergeant and clung to him, and the older man realised abruptly that this noise was grief, and maybe even shame.

The Sergeant sat for a moment with his elbows at shoulder height and his hands in the air, as if someone notionally friendly had him at gunpoint and it would all be sorted out in a moment. Then, with great caution, he lowered his nearer arm and put it around the boy's back and wrapped the other across so that he could clasp his own wrist and complete the circle in a hug. He rocked gently, and made wordless noises of encouragement. From the boy came back squalls of sorrow and remorse. Shola's death, the Sergeant gathered, was somehow all to be laid at the boy's small feet. Shola had been coming to rescue him. They had killed Shola because Shola had told them to leave the boy. The boy had done nothing to help. He had watched Shola die and done nothing. What sort of hero would let that happen? The Sergeant had been like lightning. He had been a god. He had been a warrior. He had been like Batman, but a thousand times better because Batman was ultra wealthy and the Sergeant was just an ordinary person. The boy had done nothing. The whole affair was his fault. The boy was bad.

This flood of self-despite was at the same time quite alarmingly foreign to the Sergeant and entirely familiar. True, he had no direct experience with the violent woes and self-reproaches of children. On the other hand, he was a sergeant, and the commonality in the roles of NCOs and parents was too obvious to dwell upon. He knew how very destructive that simple, unadorned 'bad' could be, how it could embrace a whole person from birth to this very present and condemn every aspect of him entire. Where a more nuanced description could be examined and faulted, something so broad was resilient. It was a tar pit. You couldn't argue it away, because reasoning gave it an undue status as something reasonable. Each attempt to unpick the nest of accusations would draw you deeper in. Your empathy was misunderstanding, evidence of your pure heart's inability to comprehend the enormity you confronted. Your effort spent on a creature so vile was a waste of kindness needed elsewhere, and this itself was a fresh crime to be registered against the villain. Your subsequent distress and ultimate frustration were read as justified anger at the perpetrator of such sins.

You did not defuse this kind of madness by treating with it upon its own terms. You answered the embracing fear, not the question. For the moment, he waited, honouring the grief. He waited until the storm had died, until the tide had risen to its highest and ebbed and the boy had noticed that no denials or affirmations had been forthcoming, and some part of him had begun to feel instinctively that his confessor must render judgement or lose his position.

'You're getting snot on my shirt,' the Sergeant said to the top of the boy's head. Translation: *the worst thing you are capable of is covering a dirty shirt in mucus.*

128

Silence.

'I don't mind,' he continued. 'I'm not saying I mind. I just felt, you know, I should say something in case you end up glued to my armpit.' Translation: *cry as long as you need to. I'm here. But the world is still the world, and you haven't changed.*

Silence.

'And you didn't shoot him yourself, did you? And you didn't hire those men to shoot him. So all this is sort of by proximity. I'm not saying you're wrong. You may be right. At the moment I just don't see how, is all.'

He didn't push. He let the tiny, shuddering thing in his arms subside, and realised from the residual tension that there was something left, that the boy had a final charge against himself, and that it was the most serious, the most vile.

'I did not tell you,' the boy said at last, stepping out of the embrace to stand in some invisible dock. 'I have obstructed the investigation and the course of your inquiries and the execution of your duty.' He was calmer now. Miserable.

'How so?' Very neutral, because there was just a chance.

'Shola worked for Bad Jack,' the boy said.

The Sergeant opened his mouth to say 'Bad Jack?' and shut it again in the awareness that he would sound like a fool. He moved through a chain of response and counter-response in his head, looking for a place to enter the conversation which would be neither condescending nor credulous: *if I say this, he will say that*. It was hard. He wondered whether it was hard because it was hard, or because he was getting old and couldn't remember being a boy.

Shola worked for Bad Jack.

On the face of it, the idea was absurd. The main thing about Bad Jack was that he was a fairy tale. There was no such person, and if there had once been a Jack, a brigand, say, or a murderer, well, he was by now at least three hundred years old: a bit long in the tooth to have been Shola's employer.

But the boy knew all this – and he knew the difference between story and truth. He read *Superman* and watched Fox News, read *Batman* and watched Al Jazeera. He was not the sort to fret about a bogeyman. A child living on an island which is itself under threat of execution for the crime of having been environmentally raped has no need of invented villains. A person trading mountain honey with the Black Fleet for shoes and DVDs, running go-between for who-knows-what deals with the shore, did not conjure crooks out of the air. So when the boy said Bad Jack, he did not – could not – mean the nine-foot-tall pumpkin man or the web-footed devil. He meant the kind of Bad Jack who did business in the world, the kind who could command a measure of actual fear. The kind who might have enemies with Kalashnikovs.

'Someone goes by the name of Bad Jack?' the Sergeant asked, having come to the end of this line of reasoning and arrived at a response which was not patronising or ignorant.

The boy nodded.

'Since when?'

'Since always.'

Which to anyone under the age of twenty meant a length of time greater than a year, but you couldn't say that, either.

'He's always called himself Bad Jack?'

'No. This Jack is new. But there is always Jack.'

It was just distantly possible, he supposed: an unbroken line of Jacks come down from when Mancreu was a wild island port halfway between French North Africa and British South-East Asia. A secret king, a pirate, a smuggler, a crook.

He pictured a Lord of Misrule on a throne, a combination of ogre and imp in a mountain hall, surrounded by stolen virgins and treasure. Translate that: a thug with gold teeth and imported slave-women, wearing a gangster's gold chain and thinking himself a monarch. Or an urbane sort of plausible sod from Boosaaso or Yangon with a business degree, taking a hand in the heroin trade.

'And Shola . . . what did Shola do for him?'

'Store things. Make rum. Make connections. Everyone went to Shola's. Like an oasis with lions and giraffes.'

'Did you ever meet him?'

The boy shook his head. 'He comes, he goes. Everyone looks away. No one sees him. No one ever sees Jack, no one talks about Jack.'

The boy was apologising now. 'I did not tell you, because no one talks about Jack. Or else.' He drew a line across his throat, made a slicing noise.

'Well, if he's so bad, that makes a short suspect list. Who'd stand up to him?'

'Other bad men.'

Fleet men, maybe. But that was a world of trouble. If this was Fleet, he had no remedy, and he wanted no part of it. He wondered what he would do if it was, how he would explain the limit of his power. Of his will.

'Bad men doing what? Why?' he asked instead.

The boy shrugged. 'This was maybe a demonstration, maybe like Alderaan?'

Alderaan. The Sergeant was the right age to know what that meant. He had been to see the film the first time around, very young and very amazed as the orange and white starship went over his head, and then even more amazed as its enormous pursuer roared after it, going on and on and on for ever and shaking the seats. Movies had never seemed so big.

As for the boy, in the flatiron days of the hot season he wore a baseball cap he had begged from an Afrikaner ship-captain. It said in yellow letters on a starry background: HAN SHOT FIRST, and it proclaimed another of his global allegiances. Now he ended his suggestion on an upward note to make it a question, and he had that look again, the one which said 'Is this my fault? Do you hate me?' and most of all 'Should I hate myself?' The Sergeant wondered who had put that idea in his head, and how long ago.

'You're a good lad,' he said, answering the important question first. *You are filled with whatever it is which makes worth. You have not expended it or negated it*. 'You did right, telling me. You're not, you're not bad. You hear me? You're a good lad. And this is good. I can use it. Find out what happened. Tomorrow I'll go and talk to those men again, and I'll talk to them about Jack. It's better when you know what to ask. They'll tell me things and that'll be because of you. You've done a brave thing here today. The right thing. And I'm proud of you.' He found he was having trouble speaking and, hearing his own voice, realised he was nearly in tears. He saw in his mind the boy standing mute and hopeful in front of an ugly armchair, its back towards him and a silence proceeding from it which could only mean a perpetual, corrosive disappointment. A moment later he realised that it was not the boy at all but himself, in that bloody room at home, and there was the electric fire and the print of a hunt and the ship in a bottle. He shuddered. Christ, he had to hold it together. It was not the time, not the time at all to be worrying over old, dead ghosts.

Sergeanting had an answer to that. When you were utterly fucked and you didn't know what to do, you got busy making sure everyone else was all right and told them not to worry and by the end of it there was a good chance you'd convinced yourself. And if you hadn't, well, sooner or later you either died or you didn't and in either case the problem went away. He hauled himself into the present and ordered a forward march, but that did require a definition of forward, and he wasn't sure where that was, so he just said 'You're a good lad' again, and stood there.

After a moment in this hiatus, the boy slipped quietly back under his arm and rested against the Sergeant's ribs. The weight was familiar, as if they had sat in this way many times over many years and the Sergeant was only now remembering.

We are changed, the Sergeant thought. *Of course we are. Whatever this is, we're deeper in it.*

He shifted slightly and brought his other arm around to make it a real hug, and heard a gasp. When he looked down, he saw under the wide boat-neck of the smock a series of stark blue-red lines across the boy's shoulders, and recognised them after a moment as bruises.

Some people knew horses and some people knew guns. There were navy men who swore they could tell you from the taste of the water what ocean they were in. You picked things up as you went along and these things became part of you whether you really wanted them to or not. He suspected that Jed Kershaw could tell from walking into a room if someone was about to get shitcanned or promoted. It was just part of becoming who you were.

And Lester Ferris was an infantryman the way the Witch was a doctor. He'd hiked through snowfields and crawled across hot rocks, marched through opium fields and jungle, been shot at and occasionally shot, and blown up. At various times and in various places he'd fought men with his fists and his feet, with broken bottles and with bits of wood picked up from the floor. Some of them had wanted to kill him, others had just been enjoying a donnybrook. Three days ago he'd broken a man's arm with a frying pan to save the life of one friend and avenge the death of another, had known as he was doing it exactly how much it hurt and how much force was necessary to make sure of the bones.

If Lester Ferris knew just one thing in the world the way meat knows salt, it was bruises.

So he knew a professional punishment beating when he saw one, and his world caught fire as if he had just been waiting to explode all along and now he was raining down on Mancreu like the volcano which had brought him here.

'Who,' he grated out, before he could hem himself in with cautions, 'did that?' It might be a parent, of course. That might be why the boy was so elusive yet so fond, so seemingly in need in a way the Sergeant could not quite reach. He had a bad dad and needed a good one he could run to when blood was not thick enough to endure. Well, if so, there would be words. 'Who?'

The boy did not answer immediately, just looked back in something like amazement at the anger kindled in the Sergeant's face, as if he hadn't dared to expect it but now that he saw it he was drinking it in like nectar. *Christ. Did I not make it obvious that I cared? Is this the only way you know?* But then the thought blew away, a frozen bird tossed in the body of the storm.

'Show me!' the Sergeant demanded, then carefully bit back the measure of his fury so that he could say 'please' and not add to the boy's injuries a disregard for his sovereignty, however badly he had already been infringed. (And how badly? If he had been, as the newspapers would have it, 'abused', there would be no place on the island for the doer. That person would simply vanish into a woodchipper somewhere, and thank you to the allied powers for their extralegal zone.)

But when the boy removed his kirtle the damage was almost surgical. There were bruises which marked where he had been held and more where the lash had fallen – no, not a lash, it had been stiff: a baton or a truncheon – but nothing below the waist, nothing which suggested that sort of interference, and his motion was easy at the hip. No. No, this was punishment, and it had the feel of what a particularly brutal man would call education. On a hunch, the Sergeant glanced over at the boy's knapsack where it lay on the floor, and saw that it was uncharacteristically poorly fastened, as if in haste. He glanced at his friend for permission and when at least no denay was forthcoming he stalked over to it and plucked at the buckles with his fingers. His hands were clumsy and he snatched and scrabbled, goring his thumb on a sharp edge, but he barely noticed.

When he got the bag open, pantomime snow fell from its mouth onto the bed, wide white pieces drifting down to settle on the blanket. He stared at them, turned them in his hands. Not snow, paper. And not all white. White and pink. White and red. White

134

and black, blue, green. He saw a face with a mask, and recognised at last the remains of a comic book, and then he emptied the bag out and realised that he was seeing the corpse of the boy's entire collection for the month, ripped beyond restoration. Carefully ripped. Painstakingly.

He felt the world pulse again, as if the room was stretching out wider, bowing to make space for his reaction. A beating was a beating and it was wrong, but there were persons – it might be a schoolmaster, a priest, or even a nun – who would claim that old adage about sparing the rod. But this was not that. This was vandalism of a calculated sort, a two-pronged assault most deliberate, to torture the body and deprive the mind, and it possessed a persistent cruelty. To rip a comic book in half out of frustration, yes. He could see that. Didn't like it, but yes. But this had taken time and effort and bespoke a refined sort of sadism.

'They did this in front of you.'

The boy nodded. Of course they had. They had. And they had done it, he knew without asking, from the back of each book, so that there was no possibility of reading them however hurriedly in the right order. The boy must turn his head away and listen, or face the destruction and suffer spoilers as well as desecration. It possessed a peculiar elegance, like the killing of the dog.

'Who?' he said, and this time it was a whisper.

'The fish,' the boy said at last, and before the Sergeant could misunderstand: 'I knew that you could not go. It is NatProMan, the fish. But I thought if I went and could take a picture, you would have something and you could show Kershaw. I thought I would fight crime, and then you would have time.' And the Sergeant wondered if the missing words he swallowed were 'for me' or 'for Shola' or some combination of both.

'I see,' he said. And then, because he had to say the name, he said it like a curse, as if it could turn good food into rot: 'Pechorin.'

The boy stared at him, eyes wide, and did not say 'What will you do?' but Lester Ferris was already asking himself that

135

question, because one way and another he was going to do something and that something must answer this most exquisitely.

He looked around at the flakes of paper on the floor, the ruined mess of bright colours and ridiculous stories of salvation from the sky, and he knew what he would do, as if he was staring through stone to the very heart of the island to find his answer written there. It was a glorious idea, one that was both foolish enough to pass for a prank and yet still savage enough, specific enough to be perfectly understood. He would lay down a law. Not a law in words, but a soldier's law. Lester Ferris's law. And the right people would know, without any ambiguity at all, where that law began and ended, and what came if you crossed it.

He would draw the line first of all for Pavel Ygorovitch Pechorin, personally, in a manner appropriate to the sin.

'Tigerman,' he gritted out. 'Whoomf.'

8. Suit

On grasping the Sergeant's intention the boy had been almost incandescent with delight. The word 'win' had filled his mouth and for several long minutes he had seemed unable to say anything else. Then he explained in a whisper that the plan was composed entirely of awesome. It was made and designed by the House of Awesome, from materials found in the deep awesome mines of Awesometania and it would be recorded in the Annals of Awesome – and nowhere else, because any other book would catch fire and explode from the awesome – and by its awesomeness it would be known from now until the crack of doom.

Then abruptly he had sobered and applied himself to the matter, eyes alight not with enthusiasm but with that almost eerie intensity of thought which occasionally marked him out from the crowd. He ran off with promises of a speedy return, and an hour later he was indeed back with an actual suitcase full of comics, the muscles straining in his narrow arms as he hauled it across the gravel of Brighton House: the rest of his trove, the Sergeant assumed, fetched out of whatever hiding place to meet the need of the hour. 'My library,' the boy agreed.

'Library?'

'Sure,' the boy said. 'Wood and brass, velvet armchairs. Many floors underground in my secret volcano base. I drink brandy, wear a smoking jacket. Take over the world. Because: that's how I roll, dude.'

'Oh,' the Sergeant said. 'Right.' His mind's eye pictured a shed or a cellar like the one he had co-opted for his own use long ago – it really was way back now, three decades gone – hung with spare blankets and scattered with books, cushions, chewy sweets and battery-powered torches. Later he had added a radio and thought himself rich. He wanted to ask more, to reminisce and share that fragment of himself, but as so often when he tried to say something ordinary to the boy he couldn't find the words, and anyway it was the wrong time.

When the boy unclipped the fastenings on the case and threw back the lid, glossy nightmares slithered out onto the floor: tentacled things in suits reached for appalled plucky girl reporters; dogs barked at half-transformed wolfmen; nameless creatures crawled from the ocean towards sleeping fisher towns. The next level down featured more conventional heroes fighting strange enemies, inhabitants of horror stories briefly making uncomfortable appearances in the primary-colour worlds of the Justice League or the Avengers before skulking back where they belonged. Below that, the boy's energetic scrabbling revealed a remarkable collection of true stories, or stories which were said by those relating them to be true: the Mothman, the Yeti, the Chupacabra and the Ozark Howler, and sundry tales of people being taken to alien places or deserted houses by entities too strange to understand.

From this landscape and palette they derived a mood, a sense of foreboding and intrusion. The theme was never being safe, and above all never being safe in isolation. In these stories, the boy said, if you wanted to be the hero you had to stand alone, but when you were alone was also when you might get eaten by the monster.

'First it is seen,' the boy explained, waving his hands at the edge of his vision, 'here. And then there are more and more warnings, and they are ignored. Always, in daylight, the warnings are funny. They come from someone a little silly, maybe. And finally it walks in the night and everything is terrible.'

The interesting thing, to the Sergeant, was how these stories were at least in one way quite true to life: you didn't know whether you were the hero or not until the end, because at any time up to that moment you could just get eaten and the rest would be about someone else. In fact you were never safe, because sometimes the monsters won.

From patches and scraps they stitched a skittering cockroach blanket and left it out for Mancreu to find.

The following morning, the fourth since Shola's death, the Sergeant carefully assembled his face and manner into an attitude of amiable vagueness. It was difficult, requiring constant attention. If his focus wandered, his shoulders tightened and his mouth slipped into the sneer he recognised from the first day of deployment to an active theatre. But it was necessary for what came next that he should appear benign to the point of risible, so he thought about what Shola would say to this new plan, and played his part.

'You're quite out of your mind, Lester, you know that?'

'Yes, Shola, I do.'

'I mean, seriously, my friend: this is a terrible idea.'

'So you like it.'

'I love it. But that does not make it smart.'

'You want to come?'

'I'll watch from a safe distance, I think. But you go ahead and have fun. Give Marie a hug for me, Lester. She's not doing well.'

But that was too close to home, and he hurriedly put the vision away, then composed a hazy smile and ambled through the streets of Beauville with his customary pleasantness. He greeted the people and gossiped, accepted their condolences and their respect, and took his ease. Wherever he went he allowed the conversation to follow its own course, to wind and meander. That sort of chatter, on Mancreu, inevitably tended to swapping gossip and rumour, and where it seemed appropriate he would laugh and mention the demon, just in passing. Then – if someone asked 'What demon?' which they mostly did – he would explain and laugh some more. If he laughed too hard, well, he was a man who had lost a friend, and he could be allowed to find humour where he might. If it didn't come up, then, well, that was fine too.

He told farmers he'd heard the story from stevedores, drovers he had it from seamstresses, bakers it came from lobstermen. Always he dismissed it out of hand, even as he spiced the pot with alarming details: the hint of missing persons, the flavour of doubt and poorly concealed official concern. He sought reassurances: 'Oh, so you have seen Old Père Lipton? Good, all right, then he's fine,' as if crossing a potential victim off a list in his head. When pressed, he would explain that there were concerns about a real monster behind the story, a ghoul in the night. He didn't outright say that it might be a human being so warped by the Discharge Clouds that he had become something other. He let the notion bubble up. He was jaunty, and called the whole thing a ghost story, nothing worth thinking about. And then in parting he would drop a reference to someone who was still missing. Every so often he sealed the deal with an earnest 'There's really no cause for alarm.'

It was so easy, he felt a little ashamed. You could have done it anywhere, in any village in the world. At a pub near Hereford, he remembered, an earnest matron had told him in great seriousness that windmills caused cancer, and the government was covering it up. A man from the *Spectator*, she said, had come and given a lecture. When the Sergeant had begun to express doubt, the whole saloon bar had laughed at him for his credulity. Myths and monsters were a human weakness, even in places not about to be evacuated and sterilised by fire.

The boy meanwhile had let the story slip to the card-players, who inevitably handed it on to passers-by and friends, and the legend grew in the telling so that one lonely ghost became a host led by an appalling demon prince. Inoue was right, apparently: the mountain people, in particular, had a lot of demons – although the fishermen had more than enough to be going on with, rising up from the frozen deep-water hell.

The boy had moved on to the waterfront and idled with the net-menders and the basket-weavers, run errands for the

Portmaster. If he mentioned along his way the matter of the disappearances, the ones NatProMan was covering up, well, he could hardly be blamed. He was a child, and, after all, everyone was talking about it.

This being the way of things, it was quite natural for the Sergeant to bump into Pechorin, pass him a routine report from Kershaw's office, and share the local colour.

'Watch out for the demon!' he said as he was leaving, and Pechorin grinned.

'Sure, Lester. I will be very careful. I would not want Baba Yaga to come and steal my balls. Unless it is young Baba Yaga. A beautiful demon would be okay.' He made a helpful gesture with his hips for clarification.

'Well, I can't help you there,' the Sergeant said genially. 'We're pretty certain it's a man.'

'Fuck!' Pechorin cried in appalled delight. 'You taking this seriously? There is a demon?'

'Oh, yes. Of course. Well, not like a real demon sort of demon, obviously. Just someone not right in the head. Or a man suffering some sort of break because of . . . everything. There's no serious suggestion that he's been affected by the Clouds. Yeah,' he mused, almost to himself, 'there's a few Leavers have been a bit mad, we tend to brush them under the carpet, sort them out at the other end. And there was one lad with longish fingernails and teeth, but he was from the mountains and you couldn't say for sure he wasn't always like that. Anyway, nothing to worry about for an armed patrol. Less good by yourself in a dark corner, I suppose, if he's really far gone. I mean, you know what crazy people are.' He sucked air through his teeth, as if this thought was just now occurring to him.

The merriment faded. Pechorin's mother was from Rostov, at one time the home of Eastern Europe's most infamous murderer. A grubby little man in a brown overcoat had killed nearly a hundred people, and ever since his execution by firing squad the town had had a ridiculously high rate of serial murderers, as if Chikatilo's spirit had passed into the air. Perhaps it had; the arresting officer had been suspicious because of a smell he detected around the suspect, a smell he called simply 'evil' but which forensics later explained as the meaty exhalation of a cannibal.

Pechorin's crew muttered and crossed themselves. It was an irritation to the Sergeant that men who one moment before had been braying for the sexual favours of a fiend could appeal to the Virgin in the next. It smacked of sloppy thinking.

'He's killed men?' Pechorin demanded. 'Women?'

The Sergeant raised his hands resignedly. 'People are missing. But people are always missing on Mancreu. They drown. They fall off cliffs. Or they Leave and don't tell anyone. It's not serious. Only . . .' He let his voice trail off as if in thought, then shook his head to clear it. 'Never mind. But if you see anything, let me know.'

'See what?' one of the men demanded. 'Only what, please?'

'Nothing,' the Sergeant said hastily. 'Nothing at all.' When Pechorin raised his eyebrows as if to say 'Let's hear it' – not in the manner of a gossip, but that of a cautious leader of men – the Sergeant shrugged unwillingly, then went on. 'Only there's a small list – not more than a dozen – that I can't account for that way, even with the Brighton House records and asking people to come forward and so on. It's early days. I'm sure they'll turn up.' He laughed. 'It's not as if the witnesses are consistent. This morning someone told me it's a man with a monster's face. Except that the next one says you can't see him because he's invisible. He has hands like a tiger, or a mouth like a heron. And he comes and takes your teeth while you sleep. It's a bedtime story for naughty children. Unless maybe there's a market for teeth somewhere. Eh? Hah!'

He nudged the Ukrainian with thunderous good humour, to indicate that everyone should laugh. They did, but politely, because it wasn't very funny. It was true that there was no market for human teeth because these days dentists could make them out of ceramic and sooner or later they'd just grow them, that was how it was going. Organs, on the other hand, absolutely could be bought and sold around the world. It was a quite legitimate medical trade, one which states regulated very carefully to prevent abuse, meaning that the abuse was profitable and sophisticated. There was a hospital ship in the Bay of the Cupped Hands called the *Reluctant Alice*, where you could buy a heart for $120,000, not including surgery. The *Alice* was one of the more receptive vessels of the Black Fleet, so much so that she very nearly advertised. The numbers were common knowledge on Mancreu: a whole body was only $210,000 and a liver was $80,000, so it was actually a better investment to plump for the corpse entire and reckon to resell the other organs. Of course, if there was a sudden lack of buyers you'd be out a lot of money, but in practice that seldom happened. Someone, somewhere, always needed something.

But suppose for a moment that the problem were reversed: you might find there was no compatible donor, and if you were in a hurry – and what rich transplant patient ever felt he or she had too much time before the situation became critical? – well, under those circumstances it was whispered certain groups would undertake commissions. If no suitable cadaver could be found, one might be made to order. Soldiers, their medical records on file, would be a particularly good source of organs for anyone with access – politicians, say, or spies – and, of course, soldiers died all the time. There would almost certainly never be any need to help them along.

'Nothing in it,' the Sergeant said. 'I shouldn't have brought it up. But if you do see anything strange, call me. And call for a medical team, just in case.'

Pechorin worked his way through that. *In case the victim has been robbed of his kidneys and is sitting alone in a room in a bath of ice waiting to die.*

The Sergeant left them to gather their gear.

The prank – he was thinking of this salutary lesson in manners as a prank, so that if he ever had to testify about it he could truthfully say that was how he'd seen it – was shaping up nicely, but there remained the question of what to wear. The Sergeant had no idea how to begin. He was not someone who spent a great deal of time on clothes. Beyond sewing on a button or a new rank insignia, he had also never done any kind of tailoring. The boy, however, asserted that he had made costumes before, for festivals and parties and for his own enjoyment, and appointed himself quartermaster. This would be better than a normal costume, because it would be real. In fact it must be perfect. Yes, perfect – and would the Sergeant stop wriggling and please allow him to take a chest measurement?

The Sergeant obediently raised his arms and waited. He had been thinking of something rather more ad hoc, but realised now that the exercise of imagination and skill in all this was as much a balm to his friend's hurt as the prospect of justice itself. In the end, it was also better by far that the boy should be party to his redress than that it should be given to him as a gift. He therefore suffered himself to be measured in his various dimensions, and tried not to growl when the waist came up larger than his vanity would have liked. Thinking about it – with his hands in the air and his back straight while the boy measured his chest – the Sergeant understood that what he was proposing to undertake was in some measure stupid and dangerous, so he would do well to be prepared for it to go wrong. He stopped the design process, walked the boy down the long corridor to the newest section of Brighton House, and opened the armoury.

After a while, the boy said: 'Holy socks.'

The weapons were all along the right-hand wall and in racks which slid out on rails to allow many men to arm themselves at once. There was protective gear at the back, and specialist situ-ations kit – demolitions and bomb disposal, engineering, survival and scuba gear on the left. The boy was particularly impressed by a row of sharkpunches – slim aluminium batons tipped with a shotgun shell for dealing with ocean predators on dive missions – and averred that Roy Scheider should have had one. Immediately next to the entrance were various sorts of chemical-weapons suits, because you didn't want to have to go any further than was absolutely necessary when you needed them in a hurry.

The Sergeant wondered what it must be like to see so much appallingly dangerous stuff gathered together in one place, so many strange and expensive tools of destruction and defence, for the first time.

Finally, the boy said: 'This is not a good room,' and Lester Ferris thought he would cheer.

'No,' he said. 'It isn't. But it's got things in it I might need.' He knocked on an armoured vest, and sighed.

The boy nodded.

Together, then, they sat with the comics and the inventory list and drew up an outline of how he should appear. They began with words:

dangerous
fiendish
indestructible
monstrous
capable.

The boy proposed also
cannibalistic
but the Sergeant demurred, and the boy in return struck off
professional

145

as being more something a soldier should be than a caped crusader. They got stuck for a while, and came up with

scary

which was redundant, and

lethal

which made them both uncomfortable, however true it might be that they wanted their creation to seem that way. And then the boy suggested

shocking

and, of course,

awesome.

The Sergeant laid down a few hard rules for equipment, and then withdrew to watch his friend work, bemused by the sketches the boy drew on sheets of paper from the stationery cupboard and by the piles of gear he fetched and discarded from the armoury. Mancreu and even Pechorin, Lester Ferris understood well enough, but it occurred to him now that he did not understand the business of superheroing at all. He knew it as a thing to be admired and as a brief diversion in childhood, but he had never considered it for what it was or how it might actually be done, or even what it might mean if one did.

He was going to put on a funny hat and fight crime. He was going, however briefly, into their world, and you didn't do that without learning about where you were going. He needed to see the fictional landscape of hopes and aspirations and the characters who inhabited them. Symbolic terrain.

He opened a comic and began to read it the way he read soil and weather.

The first thing he understood in that hour was that it was never about hitting people. It was always about proving a point. Hitting people was just a background, the way a uniform was. The message varied like the soldier. For Superman, that point was about justice and ideals. He really was a perfect American dream.

For Batman, it was something else altogether. It was a statement that no matter who you were, how tough you were or how wicked, there were some things you simply could not do. He was not primarily about punishment or even prevention. He was a living cypher, a message that the set of actions which were available to human beings did not include certain crimes, and that line was absolute, made absolute not by him but by what he represented, the human capacity to say 'no'. They could not be prevented, not every time, but they would be uncovered and they would be punished. The Sergeant found himself thinking about Bosnia, where a war had been fought by the West to achieve exactly that same result, and about Afghanistan, where the nations which had pursued Karadžić and Mladić for their misdeeds had decided that some of those things were acceptable so long as they were done for the right reasons.

The boy asked him to hold something while he marked it in chalk, and the Sergeant put down the comic book and shifted to accommodate the easy pressure of curving lines drawn across his chest and legs. Then he was detailed to cut something along the marks, and found that it was not hard at all. There was even a satisfaction in it, a simple lift in his mood for a simple task unequivocally completed. The boy squinted at his work, and then approved it.

It was very companionable, sitting and making in this way. The Sergeant and his uncle Mike had once made a go-kart together, out of a box crate and some wheels from a discarded perambulator. Mike had insisted at the last minute on adding suspension in the form of bed springs, which had complicated the procedure enormously and resulted in a strange, nauseating ride. All the same, it had been grand. The young Lester had ridden it every day until it tore itself apart. He had not had the knack of reassembling the springs, and the kart had mouldered in a corner of the garage because Mike was living overseas. More than likely it was still there.

The Sergeant found himself wondering whether the boy would enjoy it as much as he had, whether they might repair it together. The warming notion soothed him, and he drifted like a man sleeping in the bath. He considered other things he and the boy might make together: musical instruments, chemical experiments, and even cakes. He had enjoyed cakes, in his earlier life. Somehow you didn't get much opportunity to make cakes as a sergeant.

'What you really need,' the boy said at last as he tied off a thread, 'is a sign from White Raoul.'

The Sergeant nodded. He knew it was absurd, even a little mad, but it felt like the right thing. The world was being ludicrous at him, so he would be a bit ludicrous back, and he would make that small part of it around him a little better. Call it atonement, perhaps, for being the one to reveal to the boy that adults do not automatically have all the answers, and that justice does not flow like water from people who are taller than a child. If the boy thought he should have a sign from the scrivener, then: good.

So he told the boy that if it could be arranged, he would have such a sign, but that it must be a secret, and the boy said that the scrivener's calling was like the confessional, that he would die before he told a single one of the secrets he carried in his strange head.

'God is inside him like the ringer in a bell,' the boy said solemnly, and when the Sergeant glanced at him – religious faith not being part of his stated world-view – he shrugged and added that people believed all kinds of stuff.

Perhaps this lack of faith was the reason he would not enter the shop. 'I may not come in,' he informed the Sergeant as they stood at the door. 'It is not allowed.'

Much negotiation had been required to secure an audience at such short notice: a rapid-fire telephone discussion in Moitié passing far beyond the Sergeant's ability to comprehend. There had been a woman's voice first, sharp and annoyed, and then eventually she had yielded the device to someone else: a man who spoke low and slow, to whom the boy was – if not actually respectful – gentle and wheedling. Then the boy had taken some items from the costume pile and required that the Sergeant drive him to the waterfront and circle the car until called for. Favours were being called in, the Sergeant sensed, and gravest contracts signed. But none of these, it seemed, would bind him personally. The debt would rest with the boy, or perhaps Raoul was discharging some earlier IOU. The boy was stubbornly opaque on the matter, and would only talk about what came next.

'It is your quest. Your tree on Degobah!' the boy said. 'Maybe you meet Darth Vader. Full of evil win!' He looked worried for a moment, then shook his head. 'No, no. You meet only White Raoul. I have told him already what he must do for you. I have given him what he needs. He is a crazy old man, maybe also a prophet. Like Hunter Thompson found Jesus, maybe.'

'With a beautiful daughter,' the Sergeant muttered.

'She is ordinary,' the boy said reflexively, and then he looked away, so the Sergeant immediately wondered whether he was in love.

It would make sense. The boy was an enigma and so was she: Sandrine, the hallowed virgin, secret and perfect. The boy loved winkling out secrets, and it seemed there was no door barred to him. If anyone on the island could fall in love with with the princess in the tower it would be this wolf child, courting her without knowing what he was doing, losing his heart. She would be fifteen years his senior or more: a hopeless, unrequited passion. Or the Sergeant could be seeing things, making up stories like a sad old man.

He took a breath and walked into the scrivener's shop, smelling the air, tasting salt and solvent.

The first thing he noticed was the smoke, thick and blue. It was grandfather smoke, hanging in sheets and curtains, wrapping itself

149

around his hands and teasing his mouth with bitter fingers. Thirty-five-year smoke. If you could open this room to the light, you'd see that everything in it was preserved behind a glaze of solid smoke.

White Raoul sat in a basket chair which hung from the ceiling in the darkest part of the shop. The rope was old and dry so that it creaked against its hook. The man had patches of dark brown skin at the corners of his eyes and mouth and rising on one side of his neck, but the rest of his face was a stark, uncompromising white, like the belly of an eel or a clapboard church. He had a narrow face and yellow-silver hair cropped less than a half-inch from his scalp, and around his chin was a fine, soft beard.

His hands clung to the wicker of the chair, and of all of him they were the most vibrant part. The skin was stained with inks and pigments in a strange motley, so that from the elbow down he was a mosaic or a tortoiseshell of reds and greens and blues. Beneath the colours they were working man's hands, strong and scarred even now, but the nails were trimmed very precisely and the skin of his fingertips looked soft beneath its gaudy coat. Pumice, perhaps. Someone must do the manicure for him, someone with a very certain touch.

'I'm Raoul,' he said, as if the Sergeant might genuinely be unsure, 'and you're the soldier.' His voice was hoarse, but when it caught – when the apparatus of his speech unlocked from whatever spasm habitually held it – there was an echo of depth, of a tone fit for hymns and hellfire sermonising. In between times he hoarded his breath, dropped words and letters into the gaps between his inhalations. Cancer, the Sergeant thought, or poison-gas damage to the lungs. Pneumonia. Emphysema. Gunshots. Even partial drowning.

'Got a seen-the-world face. Been boiled honest, like soup. You're worried about secrets. I tell you, this is between us, whatever comes. You understand? I don't talk about it and nor do you.

150

That's part of the price for both of us.' The accent meandered from Paris and Sudan to somewhere American. The Sergeant guessed Miami, but he didn't know what a Miami accent sounded like, so he wasn't sure. Perhaps there wasn't one. Everyone said Miami was full of people from somewhere else.

Raoul waved. 'Come to me for a stele. For my blessing written down. But maybe I should write it so you don't find no more battles. Just happiness. You maybe fall in love with my girl and raise goats. Goats're a good life for an honest man. They are a pain in the ass and they smell like hell, but they give milk and they taste good when you take one f'the table. Yes. I shall write a stele for a man of peace and you go on out in the world with my Sandrine and make her content, hey?'

'She's just a girl,' the Sergeant said, then realised he had no idea. Until this moment he'd had her image in his mind, a slim-hipped almost-woman with dark eyes staying firmly behind the counter. She could be anything at all.

'Yes, she is,' Raoul said. 'After all this time, she's just a girl.' As if this was the saddest thing he had ever said, and the Sergeant had missed the point entirely. He puffed out his cheeks. 'And you won't marry her and live a life of goats.'

'I'm sorry.'

White Raoul leaned forward in his basket chair.

'No, you're no kind of sorry. Not now. When you look back and understand I was right, well, you maybe will and then again perhaps you won't see you could have done different. Faugh!' He lurched to his feet and went hand over hand along the counter, favouring his left leg. 'Dead flesh, dead island.'

'Not dead yet.' It didn't sound convincing.

'Bullshit.' White Raoul balanced, moved the bad leg with his hands and pulled sharply at a leather strap, a brace. The leg stiffened and he hissed. 'I got messed up. Should have seen it coming. Should have wrote my own stele, but it ain't allowed.' He grimaced and lifted a bucket of yellow-brown paint onto the counter, then another, of black. 'Shit. I got old. When did that happen?'

'Some time ago.'

The scrivener laughed and it was a huge sound. *Pirate captain*, the Sergeant decided. *Not poet*.

'Hah,' Raoul said. 'True as hell. But not polite, and you knew I'd think that was funny, too. Now lay your hands flat. I need to touch you and I don't want you jumping about.'

White Raoul reached out over the counter. He brushed down the Sergeant's face and chest, a clinical contact, dry and diagnostic. 'My eyes are bad.' He growled in his throat, a deep, dog noise. 'You think I'm seeing you as you are, Honest? Then you're wrong. I'm looking back from out of the future. Where's the man you want? The you who wears this sign? Oh, yes. There, and there and there he is . . . your Tigerman. Sure. You're gonna make a famous victory, all right, just like the boy says.'

But if this victory pleased him the joy was invisible. He shook his head, then pulled open a drawer behind the counter and drew out a curved grey tablet, then a second. For a moment the Sergeant assumed they were pieces of a Cadillac, a fragment of some strange Mancreu moment where the mayor of Beauville had ridden around in a huge American car. Then he placed them: ceramic plates. Body armour, the kind worn by special-forces soldiers in frontline operations, although these were his own, from the Brighton House armoury. The boy had delivered them in advance.

White Raoul slapped the first plate down on the counter and drove his hand into the black bucket, swirled the paint. Over time, the toxicity must be killing him in a dozen different ways. 'No brushes, Honest. I have to touch the stele. You and these both, becoming one through me. It's about touching and heart. So the heart: who is this Tigerman inside you?'

'A hero. Like in a comic book.'

'Tcha. Of course. That's not enough, Honest. What does he care about?'

152

The Sergeant had never had to lay his heart out for a stranger. His body, yes, for surgeries and medicals. But the heart was private and unvoiced. He tried: 'Justice.'

White Raoul sneered. 'Bullshit. I want to hear about you! The real truth. What are you doing here in my house? You ain't a religious man. Ain't born here, don't care about the island scrivener or his magic paint. That stuff's for locals, Sergeant. You make nice about it so's not to be rude, but you wouldn't ever come in, not until today. And now here you are, getting a stele from an old black native with rotting skin. Why're you doing such a thing, Sergeant of Her Majesty? Hmm? Tell me why.'

He couldn't say it was a prank. That would be unpardonable, and he was already ashamed. But he didn't know what to say instead, so he tried truth, of a sort. 'Shola. The stolen fish.' Seeing that he was making no ground: 'Missing dogs.'

White Raoul scowled like a headmaster. 'A dead man you barely knew. Tcha! Open your mouth and don't think. What do you care about?'

'I don't know!'

'What?'

'I don't—'

'WHAT?'

'Family!' It came out like an admission of guilt. 'Family.'

The scrivener exhaled, and nodded. 'You got one?'

'No.'

'None?'

'Sister.'

'You're not doing this for your sister.'

'I—'

'Come on, come on! Who's this family that you care about so much?'

'The boy,' he said at last, looking into his hands.

'The boy?'

'The one who brought me here.' And then, with sudden hope, 'Do you know who he is?'

'It's not about what he is to me! What is he to you?'

'I thought . . .' He shivered, then dropped his voice so the boy wouldn't hear, leaned across the counter to White Raoul. 'I thought I could try to take him back with me. I thought he might need a home. And a dad, maybe.'

White Raoul stared back at him. 'You doing this to be a father?'

'I suppose.'

'There's easier ways.'

The Sergeant nodded. 'Still.'

'To be a father you're going to put on a mask and be a monster?'

'A hero.'

'Oh, sure.'

'Once, one time. To show him a win. A world where sometimes someone does fix it. Doesn't just walk away.' Doesn't just sit and stare into space, and give up, and die by inches.

'For a son you ain't got.'

'Yes.'

'But that's not funny!' White Raoul shrieked abruptly. 'That's not funny at all!' The scrivener dropped his head and leaned forward over the counter, shuddering. The Sergeant started forward to help him, but Raoul waved him off, his face wet. 'Not funny!' He plunged his hand into the black paint and across the face of the ballistic shield, fingers shaping the pigment. He slashed one way, then the other, and screamed, hammered his fist down onto the worktop. Paint splashed. His other hand delved into the yellow pot and clapped down dotting and slicing, and suddenly a tiger's face leaped from the flat surface, made real by the contrast. The eyes were luminous.

Raoul reached for the second plate, and this time he used only the yellow. He moved his hand four times, and a shape like a mathematician's x appeared, the lower portions curving back up. He went to make one more gesture and then snatched his hands away, forced his breath out slowly, like a man backing away from a fight.

'That's it,' he said. 'They always want more than they can carry. That's pride, not the art. The smallest mark, the most meaning, and stop.' He pushed the plates across the counter at the Sergeant. 'There.' He pointed at the tiger's image. 'Man see that in the nighttime, he's going to run like hell. Might shoot at it, too, instead of your thick head.' The image seemed to ripple in agreement.

'And this one?' The Sergeant pointed to the second plate.

'Backplate, Honest. Sometimes you got to leave in a hurry.'

'I know that. What does it mean?'

'Mean? Means you. Tiger's face again. See? Cat's mouth?' He traced the lower part of the x, turned it around, and the Sergeant almost jerked back from it, the same tiger's face conveyed in bare lines. His tiger, as it had stared down at him in the graveyard. The smell of the paint was heady and thick.

The scrivener touched the plates. 'Touch-dry already. Waterproof in an hour. Now go. Show your boy.'

'What's not funny?'

'Most things, I guess.'

'When you were working. You said it wasn't funny.'

'I was possessed by the spirit of my future. How should I know?'

'Tell me. Please.'

White Raoul sighed. 'Nothing about this is funny, Honest. Take those to your boy and say you ain't doing it. Throw them in the sea and tell him you want to take him away from here. See what he says. Maybe there's a family for you after all. Leave your victory on this island where it belongs.'

'Do you know,' the Sergeant asked abruptly, 'who his parents are? Are they alive?'

White Raoul stared at him. 'Is that a price, Honest? I tell you, you take him away and forget all about your Tigerman? Even if he don't want to go?'

155

After a long moment the Sergeant shook his head. White Raoul sighed and sat in the basket chair again, and closed his eyes. 'Then I am sleeping now, Honest. Not talking. Go do what you do. Go.' From the corners of his weak eyes, lines of moisture ran down his flat white cheeks, and he dabbed at them with leaded fingers, and turned away.

Outside, Lester Ferris rested his back against the black oak door and let the sun bake him. The armour plates were in his hands. He felt committed, filled with the taut excitement of an operation approved and begun. It was a sergeanting state of mind: make your decision in advance, and even in disaster everything thereafter makes sense.

Pechorin and his cronies had a hideout somewhere, a place where they took girls and got drunk. They went there every week. This time, the Sergeant would follow and take his moment with Pechorin. He would introduce the Ukrainian to Tigerman, the demon of Mancreu, and if possible capture that moment of bowel-loosening fear for posterity. A handy snapshot would adorn the inside lid of his locker for evermore, and more than a few messhalls, too. Rough justice, but justice, for sure. And then he would fade into the night and that would be that.

Barracks humour. An education in Lester's Law. Nothing more.

He went back to Brighton House to put on the suit.

9. Cave

The boy had laid it out for him on the bed, and he felt a curious sense of purity as he changed. He began with under-garments supplied to work well with combat protective gear. Then he stepped into thick, blade-resistant cloth trousers and a similar shirt, then the body armour with White Raoul's scrawled insignia, and then the utility belt, heavy and tight and covered in curious things the boy had felt he might need. Next there were gloves, thick and reinforced across the knuckles and braced to strengthen the wrists. A slick camouflage webbing wrapped around the whole to make him amorphous, a little mutable – it was for urban snipers, according to the box, and why anyone had imagined he might require it here he had no idea. In a separate bag was the mask, the boy's special creation. He left it where it was for the moment.

He stared at himself in the mirror. The stele glimmered back at him, unfamiliar and slightly alive. He wondered if he was claiming it, or if the ownership went the other way around. Only one thing was lacking – but when the Sergeant reached for his side arm the boy stopped him.

'Batman has no gun,' the boy said.

'Maybe Tigerman does,' the Sergeant suggested. The boy shook his head very gravely.

'No. He does not carry a gun because he does not need one. Men who carry guns think that guns make them strong, but they are not. Tigerman is a ghost, and he has skill and he cannot ever be stopped. He doesn't carry a gun because he destroys the idea of the gun by existing.'

The Sergeant was painfully aware of how he could be stopped. The boy seemed to sense this, because he shrugged. 'Also, it would not be good if you shot someone.'

This was clearly true.

He left the gun off, though he did sneak it into the glove compartment of the tiny, rusted hatchback which had been the Consul's wife's personal runabout, and before that part of a job lot brought to the island by the chemical men. They were known locally as *toutous* because they looked like turtles. Without plates it was as close to anonymous as he could hope for. He allowed his sidekick to drive – on Mancreu, you learned as soon as you could see over the wheel – and conceded that the boy might make a video recording insofar as that was possible without revealing himself or coming into the line of fire, but it was not to be shown, shared, broadcast or otherwise disseminated, ever.

'And if anything goes wrong, you scarper. Dump the car in the alley behind the mission house.'

'Scarper?'

'Make yourself scarce. Drive away fast. Skedaddle.'

'Vamoose!'

'Yes. That.'

'If anything goes wrong, I shall totally vamoose. But nothing will.'

The Sergeant sighed, and glanced at the sky. Some high cloud, some clear sky, the promise of rain before dawn. 'Take us on a loop through the town,' he said. 'Get us under the awning at the fish market. Let a few people go past us, wait for a car like this one. We'll buy some dinner at the same time.' He drew a long coat around himself, hiding the suit.

The fish was expensive and the boy insisted on haggling, which served them well because just as he was finishing up not one but three *toutous* came in at once. The Sergeant looked upwards again. Fully half of the sky was covered now in solid cloud. The other part was gauzy. He sighed. 'Get ready,' he said. 'We leave when they do.'

The boy looked at him curiously, and then his mouth opened in a startled O. 'Satellites!' he said. 'You are thinking of satellites! That is hardcore!'

'Watch the road,' the Sergeant told him.

The boy brought the car out and around, then across the shanty to a ridge where they could watch the gate of the NatProMan barracks on the north-east side of town.

The Ukrainians left Beauville very fast, driving in convoy and heading for the central mountains. The Sergeant watched them through his lightweight binoculars, while the boy did the same with the enormous antique field glasses. The boy had parked in a drainage ditch on a hillside west of the shanty, and from here they could see Pechorin's barracks and his likely routes. It was a good lookout point, well hidden but with a broad view. 'Smuggler post,' the boy said, when the Sergeant asked. 'Keeping an eye out for John Revenue!'

The convoy passed two small farms the Sergeant had briefly considered as possible locations for the hideout, and zoomed onward towards the foothills. He had a weird moment of inversion, looking down on them. This must be how the Afghans had seen him all the time: hasty and energetic and ineffectual. He could see, from here, how you could just detonate the road underneath and watch the wreckage slide down into a ravine. It would have a satisfying elegance – a distant, clinical justice, all that busybodying brought to one climactic head and then silenced. He shivered.

In fact, Pechorin was coming this way, heading for the Iron Bridge over the white Lucretia River. The hideout must be in the mountains proper, a hillman's hut or something like it. The trucks hurtled on, not directly towards their position but off along a spur and through the sparse beginnings of the real jungle to the lower peak. They drove for half an hour, then up into the winding lanes which led over to the south side. Abruptly the lights zagged and juddered up ahead, the trucks bouncing and banging their way across terrain rougher than they were really able to deal with, and then a little later the glow vanished entirely as if covered in a blanket.

'Cave,' the boy said at the same moment the Sergeant understood.

'Give them ten minutes to get settled inside.'

They waited, watching the dashboard clock. The orange plastic hands, styled for cheery city shopping, snicked loudly as each minute passed.

'Let's go,' the Sergeant said. 'What's the best way?'

But the boy was already moving the car very slowly along a drainage ditch, over what seemed to be a precipice – the Sergeant's hands tightened on the door handle, but he forced himself to breathe out and not shout, and his forbearance was rewarded. The noise of the tyres on gravel stopped, and they ducked down between old concrete walls and rolled along on silent wheels. 'Smugglers,' the boy said. 'I told you.'

Indeed, the Sergeant realised, this was not a second route to the entrance, it was the proper one, major pirate engineering using stolen half-pipe segments no doubt intended for some bit of chemical plant back in the day. Arriving at the cave by the public road was for amateurs.

He grinned. This would be fun.

The Sergeant alighted from the car and made sure that the boy went on – just a weary traveller on his way home – then turned and slipped away into the scrub. He felt clumsy at first, and then entirely at home. That stand of bushes was tall enough to hide him, that boulder would make good cover, those trees were an ideal landmark. He felt the terrain around him, not seeing it in his head like a tabletop map but knowing it the way he knew the location of his limbs. He realised he had been committing the island to memory since his arrival. That road went down into the valley, that one to the peaks. That one was hard in monsoons but fine in the dry season – today it would be passable in the Land Rover, tough on foot. Over towards the volcano there was a small village in a valley with a defensible approach, but the headman was old and his sons were fractious. Two miles down that way was the Iron Bridge, and beyond it a strip of dense jungle and then the Beauville shanty. Brighton House was behind the curve of the mountain . . . He knew it all. He shouldn't be surprised: Always In Combat, after all. He glanced up: some cloud, sporadic patches of sky. If the helicopters came . . .

But there would be no helicopters, and no need for them.

He passed the truck, very careful in case the Ukrainians had posted a sentry. No: bad practice. Part of him wanted to shake his head and sigh. They were off duty, so they weren't being soldiers, and never mind that they were deep in a foreign land. A large part of him wanted to give them a stern talking to, a bit of parade-ground beasting. But their lack of good sense was to his advantage, so instead he peered up along the line of the path. There: a shadow in the rockface. The entrance.

The Sergeant removed the mask from its bag and studied it. The boy had taken a gas mask and decorated it with fragments of fur and bone. The long, mournful face was sinister enough, but with these additions it became feral and judgemental. The nose of the respirator hung down to cover his neck – a tongue or a stinger, it wasn't clear – and in front of his mouth was a strange echo chamber into which the boy had inserted a papery disc like a kazoo's. He breathed into it and heard a soft burr, like the first grunt of a motorcycle on a cold morning.

There was music playing inside the cave, so they would not hear him speak. He wondered how he had come this far without putting the mask on, and knew he had been avoiding it. Experimentally he raised it to his face and said, 'I am Tigerman,' and heard the words came out in a deep, insectoid buzz, as if a wasp's nest had a voice.

I am Tigerman. It should have been absurd. Here, now, he wasn't sure he could live up to it.

He looked down at the thing in his hands, lying open like a black rubber flower. There had been a moistness to the inner surface against his cheek, and the shape was fitted to embrace the human head. He wasn't sure whether it would kiss him or swallow him. He had a nightmarish flash of the shiny interior sticking to his skin for ever, turning him into . . . what? A man with a silly mask on his head; but in comic books it would be something more, something strange and awful and powerful. He rolled his shoulders. The gas mask was to complete the effect and to conceal his identity. The boy had made it while he watched. There were no old, dead gods or mad scientists involved, just tape and glue and scissors.

He ducked his head and put it on, scenting ammonia. He listened for a moment to the sound of his own breathing. Then he picked his way to the cave mouth, and slipped inside.

The passage was narrow at first, with a longish passageway leading in. He could hear the sound of men up ahead, in a larger chamber, and see the flicker of their lights. They were listening to terrible music, a compilation of 80s rock ballads he had been embarrassed by the first time around. In a lot of places, of course, the 80s had never really come to an end. Stone-washed denim and mullets and Freddy Mercury never got old or went away. If Mercury hadn't died, would the band still be playing concerts like the Rolling Stones, indomitably brash and knowing? Not that this was Queen. This was something handed down, a Polish imitation of a German tribute band, played at top volume on a sound system just a bit too small to handle the job. *But baby, oh yes I can rock you, yes, don't block me, get on top!* But the final words vanished into a gargle of distortion.

Laughter rolled down the tunnel. They were early, he gathered, preparing the ground. The guests would arrive later. Girls, he assumed, and maybe some other soldiers. Plenty of people to spread the story of what happened here, to witness the moral caning which was about to be handed out.

At his belt, in true hero style, hung a small selection of oddments: a strange collection of tools the boy had added of his own initiative which must seem useful to a reader of comics – climbing gear, a compressed-air siren, some fisherman's glowsticks. What possible use was a compass? Or a device for seeing off predatory fish? *Holy Shark Repellent, Batman!* As for the siren, it was a civilian thing for summoning aid if you were being mugged. He imagined himself using it to call for help, and trying to explain his outfit. *Loony Lester.*

Alongside this bric-a-brac, though, were two smoke grenades of a new type, sent from London without explanation six months before. He had dutifully taken delivery and stored them away. At the time, he had been entirely bewildered by them. Yesterday, they had been the first thing he and the boy had both approved for Tigerman's utility belt. On his other hip, for balance, were two more-familiar flashbangs.

He rested the first grenade on the ground, set it to 'slow' and pulled the pin.

Darkness welled up from it, oily and thick. The new gas had a very high surface tension. It rose in a plume and hung, clinging to the edges of the tunnel. You could almost feel it, shape it with your hands. Standing in the cloud was like having your eyes shut tight, or wearing a hood, and it seemed to pluck at his sleeves. It was blank. Flat. It made things feel dull, like a layer of mud. It blended smoothly into the darkness outside, had the same impenetrable depthlessness as natural night.

He judged that when he stepped through it into the cave proper he would appear to come from nowhere, from another world.

So long as he could get there, through the cloud. So long as he could make himself walk through the tunnel. From inside, it was hard to imagine there would ever be an end to the stuff.

163

Despite the filtering mask, he imagined it in his lungs, polymeric invader in a wide blue space policed by antibodies like seaweed. He realised that the images came from that film with Raquel Welch in which she – and the submarine in which she travelled – were shrunk to microscopic size to save a diplomat from an assassin's bullet. Ridiculous Technicolor images from the 60s, spacesuits with short hems. He could not recall the title, because the other film about the lost dogs trying to rejoin their family kept getting in the way. There was a moment in the film in which a man was consumed by a white blood cell. It slid down over his head and ate him. In his mind, the black smoke was the same: a purposeful, alien presence.

It could not be more than twenty feet from one end of the cloud to another. He walked carefully, picking up his feet and putting them down from the outside of the toe so as to be silent. Demons do not clump.

The music was very close now. He must be all but there. It occurred to him that this gas was supposed to be used with infrared goggles or some sort of computer linkup, something to let him see where the enemy could not. Too late to worry about that now. But how could he know when he was nearing the edge of the cloud?

A dazzling white light shone on his face, and the Sergeant ducked back. He heard a cry of disgust and alarm, and lay flat on the ground. His mind caught up. His head had pierced the limit of the cloud just as someone swept a torch across it. They had seen his mask only, hanging in thin air: a monster face which vanished into an impossible shadow. And he had seen, briefly, something which changed the game completely and meant he was deep in the shit. Bullets came, eighteen, nineteen inches over his head.

The cave was not a place for soldiers to relax. Not a den. It was bigger than he had expected, the size of a basketball court rather than a treehouse. He had anticipated some sort of makeshift bar and brothel, with soft furnishings looted from abandoned houses, maybe even curtains for privacy. Instead, the interior felt like a forward reconnaissance base, neat and businesslike and impersonal. The lighting came from vertical fluorescents which stood at regular intervals along the walls and appeared to run off a small generator vented into a natural chimney. The floor was smooth and had been swept, perhaps even bleached. There were a few chairs, but they were spindly office stools, good for taking your weight while you worked but not for relaxing. The music was the only personal touch, a medium-sized portable player sitting on what he had first thought was a desk, but which was something else entirely, one of many such somethings, and all of them bad news.

Stacked around the room in neat piles were towers of brown bricks, each about the size and shape of a shoe, glossy with polyurethane wrapping and tape. He was reasonably confident, having seen the stuff before, that these bricks were made of heroin. Heroin in this quantity was a major operation, and heroin in this quantity here, on Mancreu, implied almost incontrovertibly the extremely deniable operation of a national government. Perhaps even of NatProMan itself. That Pechorin and his men were Ukrainian soldiers meant nothing. At this level flags and allegiances were negotiable. Passports were currency. Heroin was money was information was arms was a vote in the Security Council, and all of it was power, and power was what nations ate to stay alive.

Or, Christ, it might be plastic explosive. The same truths would apply. He'd never seen plastic explosive that colour, but there were lots of different kinds. That would explain the fluorescents: you didn't want that stuff to get hot, because it sweated, and the sweat was unstable. He tried to remember if the wrapping had looked breathable.

A bullet ricocheted off the wall and down onto the plate on his back, bounced away. He realised he had been still for much too long.

He should go backwards, but he couldn't turn around without standing. The lip of the passage protected him so long as he lay here, but the moment he got up he would be in the line of fire. He could shuffle back, but that could ultimately mean being a target for longer. He had some tenuous advantages: the smoke was confusing them, the mask had rattled their composure. They genuinely had no idea what they were dealing with, and were afraid. They had not been expecting an attack, and now – his hesitation served this much, at least – they weren't sure they were being attacked. Come to that, the Sergeant wasn't sure that they were, either. Except that if he led them out into the road now, and if the boy had not followed his instructions and fled, they would see a car, and an accomplice, and that would be that. The runabout would cease to exist. Bullets would tear into the metal and plastic, twist and deform it in the unpredictable ways they had. Perhaps the car would be unravelled as if by a giant tin-opener, or perhaps it would fold down and in under its own weight. Perhaps a bullet would ignite something and it would burn, shrivel and contract, or perhaps it would explode. He had seen all these things happen, in the past. But whatever happened, the nameless driver would be rendered into meat and bone, would cease to be a person and become the other thing, the empty thing just waiting for fire or rot to make it disappear. He could not picture the boy dead. But he could see the moment of his death, the appalling havoc of the shooting, could see him understand in that instant that he was about to be dead and that his body was finished with, and that was awful.

So he did what sergeants do. He advanced to meet the enemy. On his belly, pushing with his toes so as not to abrade his knees.

He slid forward and felt the ground drop away, ducked his head and rolled close behind the nearest stack of heroin. It was heroin, thank God; someone had been kind enough to label it in neat black print, and 'thank God' because that meant it wasn't important that it was sweating and he wasn't about to be vaporised. And he could do this.

He pulled a conventional flashbang from his belt and tossed it to his right, waited a moment and then went left because ninety-five per cent of the population is right-handed and prefers to shoot, as it were, on the forehand. In the enclosed space of the cave, the blast was even more intense, and he expected it to drive the shadow gas away down the tunnel. Instead the cloud seemed to bow and ripple, passing the force through itself and shuddering before rolling back along the walls and resuming its position with a jellied shiver which looked altogether too much like a wink. He moved while they were deaf and blind, staying low. *Overwhelming enemy forces, stated objectives impossible. Sitrep: total goatfuck.*

He let the moment teach him its logic, felt the world fall into shapes in his head.

A moment later they came forward to where he had been. They used a classic fire-and-movement line, each man halting to provide cover for the next. It looked pretty enough, but they were all still too fuzzy from the impact of the flashbang to aim well, and while you could get away with firing into the tunnel, firing those weapons into the walls of this room would be unpredictable and dangerous. They could easily end up shooting one another. In fact, the odds greatly favoured it, because there were so many more of them than there were of him. That should make them unwilling to fire, make them hesitate, but only if they were good enough to realise it. He didn't know whether they were that good, to hold to common sense here, now, with a king's ransom in heroin and a demon in the room. He thought probably not. He left them to it, his mind clear and swift.

Old objectives: crash the party, induce urination in the enemy, depart. Job done, to a great extent, and the whole thing would have been hilarious without the drug stash or the weapons fire. Leave it behind. It's irrelevant now.

New objectives: secure the boy's departure, avoid capture, escape. He had probably managed the first already, although he had to make room for a scenario in which his friend was hovering with the door open like a getaway driver. *Factor it in. This is the land-scape. The best plan will flow downhill.* The last one was the problem. It was not enough to get back to Brighton House in one piece. A brief survey of the armoury records would expose him. A probe of the boy's costume purchases would do the same. Forensics, probably, would confirm it all, and if this was a government-level operation none of that was off the table. He could only survive if the question was simply never asked. He had a small advantage there in that attacking a fortified drug hideout by himself was very much not a Lester Ferris thing to do. As evidenced by the fact that he hadn't done it, not intentionally. He had done something else and it had turned into that. Even he himself had not known he was going to do it. If he'd known what Pechorin and the others were up to in here, he would have left well alone.

Well, no, he wouldn't.

He didn't know, actually, what he would have done. Something. Not this. Told Kershaw, told Dirac. Told London, even, if he had had to. Fleet business was supposed to stay offshore. Fleet business was supposed to be invisible. You weren't supposed to fucking trip over it. Standards were falling. If he'd known, he could have done . . . almost anything. There were so many ways to administer a gentle nudge: *do your laundry on the water, not in my manor, it makes it hard for me to stay blind.* And wasn't that a sorry way to carry on?

But he wouldn't have done this.

The Ukrainians were still checking the stacks by the door. They had just discovered the wall of gas, and it was disturbing them just as it had him. Pechorin poked at it with his finger, then snatched his hand back from the meniscus as he felt the cool, organic embrace. A tendril of the gas followed him and he shouted, shot it. The bullet zinged away into the tunnel. A moment later the other men were firing too, and Pechorin was yelling at them to stop.

On the stack in front of the Sergeant was a picture of Shola, and there was a loose ring of red felt tip slashed across the image. The boy's face was bright on the left of the picture, caught by the camera flash. A ridiculous thing to find here, an image from months ago. And that, yes, that sleeve was the Sergeant's own, just coming into frame.

He put the picture in his pocket. It didn't belong here.

Pechorin turned, and saw him, and screamed an order, but no one moved. They were staring. They were seeing the demon, the alien thing they had heard about but had not believed in, had chosen to laugh at. For one moment, everything was still.

'I am Tigerman,' Lester Ferris said, and saw them flinch at the ugly voice of the mask. 'I'm here to collect on a debt.'

Without much conviction, Pechorin raised his gun. Lester Ferris sneered through the kazoo.

Paratroopers had told him that jumping from a plane was easy, but doing the same into the still air beneath a hot air balloon was another thing entirely, the difference between flying and falling. He had been in a balloon, but now he was falling.

I am Tigerman.

With one hand he pulled the cord out of the generator, and dropped. The cave was plunged into darkness. Then he unscrewed the fuel cap, jammed the second flashbang into it, pulled the pin, and ran.

The blast lifted him into the air and threw him over the stacks of heroin. He could smell his own charred hair, knew his neck and arms were scalded. His boots were on fire. His hands fended off the ceiling, and he fell down onto something human, felt the man's ribs crack, rolled forward along the cave floor. The black gas was gone now, for sure, replaced by a thick diesel smoke from the generator. He could hear them coughing behind him, choking, and he hoped like hell they'd have the sense to get out. The heroin

169

was burning, too, and somewhere in there he'd seen a spare drum of fuel and soon that would go up and take the whole place apart. Were they getting high? Would the drug slow them down, even knock them out? He ran, and heard his own breathing distorted by the mask, the evil buzz bouncing off the walls like laughter.

Outside, the boy was gone. That much, at least, was according to plan.

He allowed himself to hope for one moment that he could steal a truck, but they must have taken the keys into the cave. There was a radio handset on the passenger seat and on instinct he grabbed it and clipped it to his belt at the back. Then he ran, infantry style, putting one foot in front of the other with plenty of muscle, accelerating but not sprinting, making for the trees on the downhill slope. It was steep, but that was fine, that made him faster and he was unarmed so he didn't have to worry about shooting himself as he went along. He heard them come out of the cave, a sudden burst of noise and energy, and then a bright beam of light stabbed out, and another, and he realised they had high-powered torches. A moment later everything around him was daylight and there were shouts. They were chasing him now, and the pursuit was making them brave.

He veered into the deep brush, heading for the river, and heard them behind him. He ran for what seemed like hours, forcing himself to hold his pace, breaking through the wall of fatigue and then finding it again so that he had to break through it once more. He wished they weren't so young and fit. He worried about helicopters. Satellites might lose coverage because of high cloud, but not helicopters, and helicopters had guns on them. Helicopters could follow you, personally, with infrared imaging. They could give chase.

He wondered where he was and what he was going to do about getting home. He ran.

By the time he reached the cliff edge they were close enough to stop and fire a few rounds every five or six steps. Bullets whizzed over him, and then something caught him full in the back and he was airborne. He flew, for the second time that night, end over end. Above him he could see the harvest moon, and he thought probably this was what had hit him. He could see how it might have happened: the huge globe spinning out of its orbit and barging into him, smacking him into the air. He tried to breathe, and found vacuum. Yes. This was space. He would die in space. His corpse would go round and round the world amid the junk and clutter of Sputniks and the rest. Somewhere out here there was a dog, too, an early Russian experiment. Laika. He had always felt sorry for her: surely she had been the most alone creature ever, when she died. Now he would join her. Perhaps their ghosts would go for walks. He would throw sticks for her, or moonrocks, and she would bring them back. He wondered if a Soviet dog would associate with him, a filthy capitalist. He hoped so. Dogs were largely apolitical. Had Madame Duclos's dog had opinions about what was happening to its home? He owed her an explanation, he realised, for its death. Owed her answers.

The moon hit him again, this time from in front. It clanged. Should the moon do that? Or, no. Not the moon. Something metal, something artificial. And not space. He could smell pines and dust and burning. This was still Mancreu, and the Iron Bridge across its gorge, and he was hurtling past it towards the river far, far below.

Lester Ferris, in a home-made demon suit with a magic tiger on his back and chest, spread his arms and fell.

10. Rapids

He hit the water hard, but it felt like lying on a feather bed. Or he imagined it felt like that – he didn't think he'd ever actually been on a feather bed. On consideration they probably weren't all that comfortable: not enough back support. But he wasn't running any more. He had been running for hours. His limbs felt light and tired. He breathed in, and felt the mask suck against his cheeks. Water squirted from the kazoo and splashed his face.

Self-knowledge returned, and fear, gut-wrenching and panicked. He could die here. He *would* die here. In seconds. The Ukrainians were still firing: he heard shots snip past him; the strange, strangled yelp of bullets in water. White lines, phosphorescent, told him which direction was up. He tried to swim and realised he couldn't. Too much weight. More bullets yipped past. They were inexperienced with shooting into water, he thought, were not accounting for the deflection. His vision was brown at the edges, brownish-red. He knew in a moment it would turn grey, and that would be the end.

His boot scraped riverbottom. His chest – his lungs, presumably – felt appalling. The belt on his costume was tight, and he reached down to shed it. His gauntleted hand batted vaguely at half a dozen items, couldn't find the clasp. Knife. Bandages. Sharkpunch. Pitons. Hammer. Siren.

You're kidding me, he thought. The boy's magpie instinct, covering the uniform with ridiculous things. *Siren*. It was a nonsense – almost no one ran towards the sound of a siren, not any more, not with car alarms going off every ten minutes and a very well-publicised chance that any good Samaritan would get

172

stabbed for his trouble – and these days there were electronic ones which were smaller and louder. This one was the old kind. If you were desperate, you might use it to blow out a candle.

Or if you were very desperate you might breathe it.

He jammed the nozzle under the chin of the mask and thumbed the release, felt the rubber stretch around him like a balloon and gasped stale air. Thank God, it was proper air, not butane or anything else. The noise was probably very loud but he'd just blown himself up (again) and been shot at in a confined space and it was less bad than either of those things. He let go of the trigger and the sound stopped. The bullets had moved downstream – they were assuming he'd float, which was daft but he'd made the same mistake. How much air was there in the siren? It had to be three minutes, surely? He shook it, felt liquid sloshing around. Half full, maybe, but he'd been profligate in that first, desperate heave. Now he could make it last.

Tentatively, he tried walking against the current. Not possible. He could hold his own, just about, but it was hard work and it hurt. His back was marked, he knew, with a sharp square of bruises where the armour plate had been driven against it. How many shots? Three? Four? How far out into the stream had he fallen?

The water pushed him hard against something massive. A boulder. No, of course: a concrete slab, one of the bridge supports. It must be the first span, he couldn't have gone further than that. He tried to remember if there was anywhere to get out on this side. Two more breaths from the siren – he was worried now that the noise would give him away, but he dared not remove the screamer because it seemed to be part of the trigger mechanism – and he used the concrete to push himself along with his hands. He was moving uphill. He could see the surface about five feet above him. Eddies swirled around his head. He couldn't see or hear the bullets any more, so he dared to ignite the fisherman's glowstick, cupped it in his hand to direct the light down and forward. The siren was almost empty now, but he wasn't going to

173

die. Something new was in him, familiar and predictable but not the less powerful. He had been shot at and chased, and both of these things made you enormously angry. It was just a fact; human nature, human chemistry. When someone tries to kill you, when they hunt you, you hate them. So now he hated, and with that came a confidence. He was getting out of this river. He was a few steps away from breaking the surface, he could see the rocks, the path up to dry land. He took his last breath from the canister and released it, let it wash away. Perhaps they would see it and think it evidence of his death, like a destroyer hunting a submarine.

He felt the crown of his head break the surface, and lifted his chin so that in the next step his eyes were just above the water. There was no one on the bank. Three steps more and he could breathe again, and then he was staggering through the shallows and up and out, and the river was behind him.

A soldier would take this opportunity to retreat. A soldier would call for reinforcements and retrench. But now, out of the water and with air in his lungs again, the ragged, tooth-spitting fury of a brawler was boiling in him, demanding release. *Fucking shoot at me?* And there was the picture of Shola in his pocket, the picture which said they might have had something to do with that, too. *Oh, you fucking think so? Is that right, you Chicken Kiev wankers? DO YOU FUCKING THINK SO?* He rolled his shoulders and felt the pain in his back, and that made him even angrier. He snarled. Water spewed from his mask like steam, and the sound which went with it was like the sound of hopeless triage.

He smiled tightly behind the mask, and took a few experimental steps. Nothing wrong with his legs, no shrapnel, no fractures. Ribs might be a problem. Limited mobility in his arms, but they'd loosen. Time to go and put these lads straight. Oh, yes. Time, and more than time. After a moment, he sliced open the glowstick and poured it over his head, glowing green slime. No doubt it was toxic. If he didn't die tonight, he'd probably have an itchy scalp. He laughed, and the mask made it into something very wrong.

He set off at a run, water falling from his clothes.

He knew where they were because he could hear them shooting at rocks and tree trunks in the water, hear them arguing about it. He circled to put them against the lights of Beauville, and waited until the wind was blowing off the river, carrying his footsteps back behind him into the trees. Then he charged.

Two of them were standing side by side a few steps from the others, and he slammed their heads sharply together, heard gristle and that sickening sound like the ball in an aerosol can which meant concussion. The bruises on his back screamed and he screamed back. A third man turned in shock and looked about to scream too, and then his face disappeared under a crushing elbow. He dropped.

A step further away, Pechorin held an expensive gun. It was an American thing with all sorts of clever engineering and a bottle-opener on the back: very light, very strong. He should have used it already but he hadn't, seemed to have forgotten about it, or perhaps he just couldn't believe this was happening. Now he brought it round and the Sergeant whipped the sharkpunch up and forward in a fencer's lunge. The tip touched the gun and the charge fired. Pechorin went flying back, fragments of next-gen rifle embedded in his face.

The Sergeant dropped and rolled, putting the fallen between himself and the remaining men. As he came up, he saw his nearest enemy sighting along the barrel, looking for a clear shot. He ducked left, then reared back the other way and threw one of the climbing pitons as hard as he could.

It was supposed to be a distraction, or at best a knockout blow. Instead, the steel pin went directly into the man's open mouth and lodged in the soft part of his throat. He made an appalled sound and sank to his knees, hands outstretched in appeal.

Everything was still.

The remaining soldiers stared in abject horror at the choking man. Blood was coming out of his mouth, not arterial spray but a venous welling which would kill him eventually if not treated, although it seemed he might suffocate before that became an issue. The other casualties were regaining consciousness. Pechorin looked as if he might lose part of his nose.

Tactically there was all still to play for. The Sergeant had his ace in the hole, the fast-dispersal setting on the remaining gas grenade. It would make a thirty-foot ball of darkness, the manual said, pretty much instantly and until the wind dispersed it. Although actual performance in the field did not always match the claims in the documentation. He had his hand on it, ready to use, but he knew he had overreached. The last of Pechorin's men could take him now, and if he died here he'd have no one but himself to blame.

But they didn't know that, he realised as the moment held, and they were convinced now that he could do impossible things. He could appear from nowhere, breathe under water, make guns explode and strike down men at a distance. He was bulletproof. They had seen evidence of all these, and they knew, too, that he was the Mancreu demon, the one everyone was talking about, the one who might be a psychopath or an organ hunter or something even more awful. So they stared at him, and did not attack, and waited to see what he would do. Like prey, they hoped that if they did nothing he would depart to eat his kill.

He didn't do anything. If he ran it might break the spell. If he came forward he might press them into action. So he waited, and they waited.

From somewhere across the valley, he heard the sound of a tiger growling or calling, and a reply. A mated pair.

Behind his back, he flicked the dispersal rate on the grenade to medium, and drew the pin with his thumb. He didn't move. The darkness boiled up over his back and all around him, and he kept the eyes of the mask on them all the time. When the gas finally shifted to cover him he rolled back and away, then ran for the trees.

Pechorin called for reinforcements.

On the stolen radio handset the Sergeant could hear the chatter, cool and efficient. He had worked with some of them before, here and elsewhere. Could he run towards them? Claim to have been taken hostage and escaped, even fought back? But when and how? At the fish market, or from the house? He shook his head. There might be a way, but he was too addled to see it, to account for the branching possible consequences. He imagined buying his absolution by accidentally selling out the boy. No. Run on. *Hostile contact: allied forces in the target ʒone.* Then numbers, coordinates, and yes, there *was* a helicopter after all. They would close the roads, and with the 'copter they would do so effectively – but where he was going he didn't need roads. He glanced at the sky and growled: the cloud had lifted again. He should shed this suit somewhere it wouldn't be found. He couldn't permit himself to be caught in it, for sure, but his blood was in it and if they were serious about this – and you didn't put a helicopter in the air if you were just kidding around – they would know that within hours.

He considered options. Brighton House – the phone was ringing there, no doubt – was a few miles away cross-country: over scrub and through banana plantations, for the most part. But there was a line of open ground between the house and the jungle, and in the worst case he would be at a loss to explain how – having left the house on a shopping expedition – he came to be returning on foot from another direction. On the other hand if he returned to the house in the *toutou*, between obfuscation, retasking and cloud cover he might have nothing to explain at all.

In the meantime, he was already running again, on the half-cleared paths used by hunters and animals both, between the trees.

Time became fluid. Running was something he enjoyed. After a certain point, his mind was silent. He ran. He spectated. There was a clean, moonlit purity inside his head. He was exhausted, but it was this or capture and he had no intention of being captured, so exhaustion was irrelevant. He was also high on combat and anger and for as long as the immediacy lasted he would feel like a god. He had about twenty minutes of that left, so – knowing he would walk, after – he ran now.

The jungle was wet and warm. It smelled of vegetation and life and in particular of a species of red-flowering vine. The flowers opened at night and were called something dirty in Moitié; Inoue had told him once that in the dark, to a certain kind of lizard, they looked like meat. The lizard ate them and shat out the seeds somewhere else, spreading the plant. It had no sense of smell to speak of, so no one knew why they smelled good. He wondered if you could eat them. Perhaps they were some sort of healing drug. The Witch would know. Perhaps he should go and see her. A last chance: tonight of all nights he might turn back the clock.

Nonsense.

He growled, in irritation or lust, he wasn't sure, and ran on. He was following a narrow path, probably a badger run, and yes: he was holding the compass, finding his way. He grinned, then laughed. He wanted to sing and drink and eat. He wanted to sleep for a year, to lie naked in a jacuzzi looking out over the Sahara while someone rubbed his feet, to headline at a rock concert, to tear down walls with his hands. He had won. He was a god.

Adrenalin. Let it go.

But he couldn't, and anyway it should be over by now, the high should be exhausted and burned out, should have left him hollow. He wondered if inhaling burning heroin could do this. Cocaine, perhaps. Maybe there had been cocaine, too. Or perhaps there was something here, in this jungle. Maybe the red flowers were a stimulant.

Tigerman make famous victory! Hah!

There wasn't really, in this world, a way in which burning a shitload of heroin and beating up some dealers was a crime.

He ran on to Beauville, and his way home.

His reckoning was good. He came out of the jungle at the old millhouse, checked the sky and saw clouds and no helicopter, trotted over the road into a plantation and jogged on. He felt he still had more in the tank – impossibly – but he wanted to save it in case there was more craziness to deal with before he slept. The rendezvous was another twenty minutes away. Two streets later he stopped, halted by a thought: the Witch. Her house was here, or near here. It must – he had never thought of Beauville like this before, had always stuck religiously to the road system, but in fact it was all closer together than he had realised – it must be just beyond that stand of palms.

He found that he was heading towards it. For what, exactly? Surely not to bang on the door and ask her to harbour a fugitive. To have sex with a fugitive. No. Whatever magic was working on him to vanish his aches and strengthen his legs, he remained himself, and he knew after nearly forty years on Earth that when you showed up at a woman's door in the middle of the night smelling of blood and diesel and river mud, she did not immediately lose track of her underwear, or even her common sense.

Not to admit all, either. If she was what she appeared to be, she didn't need the trouble – and if she wasn't then nor did he.

Not to serenade her, not to seek medical attention, not to steal her car. But since he was passing, and this being the day he was having, he wanted to see her front door and put his hand on the gate, and know that not everything on Mancreu was a mess.

He climbed the fence around the plantation and ran across the spongy sea-grass towards her house. The door was very solid, an old, traditional Mancreu colonial door made of salvaged wood. It looked inviting, and safe. Perhaps he would just call on her, say he had heard a noise, was wondering if she was all right. Perhaps she would ask him in, after all. Perhaps she was so worldly that his attire would hardly seem odd to her.

Don't be an idiot.

There was a light burning in the window, and to his amazement she was awake, sitting in a high-backed chair. Her hands were stretched out in exhortation or applause. Come on, come on! Did she have a child, then? Was she for some reason teaching her toddler to walk at two a.m.? The Sergeant realised he had no idea. Perhaps that was something some children did, perhaps they sat up in bed and screamed until you put them on the floor and then they took their first steps and you gave them a lollipop. He had not seen a child's first steps, not ever. Or perhaps he had and hadn't known. He had seen plenty of small children, shaky waddlers flopping into their mothers' arms. In Europe, in Africa, in Asia. Perhaps, if he had understood what was happening around him, he would have realised on some of those occasions that he was witnessing a mundane sort of miracle. Perhaps if he had realised it, he might actually have won a single, genuine heart or mind, made a connection which meant more than occupation and cigarettes.

'Your son is walking! Is that the first time?'

'Yes! It is! Well done, Iskender! Well done!'

'Here, we've got some coffee in the jeep, have a cup with me.' Because, in some parts of the Caucasus and even elsewhere, to drink a toast in beer was an eternal curse. Coffee, however much he loathed it, was universal.

And thus I make the world safe for democracy! But perhaps children's steps were private things, not to be shared with a lumbering British sergeant.

Just as this scene beyond the window was private. He turned to go, and as he did so he saw White Raoul the scrivener, one leg twisted without his cane, claw his way forward. Therapy, surely, of the most human sort. Teach the muscles, lift the spirit.

The Sergeant could hear the patient's joints protest, hear them click and grind. Each step was pain. And yet White Raoul weathered it, welcomed it even, because she was at the far end. Her arms were out to him and her face was a cry of approbation. *Brave soldier!* Raoul grunted, and the Sergeant could see her weight shift as she prepared to bridge the gap between them, but she held back, held back, and he recovered his balance and his composure. More pain. A mangled hip, the Sergeant thought, and likely a prosthetic kneecap on the other leg: an old, cheap one. A Swiss surgeon had famously used a calf's kneecap years ago, but he had been a genius and this was not his work. This was patch and repair and don't worry about it too much because to be honest this man will probably die. Car crash. Gunfire. Falling log. Bones were not strong just because they were the strongest thing a human body had.

Raoul passed the little table and the chairs, and his grin was victory. His doctor – no, more: his *reward* – lunged at him, and for a moment the Sergeant thought she would knock him down, but together they made a single, upright pillar in the little house. She pressed her mouth on his urgently, and then her dress was gone and beneath it she was quite nude. She stripped away his smock and the shapeless trousers, and then his strange, rainbow arms were around her back, corded muscle locked against tanned skin. The scrivener's body was a tapestry, tattoos weaving in and out of bands of mottled skin, over old, hard muscles and elegant ribs, and what could only be shrapnel scarring in a spray along one flank. Life must be a constant barrage of greater and lesser pain. But here, now, it all made sense, as if he was a machine made of broken parts which functioned perfectly only in this one action, only for her. They made love standing up, and White Raoul grew less unsteady and more fluid with each moment, and her breath gasped out into the night.

Abruptly, the Sergeant realised that he was spying.

He turned, and picked his way through the shadowed streets into a breeze which was unusually cold.

The car was exactly where it should be, and the boy was gone.

The Sergeant arrived at Brighton House ten minutes later, and closed the door on Mancreu with some finality. In the morning he would love the place again, he knew, but for tonight he had had enough. Enough tomatoes, enough stolen fish, enough local characters and their little ways. Enough tigers, enough trying to do the right thing. He was tired and he was not dead and that was good.

He stripped off the suit and bundled it into a bag. When he awoke he would destroy it, return as many pieces as he could to the armoury, and move on. He reckoned he had a better than even chance of having escaped identification and tracking tonight. If he had, all he needed to do was sit tight and stay clean and let the inevitable blurring of events and the imminent destruction of Mancreu wash the problem away. Dig in and let the shitstorm fly by. He laughed, feeling the euphoria of survival.

Fuck you, he told the world. *Not dead, again.*

He showered, peering down at himself and seeing the body he recognised, old scars and new bruises. He had some light scalding, some scratches, and in the mirror he could see a bold blue square where the armour had taken bullets. Green mosaic tiling gave his body a slightly fishy sheen.

He walked naked into the galley and drank water straight from the tap, then when his thirst faded he poured a couple of fingers of Scotch and sipped at it slowly, letting himself feel the burn. He did not dilute it. He wanted the fire in it, the bite.

Sensing movement, he peered at his groin, half-amused, half-frustrated. Signs of post-combat arousal: all dressed up and no place to go. He patted his penis in a friendly way. It bounced. After three decades of sharing his life with its weird, unpredictable reactions, he tended to view it as a benign alien presence and treated it accordingly. He had never given it a name, because he privately thought only idiots did that, but it was idle to pretend that he and the organ were always of one mind. He, for example, found nothing erotic in being shot at, but it inevitably produced this reaction. Seeing the Witch naked and having sex would seem much more so, but had elicited none at all. That was imponderable, but curiously appropriate. He wished her well with Raoul, truly. He felt his desire relinquish her, felt his mind remove her to that separate, respected place reserved for things he cherished and wanted to protect, but did not touch.

Not dead, again.

11. Complications

The Sergeant showered and went into the comms office, found that Kershaw had indeed called, several times. He thought for a while, then lifted the phone and called back.

'What's the news, Jed?' he asked, when the operator connected him. 'I've been hearing helicopters all night.'

'Your typical batshit insane Mancreu,' Kershaw snapped. 'While you were fucking three Bolivian pole-dancers in a hayloft, some jackass hillman went postal on a patrol. Roughed them up pretty good. You okay?'

'Aside from being roused from my beauty sleep. Big chap, was he, this jackass?'

'Oh, ha ha.'

'I was only going to observe, between Bolivians as it were, that we in the British Army give our fellows guns and train them in this thing called combat, and we tend to think of one bloke attacking a full patrol of – what, eight? – as a bit of an error on his part. We tend to expect the patrol to cut such a fucking idiot into thin strips and bring him home to us for close inspection of the parts.'

'They were a man short.'

'Oh, well, if it was only seven to one, that explains it.'

'Yeah, I guess it was a lot like the War of Independence, huh?'

'Yes, I'll tell the Queen, she loves your little japes. Here, hang on.' He yawned loudly. 'Did you say he roughed them up? As in, with his hands?'

'Hands and feet. One of them has a heelmark on his ribs.'

I'll be sure and burn the boots first. The Sergeant let a little more disdain creep into his voice. 'He was *unarmed*? Against professional soldiers?'

'I know, I know.'

'No, you don't, Jed. This is one of those moments where you sort of need to be a soldier. It can't be done.'

'You did it,' Kershaw objected.

The Sergeant's heart nearly fell out of his mouth. *He means Shola! Shola's café. Not tonight! Talk!*

'That was entirely different. Five amateurs, and I got bloody lucky with the custard. Even so, I ought to be dead. It was a bloody stupid thing I did, Jed, and I honestly don't know why except there was a child present and I thought he was next. This isn't that. You're talking about a fully armed, trained patrol. They're pulling your pisser. One bloke? Nine foot tall with green skin, was he? Warned them not to make him angry?'

Kershaw paused. 'Yeah, something like that.'

Too close to the truth. Careful. The Sergeant filled the silence with a more plausible slander. 'Probably got into a fight with one another and it turned nasty.'

'Lester . . . I'm a little bit freaking out here. I have a guy in the hospital they're telling me was force-fed a railroad spike.'

'Fuck.' Because it was the only thing to say.

'Yeah.' Kershaw sighed. 'This island . . . What the hell do you want, anyway?'

'You called me. I assume you needed my superior military knowledge.'

'I'm up to my neck in superior military knowledge over here, asshat. Pardon me if I was a little bit worried about the old British washout who lives on his own. Why the fuck didn't you answer your phone?'

'Went out to buy dinner. Had a glass of beer. Just woke up.'

'You were asleep? Asleep but hearing helicopters?'

'It was a very large glass.'

He let Kershaw bitch at him a little more, fostering the notion of chummy, earthy Lester Ferris, a bit vague and a bit hapless, serving out his time. After a few more exchanges Kershaw transparently wanted to get rid of him, reassured and aggravated in just the right measure, and the Sergeant hung on just long enough to appear a bit needy. Then he went to his bedroom and lay down. His bones hurt. His muscles ached. He realised his ears were ringing. On the other hand: full of win. From SNAFU to Mission Accomplished by dint of having balls of steel. Very nice.

So score one for the world, he told himself. *Score one for kitchens and cats and woolly hats and village green cricket and score bugger all and piss off for men in offices and men in caves making war on one another by selling smack to kids in Liverpool or New York, for the sake of things none of the rest of us give a shit about.*

At some point, he slept, and was grateful.

The Sergeant woke late and realised he was stuck to the Consul's linen. His left forearm was bleeding all along to the elbow, sluggish, grazed, and painful. The sheet was solidly glued to his shoulders where he had been burned above the armour, and he had bruises everywhere. His throat was sore as hell.

'You are an idiot,' the Witch said unsympathetically.

She stood at the foot of his bed, a leather bag hanging on a strap across her chest. It pressed her shirt against the centreline of her body, emphasising her curves. He realised that the last time he had seen her she had been naked and gasping, and belatedly averted his eyes.

She leaned away from the bag, hauled it onto the foot of the bed, and rummaged. 'Don't move. You're a mess.'

'As well as an idiot.'

She shrugged. 'I said, don't move. If you pull that off it will hurt more. For longer. Tcha!' This last in disgust, because he had turned to examine his shoulders and the movement had wrenched a wad of fabric away from his flesh. He grunted.

She stomped up the side of the bed and put her hand flat on his chest below his chin. When he did not lean back she pushed him, not with her arm but with her body's weight, so that if he

186

wanted to remain half-upright he must effectively carry her. His stomach muscles gave up the fight immediately, strain spiking from his pelvis to his ribs.

She nodded approval. 'No hernia.'

'How d'you know?'

'You're not screaming.'

She removed a pair of scissors from the bag. The Consul's linen would suffer, but there was an entire room devoted to it upstairs and none of it would last much longer anyway. She began to cut.

'What are you doing here?' he asked.

'Your little friend came and got me. Said you'd come on a grassfire and tried to put it out. Did it not occur to you to call for assistance? I see you also fell on . . .' she peered at his back, '. . . a dressed-stone wall. From a height of not less than five feet. Congratulations on not being paralysed. No, please do not tell me why it was important that you take on the inferno by yourself. If you tell me I am reasonably certain I will find that "idiot" does not do you justice. Do not answer me unless I say so. It is unwise to annoy or surprise the person who is cutting around the place where your skin is glued to your sheet.'

The scissor blades snipped. He kept silent, listening to the boy's lies in his mind, turning them over. They were good.

'Can you feel that?' the Witch demanded. 'You can answer.'

'Yes.'

'Is it painful?'

'Itchy.'

'And here?'

He hissed discomfort.

'You're very lucky.' She daubed. A welcome cold spread along his scapula and down his spine.

After an hour of more or less painful ministrations she pronounced him shipshape, at least to the extent that was possible for an idiot. He thanked her and asked how the clarinet was going and she said it was going well. He went upstairs and brought her the sheet music, a little shyly. She took it with thanks, but regarded him with an uncertain expression. She was sensing a shift in his perception of her, could not entirely place it but knew it was a respectful one and did not inquire as to the reason. Perhaps she assumed someone had informed him of her relations with White Raoul.

'Light exercise is fine,' she said. 'More than that and you'll split something and bleed. The burns are extremely minor but they will be annoying. Don't pick at them. Don't get them dirty. Don't sunbathe. I've left you a salve for the bruising, which you should apply morning and evening. You're nodding! Don't nod: listen! I cannot count, even on both hands, the number of injuries you have which could've been much worse, so don't do whatever you did last night ever again or you'll probably die. That's a medical recommendation, okay?'

'Okay.'

'You're an idiot. Tell me there was at least a puppy in a tree.'

'Just grass. My fault. Having my annual fag. Cigarette. Dropped it in the wrong place.'

He offered her tea, but she had business elsewhere, so he sat on the low red-brick wall and watched her depart. She had a workmanlike stride which spoke of important things to do. He still found her admirable, but his lust had evaporated. He liked her, and he respected the scrivener – insofar as he knew him at all – and he would not for worlds interfere with what they had, which was something he had heard about but never tasted and which he felt the world ought to respect more than it did. The world respected nothing, and in most cases that was fine because not much was worth respect the way some people believed. But love of the sort that uplifted he regarded with something close to religious fervour. The love of family. The love which builds.

He moved his shoulders cautiously, felt the slickness of her creams between his skin and the bandages.

A little while later he realised that he was not alone.

'Well done with the car,' he said. 'And the story. That was sharp.'

The boy sat down. As always when they were close together, the Sergeant felt conscious of his own bigness.

'It was okay?'

The Sergeant contemplated last night's events. 'Yes. It was good work.'

'You are not arrested.'

'No. I think . . . the longer I am not arrested, the less likely it is that I will be. Or killed. I suppose that's the other thing.'

The small head came up fiercely. 'They had better not!'

'You'll sort them out for me, Tigerboy?' Something flickered in the boy's face. The question was suddenly unfunny. There were plenty of places where someone his age would be quite old enough to do that. The best guerrilla fighters and commandos in many wars were children this age: small, quick, and desperately loyal. And ruthless, with the clarity of childhood. There were warlords not much older.

'Joking,' the Sergeant said quietly. 'In bad taste, I s'pose. Sorry.'

The boy hung his head. 'I should have known what was in the cave.'

'No.'

'Yes! I totally screwed up.' Pride. If the car was his own good work, then the cave was also his, with what that entailed. No day without night. No glory without responsibility.

'All right,' the Sergeant agreed. 'Yes. We should have done more work up front. We were sloppy and we screwed up. You and me both. But we didn't die and, fingers crossed, we got away with it. We just have to be smart. It's like . . .' He cast around. 'It's like after a bank robbery in the movies. They always

189

get away clean and then someone buys a new car when they shouldn't.'

'Yes. That is dumb.'

'It is. So we go through it. Tell me what you saw last night.'

The boy shrugged. 'You went into the cave. A few minutes later there was a huge bang, and smoke. I vamoose! Watch from a little way. You – Tigerman – come out. Look strange and scary. (Great mask!) They follow you, very angry. You run. I take the car and dump it where you will find it. Then I re-moose. I go home, erase the video footage.' Oh, yes. The boy's video. 'Which is a shame, because it is the shizzle. Simpson Bruckheimer himself has no shizzle like this shizzle.'

'Erase how?'

'Tell the computer to write stuff over – random numbers again and again. Takes a long time. Better-than-DoD-standard.' This last had the feel of a direct quote from the manual. 'I was careful all the time. I looked up high for the eyes in the sky! But there was cloud, like this way then that, all the time. I think they can see one minute in every five.'

Let us devoutly hope.

The Sergeant nodded and fell silent. He did not know how to ask his next question, but he did not have the option to put it aside. It had become his habit when talking to the boy. He avoided the things which might cause friction between them, treating their friendship like something very fragile because precious things were, to his mind, always so. But not this one, not today.

'How did you find out about the cave?'

The boy looked away. 'It is known.'

'By who?'

'Many people. It is not a secret. And in the past it has absolutely been a clubhouse.'

'Have you been there?'

'I? No.'

'Who, then?'

190

'Some people.'

'What people?'

'Some people that I know.'

They glared at one another. Finally the Sergeant said: 'Have you spoken to any of these people recently? About the cave?'

'You wish to know if someone lied?'

'No.' *Although now that you say it I'm worried about it. Who? And why?*

The boy scowled for a moment, and then he brightened. 'You worry that this person will give us away!'

'Yes.'

'No.'

'No?'

'She would not.' With absolute certainty.

She, the Sergeant heard. Not anonymous people any more. One person. A woman who would never, ever give him away. Someone who for whatever reason would not, could not change her allegiances. Someone bound to him to the point of destruction. Squadmate, family, lover, debtor.

Family.

He nodded acceptance, and made sure it was respectful. They had clashed, and they were still friends. It was only polite to acknowledge it.

The boy saw that his debrief was over. He nodded in return.

'I am going to the lake,' he said carelessly.

'Have fun.'

'There will be good water.'

'I'm not allowed to swim. The Witch said.'

The boy nodded acceptance of this overriding command.

'But,' the Sergeant added, 'I might eat later. Maybe at the café. *Kswah swah.*'

Laughter. '*Kswah swah.*' Then: 'Will you burn the suit?'

The Sergeant nodded. 'I should.'

'Now?'

191

'Yes.'

The boy seemed to concede this, then shook his head. 'But you may need it. To prove that you are helping. And if you find it then your DNA can be on it when they test. It is natural. Your fingerprints, the same.'

The Sergeant recognised this as special pleading, and he mistrusted how much he wanted to agree. He did not relish the idea of destroying the suit – it was something they had done together – but it was evidence that could hang him. But then again, yes: what the boy said was true. He might need, down the line, to produce some sort of coup to demonstrate his commitment to good order on Mancreu and to the search for the terrorist in the funny outfit. Assuming such a search ever took place.

'There is a burn bag,' he said at last. The boy blinked at him owlishly. He never said, 'I do not know what that means.' He just waited until you said it another way. 'A metal container for the storage of sensitive documents. It is a diplomatic bag, but it has a small bomb inside it. If the wrong combination is used, the contents of the bag are destroyed.'

The boy nodded. 'The suit goes in the bag.'

'And then at least only London can find it.'

'And you are London. In all Mancreu, only you are London.'

True. He would keep the suit, for now. If things got hot, he could always destroy it later. He tried not to feel glad at this decision. It was perfectly rational.

He waited until the boy had gone before he moved the suit. He wasn't sure why; it wasn't as if they would somehow be overcome by it and rush out again to foil a bank robbery, but he could not shake the feeling that it was a temptation, somehow, that he should not extend. When he picked the pieces up in his hands, he felt like a man engaged in an illicit affair with someone else's wife.

He put the whole suit in the burn bag and put the burn bag in the armoury. As soon as he closed the door he remembered the photograph of Shola he had found in the cave. Theoretically there might be fingerprints on it. He might even be able to lift them with talc. Tomorrow. It would have to be tomorrow. He was exhausted, which was natural, and he was aching. A nap would be ideal.

He took ibuprofen, drank Coca-Cola from the cellar, and kept moving. Movement would help, and he needed to be seen. By now, whatever NatProMan was doing about last night was in motion. If the whole thing had been identified as weird bullshit from a crew of fish-thieving East European wideboys then the business would be shelved. If not, investigators would be on the way. He owed London a report, so he went into the house and fired off an advisory: *NatProMan pissed off about something, no military threat apparent, no details yet available at this end*. He made it somewhat less informal, but the sense was that knickers were in a twist for no discernible reason and there was nothing to see here. He'd have to revise that later, but for now it was nicely in character.

He glanced at himself in the mirror. *In character*. When had he started thinking of Lester Ferris as a role to inhabit? He had known, in Iraq, a young man who had realised belatedly that the army life was not for him. The kid had been from some shithole, signed up half-drunk and was now seeing real bullets and bombs and wishing he hadn't. So he pretended to be mad.

It was simple enough. He went on patrol in a Mickey Mouse hat he'd got from somewhere, and he carried his gun like a swagger stick. He'd never seen *M*A*S*H*, so he didn't realise he was travelling a well-worn path. And after each patrol he'd push it a bit further until they had to take notice. They'd put him in a secure hospital cell indefinitely, and he'd carried on the game for weeks and months and faked a suicide attempt and bitten an orderly and finally he'd broken down and explained that he was faking it, he just wanted so very much to go home. And the doctors told him: 'It's okay. You're going home, and no one's going to punish you.' But he deserved to be punished, he said. He'd faked it. 'Yeah,' the doctors said. 'We always knew you thought you were faking it. But that's the thing: you never were. It was real, and now you're better.' Which was about the most disturbing fucking idea the Sergeant had ever heard, until he came here and it was just life, and then he had the *really* disturbing idea that everyone in the world was carrying on this way all the time.

Mancreu turned everyone into a psychologist. And a lunatic, as well.

Well, that sort of thing got worse the more you thought about it. So he made a list of all the things he ought to do, would normally do. Pretend last night never happened: what would today ordinarily be about?

Well, yes: he would investigate the business of the dog, and he would give due consideration to how Mancreu's new motoring enthusiasts could best be brought to consider their actions in a responsible and adult light. Somewhere in the back of his mind, sharp teeth flashed and something growled: *like the light of burning quad bikes*. He pushed the thought away. It was not exactly un-sergeantly, but it tasted of the mask and of those soldiers who couldn't ever put the battlefield away. He thought of his war on tomatoes, and shook his head.

Second – always hidden, always present – came the matter of the boy's parentage. Inoue's work said the end was coming, and that meant he could no longer afford to dawdle, which, as he looked at himself in this exhausted clarity, was what he had been doing for months. On the other hand, Inoue had also given him a lead. And so had the boy: the unnamed woman who knew about the cave. To an average copper in an average situation that would surely scream 'tart', but here and now, not so much. The Protectorate forces were like American GIs during the Second World War: they had food and access, and they were exciting. When they had first arrived, both the men and the women of NatProMan had been the subject of intense local interest. So the boy's family member – he did not say 'mother', did not prejudge, because it could be a sister or an aunt or even a grandmother – was probably lively, attractive, and might be single. She was still here. She might be a familiar face. Between the records at the Chapelle Sainte Roseline and that, he could narrow it down to a manageable number. Even if some of his working assumptions were wrong, it might work. He was not too proud to accept a bit of luck.

And not unrelatedly there was Shola, and that almost made everything else make sense. *Five days. Five days ago we were laughing.* Of course there was a dead dog on the bonnet of his vehicle. Of course there was a gang who wanted his attention, and a Ukrainian unit smuggling industrial quantities of drugs. Why not, if Shola could be slaughtered in his own house by men who would not say why? If there was still a distance being preserved between himself and the boy, then Shola was part of the bridge. Perhaps it was a fair enough price of admission, at that: *If you cannot answer this, how can you protect me? If you will not answer this, how can I trust you?* The boy would never put it that way, perhaps would never even think it, and yet it was written in him, in how he spoke. You didn't judge that sort of thing and you didn't choose it. Those calculations took place in the engine room of a person, grimy and irreducible. *Something more is needed.*

It was needed in any case: here he was, Shola's friend, who had put on a fancy-dress outfit to avenge some torn comic books and an adolescent's pride, who had blown up some big drug smuggler's hoard on a whim, but somehow couldn't do much for a murder he himself had witnessed, whose perpetrators he had in custody to question at his pleasure. He had learned a new phrase in his comic book studies: Bizarro World. It was the place where everything was wrong. He found himself wondering how you'd know for sure you were there.

Well, that was sergeanting, for sure. Something more was always needed, and your job was to get up and deliver it. Advance to meet the enemy.

He drew breath. Fair enough. He had a real direction of his own, something which came from who he was rather than the masquerade of last night. That was NatProMan business, after all, and he didn't get involved in that.

For the rest he could talk to Dirac and get some perspective. Dirac was crazy, but his craziness was the right sort, the sort which let him keep being Dirac even when the world didn't want him to. That was where to start.

He went to see the Frenchman and laid it out, and Dirac listened. They were sitting on the balcony of the townhouse where he lived, which was a proper wrought-iron thing more suited to a lovestruck Juliet than a brace of hoary soldiers. There was a pot of Turkish coffee on the table, mellow and sweet. Dirac wore a bathing suit and a towelling bathrobe, and when he moved there was always a possibility that his genitals would peep out of the suit next to his thigh. The Sergeant chose on the whole to avoid these occasional appearances and had therefore positioned himself a little way back from the cheap marble-topped coffee table and directly across it. The round white stone concealed Dirac's body from navel to knee, which still meant that the bulk of his broad chest, with its profane, nautical and religious tattoos, was visible when the robe gaped. There were flowers all around the balcony in lead planters. It seemed surprising that Dirac should be a good gardener.

He knew how to listen, though, with the attentiveness of a man who has listened to briefings in order to stay alive. He listened now to everything the Sergeant knew about Shola's death, and about the dog gang and whether they might be related, and even about Pechorin's fish, because in the story of Lester Ferris the harmless washout that was still an open case. There was no mention of the boy because that was something else, and not within Dirac's particular competences.

When it was done, Dirac sighed.

'Okay, Lester, you got two problems.'

'Two?'

'Yeah. Your third one is taking care of itself. The Ukrainian asshole is in hospital. Someone beat the crap out of him last night.'

'That was him? The patrol and all the helicopters?'

'*Bien sûr.* Pechorin is very unhappy, he is deep in shit for reasons I do not want to know, he has cosmetic surgery on his nose. That will do?'

The Sergeant nodded. *And then some.*

'So then there is the gang and Shola. The dog, that's sick. Okay? That is fucking sick. But it's kids, it's idiots. Okay? Professionals, they would kill you, and they would do it between the Xeno Station and Beauville, where there is no help and you would disappear for ever. Right?'

'I'd do it that way.'

'Me too. Also it's what those Pathan bastards would do, and they are the fucking world leaders in making you wish you were somewhere else. They come from a part of the world with death in the fucking title, you know that? The *Hindu Kush?*'

'Yes.'

'And so we are professionals and they are artists and we agree that this dog thing is amateur. It's someone who watches too much Tarantino, although I hear Tarantino likes Balzac so maybe he's not so bad. But okay: you will find those guys if you look for them. The issue is supply. You get what I'm saying? And it is in both your problems.'

'The guns and the bikes.'

'Yes. There is a supply of new shit. Overseas shit. Where is it coming from? Who on Mancreu has any money to import shit? Us. Us, and maybe a criminal who deals with us.'

'Bad Jack.'

'No. I don't think so. I think there's no Jack.' He scowled. '*Mauvais Jacques.* And the new Mancreu Demon, too. It's bullshit.

197

This island is going crazy. You know what I saw the other day? I saw a boat come from the Fleet and land on the shore. With people in it, and they got off. They had a fucking picnic on the beach.'

The Sergeant stared at him. 'Fleet people?'

'Fleet people, fucking casual. Like tourists. They came onto the island for a cheese and wine party. I choose to believe I was drunk and misunderstood.' Because if he had not been drunk, he would technically have witnessed a breaching of Mancreu's tangled covenant. The shore was a barrier between the world which was denied and the world which could never be acknowledged. The Fleet did not touch the shore. Not ever. It was how the boy made his money, by running errands and trading luxuries between land and sea. Dirac belched. 'It's all coming apart. So fine, the world's coming to an end, okay? But Bad Jack? No. Who says so?'

The Sergeant had decided he would lie about that. The boy did not belong in this discussion, not even with Dirac. 'One of the killers. "Shola worked for Bad Jack." Like that was the end of that.'

'Then go back and ask him more. Offer him a deal.'

'I did.'

'What terms?'

'Just a deal.'

'You have to be specific. If you are not specific it's just a noise you make because you want something. It's only tempting when you lay it out, point by point. I will give you this, this, this and this, but you must give me this. It is a price comparison, like shopping. And you encourage that he haggle. Once he haggles, he has accepted the principle: he will cut a deal.'

Dirac said this with the surprising certainty of one who knows, and the Sergeant found that he had raised his eyebrows at the Frenchman in what could only be a 'how the hell do you know?' expression. Dirac rubbed his eyes with his fingers and blew air through his cheeks. 'After the Africa thing, they sent this Italian,

198

you remember? I thought, "Great, he will laugh and talk about racing cars and girls and we will get drunk." But the guy was like a laser. He's inside the door and he's asking me when I decided, who did I talk to, like he already knows everything. He's asking exactly the right questions, the ones you either tell the truth or you tell a big lie, one they can check. And he has a deal. All the stuff they were worried about – that I took money, that I planned to do this, that I'm a partisan, *pahpahpah*: it wasn't true. But this deal he is offering, it's good enough that I seriously have to think about taking it and I'm not even guilty. Okay? My commander already offered me a deal, like you did: some deal, whatever, we work out the details between us. You say yes to that, you basically admit everything already. But with this guy . . . *nom de Dieu*. Him I want to say yes to. The way he puts it on the table, I want to say yes.'

'And did you?'

A shrug. 'They took it off the table again when they realised I hadn't done anything. Threw me to the military system, but I'm such a hero by then I get medals and lunch with the President, whatever. I wasn't trying to be a hero. I was just angry. But you see? You have to have a deal. You can't get him to do it, he will make up a deal he can turn down or one you cannot offer. Tell him, "For this, you get that." You find out about where the guns come from, he gets a room with a bathtub and a view, better food, whatever. He's not smart, Lester, or he wouldn't be a low-rent killer on an island the Americans are going to incinerate. That's not a growth sector.'

Let us hope.

They finished the coffee, arguing lightly about whether the Foreign Legion, the Royal Green Jackets, or the Rhodesian Light Infantry-as-was were the toughest bastards in the game. Somewhere in the house a phone rang, with an actual bell. Dirac ignored it, and the caller gave up. A moment later he or she tried again, and then again, and finally Dirac growled that something must actually be happening and stamped away. 'There's cognac,' he said, pointing. 'It's fucking awful, but when you've said that it's not that bad.'

Cognac on top of pain pills, caffeine, burn salves and unknown topical analgesics did not seem like a brilliant idea, so the Sergeant poured one for Dirac and splashed some water into his own glass, then took the lid off a small bottle of vodka and laid it on the table where the Frenchman would see it. In the event, Dirac didn't see it, because he didn't come out again.

'Lester,' he called from inside the house, 'I am completely wrong. Please bring the cognac and come and watch television.'

The Sergeant ducked through a low door and found himself in the sitting room. The television was a new one on a spindly glass table. Dirac had turned a chair around by the small dining table and was sitting astride it like Christine Keeler. The remote was in his hand, dangling down so slackly that for a moment the Sergeant thought he might have had a stroke, and the cry had been some garbled plea for help. The Frenchman was staring at the screen, and he had the sound off, either because he couldn't stand the commentary or because he simply hadn't thought to turn it on yet. With a feeling of extreme fatigue, the Sergeant turned to look.

Someone else, evidently, had had a camera at the cave. And not just one – they must have been everywhere. It didn't really look as if it mattered very much that the boy had deleted his YouTube-ready revenge footage, because this was better, so much better, and it was already on just about every channel in the world. 'Anonymous footage', the caption said, 'sent to our offices in Sana'a.' There was a parenthesis afterwards, to let you know that was in Yemen.

The first shot showed Tigerman as a shadowed figure picking his way like a heron between the trucks. Then he went inside and the picture switched over to grainy reddish-brown, some kind of enhanced view. The figure stood eerily still; a fleshy darkness wrapped him and he was gone.

Inside the cave, the Ukrainians didn't yet know he was there. Then the head appeared, ghastly arachnoid fur and parasite mouth, apparently out of thin air. They fired, and a moment later Tigerman slithered into the room. The screen went white and he was gone again, only to reappear a moment later in the air as the cave exploded in flames, and then vanish again into the supernatural dark of the tunnel. You couldn't see how it was possible, only that he did it, and he seemed almost disinterested, as if the whole thing was somehow a side issue.

He was replaced by a breathy anchorman with perfect teeth.

Dirac thumbed the remote and rewound the clip, sucking air between his teeth. They watched the whole thing again.

'He's good,' Dirac muttered. 'I mean, he's a fucking lunatic, but we knew that from the hat, right? But that there,' he paused the playback, 'that could be free running or it could be Systema, that shit they teach Spetsnaz.'

'Russians and Ukrainians,' the Sergeant said, almost automatically.

'For sure,' Dirac muttered, 'because those assholes do not live without complicating things. *Connerie de merde!* He blew them up and stamped on them. That is some shit.'

Yes, the Sergeant thought, *it's a Shit Creek tsunami, is what it is. Paddles are no longer the issue.* But what worried him was what would come after the initial high tide. Inevitably, on the heels of the outcry, there would be a proper investigation conducted by someone who knew how to do the job.

It occurred to him to run; to go and pack and just disappear. There was nothing to stop him. There would be wars to fight in, some of them pretty close by, and no questions asked. He might even get rich. Otherwise, he could turn himself in, just walk into Kershaw's office and explain everything, or throw himself on London's mercy and await instructions. They'd ship him out immediately and patch things up. He wasn't sure what would happen after that.

But he'd lose the boy, for ever. It did not seem likely that an adoption committee would look kindly on his desire to formalise a criminal partnership which had caused what would almost certainly be an international incident.

He could also stay here and stick to his programme. He could carry on being Lester Ferris. Chase petty villainies and – at the right moment – drop in on Kershaw and be absolutely amazed at what all had been going on. 'Jesus, Jed, I thought you said it was a storm in a teacup! But that looks almost professional. And what the fuck is all that in the bundles? Is that heroin?' He wondered if anyone would follow the other end of the thing, the drugs end. They must, surely, even if only as a show of willingness. At least some of the focus must head away from him, onto Pechorin and the others. Then again, Dirac had mentioned Spetsnaz. Would others make the same assumption? That would send them off down more blind alleys for a good long time. He could nudge them. A friendly word at the right time. It was plausible. And there was the distant possibility, if he were caught, that his silence would be purchased on the topic of the drugs with leniency.

So far, at least, he had not been caught. There was no hue and cry for Lester Ferris. Dirac had not been asked 'Have you seen him?' And there was a good chance he would not be. He was not about to repeat his outing as Tigerman, and if he returned to the scene of the crime he would do so legitimately, as an adviser. Meanwhile they must make do with evidence from the night before, evidence which was even now fading into the landscape or had been burned in the cave, the video footage notwithstanding. If he could hold the line, there was a solid chance he would walk away. He had beaten far worse odds and seen off far more unpleasant consequences. In those cases he had been fighting for his country.

There were problems with that: if he had left DNA traces and they found them; if the video footage included an image of him in the car before he put on his mask; if the satellites had been looking that way and the cloud cover had not been enough; if the footage was enough to use some sort of biometric recognition; if Pechorin had somehow recognised him. In any of these cases, he would be shat upon from a great height. Dismissal, disavowal, prison, even a quiet vanishing. Retribution in kind from the Ukrainians, up to and including murder, because this was Mancreu and something like that could happen easily enough.

All this, as he stood in Dirac's sitting room and watched himself, over and over again.

The question was whether what he stood to gain here was worth the risk. And that was no question at all.

12. Inquiries

The Sergeant had been going to the Chapelle Sainte Roseline before he saw Tigerman on the news, and there was no reason to change his plans. In fact, there was every reason to stick to them. He mentioned his destination in passing as he bade farewell to Dirac, so that anyone who asked would know Lester Ferris was off on one of his daft detective projects, but the Frenchman was muttering, 'Parkour? Silat? Ba Gua? Or, how is it called, that Indian stuff?' and looking things up on what was apparently an achingly slow Internet connection, and might not entirely have heard. That was fine, too. Dirac would remember being told, would know it had been somewhere ridiculous and unrelated.

The Sergeant drove gratefully, letting the shock of the video footage wash away and taking solace in his decision to stick it out. Part of him yammered questions to which he had no answers, but the mountainsides were empty and endless, and the air was surprisingly cold. Whose footage was it? Why had they released it and was there more? Was he the target, or was Pechorin? Or NatProMan? Or the drug lords, assuming these were different people?

Away on the opposite mountainside was a figure, a shepherd or a hunter. Instinct told him it was a woman; something in the movement was female. She seemed at this distance quite unconcerned. *Good for you,* he thought. *Live your way. Live and wander and do whatever you like.* He inhaled, tasted pine, woodsmoke and rain, and when he looked again she was gone, she'd ducked into the trees. There was a limit, he had always found, to the number of times you could chase the same worries round your head. If you let them run, they wore themselves out, and then you could make your choices in the quiet. It helped to be a thousand feet higher than everything you were frightened of, alone in a landscape older than empires.

When the road dipped again, he regretfully turned the air conditioner back on, feeling mild claustrophobia.

Sainte Roseline was a proud stone building held in the crook of a small river. The waters rolled and gurgled from the foot of the mountain to the western shore without ever joining the hasty torrent beneath the Iron Bridge, content to take their time. The same patience hung over the old chapel itself, as if time within the cemetery gates was honeyed and heavy. Bees buzzed and flowers grew up tall around cracked old headstones. The graves here were not tended in the formal sense; the Mancreu people who interred their dead here saw no shame in life springing up from the site of burial. They did not mistake the corpse for the person. But the pathways were well trodden and small gifts rested on some of the stones: miniatures of whisky, sweets, and cigarettes. Somewhere there was a groundsman whose job was to wait a respectable time, then come along and see that these bounties were consumed or taken away, lest their continued presence serve as a reminder of decay.

The Sergeant parked the Land Rover at a respectable distance and walked along the path to the chapel doors, then let himself in.

The interior was dark and golden, beams and a peaked ceiling following the line of the roof. High windows streamed sunlight down towards the altar and the small pulpit. There was a font made of stone close by the entrance so that the mountain folk could anoint themselves as they entered and – so long as they were modest about it – take home a little blessed water for better protection of their homes from whatever kobolds might beset them. Over the altar there was a painting on board of Sainte Roseline being assumed into Heaven. She was petite and pretty, and her face was full of a childlike joy. Looking closer, he realised with a jolt that she was flanked by tigers. The nearer one scowled at him out of the image, and he felt the imprint of its silhouette across his chest, remembered the scent of musk and fur. White Raoul's work, he would swear. He wondered what it had replaced, and why. Had the old piece been stolen? Or shipped out to save it from the coming fire? And, more importantly, when? He had heard nothing, but then he might not. This was a private place. He scented paint, and reached out hesitantly to touch the board.

There was a sound behind him: a polite scraping of feet. He turned.

The woman in front of him was short and spare to the point of scrawny. The bones in her hips poked at her grey wool gown, and her face was covered in an orthodox veil. A nun of some sort. She prostrated herself, full length, and kissed the stone at the foot of the altar, then rose and met his gaze. She did not speak. He realised that she did not need to. Her presence here was inevitable, while his was surprising. Logic told her he must be seeking something, be it absolution or something more tangible, and he would explain himself.

He cleared his throat, feeling large and intrusive. 'My name's Ferris. I'm the British . . . well, I'm everything, actually.' She nodded. Of course, she knew that. His uniform with its flag would tell her what he was, and she could not but know, even here, that there was only one of him. 'I'm looking for – we'd call them the parish records.' Her inquiring expression did not fade. 'Births. Christenings. Deaths. In a ledger. Like a big book. Exactly like, I mean. It *is* a book. But they call it a ledger, I don't know why, never thought about it.' He blathered, and she listened politely. When he ran dry, she nodded, and gestured to a table against the back wall. He saw Bibles. 'Not, um, religious ones. Not the Book of Kings, or what have you.' He was relatively sure that was the one where everyone begat everyone else. 'For local people.'

She nodded again, and then patiently plucked at his hand and drew him over to the table. Her fingers were long and dry, the nails plain and carefully cut. He caught an embarrassing mouthful of her scent, her hair warm beneath the hood of her office. Even nuns were also women, and women sweated just as men did. She had a reassuring odour, like a warm dog or an old vicarage cushion, but beneath it was a whisper of startling femininity that he tried not to notice.

At the table she took the top Bible and opened it. Blue-black leather covers clopped gently against the wood, and the paper rustled. Bible stock, they called it, thin as ricepaper but strong. She turned to the last pages and tapped again, and he realised she had understood him perfectly. Old Bibles had a section at the rear for the keeping of family records. The family Bible wasn't just a book of God's truth, it was about where you came from in a more ordinary sense, and who you were because of it. His family had had one, until his father burned it when his mother died and cut them off from memory. Burned it where? The Sergeant wondered now. Not at home. Not on the electric fire. In a bin in the garden, perhaps, or perhaps he'd imagined the whole thing and his sister had it, always had, in some neglected corner of her house.

'I'm looking for a boy,' he said. 'There's . . . he might need my help. Later. When it all . . . happens.' *Are you his mother? If I could see your face, I might know. You might be the right age. You've got the same colour eyes.* He wondered how many women on Mancreu might fit that description. He could hardly ask them all.

She picked up a pen and wrote on a yellow notepad. Her writing was unjoined and simple.

How old is he?

'About twelve. Between that and fourteen, anyway. I don't know, I've never asked.'

Name?

More unasked questions. 'He once told me it was Robin. But I think that was a Batman joke. He's very clever – proper clever. I mean the way some people are and you look at them and you know the sky's the limit if they can just get on their feet, get on

207

the ladder. One day he's going to be a lawyer or a businessman or something, I'm sure. Or a cardinal,' he added, in deference to her habit, and thought he heard a gentle snort, though whether this indicated scepticism or a general dislike of cardinals he couldn't say. 'A prime minister of somewhere. If he just gets the chance, you know. I . . . I can help with that. Not much, but I can give him a place to start.' What was it with confessing this plan to random women? He might as well announce it in the paper. But her eyes smiled.

You think he is here?

Her fingers sketched the Bibles, the chapel.

'It's all I've got. I need to know who he is.'

Ask him.

Well, yes. But. 'I'm . . . I don't want to bother him. I don't think he thinks of the island as coming to an end.' She waited. She did it perfectly, without impatience: a silence which was his to break. Waited. Waited. Waited. He sighed. 'And . . . to be honest, I'm . . . I'm afraid.' Yes, she thought that was a poor answer, and really so did he. All the same, it was true. That counted for a lot.

She nodded. She opened two more Bibles, and laid them out. Boys' names, families. The right ages. He copied them down.

'He has someone who looks after him. Someone he trusts, who knows the old smugglers' paths. You don't know who that might be?'

She shook her head. He wondered if she would lie. She must have guessed, because she frowned at him, and snorted again.

'I saw a woman, on the way,' he said abruptly. 'Walking in the fields. Is it a good life out here?'

Yes.

'Do you know who she was? On the mountainside?' He wanted to know something about this place. He had spent too much time in the port, he thought, had ignored the rest of the island and now he wondered if the rest of the island wasn't much more important.

She dances in the water, the nun wrote. *She is content.* She put down her pencil gently. Interview concluded.

She dances in the water. Perhaps that was as good as life got, after all.

The nun walked him out to the Land Rover and stared at the dent, with its bloody scratches. He sighed. 'Some lads threw a dead dog at my car. Kids on bikes. I haven't told the old lady yet, the one whose dog it is. Christ, she'll know by now.' He heard the blasphemy hang in the air. 'Sorry, I didn't mean—'

She shook her head to let him know it was all right, then blessed him. Her finger rested solidly on his forehead for a moment, dry and hard. Satisfied, she went back inside. He touched the short list of names in his breast pocket. Something attempted, something achieved. Something actually according to plan. Simple enough.

He wasn't used to the feeling; recently everything had gone the other way. He found he approved of it very much.

His good mood carried him into Beauville with renewed energy. He told Beneseffe the fish issue had taken care of itself for the meanwhile, and Beneseffe grinned and said yes, he'd heard something about that, couldn't happen to a nicer person. The Sergeant bought a sandwich and a fizzy drink and walked along the harbour front in the sun. He asked after the names on his list. One of them was gone, they knew for sure, left with his parents in the first days. The other two they weren't sure about, they'd ask around. He checked with the schoolhouse, too, but no joy. All the educational records, the schoolmistress said, were in storage at Brighton House. He realised he should have known this, could have known if he'd thought to check. It occurred to him that if the boy was in there he might have short-circuited his investigation and saved himself a lot of shoe leather by sitting down like a clerk and going through the records one by one. There couldn't be more than a few thousand in the right age range. It would have taken – assuming one photo every twenty seconds, which was pessimistic – about twenty hours at the outside.

Well, he would start tonight. If one of the names in his pocket was the boy, good. If not, there was still a good chance that by the end of the week he would have his man.

More progress. Part of him was almost alarmed, but he knew it happened this way sometimes, knew that when it did you had to ride the wave and choose your options well to keep it under your feet. It looked like a sudden turn for the better because humans saw what was in front of them, didn't look at the time spent getting to a certain point. This was not a day of success, it was the success of many days, the pay-off of effort.

He went to the prison to lay down a deal.

He chose the man in cell two because he had been easy to talk to. It didn't matter if he had lied, he was interested in dialogue. The golden hour was past, he'd have regained some of his vinegar, but the Sergeant had more to work with now, had a magic word to open doors. He let it set the tone as the marine on duty pulled the door closed.

'I want to know more about Bad Jack,' he said. 'For information relating to Jack, I will release you. I will put you on a boat. I will assume that you are just what you say you are, a man who got in over his head. That you fired into the air. But I want to know,' the door shut with a very final *clunk*, 'everything.' The marine must have heard. Well, if Kershaw didn't know about Mancreu's apparent crime kingpin already, he would know now.

'There is not Bad Jack,' the herder said.

'Oh, but there is.'

'No. It is not real. Everyone knows this. What is Jack? A silly story for children.'

'I hear Jack's real enough. I hear he runs the island. I hear the man you killed worked for Jack, so that means Jack doesn't like you.'

'He did not work for Jack because there is not Jack.'

'I think those nice guns you had – those very foreign guns – I think they came from Jack's opposition. Tell me they didn't.'

'There is not Jack.'

The Sergeant nodded. 'Perfect. Then lie to me. Tell me a lie about Jack. Tell me a fairy story.' The man stared at him. 'Go on. It's all right. Make something up. Jack comes from the moon. Jack can fly. I don't care. For a lie about Jack, I will arrange a nicer cell. One lie, about a man who isn't real.'

And now he saw fear. 'There is not Jack.'

'If there's no Jack, then lie to me.'

The man closed his eyes and turned away.

'No Jack.'

'No Jack?'

'No Jack.'

The Sergeant took a map from his pocket and laid it out, and then he came around the table hard and fast as if he was in a bar fight. He captured the herder's arm and shoved one shoulder hard into his chest, took the man's centre and locked his elbow against the joint. He held the helpless hand over the map. 'Where in particular is there no Jack?'

The man flinched away. The Sergeant wrestled with him, hauled him back. Was this abuse? If he'd been interrogating a prisoner of war, certainly. But this was a civilian matter. He was not physically harming this man. He was manhandling him, which was probably illegal in Britain, the Sergeant didn't know, but they weren't in Britain and the governments of the world had quite deliberately made 'legal' disappear on Mancreu. It wasn't wrong, he was pretty sure about that. It was nasty, but not wicked.

He looked down at the herder's hand. Hovering and twitching over the map, unwillingly giving up secrets. The prisoner's aversion to the paper was strong. He did not want to touch it. But there were some places he did not want to touch more than others. The Beauville shanty. The harbour.

211

'No Jack!' the man was shouting. 'No Jack! No Jack, no Jack!' And the marine was opening the door, though he clearly did not know what he was going to do now that it was open, now that he could see what was and was not happening.

The Sergeant let go. 'Deal on the table,' he said. 'I know about Jack. You've just confirmed it, haven't you? But I want to know who he deals with and who doesn't like him. I want it all. Because I want to know who killed Shola and why, and I don't mean you and your friends, I mean who paid for it. For that information, I will let you go. I will arrange travel. Passports, even.' He wished he could ask about caves and heroin and NatProMan soldiers dealing dirty, but he didn't dare and probably this poor sod would know nothing about it. And if he did, the Sergeant himself understood too little to tell a lie from the truth. *Don't ask questions whose answers you won't understand*, DI Burroughs had said. *Well, fine, but you've got to start somewhere*, Lester Ferris wanted to object now. What did you do when you had the middle but neither end, and nothing to reel them in with?

The herder was staring at him in dismay, and at the marine as if to say 'Help me.' The Sergeant sighed and went out. With the others he made the same offer, simple and clear, and saw them understand it, saw them try to pretend they didn't, and turn away. Outside in the corridor, he found he was incredibly angry with them all for being so stupid, so stubborn. He shouted, an explosion of noise without shape because no curse could adequately express how stupid all this was, how very much it was in his way.

The marine, evidently unsettled by this evidence of passion, followed close behind him all the way to the outer door, as if concerned he might steal the plastic spoons or the ancient, stinking coffee machine.

Being in Beauville and with a moment to spare, it was natural that he should call in on Kershaw and talk shop. Today, of course, shop for Kershaw would be the Tigerman footage, and the Sergeant took care to be genuine in his expression of sympathy.

'All right, Jed?'

'Go away, Lester.'

'I gather some of your lads got beaten up by a sex pervert last night.'

'Seen from space, your entire country looks like a gusset.'

'Be that as it may, Jed, I understand this pervert actually flashed them his man-parts. I do hope they're not so traumatised by this terrible experience that they'll never save the free world again.'

'They were Ukrainians, Lester, I'm sure they've seen scarier things than a sex pervert's genitals.'

'You mean he actually was a sex pervert?'

Kershaw stopped and appeared to consider this. 'God, I wish. That would actually be terrific. I would love that. And do you see how insane that is? I am fallen far, Lester, when I find that I am wishing, in my official capacity as chief civilian authority in theatre of the NATO and Allied Protection Force on Mancreu, for sex perverts. I don't suppose anyone's actually saying that, out there?'

'No idea. I've been out and about. I saw the telly at Dirac's place earlier. Bloody weird.'

'You think? Back in the US, we get guys who can fly and breathe under water and beat up heavily armed soldiers all the time!' Kershaw scowled. 'You tell me, Lester. You took down those guys from Shola's. What was this?'

'Commando,' the Sergeant said smartly. 'Dirac said Russian. I thought maybe Chinese, what with all that rolling and that, but he says Spetsnaz. I gather he's a bit of a connoisseur of your international ethnic fisticuffs. Was that stuff in the background really what I think it was?'

'If you think it was a boatload of fucking heroin bricks made from processed opium, then you think what I think but I don't know yet. There's a guy coming. An investigator. That side is all his problem.'

'Top dog, I imagine.'

'Arno. Dirac knows him.'

He's asking exactly the right questions, the Sergeant recalled, *the ones where you either tell the truth or you tell a big lie, one they can check.* 'Sounds ideal,' he said, thinking: *well, shit.*

'Lester, I have to ask: have you ever had any hint of anything like this on Mancreu?'

'Like what? Commandos? Well, there must be a few out there.' He nodded at the sea. 'And if that's really about a city's worth of heroin in the video, that's got to be Fleet crap, hasn't it? Cheeky sods, bringing it onshore. Maybe they were trying to cut someone out of the supply line and he got cross.'

'Yeah, but it's weird.'

'Weird, Jed, I have definitely seen on this island. Someone threw a dead dog at me the other day, you know. I'm still a bit cross about that. The culprit will feel the pointy end of my boot shortly.'

'You know who it was?'

'I'm bloody going to!'

Kershaw hesitated. 'Be careful out there, Lester. If this is Fleet stuff, fine, everyone ought to be very polite. But if it's something else . . . you remember you were saying when Shola died that maybe the next thing Mancreu was going to do to itself was crazy insane shit with a body count?'

'Is someone dead?'

'No. But they could have been.'

'And if he's a commando, if he'd wanted it that way, they would have been.'

Kershaw nodded. 'I guess that's true. I gotta work, Lester. This is not the only shit in my shitbox today.'

'I came by to offer my informal assistance. Lester Ferris in his off hours, not the Consul or what have you. Or just beer. I understand beer works wonders.'

Kershaw hesitated. 'Thanks, man. Actually – are you busy this evening? I have a thing. I was going to ask you anyway. Unofficially official or whatever. You know what, sometimes I have no idea.'

'You can record me as present or absent. At your service, anyway.'

'I'll call you later. Take care, Lester.'

'I'm a bit concerned about you, Jed. If you think Britain looks like a gusset, your girlfriends have been giving you a very strange idea of what sex is all these years.'

'Seen from space, Lester. Space. The place where British people do not go because the British space programme is, what, two guys with a really long stick?'

'In that way, Jed, it is very much like US healthcare.'

'Go now, Lester. Tell the Queen I said hi.'

'See you later, Jed.'

The Sergeant let himself out, past the grinning assistant who had no doubt been listening to the whole thing on Kershaw's intercom. He tipped the man a salute and received a careful wave in acknowledgement, and then went back to Brighton House to dig out the school records. As with his visit to the docks and the chapel, his conversation with Kershaw had been all according to plan. Not perfect – not with Dirac's Italian inquisitor on his way to Mancreu – but within the parameters he had set for the encounter.

Recalling the conversation he wondered, twitchily, whether he should try to banter like that with the boy. With Kershaw it was easy because the stakes were low. If either one of them overstepped, the matter could easily be resolved because the friendship was convenient and ultimately time-limited. It would not survive their departure from the island. But with the boy he wanted something more than that and he had no idea where he might transgress in some awful way. Or just come across as trying too hard. Adults who wanted to be cool, the Sergeant recalled, were painfully uncool.

He would have to think about it.

The school records proved to be at the back of the stack of boxes that had been piled very neatly in the east wing, sealed in plastic to keep out moisture and possibly rats. It was hard to see why – the boxes and indeed the rats would cease to exist soon enough. If this paper had been wanted, it would by now be in a new home somewhere. The Sergeant had very rarely known a bureaucracy let go of so much information, and he suspected darkly that some of the Mancreu records must contain references to long-ago British behaviour under the Mandate in Occupied Palestine, or in Malaysia or Kenya, which was now considered discreditable. The evil baby would be lost with a great deal of murky bathwater, and that would be that: a shipping error, valuable historical accounts alas gone for ever. He idly considered a trawl through the most obscure boxes for whatever it was Whitehall wanted to forget, and looked at himself, startled, in the fractured window glass. He was a sergeant, not a troublemaker.

He hauled what he needed out of the pile, wishing someone had bothered to digitise all this at some point in the last two decades, but they hadn't. Mancreu before the Discharge Clouds had existed in a sort of perpetual 1989, so hardcopy it was – nearly sixty boxes of it. He pulled at the plastic wrap with his fingers and found it surprisingly tough. He vaguely remembered a girl who had worked at a post office somewhere in Germany telling him – it had been a come-on, he realised in retrospect, and he had utterly failed to notice – that industrial cling wrap was really good for tying the wrists during sex. He tried to claw through it, then gave up and went back down the corridor for a Stanley knife.

The phone rang just as he gave up on the Stanley knife and realised that the weather-stained carving knife in the galley kitchen at this end of the house ('We use it for barbecues,' the Consul had told him) would do just as well, and he nearly took his own eye out lifting the receiver to his head.

'Jed?'

It wasn't. Inoue's laughter bubbled at him. 'I'm going to hang up now,' she said happily.

'What? No, I—'

'Bye bye!'

'I'm sorry,' he said, but she was gone. He stared at the phone, put the receiver back in its cradle, bewildered. Had he really upset her? No one really called him other than Kershaw.

The phone rang again. He picked it up. 'Dr Inoue?'

'No,' she said gruffly, 'this is Jedediah Sibelius Kershaw. I want you to come to dinner. We talked about it earlier.'

'I'm sorry about before. he just calls me more than other people, is all.'

'Lester! What the hell are you talking about?' Inoue continued, in character. 'I want you to come and eat with me. We're all going out for dinner. I told you about this when you came by today. That Japanese scientist, Kaiko Inoue, will be there, too. You're going to sit next to her so she doesn't have to discuss Pan-Arab Nationalism with that idiot from the Working Group whose name she cannot remember but who has too much nose hair.'

He went with it. It seemed the only thing to do. He didn't want her to hang up again. 'Oh, right, Jed, thank you.'

'It's a horrible nose, Lester, so don't even think about being late. And wear something smart. Do you have medals?'

'Yes, I suppose I do. Shall I put them on?'

She sobered abruptly, and her voice became Inoue's, strained and uncertain. He had never heard uncertainty in her before, and it did not suit. 'I was going to tell you "yes". But maybe . . . I think you should not. This will be a . . . well, I think it will be a strange occasion. Kershaw will announce the disposition of NatProMan and the Mancreu Project. In the wake of my recent findings. You understand?'

The finding, in particular, that another Cloud was coming. 'Yes,' he said.

'And it may be that I must say something, publicly. I would like to have you there as my friend, but you probably should not be the British Brevet-Consul, in case I am embarrassing. Is that possible?'

It was. The outgoing Consul had foreseen the possibility of unofficial appearances, and a suit had arrived and hung in the cupboard ever since, unworn. It was still his size, he supposed. He had stayed in trim.

'I'm sure you could never be embarrassing,' he said, somewhat awkwardly, and held his breath in case this was the wrong thing.

She laughed again. 'Oh, yes, I can. Did you know that there are different ways of speaking Japanese for men and women? Women's Japanese is supposed to be gentle and submissive. But English has no such division, so I am unchained. Vee-eeery dangerous.' She chortled wickedly. He tried to imagine her demure and mousy, and failed. 'But will you come?'

'Of course.' He felt a curious twitch in his stomach. He had been friends with few women in his life. It was like what he felt about the boy, a frantic awareness of fragility and a sense of making his way in the fog. 'Just me. Lester Ferris. No Consul, no Sergeant.' *No Tigerman*, he almost said, and then wondered whether he had been quite so angry about the boy's beating in part because someone had thrown a dead dog on his car in front of Inoue, and whether he should say he was looking into that, which he would, as soon as he had time. For an island with no future, Mancreu had a great deal of present.

Inoue apparently decided that enough had been said which was serious or alarming, because she dropped back into her Kershaw voice. 'Good! The doctor says she'll send a car at eight and you're to call her Kaiko or you're walking home!'

'Yes, ma'am.'

'Jumping Jehosaphat, Lester!'

'Sorry.'

'This is Jed Kershaw, Lester. You don't call me "ma'am".'

'In point of fact, Jed, I've been calling you "ma'am" since day one.'

'Never mind that now!' It was actually rather a good impression of Kershaw's bluster. 'And when you talk to her, you say "Kaiko".

In fact, say it now so that you don't forget.' She made a basso chuffing which he was fairly sure was a giggle. Was it possible she was talking through a cardboard tube?

Gamely, he said: '"Kaiko."'

'Again!'

'"Kaiko."'

'Practise, Lester. Dr Inoue was quite specific, and it's a long walk.'

'All right,' he said, and she chuffed again and rang off.

He looked at his watch, bemused. He had just enough time to open one box and look randomly through a few files, but not enough to find the one containing the records he wanted specifically, and somehow it would be admitting defeat to begin as if he had already been let down.

He put the knife on the sideboard, ready for the morning.

Not wishing to treat his half-arrangement with the boy with disrespect, the Sergeant went down to the café to leave a note, and, finding his friend already there, hastily ordered tea and made his excuses. The boy listened, then grinned hugely.

'You have a date!' he said. 'With the xeno lady! That is hot.'

The Sergeant shook his head. 'It's not like that.'

'It so is.'

'It's not! She wants a friendly face, is all. She's worried about something.'

'She has many friends at the xeno station,' the boy said, 'but she calls you. This is totally hot adult dating (meet area girls now!)'

When the Sergeant continued to protest, the boy enlisted the help of Tom from behind the bar. Tom listened carefully to the sequence of events, and grinned. 'I don't know, Lester,' he said lightly, 'I think maybe the kid has a point.'

'Not on my best day,' the Sergeant said, smiling back.

'Oh! So you would tap that?' the boy demanded.

The Sergeant, who had never really thought about it, was about to say 'no' but found he couldn't. It had always seemed such an impossibility that he might be attractive to Kaiko Inoue that he had never actively asked himself whether she was attractive to him. Now that he came to consider it, however – now that he came to wonder about what might happen between them if such a thing ever came to pass – he had to acknowledge that she was more than a little captivating.

'The situation does not arise,' he muttered, and realised he was blushing.

'Ooooo-ooooh!' cried the boy happily. '*Barracuda!*' And then, in deference to the possibility that the Sergeant was too old for this reference, 'Na na na na na na na na na NA NAAAAH! Oooo-oooh! Barracuda! Like in *Charlie's Angels*.'

The Sergeant stayed for a little longer, threatening everyone with terrible violence, and then took his wounded dignity back to Brighton House, trying to think about everything except Kaiko Inoue in his bed.

13. Dinner

The car arrived on the dot of eight, and the Sergeant stepped into it with a feeling of being on the outside looking in. Until now, insofar as he had been in this situation at all, he had been the driver, not the passenger, waiting patiently with a book while someone very influential tried to find his other shoe. He found he was imagining what he must look like to the polite young man behind the wheel, and worried initially that he must look very posh and snotty, then abruptly, in a veering inversion, that by trying to look less so he was denigrating the importance of the event which was consuming the driver's evening. Was it perhaps more disrespectful to assert that they were on the same social level than it was to accept that they weren't? The Brevet-Consul was a mucketymuck, but the Sergeant was a working man, and this was a temporary assignment. Except that, he supposed, it would never entirely go away.

It occurred to him, with a sense of wonder, that it would almost certainly help in getting a job after the army.

He didn't say anything at all while he thought about this, and when he came to himself the car was slowing outside the NatProMan admin block, the red-brick misery which had once been Mancreu's house of detention. It was lit from below by two floodlights which somehow served only to make it darker and more Gothic.

Wonderful.

He walked to the door and it opened as if God or some sort of technological whizzbang was involved, but this was Mancreu so it was neither, just a respectful NatProMan soldier in flunkie mode.

'Thank you,' the Sergeant said, and saw the kid's eyes flicker in surprised acknowledgement. He went on in.

The old prison had been largely modernised for the use of prisoners, so the majority of the cells were drab little cubicles which had readily become storage rooms and offices. The main hall, however, had been preserved – for historical authenticity or more likely because the triple-height open-plan room with its cages along the side walls was too expensive to remodel. Kershaw greeted him at the double doors and ushered him inside, and the Sergeant stopped for a moment on the threshold in utter amazement.

The hall had been transformed. It was still wrapped in shadows, still echoing and bleak. But along the middle was a banqueting table laid for forty, and the cooking was being done on gas burners in the cells. At one end, another, larger cell held a military jazz band, the drummer a striking marine corporal with her head shaved and the island of Mancreu tattooed onto her scalp. The music was slow and edgy and made him think of Shola's wake, the combination of sorrow and celebration, and the building vanished into its own darkness, so that the ceiling was invisible and the walls seemed to go up and up for ever.

'I hear you're making an announcement, Jed,' the Sergeant said.

'Yeah,' Kershaw replied. 'You were on the list, anyway. Inoue just called you first. You get that, right?'

'It's nice to be a plus one. I can pretend I'm an ordinary bloke.'

'I thought you *were* an ordinary bloke.'

'Oh, I am. But they've given me all these hats, haven't they?'

Kershaw nodded like a man who understood hats. 'This is going to be an epic party, Lester. I'm glad you're here.' He smiled and – to the Sergeant's amazement – actually leaned forward and hugged him, then dashed away to greet someone else. The Sergeant stared after him in bemusement.

He felt a hand on his arm.

'Did he just hug you, Lester?'

'Yes, Kaiko, he did.'

'Was it weird?'

'It was, a little bit.'

'You need practice.' She hugged him too, fiercely, and slipped away again before he could register that it was happening. His memory reported: *Slender. Strong. Soft in interesting places. Smells good. More, please.*

'Come on,' Kaiko Inoue said, 'we're over here. By the way, this is when you tell me how well dressed I am.'

He smiled and stepped back to give her proper consideration, and then found he was genuinely staring. Inoue was wearing a black dress, long and flowing and with a collar which fastened at the neck. She wore earrings made of tumbling gold and red links which rippled as she turned her head. Her arms were bare and narrow and surprisingly muscular.

'You look great,' he said honestly. She grinned.

'Thank you.'

There was a mirror standing in the corner of the room, and he could see himself reflected in it beside her. To his amazement, he did not look absurd. The suit was a good fit and he filled it the right way, with weight in the shoulder and chest, not much in the tummy. There was a whisper of grey at his temples – when did that happen? He looked like a grown-up, like the people he had guarded when they came to visit in Iraq and Bosnia. The two of them together were formidable. *People of consequence*, that was the expression.

Inoue followed his gaze, and made an approving snort, then took his arm again and led him to their places. Someone had spent a longish while, he thought, writing everyone's name in cool copperplate script on the little white cards at each setting. Inoue's card was in Japanese as well as English.

Even with all the places occupied, the room felt huge and echoing. When the band paused between songs the Sergeant felt an eerie moment of vertigo, reminded somehow that the sky

223

beyond the shingle roof was a bottomless abyss and that he and the building itself were held on the ground by a blessing of physics he did not understand.

The gathering had become, if not raucous, at least relaxed. The first course was done and enough wine had been drunk and enough fluff had been talked that the diners had lost their initial sense of awkwardness. The tinny chatter of the guests dipped as everyone realised they were suddenly that much more audible, their voices bouncing off the brick walls and echoing in the detention cells. Now they hunkered down and made exaggerated gestures of furtiveness to one another to conceal a genuine embarrassment in the quiet.

They were a mixed bag – NatProMan staff, foreign officials and quasi-officials, and one or two the Sergeant did not recognise who must be regional bureaucrats or factfinders passing through. He hoped very much that the thin-faced man at the far end was not Arno the investigator. His eyes were unsettlingly sharp. As if responding to the thought, the man turned in his seat and waved a graceful hand, his lips curling up in a faint, cordial smile.

It's him. I know it is. The Sergeant nodded back, bluff and a bit clumsy. Well, that was of a piece with who he was supposed to be, after all. He retreated from the penetrating gaze and hid behind his neighbour.

Jed Kershaw tapped on his glass with a knife. A high, pleasing bell-sound rang out, and he seemed happily surprised and did it a couple more times, then got a rhythm going. He tapped the glass, then stamped, then slapped his hand on the table. A moment later, to the Sergeant's absolute amazement, he added vocals, doowahbopping and tchakachahing, and people began to clap along. When the head of financial affairs began tapping her spoon and fork together he encouraged her mightily like the conductor of an orchestra, and slowly a few others made impromptu instruments and were inducted into the fellowship. A Croatian officer with NatProMan insignia proved to have a very elegant bass voice,

and a moment later the thing had become a rendition of Screamin'
Jay Hawkins's 'Heartattack and Vine' before collapsing into a
mess of laughter.

'Did you know he could do that?' Inoue asked behind her hand.

'I really did not,' the Sergeant said. She shook her head in
wonderment, and they shared a moment of complicit bewilderment. Jed Kershaw, bluesman.

Kershaw waved for calm, and banged the glass again. The
meeting came happily to order.

'Okay,' Kershaw said. 'Okay, okay. Welcome, everybody. I
hope you're having a good time. I'm having a great time. I kinda
love this island, actually. I really do. It drives me insane. But in
this business you're pretty much gonna go insane somewhere,
so it might as well be here.' Laughter. 'It's been a helluva week
at Kershaw Towers.' More laughter, Kershaw's right hand waving
to indicate the building, recognising the ugliness of the place,
the pompousness of naming it for himself, and a little bit of
pride in his ugly domain. 'We had . . . what did we have? We
had stolen fish. Yeah, don't think I didn't hear about that. We
had guys in hospital because a demon came out of the sky and
beat the shit out of them – *or* they got in a fight with one another
over a pretty girl and someone else faked up some weird film,
it's *very* hard to tell. Thank God, that's not my job, I have
Colonel Arno here for that.' And yes, the thin-faced Arno
nodded languidly. Kershaw bobbed his head as if reading an
imaginary list. 'Someone threw a dead dog at Lester and Kaiko,
which was bad for them but really sucked for the dog. How's
that coming, Lester? Bad guys on quad bikes who are mean to
puppies. We do not approve of bad guys who are mean to puppies,
do we?' He referred the question to the table, as if the Sergeant
might otherwise say that he rather did. The room booed firmly,
and Kershaw raised his eyebrows.

'We're pursuing lines of inquiry,' the Sergeant responded. 'We
anticipate movement shortly.'

'I love how he says "we",' Kershaw told the table. 'And I love that he's not kicking down doors and yelling. He's so polite, even when he's pissed. And do not mistake, my friends, he is pissed. An Englishman assaulted with a dog? In front of a lady? Beshrew me! Fol-de-rol and hey, nonny noo, there's going to be crumpets toasted over this frightful racket, right, Lester?'

'I have no idea what any of that means, Jed,' the Sergeant said primly, to general delight.

Kershaw grinned. 'So, actually it's been pretty much an ordinary week on Mancreu — assuming the devil did not actually send a minion up out of hell to torment my Ukrainian contingent. They're fine, by the way.

'Except one thing is a little bit different. You know how it's always the quiet ones? Just when I was leaving the office the other night, I got a report on my desk. Dr Inoue, couldn't you have waited until ten minutes later? I was going to play some golf, and I missed my tee-time!' Laughter, but a little strained. Everyone here knew what Inoue's reports were about. 'Yeah. So, this report. It's not the same as the last one, or the one before. It says we have . . . maybe another three weeks before the next Cloud, and it's going to be a big one. So I was lining up a big civil-protection effort for everyone who's still here.

'But we may not be doing that after all. We may be leaving. On receiving this report, the higher-ups have gotten a little windy. Yes, they have. And they are saying right now that they may push the button on this island. The final evacuation. We should get word before the weekend. So if there's anything you want to see here, do here, do it this week. If there's someone you've been thinking of asking on a date, I suggest you do that too, because there's a good chance we're all going on to our next assignments.

'Hence this party. This isn't a Leaving. That's not who we are. This is not our home. When we came here we knew it was temporary. But it's something. It's the beginning of goodbye. So eat. Drink. Celebrate Mancreu. If you have business unfinished here, get it done. Because I'm pretty sure the clock is ticking.' Silence, sombre and contemplative. 'And if you do not eat this food that I have personally made, I will come to your house and hide the leftovers in your curtain rails!' Laughter and applause, on cue, but from the chest rather than the gut.

As Kershaw went to sit down, Kaiko Inoue got to her feet. She seemed unwilling, compelled. *She's got to explain*, the Sergeant thought. *Bit harsh, to make her read the notice of death to the relatives before the patient's dead*. He shot a glance down the table at Kershaw, annoyed.

But Kershaw was looking uncertain and a bit nervous. His face, turned to Inoue, seemed to be asking her to sit down again, to stay quiet. Inoue was looking down at the table. She glanced at the Sergeant, and he smiled reflexively: *be brave*. She smiled back in gratitude. And then raised her head.

'I must object,' said Kaiko Inoue.

Oh.

Kershaw slumped slowly down, chubby hand holding his mouth as if he was receiving news of a death. Thirty-eight guests stared at Inoue, along with the military waiters and the band.

'I must object,' she said again. 'I understand the logic. It is quite easily understandable. It is absolutely sure that we will have a Cloud again soon. The wind might take it anywhere. And each Cloud increases the likelihood of the Mancreu bacterium finding a home in another environment, if it has not done so already.

'But I must object most strongly. This is not the right answer. Destroying this island is not the right answer. It is wasteful and foolish. Even if we burn the rock to the waterline, if we kill every plant and animal, if we dig deep down into the caldera and fuse the rocks to the mantle. Even then, we will not sterilise this place. Some small piece of ejecta will fall into the sea. Something will survive. And we will have ruined a beautiful thing for the sake of a security which we cannot have.' She sighed. 'I have said this in my report. I have made it very clear. And now I say it to you, in the hope that you will pay attention. What is contemplated here is not science. It is like trying to knock the moon out of the sky with a rock. It is childish fear, not grown-up action. It may make things worse. And for sure: it – will – not – help.' She bowed her head. 'Thank you for your attention.'

Kershaw nodded slowly to her, winced a bit, and stood again. 'I'm going to say two things. The first is that Doctor Inoue's concerns are well documented and I'm told they have been factored into the decision-making process, but that they are considered too sensitive for public dissemination and are covered under the Mancreu Confidentiality Resolution.' He shrugged. *You all know what that means.* The Sergeant found himself wondering about his unsolved case, those stolen papers from Inoue's office. Did whoever had them know about the MCR? Or care? Probably not. But for sure they'd burned the draft or stuffed it in a mattress, because if not, well, where was it? The time had passed for a dramatic revelation. Had really passed, now.

Kershaw held up his hand sternly. 'The second thing . . . is that it's time for the pulled pork sandwiches, made to my grandfather's own special recipe, which is even more secret than that! And for those of you who don't eat the meat of the pig I've adapted it for goat, which is surprisingly good. And for those of you who eat no meat of any kind, God help me, there are yams. Gentlemen and ladies: bring it on!'

From the wings, huge silver plates of sticky pork – and goat, and indeed yams – and fresh bread emerged, bowls of mustard and pickles, and about a hundred bottles of wine. The band struck up. Inoue took the Sergeant's hand.

'Thank you.'

'I didn't do anything.'

'I did. And I could not have done, without a friend.' She smiled. Around them, the party had picked up again, as if nothing had been said. Or perhaps because it had been. There was a desperation now which lent it an edge, a sense of urgency. Inoue pursed her lips. 'It is very loud, Lester. Is there somewhere quieter? I need to clear my head.'

'There's a roof terrace,' he remembered. 'Well, there's a roof, and some chairs.'

He stood, and – because the food smelled good – he gathered them a plate of sandwich materials. After a moment of consideration, Inoue scooped up the wine glasses, and they scurried away, to speculative glances from their nearer neighbours.

The rooftop was cool but not cold, though the sea breeze could raise goosebumps on your skin. The Sergeant took off his jacket and hung it around Inoue's shoulders. She smiled thanks, then shrugged into it and sat pensively looking out at the wide night-time sea. He knew she would talk when she wanted to, so he sat and set about building her a spectacular sandwich – food being in his experience the best cure for post-patrol funk, which he reckoned was close enough. Then he hesitated: Inoue was a small person. His usual strategy with sandwiches was to layer on as much as possible, but this might not be the best method here. He looked over at her mouth, bobbed his head to get a better view. Silvery lips quirked in a smile.

'Are you actually measuring my bite, Lester?'

'Well . . .'

'That is . . .' She flapped her arms. 'That is ridiculous! You are a totally ridiculous man!' She leaned over her knees and pecked him on the cheek. Her scent came with her, a curious mixture of fruit and tea and something deep which was surprisingly like coffee. 'I am not a tiny person. I can perfectly well eat a normal sandwich. Tcha, you are putting too much pickle. Give it to me, or Kershaw will think you are a barbarian.' She began combining the ingredients with practised proficiency. The Sergeant wondered how often Kershaw had made this dish, and for whom. The ghost of her cheek was still lingering on his face. He wondered if they

229

were assuming, in the main hall, that he and Inoue had come up here to kiss. He watched her fingers, deft and sure. She grinned at him, then lifted the sandwich to her mouth and took a defiant bite. A surprisingly large chunk disappeared from the bread. She raised her eyebrows and passed the rest across.

'Mmm! Pulled pork, pickle, red wine. Very good. And Lester Ferris to talk to. Also good. Then we will enjoy the view.'

They ate, passing the makings of the sandwiches back and forth. Occasionally, fleetingly, he felt her nails graze the back of his hand as he yielded the pork platter, and vice versa when he took it back. The contact was not unpleasant, and neither of them shied from it. They ate, and then as Inoue had predicted – ordained? – they sat and looked out over the waterfront and the rooftops of Beauville. The old prison looked down on some fine colonial townhouses, narrow and elegant, and from one cluster of old streets in particular came a warm filigree light and the sound of bustle and chatter. The street of the card-players, the Sergeant realised, its inhabitants sitting out with some disreputable *grappa* and defying the world to move them. No doubt the old women were out, too, gamely chastising their husbands and peering in the candlelight at one another's perfect white steps for spots of grease and dirt. It sounded as if someone – he suspected it was the street sweeper in her scarf – was playing the accordion. If the right song came along, he wondered if he should ask Inoue to dance.

Over the bay, a gull and another bird got into an argument. The outrage of the parties was so recognisable that both the Sergeant and the doctor laughed aloud. The mirth cracked the moment slightly, brought them back to themselves.

'Tomorrow, I'd like to ask you about—' He gestured vaguely over his shoulder. *About the end of the island.*

'We shall have breakfast,' she agreed.

'People will talk,' he said automatically, and then couldn't believe he had.

Inoue grinned a feral smile. 'Indeed, they will.' She stood up and shrugged off his coat. For one moment he thought she was going to step onto his lap and kiss him. She had that look of intent, a wicked quirk in her lips. But then she looked over his shoulder and her expression changed and she said, quite inappropriately: 'Oh! What the *fuck*?'

He stared at her for a second and then turned sharply in his chair, the bruises on his back yowling in protest.

Out above the Bay of the Cupped Hands, a single line of flame, narrow as a wire, was drawn across the water and the sky. For a moment he thought the world had gone mad and the destruction of the island had started, that they were all going to be sacrificed, that they were somehow infected and must be burned away. But there was only one trail, rising leisurely from somewhere in the mist. They watched it plot a bright curve in the darkness and then fall, seeming to increase in certainty and velocity as it neared the land. It was casual, effortless, even elegant. The sound reached them at last, a high wailing roar from the first moments of the launch, and then the impact flash as it reached its target and detonated. The Sergeant wrapped Kaiko Inoue in his arms and dropped to the floor, and the pulled pork sandwich and two glasses of wine flew over them as the shockwave hit. The chairs skittered away along the roof like brushwood in a gale. There was a huge, appalling noise, and then silence.

Half a mile away, the building which had housed Shola's murderers was ash.

Civilians would have run around, but these people walked. They had procedures, and they'd been down this road before. There were people here, technically, who were not military, but there was no one who didn't know about crisis. The Sergeant didn't know where Inoue had seen this before, but he knew that she had, knew it from the way she moved and how she checked the compass points, the sky. Together they went back downstairs.

In the main hall Kershaw was standing on a table shouting into his encrypted cellphone that he needed more information and he needed it about a fucking hour ago before some asshole blew up a part of his city – HIS fucking city – with a fucking (are you kidding me?) fucking (what the *fuck?*) Exocet *FUCKING missile*. In between expletives he was fending off two members of his close-protection team, who were absolutely determined that he should be evacuated but appeared not to know where to – because, the Sergeant suspected, the fallback location if the landside ones were compromised was out in the Fleet, and the Fleet was the source of the problem. But even this little drama was oddly restrained. In a full-on emergency they'd have carried him, knocked him out. They were drily amused to be swatted as they tried to get him to a more secure room, and Kershaw was shouting not because he was frightened but because shouting was what he did. If he'd been quiet the Sergeant would have demanded a side arm from one of the waiter-marines, and he'd have bloody got one. But as long as Jed was being profane and a little ridiculous, things were not at that point. This was an incident, not a war.

Kershaw's wildly wandering eye fell on the Sergeant. 'Lester! (I'll call you back, but get me some – yes, I *will* call you back and you *will* take the call or I will – yes – get me some answers because I cannot begin to fucking express – right. Then I won't fucking express it, just find the fuck out. Yes. I. Will. Call. You. Back.) Lester! I need someone who is not an asshole and you're it! Jesus Christ,' Kershaw added to anyone near enough to hear, 'that has to be one of the most fucked up things I've ever said.'

'Here, Jed.' The Sergeant let go of Inoue's arm, glanced an apology. She waved him away. *Go. There is work for you here. Also for me.* She began gathering the few lost-looking people into one place. He could hear her gently assessing skills and resilience. *Disaster-relief 101.* And Japan seemed to attract more than its share of horrors.

'Do you know what that was?' Kershaw demanded.

'One missile, surface-to-surface, maybe laser-guided from the ground, maybe fly-by-wire. Not huge, very deliberate.'

'What did it hit?'

The Sergeant sucked air between his teeth.

'The refrigeration plant.'

'Where the fuck did it come from?'

The Sergeant tutted, apologising in advance. 'The bay,' he said. 'Maybe the Fleet. Couldn't see. Jed, one more thing: I've heard rumours of Fleet people coming shoreside for fun. I wouldn't have bothered you with it until this.'

Kershaw stared at him for fully a count of ten, then nodded and shut his eyes. His lips moved. For a moment, the Sergeant thought he was praying, then realised he was rehearsing possibilities, seeing politics in his head. It got quiet in the room as the word spread. *The Fleet*. Because if partying on the shore was a technical transgression, blowing up the shore was something else again.

'Colonel Arno,' Kershaw said at last. 'Consider your investigation expanded to include this matter.' Arno was still sitting, dark eyes taking in the whole scene. The Sergeant wondered how much he had learned just watching all this, and thought: quite a lot. The Italian inclined his head in acknowledgement. 'Work with Lester, please,' Kershaw added.

Shoulder to shoulder with the man he most wanted to avoid, the X-ray Italian and all his myrmidons. *Oh, thank you, Jed*. On the other hand, he'd wanted to insert himself into the investigation, hadn't he? And now here he was.

He traced Kershaw's logic in his head. If Shola's killers were in turn killed, then whoever killed them was involved in whatever Shola was involved in, and that too-loud action, contemptuous of the norms and whatever laws or conventions remained in place, implied urgency or alarm. Two things had changed on Mancreu in the last twenty-four hours to provoke the response: Inoue's report and the footage of Tigerman at the cave. Of the two, the news story about drug smugglers and superheroes seemed the more likely to provoke fear in some red-lit covert battlebridge, which meant Arno and the Sergeant were investigating the same case from opposite ends.

'Lester, I'm formally requesting the assistance of the United Kingdom's representative, whose expertise and familiarity with local investigations may be of use to NatProMan at this time.'

The Sergeant's instinct was to say 'of course' but this would constitute concluding a foreign alliance, even if only a temporary one, so he said, 'I'll talk to London right away,' and tried to make his personal agreement clear by waggling his eyebrows. At the same time, he continued analysing the moment, because he couldn't afford to let them get far enough ahead of him that he made a mistake. He was vulnerable because he had more information than they did about Tigerman and the cave. There was another strand of connection joining Pechorin and the heroin with Shola: the photograph, probably for target identification, that he had found last night. But what sort of target? Had Shola been a middleman, a smuggler, or victim as example? The connection was solid, anyway, one way or another. And there was one more possible contributing factor to the missile attack: the Sergeant had himself made it seem that the prisoners were talking about Jack. The marine had overheard that part of the discussion, would have reported it, which meant it was in the military system. He'd told Dirac the same lie, and anyone from Kershaw's staff might have known about it, and relayed that to a contact in the Fleet.

The Sergeant felt a breath of air at his back. 'I'm going to the impact site,' Colonel Arno said. 'We can talk on the way.'

'I suppose you'll need to call in some experts?' the Sergeant suggested.

Arno shook his head. 'Not call in. By now they are already there. Something explodes while we are investigating, they will want to know what it is. You mind if I call you Lester?' He pronounced it 'Lay-stair'. 'And you call me Arno. It's better, between allies in different chains of command. Nobody is confused.' *And no doubt it makes everyone feel relaxed and careless.* He could see Inoue ahead of him, escorted by two marines and a mini-squad of co-opted administrators for whom she had found work. She nodded regally as he waved, and then they were in the street and he could smell burning brickdust and the aftermath of high explosive.

'Do you have any ideas?' the Sergeant asked. 'About this?'

Arno shrugged. 'I only just arrived,' he said, 'and I was supposed to investigate a guy in a costume blowing up opium.'

The Sergeant glanced sideways. 'Dirac said you could see through walls.'

Arno barked a laugh. 'I like that guy. I was sure there was something about him, but the more I looked, the more he was just this annoying Frenchman. You know him well?' And yes, there was the laser vision: *if you are like Dirac, then maybe what you are tells me about him. And vice versa.*

The Sergeant stuck to his question as they passed into the street. 'You didn't come here without a briefing. You know who the players are. You probably know better than I do because your job is to understand more about that lot.' He waved out at the sea. 'So what in God's name could induce them to blow up a bloody building?'

Arno shrugged. 'Secrets. Politics. Government shit, intelligence operations. If it's that, we may not get anywhere. What I can do stops at the water. I could know exactly inside a week and then that's it. Strongly worded note of protest to the embassy of what-ever. But you assume too much already, you know?'

'I do?'

'Sure. Suppose I'm a drug smuggler, I take a small boat and a shoulder-launched missile, fire it at the shore and use it to set off a car bomb, maybe.'

'I saw it. It wasn't like that.'

'And probably you're right. But now you're remembering and you've already decided what you saw. When you remember things you also change them, each time you remember more what you think happened. Most likely we get over there and there's one centre to the explosion, the chemical trace is right for military ordnance that is too large to be launched that way. Then it's the Fleet. And if it is, that means something but we don't know what until we dig. Dig like investigate, not with shovels. But this is very loud for guys like that, very stupid.'

'Mancreu can do that to you. It makes you crazy. The more you think it doesn't the more it does.'

Arno clicked his tongue. 'Yes. I can see that.' It was all the Sergeant could do not to twitch.

They were getting close to the explosion. He could feel the heat of the fire. NatProMan vehicles were arriving, military firefighters. There was a helicopter in the air and the sound reassured him, which made him want to shake his head in wonderment. 'All right,' he said instead. 'Turn it around. Never mind who. Why?'

Arno shrugged. 'Two reasons I can think of –'

Two?

'– either someone in the prison knew something and someone didn't want them to tell, or no one in the prison knew anything and someone wants us to think that they did.'

The Sergeant turned that around a few times, and made a mental note not to try to think ahead of this man. Bluff him, yes, that might work. Hide from him. But not deceive him directly, not outfox him, any more than you followed a tribesman into his own canyons. *Lies are his hill country.*

'But you,' Arno said, 'you're already investigating this Tiger Man?' He hesitated a little bit over the name. Some insane part of the Sergeant was irritated by the separation of the title into two words. *For God's sake, you lot, it's not Tiger Man, that's not how you say it. Like you don't say Mars Bar as if the bar actually comes from Mars. It's Tigerman. One word. And he's gone. Mission accomplished and he's not coming back.*

'No,' he replied. 'I was holding the men who were killed. For the murder of a local, a café owner. I thought there was someone behind them.' *But you knew that. You must have read my file, too.*

'Shola Girard. He was your friend.'

'Yes. I mean, Shola knew everyone, but I liked him. We boxed together.'

'You know the island, Lester.' Lay-stair. 'So: you have a theory?'

'More than one,' the Sergeant heard himself saying. They had reached Mountbatten Street, where the refrigeration plant had stood. There was just nothing there: a perfect piece of explosive surgery. The empty cannery next door was almost undamaged. The firefighters were sluicing it anyway, keeping the fire contained, but there wasn't even much of that. Shola's murderers were deleted. Gone.

Over on the other side of the notional cordon created by two support vehicles were three figures. One of them hailed Arno. The Italian waved them to come around to a side street. He looked at the Sergeant and made an inviting face. 'Theories?'

The Sergeant shrugged. *Disengage. Step away slowly.* 'Just thoughts, really. Obvious ones, I suppose.'

'That's good. Start with what is apparent. And keep me honest.'

'Well, what you said. But also, there was a burglary at the Xenobiology Institute. Months ago. Not much taken.'

'You think it is related?'

'Probably not.' *Not to Tigerman, for sure. Anything else – how would I know?* 'But Kaiko's – Dr Inoue's – report is the other thing that happened today.' *And now you're going to wonder why I brought up something irrelevant and you'll have to consider the possibility it's because I didn't want to talk about the thing we're supposed to investigate until I had time to get my story straight.*

But Arno seemed to approve. 'Good. That is good. That is obvious but hard to see. All this,' he gestured at the destruction, 'this could be very distracting. If someone wished to focus our eyes on drugs and madmen and away from Inoue and . . . whatever.'

'What would they hide behind something like this?'

'Exactly, Lester.' Somehow this time he got the pronunciation quite right. 'I think I will enjoy our relationship very much.' He slapped the Sergeant on the arm, and trotted off to meet his team as they reached the crossroads.

The Sergeant looked after him, and then up at the misty midnight sky. He wanted very much to be back at Kershaw's banquet, eating pulled pork with Kaiko Inoue. But Inoue was somewhere else now, doing competent Inoue things, and there were things he had to do too, duties and cares to be discharged.

For a moment he did not move, caught in the conflicting flow of events and priorities. He stared up at the Beauville night, the misty blue coloured now with orange flame and artificial light, and then he felt himself turn and begin to move, and knew that the night was far from over and the day beyond it would be just as full.

He did what sergeants do, but it felt heavier somehow, and slower.

14. Crisis

Since rocket attacks were an actual emergency, the Sergeant was back at Brighton House and sitting at the actual emergency desk when the call came in. He didn't know what time it was because he'd been awake for long enough that the numbers on the clock didn't make any sense. It was five, but he had no sense of what that actually meant. It could be breakfast, it could be dinner, it could be Wednesday. Being awake for long periods in a crisis was doable, he'd done it before for days. Being awake alone and in a crisis was harder: your mind stewed in adrenalin and fatigue and threw mad notions at you, random words and reveries, you lost touch with why you were awake, what you had to do. He knew intellectually that it must be morning, that he hadn't been to sleep, but he'd been moving all that time, moving without thinking, first at the impact site with the rescue crews in the hope that someone might still be alive in the rubble, then after that with Arno's team as they demanded of two shocked marines why they'd chosen exactly that moment to leave the building. 'We were relieved,' the marines kept saying. 'We had orders.' And Arno wanted to know from whom but it had become apparent that they really had no idea. Just from up the line. From someone, in the end, who had a NatProMan radio and knew what to say.

Kershaw was growling at him down the white phone, the local one which he used for any outgoing calls. He said something about being in someone else's shoes and the Sergeant realised he needed to go and burn his boots, and the rest of his Tigerman outfit, before Arno tripped over them. That was next on his list. He had been helpful and available for what felt like sixty hours, and now he had to look out for his own position. He would put it all in a dustbin and set the whole lot on fire, then throw the armour plates into the sea. Why had he put the stele on the disposable part of the uniform? Never going to wear it again, of course, never really expected to get shot, and that was just the backplate, the front one would still do, though that didn't matter because he would never need it. He was going round in circles. Sleep would be good. A necessity, actually.

He wondered where the boy was. He would call him next, this all made that acceptable. Call him and ask him to come and help. He needed company.

'—fucking journalists now, too,' Kershaw said, and then there was a soft, piercing purr. The Sergeant looked around, and then realised what it was and that he had been waiting for it.

'I'm going to have to call you back, Jed,' he said gently.

'Like fuck you are, Lester!'

'It's the red phone.' And with a certain satisfaction – *my government trumps your government* – he hung up.

'This is the phone which must not ring,' the Consul had told him. 'It's the phone you keep an eye on in the joyful expectation that you will never actually see it do anything. If it does, by the way, if it actually rings, my general advice would be to seek cover under something and refuse to come out until it's over. I'm not joking. I see that you think I am, but I'm not. You being a military man and so on I realise that you won't listen to anything so craven, but in the interest of our shared humanity, conniving old sod to real man: don't answer the bloody phone. By the time it rings, the situation is fucked up beyond all retrieval, anyway.'

'Has it ever rung?'

'I was in Iraq for a while. The one there never bloody stopped. People forever picking it up. IED in Fallujah, phone rings. British contractor taken by insurgents in Basra, phone rings. Please advise. Well, what do you say? Should have had a better bloody plan in the first place. Should have done what we said we were doing in Afghanistan and left Iraq alone. Should have given our troops the right gear and sent half a million more of them. Should have admitted we were doing Empire at the behest of the Family Bush and built an Iron Frame the way we did for India. A proper infrastructure. A decade or so of that and people actually do think you might be all right. In the end. Conduct oneself with a bit of dignity and don't let the local staff get murdered. Avoid the sexual torture of prisoners, that's always a good one. Make good on promises regarding amnesties and suchlike. It's slow. It's not bloody nation-building, it's generation-building, and it takes decades, not months. But they don't want to hear that, they want a magic solution involving the having and eating of cakes, and any talk of a zero-sum game is heresy. So as I say: let the sodding thing wail like a banshee, have a snifter, and await results. But if you must, the answer protocol is that you give your name and shove your thumb on the plate there. Biometric, they say, and unbeatable. My wife read in the *Telegraph* that you can defeat the system with a bag of jelly sweets. However, be that as it may.'

'Lester Ferris,' the Sergeant said now, thumb pressing down unnecessarily hard, and a nasal woman told him to hold, then connected him to a conference call between people with KCBs. They were not politicians. They were serious people who did serious work.

The conversation was staccato and fragmentary because of the lag between continents, which was multiplied by the number of participants. Everyone was British and most were male, although from time to time a softly spoken schoolmistress broke in and made very intelligent, salient remarks which pushed the discussion along wiser, more cogent lines. Finally she addressed him directly.

'Lester Ferris?'

'Yes, ma'am.'

'Hello, Lester. I take it you're having a pretty tense day over there.'

He could see a helicopter through the window, circling like a nervous buzzard. The Black Fleet had blown up a landside installation, linking itself with an industrial quantity of opium. Kershaw had mentioned journalists. Crap. He hadn't thought of that. They would have set out from bases in Bangkok and Sana'a the moment the footage went public. Some of them before. They'd be here now, and in numbers. More strangers, more eyes to avoid, more questions to trip over. Meanwhile he was talking to half of Whitehall – half of Whitehall was waiting for him to reply.

And the whole thing was about him, in a funny hat.

'Yes, ma'am. We tend to like it calmer in Brighton House.'

'"We"?'

'I was instructed that the house is always plural, ma'am. Even when there's just me.'

She laughed. 'I'm sure you were. I'm Africa,' she added, and he wondered for one vertiginous moment whether that was actually her name. No: she was responsible for Africa. Africa was her job, her title, and her domain. Short for Middle East and North Africa (and associated territories). Insofar as anyone in Britain was responsible for Mancreu, she was, which probably meant she'd lost a card game with Asia. He waited. She hadn't spoken to him just to pass the time of day.

'The question is, Lester, whether we should send someone. A lot of someones. Or let the Americans and the rest of NatProMan deal with it their way.'

Well, actually, the British contingent would clear it up pretty quickly. Lots of missing items from the armoury and the Sergeant himself injured in rather obviously relevant ways, and so on. If it got out, there'd be an almighty stink. Her problem. He waited a bit longer, then answered.

'I'd say no, ma'am.'

'Think you can handle it?'

'No, ma'am. Absolutely not.'

That seemed to please her. 'Then what is your thinking?'

He took a breath to acknowledge that he didn't know and found himself saying forcefully, 'I think it's a bloody mess. But at this point it's not a British mess. We're bystanders. The people still quite like us and we're helping them set up elsewhere so we're not the villains. If NatProMan can't take care of itself, that's a problem for the organisation. Mancreu very specifically isn't British soil any more, which is why it's just me in the first place. The whole island is supposed to explode soon, anyway. But if you were to send, say, an investigation team and a lot of diplomats and so on, then that would sort of acknowledge that we care what happens here and feel responsible. And since the world press is, I gather, coming here in rather a big way and a lot of things which aren't supposed to happen at all happen here on a daily basis, I'd suggest it's better you be able to say "Well, we only had one chap there, and he's a bit washed up, Afghan veteran, good man gone a bit lardy and unreliable, but gosh, it's all everyone else's fault." Ma'am. You might even want a ringing denunciation up your sleeve, just in case.'

She snorted. 'Well done, Lester.'

'Thank you, ma'am.'

'My instinct is to stay away. So in your on-the-spot opinion, if I let this ride, will I hate the outcome more than I would hate the outcome of my getting my hands dirty?'

'In my on-the-spot opinion, I wish I wasn't involved,' he told her, with perfect truthfulness.

'Then you are officially ordered not to be, and I am officially declaring this someone else's problem. Stay out of trouble and don't talk to the press except to say that you can't talk to them. If they talk to you, nod and smile and say you can't say anything and then – and this is very important – don't. Not even to be polite. I'll send you a form of words. If you have to, get it out and read it to them. They'll know what that means.'

'Yes, ma'am.'

'All right, then.'

And that was that, apparently. The call ended, or at least he was no longer part of it. The Sergeant could picture eyebrows being raised in wood-panelled rooms. *Well, old fellow, that's what I said. But if it's good enough for Africa, it's good enough for me . . .*

It might not last. She was not bound by this one conversation. But the longer he went undiscovered the more likely he would remain so. In a short enough time, the evidence would vanish, the island's notoriety would subside, and this would be over.

He realised he was wishing for the fire now, for the end, and felt like a traitor. And then he wondered when he had come to think of Mancreu as something he could betray.

He got rid of Tigerman's boots and put the rest of the gear back in the armoury, stuffed the mask in a burn bag and meant to go out and throw the stele into the sea, but his body duped him and when he slumped into an armchair with a cup of tea he closed his eyes.

The boy woke him, or perhaps he simply woke and the boy was there. Either way, there was tea, and even toast.

'They are dead,' the boy said.

'I know.' No need to ask who.

The boy considered. 'I feel better,' he observed. 'Is that bad?'

'No. People tell you that you won't, but you do. You don't feel good. It's just something less to worry about.'

The boy nodded. He looked pensive and unsettled. There was a formality between them, a distance, which made the Sergeant want to embrace him but at the same time warded him off. He told himself that happened, that it was part of their rhythm. There were days when they were just in the same room at the same time, and days when they were together, in sync.

'They are not the men,' the boy said eventually. 'Not the real men.'

No. Somewhere there was a man behind the men, or perhaps a woman. Someone who had decided Shola's death was necessary, for whatever reason. And that someone was Fleet, almost certainly. Fleet, where his writ did not reach, in a world he did not understand. A world he was not supposed to acknowledge existed. The boy glanced at him opaquely.

'There are journalists,' he muttered, as if this was even worse than murderers.

'Where?'

'In Beauville. They are everywhere. They try to film you if you stand still long enough or do anything interesting. They have found empty houses and they are living in them.' He scowled. 'We are being zerged.'

The Sergeant nodded. *To zerg (vb), from the video game* Starcraft: *to overwhelm with vastly superior numbers.* It was 101, the boy had told him shortly after their first meeting. Totally 101.

'I sorted out the suit,' he said, and when the boy looked up in alarm he added, 'I still have the mask and the stele.' *For now. For in case.* More crossed lines, more mismatched beginnings and middles and ends. Out of step. *It's as if we don't know each other. Or is it that we do and this is how that goes?* He hesitated. 'Have you heard the other news?'

'What other?'

'Kershaw said . . . He said that there isn't long now. That soon we'll all have to leave. Kaiko was quite angry.' And then quite something else which had not been clear when the missile hit.

'Kaiko?'

'Doctor Inoue. The xenobiologist.'

'The science hottie.'

'Pechorin's having his nose redone, by the way. The other man will live, too.' *The one with the spike in his mouth.*

'That is good.'

'What will you do?' *You'll have to leave. Won't you? I have no time left, but I can't say it all now, can I? Not with you like this. Or me like this, I suppose. It could be either.*

The boy shrugged. '*Kswah swah.*'

245

'That's not an answer!' It came out of him before he could stop it, a sergeant's bark. He regretted it immediately, awaited a furious response. None came. The boy shook his head.

'No,' he agreed. 'Not an answer.' He seemed to find this as troubling as the Sergeant, his face contemplative.

'I want to help,' the Sergeant said, after a moment. 'I just want to help. Do you mind if I try to work out some ways to do that?'

The boy inclined his head. 'That would be very kind.' It sounded wooden, like something from a phrasebook.

'Don't do anything . . . I don't know. Just don't. You know what I'm talking about.' Going after Pechorin to accuse him of stealing fish.

'I won't,' the boy said.

They sat together for a while, each peering at the other as if trying to see beneath the skin, and then went their separate ways.

The Sergeant pored over the files for an hour, looking without success for the two files which might be his friends. The files were all higgledy-piggledy, he discovered, shoved almost any which way into their boxes by someone who had no doubt assumed they'd never be looked at again. He got into a rhythm: right hand holds down the file, left hand traces the outer cover and lifts, right fans the pages, left seeks the photos. Check. Check again. Discard.

It was boring. He had not anticipated how boring it would be looking at one photograph after another of children who were not the child he was looking for. Once, a file caught his eye, but the boy in question would be twenty now. A brother? Not a father, however you sliced it. He shunted the file to one side. Then, abruptly angry for reasons he could not put into words, he went into Beauville.

The main street was filled with reporters for the first time ever. There were camera crews setting up in rows in front of the Portmaster's office, and Beneseffe was telling a team of Germans firmly that this was unacceptable, that the office was out of bounds, and they were responding that there was no law on Mancreu so surely they could film where they liked. Beneseffe saw the futility of arguing with them, so he went back inside and a few moments later six large lobstermen came around the corner and politely but firmly started picking up battery packs and cases and moving them away down the street. The lobstermen were big and scarred and looked as if they could handle themselves, but today there was something else about them, too, an edgy hair-trigger dismay which made anything possible. The newsmen could smell it, and they didn't fancy it. They cordially thanked Beneseffe for his advice and let themselves be moved along.

The Sergeant looked around. He was not alone in his bad mood. All of Beauville had it today, that sense of exposure and frustration and the resultant animal desire to bite something. He could hear the people bickering with one another, and over by the sandwich stand a scuffle broke out over mustard, two old blowhards he knew to talk to, shoving one another like children in a playground. Even the island was getting in on the act, making it worse: there was a strange, unending buzz in the ground. You couldn't call it an earthquake. It was more like having an electric toothbrush switch itself on in your luggage. But it wasn't stopping. It was just there, and it was distantly worrying and annoying.

He thought about the boy, about his perplexity and his unease, and looked at the faces around him, not the strangers but the locals, and realised what was wrong.

Someone had bombed them.

Yesterday, they had all been living on a volcano, and that was different in no way from every other day of their lives – or, philosophically speaking, anyone's. You could always be hit by a bus or slip and break your neck, whoever you were and wherever you lived. That was why car bombs and the like were frightening but ultimately ineffective. They were supposed to make a point, but all they did was remind everyone of the irritating, upsetting truth that bad things could happen.

But last night something had happened. A human hand had opened the sky with directed malice, reached down among them and killed people, had done so blandly and casually. It didn't matter that the victims had been by any measure pretty bad people. Anyone who offended against an unknown law could meet the same fate. Anyone within twenty metres of them. Anyone in a car with them or in their house. Anyone who worked with them or overheard whatever appalling secret they had to tell. Or perhaps it was nothing like that at all. Perhaps it had been target practice, or a mistake, and that was what they were worth to the world. It was like living with a capricious god, except that god was out there in the bay and he was just some fucking idiot trying to fake it as best he could, and fuck him. Fuck him for being so rude, so stupid, so powerful and yet so utterly powerless. He could blow up a building. Big deal. Could he put it back together again? No, and that was exactly how the whole thing worked. The chemical men had broken the island and now the United Nations would burn it. No one in the wider world seemed to do anything constructive, no one built or mended. It was lawyers, guns and tax avoidance out there. Real work, reconstruction, was down to ordinary people, and no one ever spent as much money and time on that as they did on ripping things down in the first place, because it was hard.

Beauville whispered to itself, and squirmed away from the light.

He heard voices raised in argument, saw a brief pushing and tussling between two Al Jazeera Persians and a cattleman who had been lounging by a truck. A few others stepped in to head off trouble, but not without some posturing of their own. A moment later, a slim kid passing by nearly walked into the Sergeant and he had to twist to avoid the aggressive shoulder as it twitched towards him. He recognised one of the boxers from the gym, quick as a shark, but too light to take him on, for all that. The kid scowled and opened his arms in a universal gesture of offended adolescent rage. *Have a go, then! Go on, grandad!*

The Sergeant walked on.

In the end he went to see Arno because he might as well. He was here and he had to keep up appearances, and he was too jumpy to go home and work. Arno seemed to understand what was happening. He had music playing in his office, just loud enough to wash away the tension. It was Bach, endlessly looping and sonorous, and it took the edge off the day somehow. So did the herbal tea Arno made with his own hands. He'd been bombed, too, of course, but he didn't know the island so he didn't care. In any case, he probably got bombed all the time. He was a military investigator, and his work would go where the wars went. The Sergeant didn't make the mistake of laughing at the Italians. Any country could make soldiers. Bravery was not choosy about where you were born. Generals were harder to come by, and good political leadership even more so. Dirac said Arno was a soldier, and that was that.

Arno's people were as good – or, given what they were doing here, as bad – as he was. There was a Dane called Ólafsdóttir, a broad-shouldered woman with a soft, cherubic face and maternal eyes who nonetheless was his deputy. She had spent most of her time pottering around the markets and the waterfront, buying bits of fabric from the weavers who sat on their porches. No doubt she knew the card-players by now, too, and had been blessed by the sweepers. Probably she had talked flowers with them, swapped hints about aphids. She could talk to anyone.

Guillaume was even worse. A lanky Frenchman, he was an endurance runner, and he was just about to go running in the mountains. It was a scouting trip, an orientation. He wore strange shoes which were almost slippers, with little toes, and looked to be able to run on and on for ever. He had run in the Copper Canyons on the

Mexican border, Ólafsdóttir whispered as Guillaume trotted out of the door, and he had come third in the Leadville race. That was 80km long and it started at 3000m above sea level. It would take, the Sergeant judged, about an afternoon for the young men of Beauville to discover that this guy twice their age could outrun them on their home terrain, and by evening they would be begging him to teach them, showing him the backtrails. He'd know the island inside out in a week.

There were others whose skills were more cerebral, who were no doubt equally to be feared. Analysts, and more than should be necessary, the Sergeant felt, to turn in the inevitable cover-up at the end of all this. It was wasteful. It was needlessly finicky. There were a thousand places in the world where this kind of effort would make a real difference. Christ, he'd lived in many of them, grown up in one. He imagined Arno turned loose on the petty crimes – and the serious ones, yes – of his old home town. A horde of bastards legging it over the back fence, only to find that Arno, unlike your average TV copper, had considered that possibility and taken steps to provide against it.

'I blame the government,' he muttered to himself, then realised how much he sounded like everyone who has ever been arrested for something of which they were unequivocally guilty.

Arno was pleased to receive him, or at least he said he was. His grave face gave only the faintest hint of reaction, and the Sergeant briefly wondered if he had nerve damage and couldn't smile properly. 'How's it going?' he asked the Italian.

'Slowly,' Arno said, with the air of one who is pleased to bitch about life to someone who'll understand. 'The video footage has been messed with before release. I thought we could get biometric data, run it against the files we hold for Mancreu-based personnel.' *Shit. Could you?* 'But whoever released it does not want that to happen. The broadcast material has been substantially reworked. I could not tell you at this point whether the Tiger Man is five foot or six foot tall. In the footage he is both.'

'You can't just,' he waved a hand, 'clean it up?'

Arno crinkled. Still not an actual smile, but near enough. 'Like *CSI Miami*? I like that show too. No. If there is no data, we cannot make more. With the original recordings, maybe. Not with what we have.'

'Does that mean it might not even be real at all?'

Arno shook his head. 'It happened. Maybe not exactly like it looks. But it happened. There was a person who did those things.'

'And did them at the time we're supposed to think they happened? It's not staged?'

'That . . . is a much more interesting question. I spoke to Pechorin at some length. He is remarkably resistant to being helpful. So much so that one feels he has orders. You see?'

The Sergeant nodded. 'When I was talking to the men who died last night,' he said after a moment, 'there was a name. Bad Jack. It's supposed to be a local king of the underworld. The fellow I was talking to, I held his hand over a map because he didn't want to talk to me.'

'Over a map?'

'Yes.' Uncomfortable. Not torture. Duress, maybe.

Arno seemed to approve. 'Not a candle flame. In this day and age that's . . . chivalrous.'

'He pulled away from the harbour and the shanty.'

'The access to the water and the poor part of town.' Arno nodded. 'That was well done. Bad Jack,' he repeated to an analyst, and the man immediately opened a new file. This room was a map of the island, the Sergeant realised, and there were fewer and fewer blank spaces on it.

He felt a chill. 'I don't suppose the satellite data was any good?'

Arno tutted. 'Bad coverage.' Whether it was too bad to be any use was not clear. Arno muttered 'bad' a few more times, then: 'Bad Jack. Does Jack know that you know?'

The Sergeant considered who had heard him say the name: the dead men, the marine on guard duty, the boy, Dirac,

Kershaw, the assistant. No one else. 'Maybe. I wasn't careful. On the other hand, if he does know, he has very good hearing. Too good.'

Arno sighed. 'If there is a Jack, does he trade with the Fleet? Do they do business or are they at war? Or both? Did the Fleet kill your friend to attack Jack? Did Jack kill the prisoners to protect the Fleet? Around and around and around. You bring me puzzles, Lester. Always more puzzles. Kershaw said I would do well to talk to you. I was not sure what he meant. Now I am.'

I wish I was.

On this convivial note, Arno shepherded him gently out with promises of updates and requests that he pass on any information he thought worth considering.

'Sergeant,' Arno said as they approached the main door, 'I wonder if you could answer me one question which has been troubling me?' His eyes were deceptively mild.

Oh, yes, here it comes. Save one tiny little question until you're standing by the door, when I'm all relaxed and off guard. You watch Columbo *as well as* CSI. 'Of course, Colonel.' *I'm buggered. I know I am.*

Arno shrugged. 'Well, my team, they are of necessity interviewing a lot of people with whom you have already spoken. I mean, in connection with the investigation, although obviously also people whom you simply happen to know. They come to me at the end of the day with questions about your questions. For me it's simple. You are not a policeman. You are just doing what you can. So sometimes the way you work is a little strange. But all the same there is one thing in particular I do not understand.' Under the airy tone, the slightest hint of his focus.

The Sergeant nodded. 'Well, then. Which one?' *And please, let it not be the missing fish.* That would tie him to Pechorin. Loosely, yes, but he did not want Arno getting interested in his dealings with the Ukrainians. Not at all.

The Italian spread his hands. 'You ask, quite often, about a boy. About where he comes from and who he is. Yet often this person is seen with you. Why do you not just ask the question direct?'

The Sergeant stared at him. 'I . . . Oh. Well. You know the island is to be destroyed, and the people resettled elsewhere?'

Arno nodded. Of course he did.

'Have you got kids?'

'No. I hope I still have time.'

Yes. That exactly.

'And have you ever seen an evacuation?' He had. He'd seen that African disaster which had produced Dirac's moment of madness.

'Yes,' Arno said.

'Well, this lad is special. He's very bright and he's got a, what would you call it, a good way about him. We're friends. I don't know if he has any family. Any parents. I thought . . .' He trailed off. Telling people was getting to be a habit. If he told anyone else, he would have to tell the boy before he learned about it as gossip. He should tell the boy anyway. That much was getting painfully obvious. 'I thought . . . if he was an orphan, you know, all that . . . I thought I might adopt him. I don't have a family, and it might work well for both of us. He's too smart for the system. Too good. They'd break him in half to make him fit in the boxes. I can't just let him—' He felt a catch in his throat, rode over it. 'I can't let it all go bad for him, in some bloody resettlement camp somewhere.'

'So you ask about him—'

'Because if he has parents he loves, I don't want to embarrass him. Embarrass either of us.' *I don't want to be rejected.*

It hung in the air between them, a palpable truth, and frankly truer and more important to him than the Tigerman mess or any of the rest of it.

Arno's face was moved, and even a little impressed. There was an inclination in his upper body which suggested his instinct was to wrap the Sergeant in a broad, Mediterranean embrace. He contented himself with a nod of respect.

God, the Sergeant thought, a little awed. *You got right to it, didn't you? You got the core of me so fast you missed the bit you were interested in.*

It seemed he had. The dangerous intensity was, if not entirely gone, massively in abeyance.

'Sergeant,' Arno said, holding the door. He nodded gravely, one un-father to another.

15. Fire

There was a bad feeling in the street, like the hush after someone says something appallingly stupid but just before the first bottle gets broken. The Sergeant walked through Beauville as if it was a place he didn't know and he had stepped off the plane into a siege or an insurrection. For the first time, his uniform felt less like a public service than a target for a sniper. The NatProMan soldiers could feel it too, and they hunched a little as they worked to clear the rubble of the refrigeration plant. That it had contained mostly murderers was beside the point. They had been islanders, and the marines guarding them had been saved, which made a stark distinction about the value of life.

Hearts and minds, bollocks. It was amazing how often that expression was used to describe what was already gone and could not now be clawed back. Although in fairness no one had ever cared much about what the Mancreux thought. They were small and they had no natural resources, no pressure groups. Their only important export was the Discharge Clouds, which was why everyone was here.

And the Fleet.

He didn't want to think about the Fleet, but the choice had been taken away from him. You could ignore something which was quiet and distant. You couldn't keep that up when it was bombing you.

'Hey, I know you!'

The voice was high and robust, an Australian woman which meant a journalist. And yes, she knew him, from Mali and Iraq. But perhaps she would lose interest if he didn't seem to hear.

'Lester! Lester! What is it – Harris? Morris? You can turn around, Lester, I'm just gonna follow you up the street.'

He turned, and there she was: small and blonde and with too many teeth in the lower set, so that her smile looked a bit too much like a ferret.

She stuck out her hand for him to shake, and it was almost as weathered and leathery as his own.

'Kathy Hasp,' she reminded him.

'BBC,' he replied. She shook her head.

'Not any more. They closed my office. So now it's the *Post*.' Which *Post* she didn't say. Washington? Bangkok? Huffington? Or something else he hadn't heard of, something that anyone who was anyone would know? 'So what's really going on, Lester? You're a straight shooter.'

'Your guess is as good as mine. I was having dinner, someone blew up a building.'

'But a building full of your prisoners, right?'

Not such a chance meeting, after all.

He nodded. 'Yes. My investigation. It's been rather swallowed up now.'

'And how's that feel?'

'It's a relief. I had a murder case. This has gone political. I don't do political.'

'Thought you were the Consul. All promoted and wearing a suit.'

'It's pro forma. I have a watching brief. Britain has withdrawn from Mancreu.' Belatedly, he remembered that he wasn't supposed to say anything. 'I have a prepared statement.'

She shrugged. 'Nah, I know what it says. Just wanted to catch up. If you find you've got anything you want to say, you know me, right? Fair shake.' True. She'd been straight with her sources before, mostly.

'I'll keep that in mind.'

She grinned. 'You do that.'

He glanced over at the horizon. He had plenty of opinions about that, for example. About what went on there. It wasn't his place to have them, but they were there, if he cared to get them out and have a look.

Hasp followed his eyes. 'You ever ask yourself how this place would work if that lot weren't out there?'

'No,' he muttered.

'Right old carnival of the bastards, though, isn't it?'

'It's unaligned shipping. You'd have to speak to the Portmaster.'

'The way I see it, either they're keeping this place alive or they're keeping it under the hammer. Should have been sorted out years ago, but somehow it just never quite happens, does it?'

'No doubt the world community will reach a decision at the appropriate time.'

'Yeah, I bet they will. Right about now, is what I hear. Now that Dr Inoue's team are saying it's gonna be the Big One. Except I also hear she says boiling the place away won't help.'

'Dr Inoue is very highly qualified. I'm sure her opinions will be given due weight.' He was sergeanting now, stone-faced and literal. He could do this all day. *Yes, sir. No, sir. 'The mission will achieve the assigned objective.' And never mind that the assigned objective is asinine, or that we'll just have to retreat the day after.* He could hear Africa telling him to turn around and walk away, but he didn't. Something in him needed to hear the lies in his mouth rather than in his head. He knew what the Fleet was. Everyone knew. He just chose not to.

Shola and his killers and the missile; the heroin and Pechorin; the quad bikers and the dog. It all wrapped somehow into the Fleet, maybe more than once. The photograph in the cave, the new guns, and Bad Jack. Round and around and around it went, and he chose not to look too closely because if he did he must, inevitably, see things which were invisible.

I say I'm the police, but I choose not to see because that's my real job. To look the other way, because it's expedient. Except that killing Shola isn't a matter of national security, is it? It's just a crime like any other, and they can do it because everyone looks the other way.

And they can kill the witnesses in my custody, too, because apparently I don't care. Because a sergeant in the British Army, and a Brevet-Consul, couldn't be allowed to see what's under his nose and make a stink. That blindness was the whole point of the island.

A sergeant. A diplomat. Words to hide the same shame, it seemed.

He could hear the tiger's tread behind him at Shola's grave, smell its breath. In its box at Brighton House, the mask was waiting for him to produce it, to give it to Arno and buy safety, even promotion. That was the sensible course. But that would mean no more Tigerman, and if the Sergeant couldn't do anything resembling what was right in this situation, Tigerman could. If it came to it, Tigerman could. That was the point of him. Tigerman wasn't a soldier. He wasn't even real.

Tigerman could do anything.

Lester Ferris shook his head so vigorously that Kathy Hasp stopped talking and stared at him.

'Tinnitus,' he muttered, when she asked if he was okay. 'It comes and goes.'

He went back to Brighton House and started working through the school files. Life was what was important. Life, and the boy, and whatever would happen at the intersection of the two. There would be a moment – and it was coming very soon, maybe in a matter of days – when he would have to make the offer of adoption, even if he didn't know whether there were parents to be considered. Even if the mood between them was still strained. And in that connection: perhaps that was why the mood was strained. He had had that experience with a girl once, had waited and waited for the right moment to ask her out and it had never come, and their friendship – which they had both vowed they wanted to preserve above all else – had decayed and faded away, because the central plank of it was that question. There came a time with any unconsummated desire of whatever sort when you simply had to speak up or let it go.

More faces stared up at him, more files in random order. No, no, no, maybe . . . no. No, no, no.

After an hour, he found the first of his possible names, resting between a baby born the year before and a man in late age. Mustaffe Etienne Gerard was tubby and already showing the barest whisper of a moustache. He was the right age and he had something of the boy about him, his look, his bones, but he was utterly different. In the picture, he had a placid face and wore an oversized hockey shirt saluting a team in St Petersburg.

The Sergeant laid Mustaffe's file gently in the discard pile, and carried on. To his irritation, his mind threw up accusations and spectres of guilt, as if he had better things to be doing. He didn't. This was his heart, the thing he needed: *Save the boy. At least find out if it can be done. Save one future, make one good thing come out of this.*

And: *May I not have one good thing which is just for me?*

But he had promised the boy he would find Shola's killers, the men behind the men, and now he was doing nothing about it and time was running out, and to take his mind off that decision he was leafing through government paperwork on thousands of people in the hope of finding out whether the child he was thus swindling was an orphan, because if he was that would make the Sergeant's own life neater and easier.

That was unfair. This was important, too, and it couldn't wait much longer, either. And it wasn't as if he was particularly guilty of ignoring the other stuff. Everyone on Mancreu ignored the Fleet, except the boy himself, and Kershaw. Kershaw couldn't, because Kershaw was saddled with some sort of role in the Fleet's world. He was the gatekeeper. Did that mean he was Bad Jack? The Sergeant pictured Kershaw in fatigues: Black Ops Jed; wily and ruthless Evil Jed. Still primed with comic books and parallel worlds, the Sergeant's imagination awarded the image a goatee and maroon jackboots. Jack Boots.

Absurd.

Beneseffe, then. The Portmaster was ideally placed to smuggle and conceal. He wouldn't even have to pay himself to turn a blind eye to shipments, he could collect them off the dock and no one would object. He need only be skilled with obfuscatory paperwork.

This was idle. Bad Jack was not the problem. It was Jack's trading partner or his enemy who was the issue: his unfaithful friend, and surely Jack must have known that would happen, that he would be betrayed. Had Shola himself been Jack? Jack had not retaliated because Jack was dead. Except that perhaps Jack *had* retaliated. The men who had killed Shola were ash. Maybe that explosion had been Jack declaring war on the Fleet, in which case . . .

Jack could be my ally. If he is alive. If I was taking the case.

Which the British sergeant never would, however much Lester Ferris might think it was the right thing to do.

A team-up.

It was a staple of the comics world: the moment when a situation so dire emerged that villains and heroes had to fight back to back, each fearing the moment when the other turned on them, each preparing and holding back, until finally both were threatened and must commit fully, come what may.

And it was irrelevant, because he could do nothing about the Fleet, however much he might wish to and whatever he had promised, and the boy understood that. One man could not move the Fleet any more than he could shoot lasers from his eyes. The Red Cross and the International Court couldn't move the Fleet, couldn't even get on board.

Perhaps he is waiting for you to do the right thing. Perhaps it has no value if he must ask.

He lost his place in the files, and realised as he went back that he had not looked at any of the pictures in front of him for a while. He had been opening the folders, leafing through the pages, and putting them away. He went back through the discards painstakingly until he was sure he had not missed the crucial one. He worked into the night, only aware of the passage of time because he had to switch on a light, and then another, and finally to bring in a third from another room. The high ceiling and the dark wood devoured illumination. When he grew tired he went to the bathroom and splashed water on himself, then washed his eyes with drops from the first-aid kit. He made a pot of tea and went back to the desk, conjured another hour from himself, and another.

Sometime after midnight, he became aware of a new sound, like geese and thunder, and the smell of woodsmoke touched his face.

He walked to the east windows and looked out towards the bay.

Beauville was burning.

The descent into the port was a delirium splashed in bad colours across the dark. The shanty was scored with the bonfires of abandoned farmsteads and upturned cars, and columns of smoke rose and spread and reflected the flames. Beauville was washed in the light of its own conflagration. Here and there, knots of angry people destroyed the streets through which they had walked all their lives, with special attention paid – it seemed at least to the Sergeant, gazing in mute horror through the windows of the Land Rover – to those places which were particularly beautiful or welcoming. Here a façade painted a hundred years ago with scenes from the lives of fishermen split and boiled; there a small mews, with its absurd front doors like tiny portcullises, crumbled and fell in. Looters brandished their trophies, fought over them like gulls, and then lost interest, letting them drop or adding them to the nearest blaze. Almost every item could have been had at any time over the last months, taken with respect from empty houses left unlocked by those who chose not to destroy what they could not carry away, but now Beauville was delivering judgement on those who had departed and all their worldly effects, declaring them dead and exiled and showing its contempt for anyone too cowardly to see the island to its end.

He drove past the Witch's house and saw that it, too, was in flames, the solid porch and the high-backed chair from which she had encouraged the scrivener fuelling the blaze. The flowers were strewn all about. Because she was foreign? Or because she was kind? He slowed the car, wondering if he should search for her, but the fire was old. If she had been inside, she was dead now, and no amount of stupidity on his part would change that, even if it did make him feel better. If she was not inside, then entering wasn't even brave, it was asinine. He cursed. There was gear in the armoury which would help with this: firefighting equipment, oxygen. He should go back and get it, but to turn around now smacked of desertion, so he drove on.

At the next crossroads he chose the harbour road, aiming in part for the scrivener's shop. Breanne would have gone there, he suspected, if she could. He would go past, see if they were all right. He could offer to put them up at Brighton House. He pulled out his cellphone, slapped the battery in and called the boy, got a synthesised female voice telling him the person he was calling was not available. He left a message: 'I'm in the car. Beauville's gone to shit. If you need me, call or go to the house. Bring whoever you want,' he added after a moment, thinking of the elusive guardian. 'There's room for quite a few.' He wondered if he would come back to find a horde of street children or a family of twenty seeking refuge in what was still technically consular accommodation, and what diplomatic shit that might kick off.

Towards the seafront, where the buildings were closer together, the fires faded as if the riot was saving the best for last. An ugly calm lay over the streets like the anticipation of a beating. Away from the source, the Sergeant heard the sound of the mob as he had from up on the hill, a kind of birdlike laughter on the wind. He realised too that he had been driving through fouled air, that there was ash in his snot, clogging his nostrils with black slime. He blew his nose, then cleared his throat and almost vomited, jerking to open the window and spit nauseating burned rubber stink onto the street. He sluiced water from a bottle in the back seat into his mouth, partially inhaled it and snorted it out, then abandoned his handkerchief to the gutter. And now, standing outside the car, he could smell something else, a grim mix of animal and hair. He looked around and about, then caught it again. *That way.*

He got back behind the wheel and rolled the Land Rover slowly forward. *Let it not be a person*, he thought. *Let it be a fox or a cow. I don't really care. But not a person and not anyone I know.* And then he felt, when he saw it, that he had brought this on himself, that he had conjured it.

Spartacus. He couldn't remember the name of the general who had ordered it and that pleased him, but he recalled the rest. Westcott had talked about it endlessly, the moment when savagery had transformed the wobbling Roman Republic into an enduring empire: security at the price of freedom. When Spartacus's rebellion was defeated, the Via Appia was lined with six thousand crucified slaves as a warning to the world.

From each of the telegraph poles on the road leading down to the waterfront dangled the corpse of a dog, front paws nailed to a coarse crosspiece ripped from a packing crate. Not six thousand. Not even a hundred. But still a manifest monstrosity and an earnest of more.

He got back into the Land Rover, hating the world.

The Portmaster's office was shuttered, heavy steel blinds chained to the concrete pediment, and the waterfront was almost deserted. The lobstermen had taken their boats to more amenable moorings and the lines of storage shacks along the docks gaped open, corrugated-iron walls bare and so rudimentary that burning them was an empty gesture. Twenty minutes with a hammer and a few bits of wood and the same metal would be in the same position, if anyone cared.

The scrivener's shingle hung halfway along the waterfront, a single lantern glowing dimly beside the papal writ. The windows were dark, but they always were. White Raoul never drew the curtains. His den was a mystery, a magician's cave. All along the road was rubble and splatter, dark stains which might be blood, and others – paint, booze, water and piss. This was a battlefield, sure as any Lester Ferris had ever seen.

Rolling the Land Rover onward, the Sergeant was starkly aware of how wide and exposed the promenade was, like a medieval killing ground. He had been driving without lights anyway, and now he stared out into the night, cursing the limits of his eyes and wishing for night vision goggles, for a partner to watch his back. And where was the boy, anyway? The Sergeant tried not to think of him running with the pack, putting Beauville to the torch and screaming like a madman, but if he wasn't doing that then he might be in trouble, be hiding, be burned. He didn't seem the type, but no one ever did. This kind of thing came from nowhere and washed you away; it was elemental. Or had that strange parent come for him, whisked him off to some mountainside for safekeeping, and was he even now looking down on the orange pall and wondering where in all that stink and flame was his friend the Sergeant? But if this last, he had only to pick up his phone messages and respond.

Call me. Is that so much to ask?

The Land Rover crunched over something brittle, a vase or a bottle. The noise was shockingly loud and made him jump. He lurched the car one way and then the other to throw off the first shot from a sniper's rifle in case that same sound excited a response in some lethal watcher on the rooftops, feeling sure there was no sniper, not here, but doing it anyway because you did, you followed your instincts and asked why later, or sooner or later you paid for it.

An improvised explosive device, now. He wouldn't rule out something like that here, not tonight. A big drum of diesel oil lifted from the harbour. What a fine blaze that would make, if a fellow knew how to rig it – and no doubt some did.

The car jiggled again, this time riding over a long piece of hosepipe. No, not a hose: a cable, and fat as a man's arm. He stared at it, following the long spaghetti line around in a wide spiral and down to the edge of the water. It was draped in seaweed and muck. In fact . . . Yes, it was the cable TV connection to the Black Fleet, he realised, ripped up and severed, and for the first time he felt a sense of sympathy with the marauders. Let the Fleet feel something, even if it was just having to fall back on DVDs and movies on highly covert iPads and laptops.

He drove on, feeling the cable squirm under his tyres, and stopped outside the scrivener's door. He debated whether to hoot, whether to leave the engine running in case he needed to make an escape. But didn't want to lose the car to some wandering sneak, so he took the keys and went to the door.

She opened it before he could knock. 'I'm okay.'

He breathed out slowly. 'I was hoping.'

She didn't ask how he knew to look for her here. Well, he was supposed to be a detective, and perhaps everyone had known except him. Gossip was like that.

'Have you seen the boy?' he asked.

'No.' And he saw her face mirror his own worry: *If he's not with me and he's not with you, then where?* But at least she was not the boy's mother, that was something. The world she could offer was so big. He could not compete with that, wouldn't try. Johns Hopkins. Ivy League schools. A woman who could open doors. That would be a fine place for the boy. Just not his boy, any more. But it seemed he was spared that moment. He felt a guilty triumph.

'Your house . . .' he began, but she raised a hand.

'I know. I heard. But it's fine. You know, it's just stuff. My clarinet, I suppose, I've had it for years, but in the end it's a thing. It's not like a violin, like a Stradivarius. Just a decent Yamaha, I can get one on eBay and it'll be exactly the same. It's just stuff,' she said again, and with the repetition it seemed to hurt her a little less. People she had known, probably, had come and destroyed all that they could reach of what she owned. That and her garden, he suspected, hurt more than the material things. She wasn't a soldier, used to showing up and being shot at.

He cast about, wondering how she would regain her sense of the world. Not by hitting someone or shooting at them, obviously. Not by arresting them. She would want to reconnect, to help. He pursed his lips. 'I can tell Kershaw to sort out a medicine bag for you, if you like.'

She smiled wanly. 'Thank you.'

He looked at the road, the residue of conflict on it, then back at her. 'What happened here?'

'The crowd came, obviously. Beneseffe and the dockmen stood them down. Well, I say that. It was pretty much a medieval battle. They even had drummers, or near enough. It was . . . insane.'

'Raoul?'

'He wanted to go out and tell them off! I told him no, so he's angry with me. He's inside painting a curse, I think, on anyone who burns their own town. On people who smash what's beautiful. It's like they can't bear to see anything good now that they know it's going to go. Know it properly, I mean. The word's out on that: that the end is nigh. So now this. If it's special you smash it before someone else does. I said anyone who does that doesn't need cursing, and he told me I was a hippy.' A lovers' tiff, and a proof of mutual affection. She waved her hand. 'Do you want to come in?'

But the Sergeant was already running for the Land Rover, because if there was one place in Beauville which was beautiful it was the street of the card-players, with its white steps and trailing flowers.

'Ferris,' the Sergeant shouted into his phone, 'and you know bloody well how to spell it. Now get Jed Kershaw on the phone and tell him it's the Brevet-Consul of Her Majesty's United Kingdom of Great Britain and Northern Ireland, and I need to know why his lads are sitting in barracks with their thumbs up their arse! I'm not pissing about – this is,' he groped for the form of words, 'this is a matter bearing upon the United Kingdom's willingness to cede sovereign claim to this island to the international protection force.' The Consul had told him if he ever seriously wanted to get Kershaw's attention, this was the way to do it. *It'll scare the living shit out of him*, the Consul had said, *and he'll be frightfully cross, so don't do it unless you have to. And for God's sake, whatever you do don't imply that you're actively asserting sovereignty. That could really start some sort of war.*

Kershaw came on the line a moment later, and he did indeed sound very pissed off. 'What the actual fuck, Lester?'

'Sorry, Jed, I don't have time to piss about. There's a bloody riot happening! Get your lads out on the street and do some good!' He threw the Land Rover around a tight turn and saw the back of the crowd, torches and spars dangling in loose hands. All moving the same way, yes, somehow drawing together again into a mass.

Kershaw snarled at him down the phone. 'Oh, thank you, Lester! I did notice the fucking riot, but I decided that since NatProMan is specifically charged with exploding the entire island when the time comes, just maybe my guys were not the ideal fucking choice of policing for the streets of Beauville right now, but I'm sorry I didn't fucking check with you first! And by the way, *Sergeant*' – he spat the rank as if it tasted of rot – 'don't you ever fucking bring the diplomatic incident with me! You're a nice guy, Lester, and I'm sure in a bar in Shropshire you're tougher than shit, but in this world you are a fucking minnow and I am a shark, do you get me? A *fucking* shark! And this is where I swim. So unless you have the Queen standing behind you in her armour, ready to fucking joust for this shithole, get off my phone and go back to your castle and stay there until you get orders from your boss!'

The Sergeant stopped the Land Rover and stared into the handset. He left the line open and he could hear Kershaw's breathing. Over on his right was the mob, about five or six minutes from the street of the card-players. He could hear them, no longer like a mad laugh but a sort of sigh, as if the joy had gone out of their destruction but they had a duty to see it through.

'Good night, Jed,' he said gently, and hung up. Shouting worked on enlisted men and sometimes on junior officers, but it was never really an answer, just a way to get the discussion started. You drove them off until you could welcome them back, and that made them grateful. But he couldn't do that here, with Kershaw. The two of them were in balance, each sovereign and neither truly in control.

He put the phone in his pocket and drove the Land Rover around the back of the old market square, then got out and walked the rest of the way.

The white stone gleamed in the orange light of the sky. The vanguard of the mob was arriving, but the street of the card-players was so neat that there was almost nothing to tear up or burn. The window boxes had been raised to the upper floors, the doors were shut. The flags were sheer and perfect. The Sergeant wondered, briefly, if it was all going to be all right.

And then he saw, under the one soft lantern, the dealer sitting at his table with a deck and a bottle, waiting.

The mob saw him at the same moment and surged forward around him, mocking and plucking. A young boxer took one free chair away and smashed it against the road, then when this met with scattered laughter and encouragement, slouched down into the next seat and poured himself a drink. He knocked it back, then threw the glass away, moved to the last free chair and repeated the gesture, staring at the old man.

A door opened, somewhere, and the sweeper came out with her broom and started to sweep up the broken glass.

The card-player gently retrieved his bottle and took a swig, then handed it back before the boxer could object.

For a moment, it seemed to be working. The sheer, brazen normality of it was waking them, bringing them to themselves. A moment more, and they would have names again, and a sense of self. They were tired. The bacchanal was run out, and the dawn was coming. It was cold and the air was blowing dust. It was working.

And then a woman near the sweeper said: 'You missed a bit here, by me,' and when the sweeper went to get it she kicked it lightly away.

The sweeper pursued it patiently, but the woman chased and kicked it again, and the sweeper slipped and went down, and the whole street heard the crack as she landed hard on one hip, and the reedy cry which went out of her. Her outstretched hand, reaching for solace and assistance, caught the woman by the ankle.

'Get off me!' the woman shrieked at her, and kicked out, and the toe of her shoe clipped the sweeper across the mouth. It was – it all was – an accident.

The dealer shot to his feet and started to speak and the boxer came up with him, drawing back his hand to silence what he assumed would be a furious denunciation with his fist, and the Sergeant shouted: 'No!'

He stepped into the silence awkwardly, wishing for his full uniform, for something which spoke of what he represented, what he was, but he only had his parade-ground voice, and it would have to be enough.

'Siddown!' he barked at the dealer, and the man sank to his chair again. *I am obeyed.* He knew the mob had registered it, could feel them making space for him. Authority, exercised on their behalf. 'And you,' he added more gently to the boxer. 'That right hand of yours is used to gloves. You hit that old fart with it and you'll ruin your knuckles for months. Don't be a twit.' He turned before the young man could object. He had to keep moving, keep making sense. 'I'm Lester,' he said. 'I'm supposed to be up at the big house hiding under the carpet, but I've got friends down here and I didn't want them to get hurt so I came. I've seen him fight at the gym,' he added, pointing over his shoulder with his thumb. 'He's a terror. Faster than you'd believe. Drops his shoulder a bit, mind, but a good coach'll break that habit. Someone take off their coat for that lady, please, she's old enough to be my mother and shouldn't be lying in the cold. You, miss, would you mind stepping back aways?' This to the woman who had felled her. 'I think you've had a bit of a shock. It's always hard to be close to something like this, you always feel it's somehow your fault and it never is.' Bemused, the woman backed away and was embraced solicitously by those around her. A moment later, the sweeper was covered in a makeshift blanket.

'Now,' the Sergeant carried on, 'we're all alone out here tonight. Those arseholes,' he gestured vaguely in the direction of Kershaw's office, 'aren't coming, so we've no emergency services. We'd best do it ourselves, hips can be tricky. I need a few strong lads to get this lady into my car and I'll take her to a doctor. You, sir, you better come along so she's got a familiar face.' This last to the dealer, who got unsteadily to his feet, assisted by the boxer.

They were carrying the sweeper down the side street with surpassing gentleness and loading her into the long back of the Land Rover when the Sergeant heard engines, and felt the mood thicken around him. He shook his head. *I had them. I bloody did.*

But he had lost them now. He pressed the keys into the dealer's hand. 'Get in the car. Go to the scrivener's office and get him and the Witch and get up to Brighton House – she knows where to find the key. If it gets nasty use the red phone in the office and tell the snotty prick on the other end that I'm compromised and the diplomatic premises are under direct threat.'

And before the man could say anything he stepped back and waved cheerily. 'Off you go, now, sir. I'll be right behind you. I want to help these folk clean up a bit.'

The dealer got the Land Rover started and went, and the old woman's eyes locked on the Sergeant's in mute concern as they pulled away.

Lester Ferris turned, and saw the boys on their quad bikes rolling slowly through the crowd, and with them a kind of bitter recollection of anger. They had work to do. There were things to be broken, statements to be made.

'English sergeant,' the leader said from beneath his mask.

'Shame we got no dogs left,' said the next.

The Sergeant felt the crowd respond. *No dogs left, and someone's got to be nailed up.*

Shit.

There was no retreat from this situation. He was cut off. There would be no help from Kershaw, either, that was clear. And no blather he could muster would soothe them. So he pointed his index finger at the leader and scowled.

'You're the toerag who kills broken-down old pups, is it? The limp-dicked, shrivel-sacked little puswad, the best part of whom dried up on a hankie, who thinks nailing a dog to a telegraph pole will make him a hero. Is that right? Is that the fucking size of it? You miserable excuse for a shitheel? Well, then. Well, then. WELL, THEN. Let's have a bit of fun, you and me. A man-to-man discussion, eh?' He was walking forward now, and that was pretty unlikely, unlikely enough to stop the momentum, change the game. But it had to be just right. He had to be offensive enough to challenge, but not enough to be dismissed as disrespectful of the game. 'Or are you a bit too scared of an old geezer for any of that? You can always hide behind your mates. You can have them soften me up a bit first, can't you? Let them take some of the sting out of it for you.' And they backed away, bless them, at this ignoble suggestion. *Oh, for a few of my lads behind me. We could actually win.*

The leader got down off his quad and stretched. He was loose-limbed and fluid, with a dangerous reach. His hands had seen proper work and proper fighting.

And then he produced a long-barrelled revolver from his belt and levelled it.

'Beat the shit out of him,' he said simply.

And they did.

The first blow came in low and numbed the Sergeant's left leg, the second across his back. They had pieces of timber, ungainly but none the less painful and bruising. The third blow knocked him from his feet and he knew that it was all up, that he would almost certainly die on this clean white street, and he rolled into a ball, saving his head as best he could and wondering when the first bone would crack. They were unprofessional and not particularly enthusiastic, but their anger was growing as they struck and quite soon they would start to mean it, and shortly after that he would lose consciousness and then it really would be over, because they would kill him without even really meaning to. It didn't matter who you were, the human body was just not that tough.

And then he went away, until curiously he smelled fish and bad cigars.

He came to in his own bed, again, expecting to see the Witch or the boy and slightly hoping for Kaiko Inoue. The unexpected smell of fish was gone, but the bad cigars, stale and grim, hung in the air along with a pungent male odour. He opened his eyes and saw a man with a bandaged nose.

'Holy shit, Ferris, they hardly touched you,' Pechorin said. 'When that fat bastard came and got me I thought maybe you'd lose a kidney at least, but look at you. The doctor with the extremely Ukrainian tits out there, who claims to come from Kansas? She says you're not even going to die a little bit.'

'Who . . . came and got you?'

'Beneseffe,' Pechorin growled. 'He and his lobstermen. We had a little conversation about fish this morning. Some opportunities were discussed. Some possible business. They send some local kid round to check me out, I figure they know what's going on, so I go see them. We make friends. Then a couple of hours ago, "Pavel, Pavel, we have to save Lester" and blah blah, and I say okay, because you will box with me and you're good when I lose my temper, which is not everyone. The world is not full of people who will decline the opportunity to hit me in the head.'

You have no idea.

'I like this house,' Pechorin went on. 'You got some architecture here. Where I come from there's some stuff like this but all the wood and paint is gone. You can go visit but the guide will tell you "here used to be very pretty, now it's shit," and leave you to imagine the rest. But it's full of invalids. You got an old lady down the hall, two lobstermen bleeding on the couch. You are the last British colonial hospital all of a sudden. Is this place still a consulate? That's going to throw some egg.' He considered this last, shook his head. 'Whatever. The tits say you should go back to sleep, get your strength. I'm not to wake you, blahblahblah.'

The Sergeant could feel himself slipping into sleep again. 'I thought you were arrested,' he murmured.

Pechorin shrugged. 'I got unarrested. I tell you another time.' He hesitated. 'You keep a secret, Lester?'

'Yes.' Lots.

'I don't want that you think I'm a fuckhead war profiteer drug pusher, okay? Let's say I maybe had some orders to do what I did. When a government does something it's not a crime, is politics. Maybe I fight war on terror. Maybe I do good work, get tip-off. Maybe my job, it's not completely clear. Okay? Like the CIA in Vietnam. I tell myself I'm sending drugs home to hospitals. Maybe it's only my boss is a fuckhead war profiteer drug pusher and I'm a stooge.' He shrugged. 'I do what is necessary. It's Mancreu. Makes no difference, anyway.'

It does. It does, it does. It does to Shola, and the others. It does to the dogs. To the boy, it does.

273

He tried to fix Pechorin with an interrogator's eye: *Are you lying? Is this bullshit? Tell me what you know!* But the world was brown and warm and then he was gone again.

By late afternoon he had shaken off the Witch's insistence that he stay in bed and was walking around, complaining with every movement but convinced he was doing himself good, and she averred between curses that he might be, but that he'd be happier if he didn't. She had no time to chase him, however, because the sweeper's hip was broken and she was concerned about clotting. One of the lobstermen had an infected cut which required medicines she could not get without crossing Beauville to Kershaw's building, and the riot was still going, so she had instead to make her best alternative from plants by boiling them in a pan and supplementing the mix with powders from the medical supplies at Brighton House, which were for the most part out of date.

He couldn't escape the feeling that all this was his fault, that he could have done more – that while Lester Ferris could never have stood alone in front of the gang and faced them down, he was no longer only Lester Ferris and he had in some sense abandoned his post, at great cost to an old woman and he had no idea how many others. He hoped Inoue was out of it, firmly on the far side of the island. He even hoped Kershaw was okay. He was sure Dirac was.

He barely dared to think about the boy. There were so many things that could be wrong. Perhaps he slept in an abandoned house and it had simply burned around him. Perhaps he had defended a dog, or perhaps his trading association with the Fleet had been viewed as treason. It was all equally possible. A father would go out and find him, risks or no, injuries or not. A real father would have no choice, would feel, surely, the tug in his blood and his bones and the need beyond common sense. He would go house to house. He would find the corpse if he must, the living child if he could, but he would be out there.

And, the voice of experience told him, that man would be an idiot. A noble, short-lived idiot, searching a burning town for a child who knew its alleys and its secrets, who was better suited to it than a clumping parent could ever be. More than likely the would-be rescuer would bring the mob to his child's door, and they would both burn. Nightmares boiled in his mind's eye, multiple scenarios of doom and folly, and each one grew more grotesque, more self-defeating.

'Dude! You got ganked!'

The boy stood in the doorway and stared at him, mightily impressed. 'You got really messed up! That is . . . that is *roarsome*!'

When merely 'awesome' is not enough.

The boy was still going. 'This is your Bespin! You failed, but you didn't die, and you totally kept your integrity—'

And then he could not continue because the Sergeant had wrapped him in a vast embrace, painful and absolute, and was having trouble letting go even as panic gripped him that this was absolutely outside their way of being, this absolute and unequivocal hug so full of worry and dismay. He wrenched his arms open and stepped away.

The boy gazed at him, wide-eyed.

And then hesitantly crossed the space between them for a second, half-hug, resting his head against the Sergeant's shoulder.

'It is okay,' he said, his face very sombre and eerily old. 'I was fine.' He stayed there for a moment, and then slipped away. 'By the way, you have mail. The Italian said to bring this to you.' From his bag, he produced a slim envelope. 'Said it would help with your investigation. Check it out! Maybe it will tell us how to beat those badmashes on the bikes! I will make tea!'

He scampered away, and the Sergeant found he could breathe, despite his aching ribs, for the first time in a day. He opened the envelope and glanced at the contents, then stopped and stared.

Sergeant —

You have been doing my work for me. It is only fair I do yours. It is busy here, but there is no better time for this. I wish you well.
— A.

Not the bike gang, and nothing about Tigerman or Shola's death.

The boy's face stared up at him from the file, his birthday, his given name. His parents.

The Sergeant retreated to the study and closed the door. It was not privacy he needed but calm, a sense of constancy. This was the thing. This was the file. The boy's file. Everything he had wanted to know was here, and yet reading it all would be cheating, of a kind. He did not have to read it all. He would leave the boy his mysteries. He had read the name at the top, had already forgotten it. Saul? Sullah? Simon? It began with an S. Or possibly M, or X, or J. He could check, but he would not. The boy was the boy, complete in himself. It was idle to give him a name beyond that unless he wanted one. The Sergeant needed only the names of his family, and where to find them.

He began to read. He tried to avoid the detail but it was impossible, the truth was buried in the text, so he had to intrude at least that much. Not a problem. He could forget it afterwards, could wait to have it explained and never let it be known that he knew.

The boy's father had been a longline fisherman from Malé. He had come to the island after a storm and stayed just long enough to fall in love and father a child. Arno had written in the margin that he thought it really had been love. He must have been out gathering information before the riot, or perhaps the investigative team had simply gone on about their business, backed by a few marines and moving carefully to avoid the mob. They must have worked in worse places; in Somalia, at least, and maybe Kashmir or the West Bank. The young sailor, anyway, had gone back to his ship and headed home to acquaint his family with his intent to marry, and had got caught instead on an outgoing line and drowned. It happened, Arno noted, quite a lot. He knew families at home who had suffered by the same thing.

The Sergeant turned the page, and – seeing what was written there – nodded in a kind of acknowledgement. The boy's mother was alive, of course. She was not a nun, or a bar fly. She was no one he knew. But he knew of her, as everyone did, and he knew that he had been in some way expecting this.

Once upon a time, he thought, *only it's not like that because it's not fucking funny.* And where had he heard that? *'Throw the stele in the sea and tell him you want to take him away from here and see what he says. Maybe there's a family for you after all. Leave your victory on this island where it belongs.'*

The story went on, relentless.

Once upon a time, White Raoul knew a lover from the mountains, a weaver woman of the old stock. They made no marriage and no contract. She would not have him, because he was a foreigner. He amused her and adored her and perhaps his feelings were reciprocated. But when she conceived a child she told him that Beauville was too modern and too cold a place to raise a daughter and she went home, and would not see him any more. Sandrine was born on the floor of a herder's cottage, midwifed by a cowman. She visited her father as she grew. He kept a place for her always in his house, and she was famed for her looks. Her father's fierce protectiveness was misconstrued. He was not guarding her virtue, just his small allotment of time with the child as she grew and changed from month to month and he missed each waystation of her life: her first tooth, her first word, her first love.

Until she too bore a child, to a longline fisherman, and when he died she mourned and healed and in time the boy attended school in Beauville, for the dead father had persuaded her the world beyond the island was worth knowing. She obtained by some haggling an old computer and a solar mat to charge it, and they learned together of the history of Mancreu, and

Europe and Africa and more, and together they were angry and impressed and afraid. She studied correspondence courses and prepared for the day she must travel with him to the mainland and enrol them both in some manner of university. It was possible. There were bursaries, charities, husbands and even sugar daddies, and if these failed there was always crime. Her family knew crime.

She was methodical, composing options and plans, laying groundwork. She networked, by phone and by email and later by the new avenues of social media. With the assistance of a passing photographer and a local flautist she created a YouTube slot which picked up thirty thousand views. And she got her wish: scholarships for them both one autumn, with all the trimmings, at an institution in Qatar.

That summer she walked the high passes every day. She took pictures of them, inhaled them, sketched them and sang to them. She slept under the stars, sometimes alone and sometimes in company, drank and danced and visited her mother and her uncles and aunts. She and the boy together toiled over their English and their Arabic both, watching movies and listening to CDs and reading books, so that the way they spoke was a muddle of Scotland and Baltimore, Tikrit and Tunis.

On the last day of her sabbatical, the first Discharge Cloud came. It rolled down along the high valleys, and she was caught in it and changed. She was vibrant and beautiful still, compassionate and energetic. But from moment to moment she forgot almost everything and everyone, living in an endless now which seemed to worry her not at all. Of all things, she remembered most of all the island, the endless smugglers' paths and narrow goat tracks, the rivers and waterfalls where she swam. She was content and even joyful in her new state. But she never spoke, and she did not know her son.

And he, of course, still knew her.

16. Houseguests

It had been quiet enough during the day, the Beauville mob sleeping off its rage on stolen mattresses dragged out onto the street or in the bedrooms of departed neighbours, but as dusk fell fresh fires were already being kindled in the shanty and the weird gabble of the riot began whispering on the wind. The rage was building again, the furious rejection of an intolerable circumstance. The Sergeant could feel it in his teeth, in the line of his jaw: the cold wash of coming violence. It whispered between men and women camped in town squares, in ditches and ruined houses. It sparked and glittered. In another place it would have meant revolution and civil war, but here there was nowhere to put it, nothing to be done with it which was even as constructive as tearing down statues, so it zinged back and forth and grew, and as it grew it grew uglier.

He stood on the flat roof at the edge of the wing and peered over the lip of the house down towards Beauville. From up here – the highest point of the building – one could see the whole of the town. When the wind came up he could smell the sea, and the stink of burning.

Beauville would burn again tonight unless someone stepped in, and there was no one to do it. Kershaw would not, and perhaps he was right that he could not. NatProMan might become the occupying enemy as opposed to the tolerated presence of the outer world. The Fleet was even more disbarred, had its denizens had any desire to intervene. Beneseffe's little army was simply too small, there were no NGOs to mediate, and the global press pack was getting great TV out of the collapse. How often did anyone get to cover an actual apocalypse, however local and small? Crisis was commonplace; endings were not.

The thought did not make him happy, and even less so because he was in some senses not affected. Up here on the hill, Brighton House was a long walk from the centre. You could herd a mob – if you had, say, quad bikes and a willingness to deploy violence – but you couldn't push them to walk an hour in the dark. That was a little too cold and considered. Brighton House was a symbol of the good old days as much as the bad ones, which was why Lester Ferris had been made Mancreu's bobby on the beat by acclamation.

So he was safe enough so long as he kept his head down, and when it was all done – in a fortnight, he guessed, not much more – he would go home and he would have some photographs and probably quite soon a new job, and that would be that.

But down there it would be bad, and really the end of the island would bring no release. Mancreu's last ten thousand would be evacuated and resettled and they'd be a people dispossessed and perhaps unwelcome, in places they did not know. He was a tourist, a spectator, as surely as Kathy Hasp and her pals. He might help the boy – though how, he did not know, and he had no notion of what Sandrine meant to that plan: would he have to adopt them both? Fake a marriage with her? – but that would be the extent of it, and a pisspoor extent it was. And he was a man under authority, specifically instructed to stay out of the way. In films that might not mean anything, but for all his adult life he had taken orders and it counted with him. It was a piece of who he was, a thing made not of duty or queen and country, but self.

He realised guiltily that he was picking and choosing. For the boy, he had done things far outside what he was permitted. He just didn't care about the people below him enough to break the rules. They were far away and he didn't know their names.

He went inside and looked in on the Witch, and she shrugged. Her patient was stable. White Raoul was sleeping in a chair. Nothing to report.

He found the old man from the street of the card-players reading one of the Consul's books in the kitchen, a Russian novel he hadn't heard of.

He knew he was avoiding the boy, and the conversation they must have. He went to look for him.

The boy was watching television in the spare room, inevitably the news coverage of the island. Kathy Hasp frowned out of the screen, her fluid, Antipodean English lending her authority and a species of gravitas while the strangely emphatic cadence of network news tried to take it away: '. . . a *grim night* here on Mancreu and most likely another one to come, with more arson already going on around me – although it's hard to know if you can really *call it that* on an island *without law*, and without a *future*. These are the actions of a people *on the edge* . . .' Her eyes flicked away to the horizon, but the cameraman had his back to the Fleet. It was just an editorial decision, a question of what was news. Rioting, yes. Shipping, no.

The Sergeant lowered himself to the floor, his shoulders resting against the side of the bed. He looked straight ahead, towards the television but not at it, and the boy thumbed the remote. Hasp was replaced by a cadaverous Brit the Sergeant had met once or twice, who stooped like a stork and seemed on the screen to take joy in nothing. In person he was a voracious eater and drinker with a high, startling laugh which seemed to erupt from the narrow face. He must have been up on the roof of the old prison house last night: the footage was excellent, like something from Tahrir or Beirut, all darkness and flame. Again, the Fleet was no part of the picture: '. . . *pall* of smoke hanging over the town, and the *very real* possibility of more violence to come . . .'

The television went mute, and the Sergeant realised the boy was looking at him, and waiting. There was no time in this moment for his hesitations and his fears, so he went ahead.

'Your mum. Your mother. I know who she is now,' the Sergeant said. 'I mean, I know the story, or something very close. Arno found it all out, I never managed it. You must have known I was trying.' And that was true, he realised. The boy could not have missed the inquiries, would have been informed by the same network of gossips from which he got all his local knowledge. And he had neither helped nor hindered. *But is that yes, or no? Don't try to decode. Just talk.* It would all be so much easier if everyone talked more.

He realised he had stalled. 'I don't know where she is. Is she safe? Do you want,' he swallowed, ploughed on, 'do you want to bring her here?' It was very hard to say. *Please bring the person who owns your loyalty into my house. The person whose claim on you I cannot hope to match.* But he was not in the business of claiming the boy, had promised himself this was not about possessing him. It was about uplifting, about supporting. He would give what he could, take what was offered, and that was all.

The boy looked at him for a long moment, and his face was inscrutable. Was this measurement or verdict? Was this silence a judicial sentence, or the time taken to uncover his own response?

He went back to looking at the silent television, the endlessly looping images of his burning home. The Sergeant sat with him and let his fear and his hope drain away into the floor, until they were both just there, in the room. In a moment, something would happen, but not yet. For now, the offer was there, and all its capacity for hurt.

'She is there,' the boy said, tonelessly. He pointed at the shanty. 'In the south side, at the edge. Sometimes she is there. Sometimes in the mountains. She comes and goes.' He named a street.

The Sergeant nodded. 'Is she there at the moment?'

'She wasn't,' the boy said. 'But now she may be.'

'Won't she stay away?' The Sergeant pointed at the screen.

'No,' the boy said. 'The fires are pretty.'

'Will she . . . will she be all right?' Amidst the burning town.

'No. Yes.' The boy shrugged. 'Unknown unknown, right? But she will not be kept safe. She does what she does. They will come to her house or they will not. Burn it or not. She will be there, she will flee, she will stay. *Kswah swah*.'

No, the Sergeant realised. *Of course. He cannot compel her, in this or in anything. Anyone else he can bargain with, cajole and haggle. He can trade or finesse. But for her he has only himself, and he is a currency she does not recognise.*

'Like hell.' The words slipped out of him, and he smiled to take the sting. 'I've dealt with refugees before, who didn't want to come. Done medical evacuation, too. Done it all. You can't pick her up and pop her over your shoulder because that would be disrespectful and I understand that. But I bloody can, if that's what it takes.'

He saw the boy's eyes widen, as if this was an answer he had never considered, and perhaps it was. Then the Sergeant's shoulder was once more being hugged, fiercely and breathlessly, and his sleeve was wet with tears. *You do a lot of crying, don't you?* he thought, wonderingly. *But then, I suppose I did, too, when I was little.* And wondered why he no longer did. It wasn't as if the world was notably improved. Although here, now, with the boy looking to him for support in something so important, and accepting his help, perhaps the situation was all right, after all.

The doorbell rang, long and loud, and then again and again, with anger or urgency. *Not rioters*, he thought. *They do not ring the bloody bell.* Someone who respected his house. Inoue, or Kershaw, or even Pechorin.

But it was none of them, and when he opened the door the world was once again upside down.

'It's the only place, Lester,' Dirac said.

The Frenchman stood on the stoop, and beyond him was a small woman with two children, both of them wearing makeshift bandages. The woman was coughing: smoke inhalation, but not terrible. Behind her was a man with a gash down one cheek, and behind him there was a family, and behind them more and more in a straggling line which wound away into the dusk.

The wounded of Beauville were looking for help. And for shelter from the gang, the Sergeant realised. It was medieval. When all else is lost, you go to the keep. He had set himself up for this: he had played the role of British Imperial person, and they had seen him do it and had not needed him. But now they did, and so here they were, and he must open the door and let them in or turn them away into a night filled with likely horrors. He felt the colour drain out of his face.

Dirac shrugged. 'You've got room.'

Which he had, and orders to keep a low profile – but now that they were here, sending them off again would be a story. A better, louder one than just taking them in. No doubt Dirac must be seeing double, leading a snake of fleeing families to the dubious safety of a house which might not want them. And just as surely, he must know that the Sergeant could see the image too, and could not in face of it default, even if he had wished to. *But this is trouble, real trouble. I can feel it coming.*

The Sergeant stepped aside, and waved them in. 'All the way through to the west wing,' he said. 'Get them settled in and I'll turn on the power. The water won't be hot for a few hours. Do they have food?'

'Some.'

'Bloody hell. How many?'

'I did not count.'

The Sergeant threw his hands in the air. Dirac laughed. 'That was almost French.'

'I'll give you French. Good evening, ma'am,' he added automatically to the corpulent matron passing his threshold. 'All the way down to your right and perhaps you'll take charge of the bathroom facilities and make sure decency is observed?'

She nodded stoutly, and carried on.

The boy gazed with wide eyes at the incomers, as if they were something he had never imagined and could not now entirely account for.

'If they fill up the west wing, shove them in the east one, we'll have to board up the windows but it's sound,' the Sergeant said. 'We're keeping this floor for a hospital and the upper rooms here for storage and so on. No one goes in my room or yours, at all, and no one in the comms room or the bloody armoury unless I say so,' *and please let me not have to go that road,* 'and keep a space for the lady we were discussing close to you.'

The boy nodded. 'And the hot Barracuda,' he added firmly.

Dirac choked a little. The Sergeant stifled the desire to argue or to shout at both of them, and ran to the comms room.

'This is Ferris for Africa.'

'Hold, please. Put your thumb on the plate.'

The Sergeant did so.

'Once more, please.'

'Sonny, I will put my thumb somewhere so appalling your grandchildren will walk like Gloucester Old Spots. Get Africa and tell her I said it's a codeword BOHICA.'

There was a suffused silence, and then Africa came on. 'It's me. He's Googling that now, I can tell from the absolutely scandalised expression on his face. Why BOHICA?'

'I have civilian refugees, locals.'

'How many?'

'Lots. A couple of hundred, maybe. Maybe more.'

There was a pause. 'Fuck,' Africa said meditatively.

'Yes, ma'am.'

'And you're letting them in because you have with your usual intelligence spotted the fact that keeping them out would be a front page we can all live without.'

'Yes, ma'am.'

'Good boy.'

'Thank you, ma'am.'

'How did they come to this solution to their problems, Sergeant? Have you been thumbing the scales over there? Flying the flag?'

'A member of an allied force took it into his head to bring them here. He feels it's the safest place within reach of the town.'

'An allied force? Not NatProMan, surely?'

'France, ma'am.'

She snorted. 'I should have known. All right, then. Continue to use your initiative, very discreetly. Take necessary steps. And yes, I will fall on you from a great height if you bollocks it up, so don't. Familiar?'

'Story of my life, ma'am.'

'You and me both.'

Kathy Hasp arrived a few moments later on a Triumph motorcycle which must have been more than sixty years old. She rolled the bike directly into the shack which served Brighton House as a garage, tacitly claiming its security in the face of the desperate line of men and women queued up outside the door. There was a rifle carrier by the front tyre and Hasp had adapted this to hold a small digital video camera, which she slapped onto her shoulder as she walked over to the door. Her face was devoid of the overly demonstrative expression she wore for the network. She looked tired and grey.

'Hey, Lester,' she said, by way of greeting.

'Ms Hasp,' he replied.

'Seems you got yourself a relief effort here.'

'Seems so.'

'I thought Her Majesty was sitting this one out.'

'Her Majesty is. But I've got space and a roof and no orders to the contrary, so I can put up a few friends in their time of need, can't I?'

'Old-fashioned hospitality, then.'

The red light on the camera was alight. He'd known it would be, then forgotten. Now he glanced at it for an instant, then away. 'If you like.'

'I do like, Lester. I like very much. It's bad down there.'

He thought of Sandrine, felt the boy somewhere behind him, the acuteness of his focus. 'How bad?'

For answer, she unlimbered the camera and reversed it. In the grainy screen of the eyepiece and without sound, he saw the mission house in flames and a man lying bleeding on the lip of the fountain. Another man, walking by, paused for a moment and rolled him into the water. The bleeding man held himself up for a moment, and then looked straight at Hasp's camera.

He lay down on his back in the water, and breathed out.

The other man watched for a while, and then walked away, vanishing into an angry crowd.

The Sergeant leaned away from the eyepiece. Kathy Hasp looked at him.

'They'll see what's happening here, Lester.'

'I know.'

'They'll see and they won't like it and they'll come up here like a fucking Frankenstein movie with torches and pitchforks and they'll burn this place down with everyone inside. You're making an opposition, someone they can get to.'

'We're not hurting anyone.'

She looked at him curiously. 'You do know that never makes any difference, right?'

'What will you do?' he returned a little sharply.

She patted the camera without pride. 'It's all I *can* do.'

He nodded. 'Same here.' She winced in acknowledgement. *Well, good.* 'Do you want to come inside? Get some shots of the before?'

'Sure. We've got time.'

'How much time?'

287

She thought about it. 'Maybe an hour and a half before they set off. But they won't walk it, not all of them. There'll be trucks. You know there will.'

He hesitated. 'We have some guns, you know. Some other stuff.'

'You gonna use 'em?'

'I'm a soldier.' She knew he'd dodged the question, but she didn't follow up. He suspected she wanted to run away, but that she wouldn't because that would be worse. He wondered how often she felt that, if she just lived from one bloody awful obligation to another. A lot of the correspondents drank, or drugged, or fucked up a hurricane, and a lot of them did all of the above, but what they were addicted to was horror, and that was the thing they'd never kick.

She walked past him into the house.

He set the boy to showing Kathy Hasp around, made sure everyone knew Dirac was in charge if he himself could not be found, then slipped quietly away. He took a moment to wonder whether this was still the right thing to do, whether Sandrine was better off where she was. *Yes, and no.* Brighton House was defensible, if it came to it. Her own, these nights, was so much kindling.

The armoury corridor was long and very quiet. The Sergeant could hear all the noises from the rest of the house – people shuffling and settling, the sound of the Witch complaining about a lack of something or other, a child wailing, even quiet laughter – but they were far away. The corridor belonged to him and his footsteps.

He had locked the partition behind him and the closed space felt thick, as if he were going down the aisle of a great cathedral and at the far end his bride or his confession would be waiting for him.

The metal door resisted. He leaned on it and there was a brief moment of stasis before it swung open. He went inside and opened the burn bag. The mask was just as he had left it, a whisper of silica spray around the cheeks. It looked like a cast-off undergarment from a very particular sort of brothel. The front armour plate was perfect, the back one ruined.

He discarded the useless plate, selected another from store and slipped it home, then found a combat firefighting suit and put the bottom half on, added the armour and then the long coat over the top. He pulled on the utility belt, stuffing random items into the empty places: flare, truncheon, taser, hand-strobe, smoke canisters and anything else which would fit. On reflection, he reloaded the sharkpunch and tucked it away, then looked in the mirror. Without the mask and with the coat zipped up, he was just a rescue worker, just good old Lester come to help.

He slipped out of the side door into the garage shack, and saw Kathy Hasp's motorcycle. On instinct, he walked over to it. The key was in the well under the saddle.

Two hundred metres beyond Brighton House along the coast road there was a track leading down to the sea. It was overgrown now – the tiny hamlet it had served having faded not in this most recent upheaval but long before, when the chemical men first set foot on the island with promises of wealth and modernity – but the baked earth remained solid underfoot. The Sergeant rolled the bike silently onto the path, and then stood for a moment in the dusk, scenting tomatoes on the wind.

This is the world, he thought. *And I am in it.*

He held the mask in his hands like a communion cup, and ducked his face to meet it. The moist interior surface sealed against his skin. The tomato smell faded, replaced by the antiseptic base note of the mask and a whisper of his own sweat.

He climbed aboard the motorcycle and started it up, then charged it out onto the road in one convulsive movement, waiting until he was pointed at the town of Beauville before turning on the lights. The nearest refugees flinched away from the sudden clap of sound, then ran from the road. *No. Not the Quads. Me.* He was seeing one face in ten, a brief impression as his eyes

289

skipped from one to the next, but Jesus, there were a lot of them, on makeshift crutches and leaning on one another, bleeding and beaten and burned.

He must seem to come from nowhere, the clap of sound and then the light: a ghost rider – or so he hoped – like the ones in the song. He roared past them, down to the town and the flames.

The endless line of refugees flew by, occasional single faces sticking briefly in his vision, their desperation or fatigue or plain boredom filling his mind for an instant before being swallowed by the sound of the road and the certainty which he felt now.

This was rash. There was no cloud cover, no concealment. If NatProMan was watching, they would see him, they would be able to trace him back to the house – although the house was full now, he realised, rather than empty, and his address would yield nothing more than confusion. The refugees sheltered him even as he sheltered them.

He had learned from watching Shola's body fall: a single man could not adequately defend himself except by attacking. If he had known that Shola's killers – now ash on the wind, and falling probably on the ship which had ordered both their original mission and their subsequent destruction – if he had known that they were coming, he could have met them, stood them down, or beaten them before their attack could find its place. After they had begun was already too late, the shotgun blast tearing through the foppish silk shirt.

But tonight, in the same position almost exactly, he did know. There were killers preparing now, and they would come into his house to do murder.

He would go to Sandrine, and then he would see about the Quads.

He took the north road towards the shanty and left the refugees behind, the seemingly endless line of them and their need.

17. Sandrine

He passed around the edge of the town proper, where the fires were far between. The buildings were more cursory in the first place, tin roofs and breeze-block construction, poverty in the spliced power lines and the drainage ditches which were not quite open sewers. He saw stragglers from the riots, either fleeing or looking for something worth the trouble to destroy, and turned the bike into the cheek-by-jowl warren of the shanty. Immediately he heard shouting, veered towards it knowing it for trouble, for a wrong thing. Beauville, something inside him still insisted, was a good place. It was filled with good people. They were ordinary people, venal people, even stupid people, but they were rarely mean and this was beyond them, should be beyond them, should have stayed in the pit of wretched possibility for the island even in its dying. It had been created out of malice.

The bike slid and skittered on the loose rubble in the alleys, so he abandoned it. He was close enough to Sandrine's house to walk, and he would need in any case a better transport if he must abduct her. He could hardly ride with a screaming woman across his handlebars – in his mind's eye he saw the journey, the slender, fragile legs of his patient-captive thrashing and distracting him, catching on some obstacle at speed and shattering, pulling her from the saddle to a red ruin on the road. He pushed the thought away and walked on, hanging close to the walls as if he was back in contested Baghdad.

In a marketplace he came upon a living fragment of the mob, perhaps two dozen strong. The square was illuminated by the headlights of a quad bike, and the Quad himself stood full height on his saddle and snarled as the mob tormented a small family group cowering by the water pump. In one way that was good: the Quads were dispersed rather than gathered, which meant that there was time to see to the boy's mother before dealing with the attack on Brighton House. But for these people, it was bad, because the Quad was here and so were they.

In the hard white light the victims looked stark and ill: a woman, a young man, a child. He didn't know whether the child was male or female, not that it mattered, and he couldn't imagine what their crime had been. Perhaps they had dared to try to put out a fire, or perhaps they were identifiably from the wrong part of the shanty, or possibly the woman had refused to sleep with someone, or the young man had, or just had the wrong sort of face. Tonight it was all one. Tonight it was a lottery, and they had lost. The first bottles were flying, smashing on the ground in front of them, splinters spattering over their feet and lower legs. The child flinched and howled, the young man lifted it and offered his back as a shield. *Good lad.*

The Sergeant moved around the shadows of the square until he was directly behind the Quad. He made no particular effort at concealment, and on the fringes of the mob people glimpsed him and turned, so that by the time he had reached his chosen position fully half the mob was looking not at the Quad nor his victims but into the darkness for something they could not see, blinded as they were by the bright light from the bike. The bottles slowed and stopped, and a hush fell over the square.

The Sergeant whispered, 'Go home.' And heard the mask turn it into something harsh and cold. 'Go home,' he said again, louder, and then he shouted it and heard the echo bounce off the far walls of the square, a noise from a torture room or a surgeon's cutting station.

Between him and the Quad was an open space like a road, and he stepped into it, his anger mounting until he was running and the Quad was staring open-mouthed, so the Sergeant drove his fist into the offered target and followed the staggering man over the front of the bike and down, landing on him with both knees and hearing a gasp and a crunch of collarbone. He reared up and hit the man three more times, feeling the gloves soak up punishment which would have cracked his knuckles, knowing the Quad's cheekbones were not so protected. The man slumped, coughing, then gasping as each convulsion shook the broken bones in his face. The Sergeant dragged him towards the family by the pump and left him lying in the broken glass. He looked at the mob.

The square emptied. He turned and found the family had vanished too, into the night.

A few minutes later, when he found Sandrine's house, it was already burning.

He went in anyway.

The lower floor was filled with smoke, and breathing through the mask was like taking a mouthful of tea straight from the pot. He trusted the filter would protect his lungs, but there was no saliva in his mouth and his throat felt like dry wood. His teeth grew uncomfortably hot to the touch. He was an astronaut on Mars, or Venus, or whichever of them was hot and dark. He saw porcelain ducks on the wall. His parents had had ducks like that. They might even have been from the same factory. For all he knew they were the same ducks, travelled by some weird route across the world to see him die just as they had seen his first days after his mother brought him home from the hospital.

The house was one of the old farm cottages which had been swallowed by Beauville's expansion and hemmed in by concrete-slab homes, lean-to shacks and the permanent tents of the inner shanty's markets. The walls and stairs were made of stone. Everything else was dry wood. He judged he had less than two minutes.

On the upper landing there was more smoke but less flame. He slammed open one door, then another, sure he was getting the firefighting all wrong, but sure as well that it didn't matter because the house was doomed anyway and anyone in it too unless they got out right now.

He found her lying in the middle of the bedroom floor, a roiling cloud stretched above her like a comforter, and thought with relief that she had made a good choice, up to a point. He could have wished that she would just abandon the house through the window onto the adjoining roof – he glanced out, saw that it was the side to which the fire had not spread – but then he would not have found her, would not be able to take her back to her son. The son she didn't know.

But she ignored him, flat on her tummy and staring down at the wooden boards. They must be painfully hot, and the steam coming up through the cracks must be scorching, but she was resting on some sort of tray or panel. Her expression was intent. What was she doing?

A tendril of flame leaped up a few inches from her face, and she smiled in delight.

He realised she was lying on a full-length mirror on the floor of her burning house, watching the fire. A moment later another jet was erupting between the cracks and then another and he knew the house was giving up, that the time was now. She clapped.

He offered her his hand but she did not acknowledge him, so he scooped her up by the hips and lifted her, his legs and lower back protesting, until she was a wriggling, objecting burden in his arms and he was lunging for the window, feeling the boards sag under him as he went and expecting at any moment to fall into the inferno below, a thing he might just about survive but which would see her roast in his arms in an instant, and that would make an end of Lester Ferris, he was fairly sure, in any form he recognised now.

He lowered his head and hunched as he dived out of the window, felt the catch give way rather than the wood and glass, so no shower of razors, thank God, followed them down onto the next roof. He landed too hard and felt something crack, then realised with relief when no pain followed that it had not been his ankle. He had just enough time to wonder what that meant, and then they crashed through to the ground floor. He picked himself up, ready to fight, but the room was quiet and when he turned on a torch he saw it had until recently been some sort of vegetable stall. A mongrel pup had been sleeping in the corner, and the woman immediately shied a cobble at it, glowering. The mongrel yipped and scuttled out, and she mellowed again immediately, as if that was all it took to restore order to the world.

Sandrine – he had no doubt that it was she, he knew the lines of her face by proxy, and there was a weird disfocus to her expression which spoke of a damaged or remade intelligence – peered at him. Her hand reached out hesitantly to touch the mask, then sank to poke experimentally at the proboscis.

'I've come to take you somewhere,' he said, then cursed himself as the reassuring words came out metallic and wild.

But she smiled in approval and poked the mask again as if he had done something clever and interesting. She dived forward and began to investigate him, pat him down and follow the contours of his body in frank appraisal. It was not a sexual curiosity, but something else. She had never seen a man in a mask like this. He was a new thing. New things pleased her, so she wanted to know as much as possible about him. When she had roved, rapidly, all over him, and established that he felt essentially the same as other men, she frowned in disappointment and stepped away.

'It's not safe.' He tried again. 'You have to come with me.' He made a beckoning gesture. Did she understand language, even though she could not speak? Did waving your hands count as language? Or was she so completely alien now that it didn't matter, that anything he might attempt to tell her would just be sound and light? Operationally speaking, he realised, he should probably have asked more questions at the beginning.

'There is a boy.' He was pantomiming a small, slim person, her son, knowing that she would make nothing of it. 'Your son, the

295

one you don't remember. He still loves you and I love him,' and that was his first time saying that aloud. 'I came to rescue you. To bring you to him.' He thought he saw a glimmer of understanding in her face, of happiness or assent, but then she shrugged and wandered away to look at the damage they had done.

He could not leave her here. She was vulnerable to the burning town and to the mob. She was an infant. He realised, in passing, that he had been wrong about something fundamental: no one looked after the boy. When he went away, it was not to be cared for but to care. His mother was his unwitting ward. All seeming evidence to the contrary was proof rather of his self-sufficiency. The comic books he provided for himself; the laptop, the phone, the food – for both of them, no doubt. He was in many ways already grown, waiting only for his body to catch up with his life.

The Sergeant felt a twinge of fellow feeling, unexpected. He had up to a point taken care of his father, when Arthur Ferris had withdrawn to his television set and his late-onset diabetes and smoked himself fiercely towards the plot beside his wife. Young Lester had forged school notes and worked odd jobs and thought he was looking out for number one, but somehow he had put food on the table for his dad as well, and seen him through the few remaining years. His sister, too, of course, but she had been older and already on her way. She had never entirely understood how much their father had ground to a halt, because he freshened up for her, at his son's insistence, and they were complicit, if in no other way, in concealing the decay. But it had been nothing like this, not really. Or, only somewhat.

His vision flashed white and he was lifted from his feet, a solid impact taking him in the right kidney and hurling him forward. A knife blade, he realised, deflected by the links of chain woven into the vest, the power of it still passed to his body, if spread wide enough to avoid penetration. *I'll piss pink all week*, he thought sourly, and rolled as fast as he could to avoid a stamping boot. *If I get the chance.*

He kept rolling and surged to his feet, bounced off a wall and swirled the torch around the room. There were two of them, ordinary thugs with ugly expressions. Their attention was on him but their goal was Sandrine. He looked for hunger and rape and, curiously, couldn't see it. Just intent. The nearer one was flourishing the knife at him, the other had a short billy club. *Take the blade, but don't imagine the billy's not a problem.*

The Sergeant slowed, feigning disorientation, lashed out wildly when the man feinted, and invited a circular stab low at his left side, blocked it early and clipped the elbow with the torch to bend it, driving the weapon hand up along his enemy's spine until the shoulder dislocated, then putting his knee upwards through the man's face. Shadows danced and he kept moving, trusting in motion to keep him safe. The billy man rushed in belatedly – they weren't used to working as a team, probably wouldn't do it again – and the Sergeant threw his first target into the line of attack to ward him off. The knife skittered away and its owner collapsed, moaning.

The other man came on. The Sergeant remembered the taser but had no time to reach it as the man attacked, leading with his weak hand, the billy held in reserve for a quick finish. The Sergeant thrust the torch forward instead, directing the blinding light into the billy man's face. The man scuttled back and reset his feet.

Sandrine drove the discarded knife in a straight line from the shoulder, hips twisting, power coming out of the legs and the strength of her entire body. The blade went through the back of the billy man's skull and continued until the point made a soft sound against his forehead. She continued the spiral to bring the arm back, heel of the hand leading and the blade outward, then dropped the knife. He thought it was completely mysterious to her how she had come to be holding it in the first place. The corpse fell at the same time, like a sack.

She looked at the Sergeant, then dropped to her knees and drew the tiger from the stele on his chest, perfectly, in blood on the floor. She looked at him again as if to say that finished the matter, and walked out of the door. He was fairly sure she had no understanding of what had passed, that she had killed a man, and a worm of suspicion was gnawing in him that this was because she only barely grasped what it meant that he had ever been alive. The world – the island – was one piece to her. Some of it moved, and some of it did not, and that was all.

He stared after her, wondering how he would get her back to Brighton House, because force seemed a far less practicable option than it had five minutes before, and by the time he heard the engine outside and launched himself at the door he was too late.

Sandrine was in the back seat of an open white jeep, and beside her sat a woman the Sergeant did not recognise. The woman was actually singing, high and clear, and Sandrine, with blood still wet on her fingertips, was listening to her in placid fascination.

The driver saw the Sergeant and took off for the main road.

He ran flat out and kept the jeep in view, pale and angular and framed by the weird brown clouds at the edges of his vision. He sucked air, spat, and pushed his legs harder. The jeep meant Sandrine and Sandrine belonged to the boy and he had promised to get her. For as long as he could see it he could catch up, and that was the target, the plan. That was the order from authority, even if authority in this case was him.

He could keep up and even gain ground while they were in the shanty, because the narrow streets twisted and turned and the jeep was restricted to a few larger roads and even those were treacherous, especially now. He could run in a straight line and know roughly where they would have to turn and slow, where he might make up for time lost when their route was clear and the engine powered away from him, impossibly far ahead. For a few hundred yards he found himself running along the roofs of market stalls. He wasn't sure how he'd got up there, vaguely recalled climbing some stairs to avoid a pile of rubble which had slouched sideways from a burned brick bakery into his path, remembered leaping insanely and making it, stumbling on and regaining his feet. Faces turned towards him, rioters and others peered up and wondered. He was drawing a crowd and that was bad, he was moonlit and that was bloody stupid, a good sniper would take about a second to pick him off. He should get down onto the street but then he might not be able to see the jeep when it turned at the T-junction ahead, might pick wrong and lose her. Then the stalls just stopped and he dropped off the last one, muscles white agony, and found that he had not fallen, was not flat on his back, but still moving. Behind him there were people shouting, pointing. *Tigerman! Tigerman!* He didn't care. They had torches, both electrical and the old-fashioned kind, and they were following, watching. So long as they stayed back. So long as no one shot him, tripped him, ambushed him, the only important thing was ahead. This was running you could die of, the kind that had killed – the Sergeant, irrelevantly, had always been able to remember the man's name since learning it at school, a piece of military trivia which hadn't impressed the recruiter – Pheidippides of Athens after the original Marathon.

Bugger Marathon. And then, irrelevantly: *And they call them 'Snickers' now, anyway.* Old anger. Chocolate bars should not take on new identities. They should be content with who they were.

He rounded a bend and saw a man threatening a woman with a broken bottle. Not Sandrine, no. Just a woman. Just a man.

He surged past, twisting his body and scything his elbow as he unwound. He was in the air when the blow landed: perfect technique. The impact took the man across the ear, snapped his head around. He fell and stayed down. The Sergeant's motion was pure and unaffected, and he ran on. Behind him there was another shout, like an amen in a charismatic church or the roar of fury from a football crowd. The jeep went left. So did he. The road seemed to bear him up, as if the island's constant vibration was for this purpose, to power his feet as he chased the jeep. Was he catching up? Maybe. Not long now. Not long. Close enough, soon, to do something, use the belt. Flashbang? Taser? Fire extinguisher? Something something something. Anything. Catch up.

In between accelerations, he could hear the woman in the back seat singing. *'Danny Boy', for fuck's sake. Enough with Danny bloody Boy! Change the record.* But 'Danny Boy' seemed to be working well enough, Sandrine was still calm. Or perhaps she was just enjoying the ride. She glanced back and saw him, watched him run. '. . . *From glen to glen, and down the mountainside* . . .'

Shit.

The jeep swerved and knocked out the supporting post of a wooden awning just ahead of him. He had his hand at his belt for a stun grenade, had to abandon it for balance, saw a girl not five years old staring up and lifted her, lifted her away and she wailed because he'd banged her head against the metal plate on his chest, bloody HELL she was heavy, so small to be that heavy, and the fucking awning was coming down on them both and of course it would have a water tank on it this end, it just would, so he swerved and smashed his way through a plywood board as the structure came down behind him, sprawled and let her find her own balance, scraped himself up and carried on but he was slowing, slowing, too slow and the jeep was escaping and FUCK FUCK FUCK! All for nothing if he didn't find more.

He found more. Hadn't run like this from Pechorin's lot. That had been rehearsal. Light training. Hadn't run like this in his life, never cared this much. Stupid old man. Water sluiced across the road behind him, the crowd splashed through it. *Tigerman!* With his luck he'd catch Sandrine and they would burn him, burn her, stake them out like a dog on a telegraph pole. Nothing left in the tank. His tank, not the jeep, fucking jeep was fine. Fucking John Henry this was, man versus machine and all the odds stacked. He had seconds. Seconds. Make it count make it count make it—

And here was more trouble, more stupid, stupid, in-the-way trouble. Beneseffe and his dockmen – *thieves and brigands and smugglers all, if we're honest,* so what was happening was not so much good versus evil as it was demarcation and turf – were facing off against a few Quads and their hangers-on, and the jeep piled on through them, and no, no, no NO, of course it wasn't just a few Quads it was all of them, and here were the trucks, the waiting trucks to carry the mob up the hill. This wasn't a chance encounter, it was a last stand. He'd been unfair to Beneseffe, this was pro bono after all. Trucks and flatbeds and bikes and all for Brighton House, all ready for the burning, that was how you got a mob to go up a hill: you laid on transport.

And press. Press bloody everywhere, Kathy Hasp following her nose and commandeering someone's car, everyone else following Kathy Hasp, all there to cover the endgame of British Colonial rule on Mancreu. See the kick-off, rush up the hill to catch the first Molotov cocktail and then be in time for the massacre, win a Pulitzer and home before bedtime.

He looked around and realised he was standing by the mission house. Up on the weathervane was the pelican, dislodged from her perch and apparently looking to him to sort it all out. Like everyone else. He stood at the intersection of a huge number of paths and powers, all gathered by accident in this one place. He: Tigerman.

And he had stopped running. Where was Sandrine?

The jeep rolled out of the far side of the square onto the main road. Clear path to the docks now, to the Fleet, to NatProMan, to anywhere – wherever they were going, it didn't matter. If he'd been faster. If he'd been twenty instead of nearly forty – although, no. Never, really; not unless he'd been Mo Farah and he wasn't. And this was his business, right here, right now.

He heard the sound of the engine fade away, and turned to face the Quads. If he took off his mask, Beneseffe might help him. But if he took off his mask, the mob would tear him apart and Africa would scatter what was left to the four winds, and it still

301

wouldn't help anyone and he'd never have a chance to get Sandrine back from wherever she ended up.

He rolled his head around slowly on his neck as if this was what it had been about, as if he had planned everything to bring them all to this moment. The sound of his breathing, amplified and alarming, filled the square. He took the sharppunch from his belt and held it in his right hand, twirled it like a swordsman, then threw his left hand forward in a stabbing gesture that reminded him instantly of Sandrine and her knife. With his index finger, he indicated the biggest and ugliest of the Quads, hanging by one arm from the fountain, and fixed his eyes – the mask's eyes – on the Quad's face. He did not speak. He just pointed, and waited, and let the challenge stand.

Waited.

And waited.

And the Quad did not come.

The Sergeant would fall on his knees soon. Would pass out. Nothing in his life had prepared his body for that pointless dash through the backstreets. He measured it in his mind. Three miles? Four? At top speed, desperation speed. He would fall, surely, any moment now. He shifted his feet, feeling for the vibration in the ground, and realised that it had stopped, that for the first time in days everything was still. He saw everyone else realise it too, with relief and an unlikely sense of loss.

Something was happening at the back of the crowd. A weird susurrus was spreading out in waves, words exchanged and shared, accounts of witnesses and testimonies, and out of all of them emerged that one word so that it ebbed and flowed in the tide of whispers but never vanished, and moment by moment it actually grew, strengthened and unified, and here was a young man with a phone holding it high for others to see – video, more bloody video, always someone. But now it seemed there were more cameras, more angles, and the square was lit as if by candles with glowing screens and tiny cameo recordings. Tigerman flew from

302

a burning house with a sick woman in his arms. He stopped a rape, or a murder. He rescued a child. He chased, always, impossibly and indefatigably, chased an abduction by someone in a foreign car, a Fleet car, chased and would not give up even though his breathing rasped and his feet twisted. *Tigerman*. And then, here, at last, he let it go, because for all that he had done in his quest, this moment in the square was more important, not to him but to them. *Tigerman. Tigerman. Tigerman.* He was not Fleet. He was not Britain or America or France or anywhere except Mancreu, Mancreu looking out for its own. *Tigerman, Tigerman, Tigerman*, and the noise was louder than anything he had ever heard. *Tigerman*, for Mancreu, because they needed him so very, very much.

The Quad shook his head, threw his mask down on the ground.

They carried the Sergeant through the town, and where they went they put out the fires. Small groups broke away from the main throng and became anything from street sweepers to civil engineers, and road by road and house by house the sound of Beauville became a goosegabble of hammering and mending.

The Quads were gone, not merely vanished or fled but publicly retired, even unmade. As one they rolled their bikes into the harbour and knelt – to the Sergeant's vast embarrassment – to receive his absolution. He wanted to tell them all to apologise to the old lady for killing her dog. And to anyone else whose beloved pet they had crucified. But then he would have to take them to task for sins more dire and ultimately there would be blood, again. It was not his choice to make, and he had no desire, anyway, to see them dangle and kick from the dockyard cranes. This, though, surely this was too much?

He cast around for an escape but found none, so he duly placed a gloved hand on each of twenty heads and pressed down without words, and saw that half of them were weeping and prostrating themselves and had to be lifted up by the crowd. They would make redress where they could and carry the guilt otherwise, and that was all that the world offered anyone, for crimes and omissions large or small.

Everywhere, the press pack followed. They spoke to men and women on the fringes of the crowd, but when they occasionally ventured closer the crowd drew together to keep them away. Tigerman was a mystery, and they did not want him unmasked, did not want him to promise things or demand things, did not like it when he spoke at all. His existence was his meaning, and if he tried to encapsulate himself he might get it wrong. Which was entirely acceptable to the man inside the mask, whose stubble was beginning to itch against the slick surface, and who wanted above all else to get away, to lie down and sleep. He had work. He had work and he must find Sandrine for the boy, he must pretend again to look for himself, to track himself across the island. He must speculate with Arno. He must find out about his powers and responsibilities towards adopted quasi-orphans and how he could account for and care for the boy's mother.

The boy. The boy had a name. He had read it, but it had felt unfitting and he had forgotten it. Boy. Boy. Son? He whispered the word and heard it echo, saw the nearest members of the crowd flinch slightly.

His focus was fading, his eyelids appallingly heavy. Soon he would black out or sleep, and there would be very little difference. He had to get away. But they were relentless: he must see everything, bless everything, and how long before they took him to the NatProMan building and expected it to fall before him like the walls of Jericho? And would Kershaw and Arno be circumspect with the Tigerman at their gates, or would they reckon to snatch him first and apologise later, to unravel the mystery? He was walking through water, through thick, clear oil, and it was cold.

And then he was rescued.

As they walked along the harbour front and he nodded to the teams of men and women clearing away the rubble of Beneseffe's line in the sand, five men emerged from a side road wearing gas masks and firefighting gear and stood in a silent line, not so much like soldiers or workmen as monks at their offices. There was a solemnity about them, a sense of ritual and place.

The gear they wore was not his gear – not from his armoury – but a hodgepodge of local stuff. All the same it had been cobbled together somehow to make it just a little Tigerman-ish, to suggest his suit without actually being like it. They wore long coats and let their arms hang by their sides. They did not move or speak, they just waited in the faint light of the predawn. The crowd slowed and stopped, and somehow knew that they must let him go, that it was time.

Knowing it was intended, and too tired to doubt that it was wise, he walked slowly through the crowd and felt reverent hands reach out to touch him as he passed, to take a blessing from his back and shoulders, touch the stele on his chest.

The masked men did not acknowledge him as he walked between them. They did not turn their heads. Instead, as soon as he was through them they folded in behind him like an honour guard, and then streamed around him, ahead of him into an empty house and out again, heading in different directions all at once so that his own path became curiously invisible. As the last one peeled away he gave the Sergeant a gentle push: *go straight ahead*.

He managed one last effort, made his feet work, wished he could take off his heavy coat, the utility belt with all its useless toys.

Outside, in a backstreet, a car was waiting for him, battered and a little scorched. Flotsam, like him. He climbed in.

'Just friends,' the boy said hastily, gesturing back along the side road as he drove off. 'They do not know you. Know only that Tigerman must disappear now, that we help him. They do not ask how I know. It is holy now.'

The Sergeant nodded, too tired to worry.

'That was leet,' the boy said after a pause. 'It was the most leet. Onehunnerten pro cent thirteen thirty-seven. You are full of win.'

'I didn't get her,' the Sergeant murmured.

'I saw. Everyone saw. Everyone in the world. You tried so hard and it was not possible. You are Elvis. More famous than Jesus Christ. Also higher approval ratings. You saved everyone. No riots. No fire. All good.'

'But I didn't catch up. Too slow. I'm sorry.' He looked over. He had taken off the mask but he wanted to take it off again, to meet the boy's eyes more frankly and make him understand the failure. *Please don't forgive me. Please. I can't stand it.* 'I didn't get her. I'm sorry.'

The boy looked back at him with a strange, merciless certainty. 'You will,' he said simply. 'You are full of win.'

306

18. Invisible

Yesterday, Mancreu had been a footnote. Today it was the world stage. If the press pack had been unprecedented before, now it threatened to sink the island with its weight. More journalists were arriving every hour. They had their own helicopters, their own boats. One of the big networks bought and reopened the Post House Hotel, bringing in generators and satellite dishes and even carpet, and Beauville looked suddenly as if it was enjoying a new heyday, its bars full and money flowing in.

There had been, indeed, cameras everywhere, small and mostly crappy but good enough for TV – good enough to give live news some real verisimilitude. And when you cut it together the way they had it was like a movie: Tigerman bursting from a burning building, smashing through a wall. He raised an army and faced down a gang. He chased a car on foot and near as dammit caught his prey. And then he vanished with the aid of his mysterious minions into the night, leaving his deeds unexplained and self-explanatory. Meat enough for a dozen stories and substories, for analyses and commentaries, and all of it allowed them to play that footage again, to show what one man – one hero – could do on a dark night in a town on the edge. And – despite all editorial efforts – the question was beginning to form in the unspoken and the tacit: how much did all this have to do with that cluster of dark ships glimpsed in the corner of the frame?

The boy reported – after the Sergeant had slept for a few hours, which was not nearly enough – that YouTube had actually gone down for ten minutes under the weight of traffic. The story was truly global, truly immense: not Obama, not Justin Bieber, not

Psy and not Bin Laden had ever touched this, he said. Not Khaled Saeed and not Mohamed Bouazizi, either. If Pippa Middleton and Megan Fox had announced their intention to marry during a live theatrical production of *50 Shades of Grey* starring Benedict Cumberbatch, and then taken off their clothes to reveal their bodies tattooed with the text of the eighth Harry Potter novel, they might just have approached this level of frenzy. But probably not, the boy said, because not everyone liked Benedict Cumberbatch. If you asked the boy, personally, he would say that Robert Downey Jr's Sherlock Holmes possessed fractionally more win, although no one could replace Basil Rathbone because he was entirely the godhead.

'The godhead,' the boy repeated. And then: 'I must go. Find out stuff. Do things. Mojo never sleeps.' But perhaps the boy might, the Sergeant thought: the effervescent eyes were strained and red. Even this prodigious child was not endless.

As if in answer to this thought, the boy turned and very deliberately went into the guest room which was set aside for his occasional use and put his bag on the bed. 'I will come back here,' he said.

The Sergeant called Africa, but she was engaged elsewhere. The secretary promised he would have her ring back. It sounded very much as if he wouldn't.

Kathy Hasp caught up with him in the main hall.

'Fucker stole my motorbike,' she said. 'That is fucking cheeky, is what that is. But it's also a great story, right?'

'I suppose.'

'So come on, Consul. What's the word from on high?'

'Oh, nothing. Carry on as usual. And it's Brevet-Consul. I'm not a diplomat.'

She shrugged. *You're in the chair.* 'Well, okay, what do you think? You were pretty brave yourself, Lester. You were ready to have a real old siege here, face down the barbarians, hey?'

He realised she was interviewing him. 'I'm afraid I can't talk about it.'

'But it was a pretty big deal. And what happened down there, that woman in the jeep, what was that about?'

'I can't talk about the kidnapping, either.'

She shrugged. 'I suppose. But was it really a kidnapping if there's no law?'

He growled. 'Yes, it bloody was, and whoever did it should be in prison. That woman has a family.' He shook his head. 'Personal opinion, that is. Not official. All right?'

'Personal opinion,' she agreed, and wandered away again, humming. He stared after her for a moment, knowing he'd gone wrong and not knowing how, by what arcane rule of journalism she had won and he had put his foot in it.

Bugger.

The less seriously injured refugees drifted away to assist in the clean-up, and to see the sights. Tigerman's Run had become an instant local pilgrimage. The more sorely hurt remained where they were, though the Witch was able to recruit some assistants to tend them and get some rest herself. White Raoul sat over her, watched her with his hand on her head, and she pressed against it as if plugging in. The scrivener eyed the Sergeant for a long moment, and then slowly nodded. The look on his face was not exactly approval. It was more that inevitability had arrived without as much pain as there could have been. *You're doing okay, Honest. But it's still a terrible idea.*

Except that the Sergeant wasn't sure about that any more – and even if he had agreed, there was more work for him under the mask because Lester Ferris couldn't retrieve Sandrine, and he had to try. He had made himself the sheriff in this town, and the bad men had come and done a bad thing right in front of him, and that was unacceptable. The more so, because Sandrine's vanishing was convenient to himself, in his quest to make the boy his child, and he would always wonder if he did not go after her whether he had let her slip away last night so that he could steal her son. And the boy would wonder too, or might, and that would be appalling.

So he must have her back from them. From 'them'. There was so much 'them' in all this, so many factions and shadows. Mancreu looked peaceful but was not. The quiet was war in deadlock all the time. A cold war, painted on a grain of rice.

Someone had taken the boy's mother. Someone with resources, most particularly of information, and there were only so many someones of that description around here.

Who profits? The Who or the Why would tell me the Where.

Well, then: what was she that someone should take her away? A mother, a pretty woman, a civilian. She could not be political because she was barely human in her thinking. She was a poor and a dangerous hostage unless one proposed to threaten a child with his mother's execution – again, to what profit? – and they had not released her in favour of someone else when they realised, as they must have, how public their action had become. Sandrine was important because she was Sandrine.

Because she was a victim of the Cloud? Was she special for that? A cure or a commodity? Or a guinea pig? And if the last: a subject to be healed, or a specimen to be dissected?

He considered very carefully how to ask the question, and then went to the comms room.

'Kaiko, it's Lester,' the Sergeant said. 'I have a professional query, so I am calling you on a secure line. Do you have an encrypt button?' He did not say, 'Sorry I haven't been in touch.' She would understand why not, and to imply otherwise would be rude.

'Lester,' she responded gravely, 'this is a Japanese science station. I have more flavours of encryption here than you can possibly imagine. I have a button I can push to delete the entire conversation from your mind after we have had it.' It took him a moment to realise she was joking, and then he found he wanted very much to ask what she would say if she knew he would forget.

He said: 'Oh. Erm.' *Very slick. Brings all the girls to the yard, that does.*

Inoue gave a low snigger. 'Now you are wondering if I really have such a button. Perhaps I do and I use it on you all the time. Maybe we have had many, many extraordinary conversations you do not remember.'

'But *you*'d remember them, right?'

'In every detail, Lester. I have a very good memory.'

He had not really had time to regret the interruption of their rooftop dinner by a missile, but it had niggled at him between waking and sleeping, in rare moments of calm. Now he smiled. It seemed there might, after all, be other rooftops – though when and where? His smile faded.

She took pity on him. 'Push your secure button, Lester. We will see if our wires are compatible.'

He did. He heard a click. Inoue spoke again, and for a moment she was some sort of duck or a coin falling down inside a metal pipe. Then: 'Okay. Can you hear me?'

'Yes.'

'I can hear you. Go ahead and ask your question.'

'What could you learn from a Discharge Cloud victim?'

'What sort of victim? Like burns?'

He shook his head, realised she couldn't see him. 'No. Brain stuff. Language problems.'

'But not a child from the Broca Cloud?'

'No. An adult.'

'Well, maybe a lot. If they were directly affected by the bacteria rather than just the Cloud, a great deal.'

He thought some more. 'What would you need to do?'

'Many examinations. MRI, for sure, lots of blood testing, EEG, maybe interviews.'

'She can't talk.'

Inoue stopped again. 'This is not hypothetical. You have such a person.' Her interest was sharp.

'She's gone now.' He hoped she would not follow that thought. He hoped Arno wouldn't happen to ask her about it.

'How gone?' Again the sharpness.

'I don't know exactly.' He made a leap. 'You said there was a tame team studying the Clouds. A political team. Would they want to see her?'

'We all would. I know who this is. What she is. There was a rumour, but I could not find her. The woman who runs in the fields, dances in the waterfalls. They say she is always joyful, that everything is a mystery to her.'

Yes. Even her son. Even killing a man. He shook the thought away. 'Would they, is there anything they could learn from,' he didn't want to say cutting her up, 'her body?'

'Of course,' Inoue said immediately. Then, 'Oh! You do not mean from a standard physical examination. You mean from vivisection and autopsy. Obduction.'

'It *is* Mancreu,' he said simply.

She made a non-committal noise, and he realised she did not wish to consider that a proper scientist, even a politically motivated one, would do such a thing. 'No,' she said finally. 'Granting that it is a real possibility, which I must because the world is full of bad people and many of them are here: there is nothing to be gained, at least not for a long time, and much to lose. It would be wasteful and there would be no way to get another subject.'

Unless you were prepared to make more like her by hand, as it were, by exposing people to the Clouds at close range. But if you were prepared to do that, and if you could, there was no need to take Sandrine in the first place. Inoue's instinct said no. 'Do you know where the tame team is?'

'Fleet,' she said. 'Of course.'

'Of course,' he echoed.

'You are investigating this?'

'Yes.'

'Good,' she said stoutly. 'They are assholes. Go get 'em, Tiger.'

He felt the bottom drop out of his world, felt his knees turn to jelly and his feet to water, and realised before saying something totally insane that she had no idea, that she was just using a common idiom. 'Thanks,' he replied.

'And after, come and have cookies. I may even make actual food.'

'How's your cooking?'

'If I answer that, Lester, I have to use the forgetting button or you won't come. Go now. I am a very important director scientist, and my minions get confused if I do not oversee their every action.'

'Goodbye, Kaiko.'

'*Au revoir*, Lester.'

He dialled again.

'Jed, it's me.'

'Hi there, Lester.'

'I'm sorry I shouted.'

'So am I. Shall we hug?'

'Fortunately, the telephone does not yet afford us that option.'

'I'm going to come up there and hug you.'

'I would very much prefer not.'

'You stone-faced British jackass! I am calling the car and I'm going to come up there and hug you until you squeak like a giant puppy!'

'This is a consulate, Jed, you can't come in unless I give you permission.'

Laughter. Then: 'It's possible that I got a little pissy back there, under stress. I can completely see where you were coming from. But you see what I was worried about, too.'

'I do.' *I think you were wrong, but I do.* He wondered what unsaid words were hanging in the air on Kershaw's end.

313

'I hear,' Kershaw cleared his throat, 'I hear you pretty much picked up our slack. Took in the wounded, that stuff.'

'It was Dirac's idea.'

'I heard that, too. But it was a good thing, Lester. I can see all the politics of it. You could have sent them away. That would have played, too, in the long run. No one would have blamed you.'

'Jed, I have a question. Feel free to tell me to get lost.'

'Shoot.'

'Who took the girl?'

'What girl?'

'In all the world, Jed, there is only one girl today.'

Kershaw didn't respond immediately. The Sergeant thought he was probably nodding glumly, or pressing the heel of one hand against the middle of his head to ease a headache. 'I don't know, Lester.'

'Off the record, between you and me? Not even a whisper?'

'Cross my heart. It's a mystery. It's like all of a sudden there are these ghosts in the system, these crazy fucking events which are part of someone else's shit and they are playing out in our town. The Tiger Man, for Christ's sake! I'm living in a comic book. It was bad when he just uncovered drugs and beat up soldiers, then it was fine because he went away, then suddenly he's chasing cars full of secret agents through a riot and then he fucking Gandhis the whole thing and everyone goes home! NatProMan is basically a primal-screaming therapy group right now. The Dutch called me this morning to yell at me. The Dutch! Do you have any idea how bad it has to get before the Dutch are pissed?'

'Arno must be doing his nut.'

'If that means what I think it means then yes, he is. All of a sudden no one's taking his calls. He says they're all worried they're part of it and they haven't realised. They're scared they're being manipulated, and they're even more scared he's part of the con.'

'He released Pechorin. I thought that was odd.'

'It was odder than fuck, Lester, and we had words about it, but he made funny faces at me which I assume were supposed to mean that Pechorin is either some kind of secret squirrel from Interpol or the King of Jackassistan's one begotten son.'

'He hardly seems the type.' *Please, oh, please let me not have beaten seven bells out of a policeman undercover.*

'I know, all right? It's post-Sov stuff,' Kershaw grumbled. 'There's a real fine line between government and crooks over there at the best of times, and you did not hear me say that because I greatly respect my colleagues from Kiev and their massive integrity, even if they do occasionally poison the shit out of one another as part of the natural flow of democratic give and take. If there is anyone in the world more fucked in the head than you Brits, which I doubt, it's those assholes. They would totally send a guy like that out into the real world. Although the other thing is, maybe Arno just didn't want someone to blow up the hospital. And I would be totally fine with that logic right now.'

That was something the Sergeant had not even considered. Pechorin might be a target. He knew things, for sure, that the Sergeant wanted to know. *I should have kept hold of him. But if he was disposed to tell me he would have, and if he wasn't I'd be abducting an officer of NatProMan for a hostile interrogation, and London would not be standing foursquare behind me on that decision. Above my paygrade, outside my need to know.*

He was really tired now. How long had it been since he'd slept through the night without fresh bruises? Since he'd just had a cup of tea and a slice of cake?

Kershaw's tone changed, warmed. 'You did good these nights, Lester. Really good. I'm writing a report. You know what Dirac did after he came to you?'

'Sat around and drank booze, I think.'

'Jesus, that guy. He's like a rescue dog in reverse. Okay, I'll put "probably stinko".'

'All right, Jed. I've got to go. Tell Arno I'm still around to consult if he's got time. And thank him for me.'

'Thank him?'

'He did me a favour. Personal thing, but it meant a lot.'

'I will. Oh, Lester?'

'Yes?'

'Is it possible that you are schtupping Kaiko Inoue?'

'You mean Doctor Inoue?'

'Oh, fine, be like that.'

The red phone rang just as he was getting up. He lifted it and the secretary said 'Hold for Africa' in a voice which suggested 'Into Thy hands, O Lord'.

The Sergeant said, 'Okay.'

Africa said: 'Ferris.'

'Here.'

'Why have you pissed in my mead bowl?'

He had never heard this expression. 'What?'

'My mead bowl. My sweet ambrosia, if you prefer. My wine glass. It doesn't really matter, Lester: what I want to know is why you have got up on the table, dropped your trousers, and pissed in it in front of my fucking face?' He found it hard to understand that she had sworn at him. She was not that person. She must know those words, but that she might use them in anger had never occurred to him.

But there was no question that she had. Fury bubbled in her as she went on. 'If that doesn't clarify matters, let me rephrase the question: did I tell you not to talk to reporters?'

Oh.

'Yes, ma'am.'

'And did you happen, in spite of this, to give an interview to an eel-faced little bitch called Hasp? About, I would imagine, twenty minutes ago? So it can't have slipped your mind.'

'I didn't know she was interviewing me. And I said it was a personal opinion.'

'You don't have personal opinions, Lester! You're standing in the house, wearing the bloody hat! You are Britain! Do you understand? You are your country, you are your uniform, and you are me!'

From nowhere, it rose in him, unexpected. 'I thought you were Africa.' He heard her hiss, hurried on. 'I mentioned one issue which is not a major part of the picture here in response to a query I took to be off the record.'

'She is a journalist, Sergeant Ferris. Nothing is off the record if she is within earshot. The interview is happening if she is in the room. The camera is always rolling. The microphone is always live. So now your interview is up. The audio is on the Internet. Your little informal chat is playing, on a loop, on her nasty little news channel. You have added to the burden of what was already shaping up to be a shitty day and I am unhappy with you. Do you understand?'

'Yes, ma'am.'

'And with reference to this specific issue?'

'Ma'am.'

'It is a non-topic. You have no opinion on it, personal or otherwise. Like everything else on Mancreu, it is invisible. All things there are invisible but some things are more invisible than others. Like this. Is that clear?'

'Yes, ma'am.'

'Because if it's *not* clear, Lester, then get a sewing kit and just stitch your fucking mouth closed for the duration. You can eat through a straw. All right?'

She hung up before he could say 'Ma'am.'

More invisible than others.

He sat with the phone in his hands, and knew that he had reached the end of reasonable hesitation. There were two more things which might be permitted to him by integrity before he had to act, or not act, and bear the consequences of the choice. The first thing he might do was go to the headland and look out at the Bay of the Cupped Hands, really look, and see what it was he had ignored since his booted foot first touched the grimy dockside of Port de Beauville, since the Consul had met him and taken his hand.

'It's a good place,' the man had said. 'No, no, keep looking at me and pretend we're exchanging information of towering importance. That's it. Yes, as I say: you'll like it here. But don't get involved. The sheer appalling fuckup of it will eat you alive. Just sit on the veranda and finish the booze. I've laid in extra. That fellow Kershaw's all right – you'll meet him later. Looks like a rodent, but he knows what food should taste like. Don't in the name of God let him talk to you about the war.'

'Which one?'

'Any of them, but most particularly the one with the Nazis. He has that extraordinary idea that the Americans saved us out of the kindness of their hearts rather than us digging in for two long years while they tried to pretend they weren't involved. Oh, no, don't look at the ships out there, the locals consider it rude, just keep your eyes on me. That's right.'

And he, bewildered and barely out of bed, had taken that at face value and never questioned it, had shaped his world around it because it was Mancreu's underpinning, like the dog beneath the flea. *Don't look at the ships.*

So now he might go to the headland and say, 'I see you.' A formal declaration. He had done it before, elsewhere: stared into the dark or the mountains or the sand and made some sort of pledge, given himself a goal or issued a warning. 'I will bring you home'; 'I know you're out there.'

But the Fleet would not hear him and in any case it wasn't the ships out there he had to acknowledge. It was the ones here, in Brighton House, at the back of the comms room.

The comms room desk was a nasty, modern thing, more a trestle table with a laminate top. It was covered in a hotchpotch of digital technology: two phones, an actual one-time pad, a desktop computer and a large brick of plastic which was copier, scanner, fax and printer. The chair in front of it resembled some sort of gibbet or mechanical stork, but was surprisingly cosy with a fleecy airline blanket draped over it. Two desklamps sat at either end of the trestle like bookends, defining the world – and if you turned towards the door they threw a stark shadow from the reinforced lintel across the wall, reminding you that, yes, the comms room could withstand a significant amount of punishment before any hostile force gained entry, giving you time to destroy the files.

And what files would those be? What, on Mancreu, could still be important enough to worry about? The ones in the inappropriately cheery orange filing cabinet – with built-in hard drive and shock-protected battery power supply – in the far corner. The copies of the daily correspondence arriving by email and encrypted transfer, and occasionally by courier pouch, which the Sergeant routinely stamped and put away but did not ever read. The bureaucratic echo of the actual Fleet and the legal niceties surrounding it, all indexed and – there was no verb, he realised, or not one that he knew, for the modern process of tagging with keywords. Indexed, then, and categorised, and sitting there like a crab bloated with rotten fish and carrion.

He did not need to go to the headland to make his challenge. He could do it here. Must, indeed, because the headland was an evasion. This was the stinking corpse in his own house.

The second thing he might do – the only thing, in his adjusted perception – was talk to the boy.

Things were moving rapidly, but not nearly so fast as they would once he possessed himself of the knowledge in those folders and took direct action against a ship in the Bay of the Cupped Hands to retrieve Sandrine. Stumbling over the heroin in the cave had been bad, but it was in the worst event a defensible position. Trading in drugs was too embarrassing to make much of a fuss over in public. Launching a commando raid on a non-official but very much sanctioned intelligence operation would be another sort of thing. It was more than likely that he would fail, and in failing he would be revealed. He had undertaken missions like that before and been lucky, but you had to be clear about the odds and the consequences of failure. The political leadership had to be clear about the cost.

The boy was to all intents and purposes the political leadership. One could argue that he needed to know the extent of the Sergeant's exposure, and what he might otherwise offer: a home, a name. A father.

But one might also say that the boy was a child and that it was the job of a father, for just a little longer, to spare his son this sort of choice: *I can try to save your mother, but it may mean that I die or am taken from you.* An absurd decision, grinding one desperation against another – the sort of dilemma beloved of the four-colour villains in the boy's comic books. Forcing him to choose was a destruction in all directions: whatever answer he gave he must hate, and by extension hate to some degree the object of his love for pressing it upon him.

And then, too, it smacked of cowardice, of a request to be let off the hook – and laying that at the door of the boy wrapped in the guise of partnership was unconscionable.

So instead of going to the café or the docks to look for his friend, or using the phone to call a summit conference, he made a cup of tea in silence. In the tradition of sergeants he stewed it orange-brown and loaded the cup with sugar so that it was less tea than it was a rich liquid caramel filled with tannins and caffeine. You could have used it for caulking.

With this in hand, he returned to the comms room and rested his backside on the trestle table. He took a sip and winced at the sickly, too-hot stuff as it mixed with the saliva in his mouth. He swallowed. Seven cups of black tea a day increased your risk of prostate cancer, he'd read somewhere, and drinking liquids above a certain temperature did the same for the sort you got in your throat. If it wasn't one thing, it was another.

He glowered at the filing cabinet, listened to the background hum of the hard drive.

'I see you,' he said.

He opened the top drawer, and began to read.

19. Fleet

Next to the comms room was a large high-ceilinged space which had been the operations section back when Mancreu still merited operations, and before that the map room of the colonial house. Victorian Mercator maps complete with sea serpents decorated one wall, but the other was a single blank space twice the height of a man. It was a perfect canvas, he thought, for making information visible and tangible. He fetched a stepladder.

By sunset he had covered the whole wall and was still working, pins and colour coding and lines of ribbon and tape making a webwork across the paint. On one side he had already been forced to create more space, bringing in a whiteboard and some Blu-Tack to continue the chain of inference and connection out into the room. Satellite images and actual schematics of different ships were piled at the foot of the whiteboard waiting their turn. He stretched lines of string and wire through the room and stapled the sheets together over the top so as to make a completely immersive experience. Finally, realising that he needed an actual chart of the ships and their relationship to one another, he turned to the map. The British Empire stretched pinkly across a great swathe of Africa and Asia.

This is all your fault, anyway.

He clutched up a brace of images of the merchant ship *Young Eidolon* and drove the pins in hard with his thumb. Who owned what. What went where, what did it do and why.

Pride of Shanghai II, liner, retired. Slave ship, bulk transfer rather than bespoke. Temporary goods warehouse. Somali registry.

Life of the Party, factory ship out of Delaware, converted in Newcastle. Pleasure yacht: an offshore brothel and drug den for an international clientele. Mostly what it seemed to be, occasional staging post for political rendition within Asia. Probably Chinese.

Champs Elysées, Very Large Crude Carrier, now a prison ship. Owned from the Horn of Africa, almost certainly a US proxy vessel, but they wouldn't say, not even – or not especially – to the Brits. Unconventional interrogation and long-term detention for unreportable prisoners and persons too damaged to be tried in public. Oubliette.

Benthic Minogue, pocket dreadnought. Unsubtly disguised iron hand in the Fleet's glove. Deterrent. Post-Soviet retcon.

The *Reluctant Alice*, hospital ship. Former whaler. Non-legal medical treatments, reconstructive surgery, organ harvesting and corpse disposal. Also chemical, electroshock and deep-brain stimulated questioning. Brainwashing. Owned by a transnational infrastructure and security company through a variety of cutouts. Parent entity in Iceland, kindly staff speaking good English with Canadian accents.

The paper forest grew up and up and out. More ships, more connections. There were always more, possibilities the Fleet itself probably had not understood. Did the German government realise it was paying two separate services to spy on one another from each end of the bay? Did the Japanese know that their drug-enforcement team was entirely in the pocket of a Kosovar smuggling ring pretending to be a French Interpol squad – and pretending so well that it had scored some notable successes against its own side? It was chaos. And in the chaos, here and there, was Bad Jack: doing favours, greasing the wheels, carrying water. Nothing worked properly without Jack. It must drive them all crazy, except that it was so convenient.

The Sergeant found he was surprised by none of it; suspected sickly that no one would be, that no one would care if he sent it to Channel 4 by overnight bag. A brief scandal, questions in the House of Commons and a lot of braying from the front-bench donkeys on either side of the aisle, and then on to the next thing.

The exigencies of security in the post-9/11 world. A nod and a wink: you got caught, but of course we'd have done the same.

I could have known all this weeks ago. But it wouldn't have helped. These were national secrets, and they were big and awful and dull. The small ones – who killed Shola and why? Who sold guns and bikes to the shore? – were too trivial to be written down.

But not to be spoken, he realised. Small secrets still had to be shared with those who needed to know them, and while there would be no transcript of those conversations, the fact of their occurrence would be noted.

He looked for signals traffic.

Found it.

There, at the time of Shola's murder, jots and tittles of radio. But not one vessel, not one point of blame. No. A joint effort. He held the sheaf of papers in his hand, traced backwards in time, forwards, ran from one ship to the next with a red high-lighter pen, scrawling along the wall. He had the feel of it. This was a favour, and so was this, and here a debt was discharged. Five, ten, fifteen small IOUs were traded, cancelled out. Someone took on the job. It needed doing, so it would get done. He drew more red lines. Four minutes before the shooting. Twenty minutes before. Twenty-five, thirty, thirty-one. Here, there, and every-where, and look who's very agitated when it goes wrong. The red marker circled back around and around. There was so much of it. Too much. He would find out, but it would take days. He didn't have days. Shola's ghost was jogging his elbow: 'Lester, for God's sake! I can wait, I'm already dead! Find her! Find Sandrine!'

But it had not been a waste of time. No, this was how it was done, this was exactly the way. Signals and contacts. The briefest touches. Who was interested when Inoue spoke? Who responded when the seismographs twitched? Who would steal a damaged woman from her son?

A copper's first, last, and best question: who profits?

He ditched the red marker for a green one, started again. Endlessly and meticulously, he connected and pinned and sketched, knowing that to someone standing in the doorway he would look like a madman, a drooling Renfield hunting flies and spiders back and forth. Green ink zigzagged, looped. He discarded duplication and irrelevance, classified cables and incidentals, policy statements. Facts were everything, tangible and physical. Connect the dots. Here, across the plaster, there and back again. Numbers. Times. Signals. Ships. Over and over. His fingers cramped, tried to fail. He kept going.

Then there was nothing left in his hand. The files were empty.

He stepped back, and stared. And saw a monster's nest or a cave, a dark blot woven into the fabric of his map.

In the midst of a scaffold of tape and rubber bands, picked out by a weird inward spiral of indirect requests and stark green lines, was a single ship: the *Elaine*. She was registered out of the Virgin Islands, and flagged in the orange cabinet's files for special care and consideration. *Some things are more invisible than others.* Not owned, obviously, by the government or by any actual British firm, but by a shell company beneath a shell company beneath a corporate umbrella to keep off Liverpool's abysmal rain: a specialist facility working in the field of contagion and containment, making use – according to the company's relentlessly cheerful web page – of the Mancreu area for its 'unparalleled opportunities for advanced biomedical research'. And in that enthusiastic admission, and in the schematics attached to the file, he saw Inoue's tame team, unpacking her best efforts and recasting her conclusions: staving off Mancreu's end, but retaining the threat and therefore the legal vacuum around the island because it was convenient. Because the shadow that hid the Black Fleet was so very useful in this morally complex time. Because if the Mancreu problem was not really soluble, then at least that insolubility could be useful for other things – for all that discreditable business good chaps do to keep us safe in our beds.

Sandrine.

The Sergeant stared at the images of the *Elaine* and wondered if it was even possible. How could he invade a ship amid a host of others without detection, find Sandrine, and take her away without being seen? Without being himself detained and exposed? Without drawing down the wrath of his nation on the head of the boy he hoped to bring under its protection?

Or without killing. He was treating this as something for Tigerman, because he could only perform it as Tigerman, in Tigerman's mask. Lester Ferris must be a million miles away or the whole show was a dud. And Tigerman did not kill, or had not, and did not make his plans with killing in mind. The Sergeant, in the normal run of things, would expect to kill his way into this ship, loudly and messily, leaving no enemies behind him to close off escape. He would treat the whole thing as a building to be cleared, as a standard if dangerous tactical mission of a sort he had carried out countless times in the urban infighting of his other wars. And then being alone was just a matter of a bad ratio of friend to foe: move, clear, hold, repeat. Room by room, with the right equipment, the right ruthlessness and a following wind – and if he made the right guesses about security – he could hollow out the *Elaine* until it was just him and Sandrine. And then he would bring her home, leaving the ship a floating bloody hulk, in memory of its dishonourable service. The name of Tigerman would take on a sharper edge. Not just a crime fighter, but an avenging angel. He imagined the sticky slipperiness of the metal deck underfoot, and part of him made a mental note to choose the right shoes.

But that would end it all. Even in this pass, the boy would see the shift in him, in the fiction they had created together, from knight to dragon. He would shy away from a red-handed killer even in his gratitude. He had not seen Helmand or Baghdad. It would be new to him, and of all the things he had seen or heard about, it would most resemble Shola's death, with the Sergeant forever changing sides.

Lester Ferris saw himself gunning down a ship full of cheerful barmen, saw them explode backwards, saw a dozen ridiculous shirts billow and split behind the heart.

He pushed the image away.

Tigerman, then. It had to be Tigerman, doing things Tigerman's way. *A famous victory*, the Sergeant sighed to himself, *not an infamous one*.

He started again. What were the tools of Tigerman's world? How did one hero take on the hordes of evil? With almost supernatural skill – and he'd have to do without that – and guile. Diversion. Twice, now, in his confrontations, he had relied on explosions to get everyone pointed the wrong way, then come in fast and hit them very hard. Yes, diversion. Then also: reputation. When he had fought Pechorin's men, he had been let off the hook at that last minute because his enemy was scared of what he was reputed to be: a demon. And last night the rumour of his pursuit had run ahead of him, had somehow turned the mood of the riot until even the Quads had backed down. Reputation, momentum, and allies. He had had allies last night, sudden and unexpected: the crowd themselves, and then the boy's stooges in their firefighting gear. Could he find allies for this, too, knowing or not?

He looked back at the Fleet, at the tangle of interests and lies, and felt a new understanding take hold of him. *I saw the sky rolled up as if a scroll*.

The Fleet was one thing, but it was also many things bound in an uneasy union. They were opposed and they distrusted one another, and they were right to do so. Their coexistence was convenient, not perpetual. That fatal missile had scared Kershaw, had done the same to the captains of the Fleet. He could read their dismay and their amazement on the wall by the door, and that dismay was not assuaged by the fact that every single one of them displayed it. One or more of them could be lying, almost certainly were. It was hardly paranoid to wonder about a false-flag operation when you lived in the middle of the largest, most public, most permanent such scheme that had ever existed.

It was not that there were cracks in the alliance. There was no alliance, only a tenuous concert which lasted for as long as each ship held its station and each nation turned its eyes away.

So long as each ship held its station.

Which in turn called one to consider under what circumstances a ship might do otherwise.

Each vessel took orders from its home authority, of course, by whatever devious backchannels had been established. But operational control was passed to the individual captains so that local and immediate matters could be dealt with appropriately. It was bad practice to shackle your commander in the field to the whims and prohibitions of a faraway master.

If those captains were like soldiers on land they would be slow to waken when crisis struck after a long period of quiet, then overcompensate. They would mistrust one another because the likely source of any attack on a vessel of the Fleet was from within the Fleet. However good they were, these were the realities they lived with. They must ask: *who is my friend? Who is a threat?* and with so many players in the game in such close proximity, the ramifications of any change in the lines of power and alliance multiplied appallingly, possibilities and dangers expanding to every horizon in an instant. Every captain must ultimately accept paranoia, incomplete understanding or paralysis. The best would act decisively but with restraint. The others would dither and lash out, and in doing so they would further cloud the situation around them, each round of response and counter-response becoming more impossible to navigate.

One thing guaranteed a great movement of the ships in the Bay of the Cupped Hands: a storm. And if, during the preparations for such an event, when ties to the land were severed and all the many vessels must move out and around one another in accordance with the instructions of the Portmaster, one were able to inspire mistrust between them, and at the same time cause one or more to act in a manner which might be seen as a threat – say, by persuading the Portmaster to set them on what might appear to be a collision course – well, then, anything was possible.

The Fleet at rest was a glassy ædifice, smooth and unscaleable. The Fleet afraid was a chaos in which a single man with a clear understanding might do much.

If only one knew when a storm was coming, or could create one.

But then, the Mancreu Meteorology Station was an unmanned post a mile up the road, and the key was held in the offices of the former authority – the British Met Office, whose branch director had been a member of the consular staff. In other words, it was down the hall, on a hook.

By the predawn the Sergeant had a plan. Since discovery was inevitable, he would provide the *Elaine*'s crew with too much to think about, too many confusing imperatives, splitting their attention in as many directions as possible. First the warning of a sudden storm, then some explosives in a dinghy or two floating among the ships. Everyone would be out on deck and nightblind, seeing patterns in the waves and shadows, seeing other ships moving in unanticipated ways. They would simply have too much to pay attention to. While they were overstretched, he would sneak onto the *Elaine* and taser anyone he met, flashbang any large groups, until he got Sandrine out and they could escape into the confusion. It would be nice to think that no one would shoot randomly into the water, but he thought they probably would, so he'd need to head away from the main body of the Fleet. *Elaine* was out on the edge, anyway.

It was a bad plan. It was all he had. He would improvise the rest. He would need to be fresh for that.

The crushing weight of fatigue landed on his shoulders all at once. He pushed it away again, found grit somewhere deep down and clawed his way back into his own head.

Bad Jack. Arno. Kershaw. Pechorin. All and any of them might be added into the plan, for good or ill. *Lies are his hill country.* Quite. Not Arno.

Pechorin, then? But he was with Arno now, and Kershaw would trust only so far.

Which left Jack. Jack was in this. Back to Jack. He stared at the nest around the *Elaine*, the madman's curve of string, and wondered if Jack would yield to the same analysis. Except that he didn't have schematics for Jack. Jack wasn't owned by London. Jack, who had been Shola's boss. Who had been the target of the original attack. Jack who was everywhere. Jack Jack Jack.

He whispered it as he walked through the house alone, hearing his voice echo on the black and white tiles, the wooden boards, the white walls, hearing it inside his own head like a whistle, seeing brown swirls and circles at the corners of his eyes. Sleep now. But he was moving too fast, still thinking. He poured milk from a bottle and made Ovaltine, still in his mind called Ovomaltine because that had been the name on the giant tub of it his mother had brought back from France when he was little. He stood in the conservatory and looked at the tomatoes, wondered if he was fighting them again, their impossible thicket of fibrous green.

He drank deeply, tasted the dregs, felt the malted powder against his teeth. His father had been sparing with the contents of the tub, afterwards, where his mother had always been generous to a fault. In the end, guessing that this was more to do with an un-willingness to let the physical evidence of his wife disappear than with an actual preference, the young Lester Ferris had taken to buying refills and heaping them in when his father was watching television – but even with the tub mysteriously getting fuller with each month that passed, his father made the bedtime drink weaker and weaker. When Lester had moved out, he'd taken the tub with him. Still had it somewhere, back home.

He put the cup in the kitchen and went to his bed. There was a faint light on in the boy's room, the glimmer of a laptop screen. He paused, knocked. Should he explain about Shola? About death by IOU? No. Not now. Later it would be a final debt to be settled, but you did not burden your soldiers with side issues before the fight. That was how they died.

'Yes?' the boy said.

'Got a minute?'

The boy ushered him in, pointed him to the chair and sat cross-legged on the bed. His face was curious.

The Sergeant sighed. 'I need something and I don't know where to get it. I can't ask anyone else.' The boy nodded cautiously.

You're not going to like this. He looked for a way to say it which wasn't bad, couldn't find one. 'I need to talk to Jack,' he said.

'Talk to Jack?'

'To Bad Jack. Yes.'

The boy considered this for a long while, his eyes shuttered and perhaps a little dismayed. 'Talk to Jack? Why, talk to Jack?'

There were so many ways to put it, to soft-pedal what he needed. But he wanted to tell the truth. Finally he said: 'Superhero team-up issue.'

And saw the boy's eyes open very wide. 'Tigerman and Jack.'

'Tigerman. And Jack.'

The boy had gone off to work mojo. It was some pretty serious mojo, he said, and would need time. The Sergeant should go and do Sergeant things. 'Go Wayne,' the boy had said.

'Do what?'

'Wayne! Bruce Wayne. Be ordinary.'

Ordinary people did not have days like this. The Sergeant slept a little, then woke and went to see Inoue, because he didn't want to feel that he hadn't when he put on the mask. It wasn't good to have outstanding business.

Inoue greeted him with a strained smile. 'Did Kershaw ask you to come out?'

'No,' he said. 'Just doing my rounds.' *I came for you.*

She smiled bleakly. 'There have been significant developments in my work.'

'Significant.'

'In two ways. The next eruption will come very soon. Three days, perhaps less. Kershaw is aware. They will announce the evacuation later. But here, we are already packing. And I am most particularly to bring my things and not . . . talk about my views. At all.'

'You're in trouble?'

'Mm. Maybe not yet. But I am to understand that I can be if I want to experiment.'

'Then don't,' he said earnestly. 'There's enough trouble coming out of this already.'

She sighed. 'They will not give me a choice, I think. I am urgently required on a project back home. A very good one, apparently. There will be no time for me to oversee the departure here, I am to board a light aircraft later today. My luggage will follow. It has the form of a promotion, all very flattering.' Her tone made it clear she was not flattered.

He stood in front of her and felt cheated. He had somehow assumed there would be time. Where that time was going to come from he had, in retrospect, no idea. There was never time. He stared at her helplessly.

'Come,' she said abruptly. 'You must see the forecast data. It will help you understand.'

'I probably won't understand it, to be honest.'

She snorted. 'Don't be absurd. I will explain.'

332

She led him into the small, oblong room which was her private space. 'Ichiro!' she shouted into the hall. 'I need the big chart in two minutes.' The Sergeant heard an answering shout, and she shut the door. 'Sit.'

He sat.

Inoue unrolled a piece of paper from a cardboard tube and weighted it down in front of him with a stapler and a pot of pens. Then she turned. 'This is the pressure chart for the upper chamber,' she said. 'In the normal run of things I would now explain each spike and trough, and you would nod as if that meant anything outside of this building.' She drew a breath. 'But it is not a normal day and there is something I wish to make clear. I decline to go back home without doing so.'

She took a quick step towards him and leaned in, held his head between her hands and pressed her mouth fiercely against his. Her lips were narrow and strong. Her tongue flirted, teased. She opened her mouth in a frankly wanton invitation and growled happily when he accepted it.

And then she stepped back and it was as if the whole thing had been a dream. The door opened and Ichiro the genius came in, passed another tube to his chief and – with a rather approving expression – wandered out again.

'The eruption is coming,' Inoue said seriously. 'A big one.'

I should bloody think it is.

But he nodded. 'I understand.'

She fixed him with a stern look. '"I understand, *Kaiko*. And I have always wanted to visit Japan. Perhaps, *Kaiko*, I might come and see you when I travel."'

'Yes,' he said. 'That.'

'Good. You would be very welcome.'

She loaded him with technical information and sent him away. They exchanged a formal handshake in parting, on the same gravel drive where poor Madame Duclos's dog had landed on his car. All around, there was bustle and packing going on, and he drove back to Beauville feeling by turns elated and bewildered. How would he ever get to Japan? But on the other hand, why not? But what about the boy? And what if he was arrested? He couldn't use chopsticks, that was a concern. He could learn, of course: it wasn't like learning to play the violin. Japanese would be harder.

He listened to this strange, unfamiliar yammer in his mind and asked himself how long it had been since he had been truly interested in a woman, in her thinking and her laughter rather than just her body. A long time. Perhaps never. Not that he wasn't interested in her body. My God, he was interested. He couldn't believe – he could, actually, readily believe it, but he was appalled at himself – that he had not explored her even a little in that frozen instant. He hadn't wanted to grab. He suspected now that she would have been quite amenable to some grabbing, might well have grabbed back. Ichiro had been an alarm clock for her, he thought, as much as for him.

At Brighton House he found a message from the boy: *The Grande, side door, 7 p.m. It will be open. I am not invited. If there is trouble, I am off the books and off the hook. Do not lick anyone, they put drugs on their skin to make clients fall asleep.*

PS I am serious.

PPS Bad Jack is an end-of-level boss.

The Sergeant knew what an end-of-level boss was. He was the age to have played the original Space Invaders machines, the ten-pence-per-game uprights which had stood in pub corners and kebab shops, stained with grease and beer.

The end-of-level boss was the monster who came when you'd beaten all the easy ones and then all the hard ones: the kind no ordinary mortal could fight.

Kershaw made the announcement at four. Beauville would be evacuated first, any outlying settlements thereafter. The

334

boats would arrive in three days. Everyone would receive instructions and an evac number. Luggage was strictly limited. Livestock would remain on the island. The risk of infection was unacceptable.

People shrugged. It was old news, and Kershaw's authority seemed contingent now on the indulgence of the world, in a way it never had before. And the world was actually watching. There was no unrest. Instead, there was a curious anticipation, as if the people had done their part and now it was the island's turn. There would be a Cloud before the evacuation was complete, and that was one thing, but even more than that: Mancreu had decided not to give up. In the street of the card-players there were fresh flowers in the pots. The sweeper was back, hobbling and directing a small army of younger women. The press pack photographed her endlessly until she chased them away. They, too, were waiting for something they could not describe, knew in their fingertips that it was coming.

Three days was a long time. Anything might happen.

The Grande had been Shola's competition, at least up to a point. It was a not very grand sort of place at the other end of Beauville, close by the warehouse district and the road out along the coast. It was somewhere between a seafront bar and a brothel with a strong flavour of clip joint, but at the same time it was a real place which had regulars who drank and chatted. Dirac claimed, against all likelihood, that the wine was passable and the Thursday stew excellent.

The Sergeant had parked the Land Rover a few streets away and carried the mask in his pocket. He was wearing a long dark coat over his armour. He felt a little excited and a little absurd. The recollection of Inoue's kiss was still with him, lifting his mood.

He looked both ways and put on the mask, gasped a little at the smell of fear and exertion which clung to it, and at the sense of homecoming which burgeoned as he dipped his face into the dark. Always before he had to some extent been forced by circumstance. Now he felt he was choosing this, and with the choice came pride.

What they are saying about Tigerman, they are saying about me. They're wrong about all of it, but still.

I am Tigerman.

He felt it put authority into his step the way his uniform did. He rolled his shoulders and breathed out, letting the mask growl.

The side door was unlocked.

He went down a sloping corridor into a back room. The walls were dark red, and there were faded poles for the dancers, chrome flaking off them onto the illuminated disco floor. At the far end were two booths, one of them empty. A small fat man with no expression on his face gestured politely to the empty table. Perhaps he received guests in rubber masks all the time.

There was a single glass and an unopened bottle of water waiting on the table. The Sergeant doubted he was expected to drink it. It just told him where to sit.

The allotted seat would mean putting his back to a broad, still figure in a pea jacket at the next booth. He didn't particularly want to sit at all, tangle himself in a table. Bad tactics. But the scene was obvious: they would sit back to back, and they would talk.

Jack is analogue.

He sat down and waited.

'Good evening.' The voice was distorted, gargling. You could buy things in toyshops now to make you sound like whatever monster was dominating children's television this year. Godzilla. Vader. Voldemort. But under the growl it sounded almost affable.

'*Bonsalum*,' the Sergeant replied. 'I should call you Jack?' The mask's buzz made him smile. They sounded almost the same.

'Jack will be fine. What can I do for you, Monsieur Tiger?'

'I understand Shola worked for you.'

'Sometimes.'

'He was working for you when he died.'

'Perhaps.'

'Didn't that offend you?' They were working from the same script: *I am a knight, you are a monster. But I am not interested in you today.*

'It was commercial,' Jack said, with just the right amount of hesitation.

'Still. He was yours. He was killed.'

'True.'

'I might do something about it.'

'I would not object.'

'I have another piece of business that needs settling first.'

'I would be interested to hear about it.'

Just a flicker of intensity. Jack was in the mood to buy what the Sergeant was selling. *Gotcha, you cold bastard.* 'I need someone to vanish from Mancreu and end up somewhere else with a new identity. And I need to make the Fleet very unhappy for twenty minutes.'

Jack wheezed, and after a moment the Sergeant realised he was laughing. 'If anyone can do that,' Jack said, 'it is you.'

They both laughed then. It sounded like nails in an iron pipe.

They talked for ten more minutes, and then Jack said he would look into what was possible. The Sergeant got to his feet and went to the door. He looked back over his shoulder and realised that the pea jacket had been thrown over a mannequin. He went back and poked at it curiously. A narrow speaking tube emerged from the wall and lay in the dummy's lap. He shrugged a Tigerman shrug, and turned on his heel. The coat billowed around his calves in ironic salute. It was almost fun.

When he went outside, there was a storm on the horizon: a great band of looming rain and lightning, two hours out at most.

20. Admission

I t happened sometimes, and he had relied on that. No one would have questioned his meteorological fraud because it was a known risk, a pattern in the weather having to do with the Somali Current and the temperatures in the Persian Gulf. A monsoon wind calved from a bigger storm would spin off from Socotra and rebound south and east, then meet the wind blowing off the Indian Ocean and suddenly something like a cyclone blew up almost out of nowhere.

It happened. That was a given, indisputable. And it was happening now. He hoped Inoue was safely away, that she wasn't flying into that. He saw her in his mind, drowning in the aisle of a tiny plane sucked down into the deep black water. Her fear. Her regret.

He shook his head inside the mask, growled and heard it echo down the empty street.

The Fleet would be preparing to move. Beneseffe would be scurrying to provide the ships with estimates and safe distances, dispositions and instructions. Exactly as planned. Except that everything was planned for tomorrow, and the thunderheads would not wait. What he had thought to fake was real, and jogging at his elbow, and he must keep up or be swept aside. Every plan was overtaken by events. Some few were overtaken before they had begun. He had chosen a plausible scenario to hide under, and here that scenario had come true. So. That was the world, and he was in it.

He snatched the mask from his face and ran for the Land Rover, heard the tyres screech as he hit the accelerator, and let himself reconsider the plan as he hurled the car up the hill.

There had been no time to seed paranoia in the Fleet captains. He weighed the pros and cons of a call to Kershaw quietly suggesting some outrageous betrayal, asking that Kershaw keep it under his hat until the Sergeant could confirm. *The Chinese are coming to take North Africa for its oil.* That would do. It was insane but not absurd. China was hungry for resources, had been buying rare earths and shale gas reserves everywhere. The American hawks would believe it. India and Pakistan had night-mares about Chinese expansion. The Chinese would know it wasn't true but would worry about where it was coming from. The Europeans would try to cool things down, but individually each nation would be trying to gain advantage.

And telling Kershaw was like whispering in the ear of the Fleet, talking too loudly at the next table. Although it might conceivably start a war somewhere, which would be a crime on a level for which the Sergeant did not have a word.

The road was slick. He had to pull back from the urge to accelerate. Brighton House was seven minutes away, but it would be much longer if he went off the road. More haste, less speed. In his rear-view mirror, Beauville lay quiet against the sea and the hills. The warning howled in him, the bone-deep certainty: something is bad. Something is not as it should be.

I am holding the gun by its barrel.

He could feel the edges of it, knew it for a real thing. But until it was clear, he had to keep moving, keep advancing, because if he stopped now the window of opportunity would close – and the opportunity was there, he knew that, too.

Already the storm was ominously close. He needed to be in the water, sneaking between the ships. He needed to talk to Jack again, revise the plan. Half of him wanted to turn around and go back to the Grande, but the wiser part knew there would be no Jack. Jack did not hang around, could not afford to. Arafat, it was rumoured, had never slept twice in the same bed. Jack was more invisible, more cautious, in a smaller place and with a less loyal following. He was somewhere else by now, if he had ever been in the room at all. The speaking tube suggested that he had, but there might easily have been a radio on the other end.

Lester Ferris snarled and thumped the steering wheel. Everything was obvious. Nothing was simple. He was trying to hold it all together with his mind and his will but the pieces were not elastic and they were pulling away, coming apart in his fingers.

He had the gear, at least. He was getting through the armoury's supplies, but he was nearly finished. God knew how he'd account for the wastage. The riots, perhaps, and some shipping errors. A timely fire. Opportunistic crooks among the refugees. Small potatoes for now. At worst, he'd just say he'd grown bored and tried the stuff out, offer to pay for it. It would be in character. So he had grenades, a couple of inflatables with outboards, remote detonators and flares for his diversion.

Which left Beneseffe. A bribe might be out of the question now, he might just have to go in there and stare him down. What if Beneseffe regarded his job as a sacred trust, or if he was more frightened of the Fleet than he was of Tigerman?

Will you make him afraid? And then trust him not to betray you when you have gone? Or will you tell him everything and hope he doesn't sell you to Kershaw or Hasp?

Gravel crunched under the Land Rover's wheels, and he put the handbrake on too hard, felt it complain and shudder, released the brake a little and ran for the door.

Inside the door he stopped cold. There was someone waiting for him, and it wasn't the boy. He could tell from the feel of the place, the nature of the quiet. The refugees had moved to the far wings, and the house murmured with them, but his little space was still his own. None of them came here without asking. The boy did, but he was at home here and his presence was calm and unobtrusive. This was not him. It wasn't soldiers, either, with an arrest warrant, or Kathy Hasp hoping for more indiscretions.

For one moment, the Sergeant thought it must be Jack, then he hoped it was Inoue, and then he was terrified it might be Inoue, because he would have to get rid of her or tell her everything and he could not get rid of her. Could not. If she was here she had chosen to miss her flight out, and something in him would not permit the vandalism in turning her away. It would – he was amazed and delighted to find – break his heart.

He had given himself most improvidently in these last weeks.

It was neither of them. He knew as soon as the other man moved. He could hear the breathing, the sigh of effort with each step.

White Raoul.

He was alone, and he had abandoned his crutch. Perhaps he no longer needed it, or perhaps for moments of great significance he rejected it. The Sergeant was amazed by the force of certainty that he carried. It was like meeting a general in your living room, an unexpected eminence too big for the space. He wondered how much courage it took for the man to stand there. The scrivener could tell the world, if he chose, who had made the Tigerman stele – and for whom. Was it courage or trust that let him stand there unafraid of the man who wore it and did mad things? Because surely men had been murdered for less dangerous knowledge.

There was no time for whatever this was, but the Sergeant was caught in it, and somehow it was of a piece, it was important.

'I ain't here to stop you, Honest,' White Raoul said. 'I think you're crazy, but I ain't going to tell you to stop. You done well enough, I guess.'

The Sergeant nodded.

'And now you goin' to do some other fool thing for that boy.'

'Yes.'

'Honest, you are a very strange man. You ever consider just telling him you love him like a son?'

Considered it every day. But never done it, and it was hard to say exactly why. Well, no, it wasn't. 'Too scared, I think.'

341

White Raoul snorted. 'Face down guns. Can't talk to a boy.'

'Seems funny when you put it that way.'

'You need practice, is all.' White Raoul eyed him. 'Why don't you tell me now? What you'd say to him if you weren't too chicken. I'm his grandpappy, after all. If you die out there, someone oughta know.'

'Not planning on it.'

'Tcha. Whoever does?'

And this logic seemed abruptly unassailable. 'I'd say . . . what would I say? I'd say he's my friend. He's not the sort needs a dad like a straightforward sort of dad, not any more. But he needs a place to hang his hat. He needs a bed and a roof and someone to dust him off when he falls, take him out for his first beer. He's probably had his first beer, I suppose. But his first beer as a man. You know what I mean. And sort him out when he gets in a tangle over a girl. And teach him how to change a tyre, or . . . well, I suppose he can do that already too. And he knows computers, which I don't.' He was drying up. What exactly could he do that the boy couldn't do for himself? Not much. 'I can show him how to be the right sort of stupid. How to put your hand in the fire for someone you love. I can do that.' *I do that quite well, it turns out.* 'But I think I just want him to know he doesn't have to be alone. I don't want to buy him, I want to give him whatever I can. Me. For a dad. For however much he needs me.' He hung his head. It sounded very small. 'I just want to be there to help. To be who we are. I don't care where. Mancreu. London. Japan, even. I do wonder about Japan. He'd like Japan. They have ninjas there, and crazy blokes who go scuba diving to rescue their mothers-in-law, and temples and Zen and that. It's been amazing being a superhero, by the way. It's totally mad. But I don't need it. I don't want to be this . . . character. Not much. What I want . . . I want to be his dad. And that's all.'

White Raoul gazed at him, then walked wordlessly past him to the front door. Shuffle, clump. Shuffle, clump.

'Well?' the Sergeant demanded. 'You wanted to hear it. You said I needed practice. How did I do?'

White Raoul shrugged. 'Lied about that,' he said.

The Sergeant had no idea what he might mean. Lied about what? And then he felt his stomach vanish into his boots, felt an explosion pass through him from his chest to his fingertips, and, turning, saw the boy in the doorway of his room.

They stared at one another. *How did I do?*

The boy swallowed. 'The storm,' he said. 'You need to talk to Jack.' He ran forward then, slammed into the Sergeant and embraced him. 'You need to talk to Jack. Promise me!' He pressed a square of paper into the Sergeant's hand, then unwrapped his arms and stared in what looked like absolute despair at the man who said he wanted to be his father, and ran pell-mell from the house.

'Follow him,' White Raoul said.

But there was no time. Somehow, recently, there never was.

In preparation, the Sergeant put the gear in the back of the Land Rover and prayed with foxhole devotion that the car would not be struck by an errant bolt of lightning. Between the phosphorous flares, the gas and fuel for the inflatables and the box of ammunition and flashbangs he proposed to use to create a credible threat, he reckoned they'd maybe find the roll cage and the engine. But a human body at the heart of the fire would to all intents and purposes cease to exist.

He realised that not long ago the idea would have seemed almost restful. He had not wanted to die – very much not – but the notion of being smoke, blowing over the island and chasing the wind, would have appealed to him in those strange endless days when he had been somehow absent from himself.

He placed his call to Kershaw, dropped hints about 'possible non-allied East Asian involvement in the Mancreu theatre through proxies under cover of existing and legitimate false-flag water-based operations' and hoped the intelligence analysts at NatProMan were creative enough and nervous enough to decide it was something to worry about. When they asked later, he thought, he could claim he had received information from a local source acquainted with activities in Mancreu's shadow world – that would be Jack – and passed it on. If the tip was bad, well, that was informers for you.

Which meant he was as ready as he could be. Gear, diversion, storm, exit strategy. As long as Jack had good things to say about it all, even in a hurry.

Bad Jack, Bad Jack.

Jack is analogue.

Bad Jack. Jack Jack Jack. He muttered it over and over as he drove, glanced down at the paper in his hand. An address. A bad address, for Bad Jack.

The Hotel Vulcan.

The Vulcan was a big, empty slab of concrete like a parking structure, hard by an overhanging cliff. It had been intended as a bit of luxury, a stopover for the jet set. Break your cruise at the Vulcan. Party in absolute privacy, play in the casino, no paparazzi allowed. It had a James Bond look from back when Connery had had the role, as if it might at any moment unleash a space rocket into the atmosphere or gape to reveal a diamond raygun. And it was derelict, or supposed to be, because the money had run out almost before the thing was finished. A rockfall during one of Mancreu's fiercer seismic events had sheered off one wall of the main structure – incidentally revealing that the contractors had not used specified materials and the whole thing was unsafe – making it into part of the island's landscape as much as the empty chemical plant on the other side. In another place it would have been a spawning ground for Mancreu kids looking for somewhere to go crazy, but Beauville was filled with those and the Vulcan was genuinely inhospitable. So it was just there, like a backdrop.

There was a utility entrance halfway along the cliff road. When the Sergeant pressed his palm against it, the door swung open soundlessly. He made sure the mask was in place and went in. A light burned somewhere ahead, but the corridor was black.

You do love your underground hideouts, don't you?

He felt the chill again, caught a flash of understanding as it surfaced in his mind. He reached for it. Corpse-white and alien, the idea slid away from him into the dark.

He went on.

The sound of his own breathing echoed, reassuringly vile, from the walls. He was careful, checking the path ahead for trips and plates, letting the sound and the airflow tell him there was no one sneaking up behind. The sharkpunch lay along his hand. But that wasn't it. This wasn't a trap. Not this.

He saw the monster again in his mind's eye and let it flee, let the rhythm of his steps take him inside his own head. *What are you afraid of? Where's the dance going, that you don't want to be?*

Tigerman, the boy, Jack and Sandrine. Kershaw and Dirac and the Fleet. Inoue, but she wasn't in it, she was near it, through him and not. Raoul. Mancreu, Beauville and dead dogs. The dogs were bad, but this place was worse. He didn't know why, knew that he should. The Vulcan. Vulcans. *Star Trek*. Romans. Gods . . . None of that. Sean Connery, that was the heart of the problem. Sean was bad news. Sean and Vulcan and the underground hideout. Jack, and the photograph in the cave: the boy and Shola. Pechorin and the killers and Sean Connery in his dinner jacket. The missile. There's always a missile, always a ticking clock, always a double agent and a beautiful girl who needs saving. Pechorin released by Arno. Pechorin, who might be undercover. *I tell you another time*. Where had he got the heroin? If it wasn't his, had he seized it? Stolen it? And the photograph of Shola along with it? How had he known about it? Someone had told him, had let him know. Jack, of course, Jack who knew everything, setting up Pechorin as his cat's paw. Jack, who used everyone, who was everywhere, who saw everything.

Pechorin, and the cave, and the night which had forced him to be Tigerman in earnest.

Which he had enjoyed, and been terrified by, and which he had wisely put away because it was mad. But someone had made it news and the press had come.

But then he'd had to do it again when the Quads came and he took in the refugees – and where had the Quads come from, with their shiny bikes? Just like Shola's killers, out of nowhere. And he'd been a hero right in front of those cameras, and Mancreu was in the news again, right now, when it was dying.

And now Sandrine needed saving and here he was again, because it let him be who he needed to be. But he had not exactly chosen it, had he, more been chosen *by* it. Tigerman thrust upon him, oh, yes. Reluctantly made a hero. Helped along, every step of the way, his paths made obvious and unambiguous by love, and need. Helped, or herded.

The corridor broadened into the lobby. The lobby of the Hotel Vulcan.

Vulcan and Sean Connery. James Bond and the space-rocket hotel.

Bad Jack's home. His secret base.

Secret Vulcan base.

No. Not quite.

His secret volcano base.

Oh, please, no.

He stepped into the room, and knew he was right.

The lobby was a huge open space, and along the inner edges it was still very much itself, a little cracked: gold chandeliers and a huge pop art rendering of Marilyn Monroe singing for Kennedy printed onto one wall. The outer section was gone, and the huge plate of stone which had cut it away made a tolerable seal against the concrete and rebar. The space was neatly kept, and forty yards along a side. The furniture from the casino had been dragged here, so half of that was roulette tables. The light was from looped industrial working lamps. A thick trunk of cable ran out beneath the cliff and was probably spliced into Mancreu's power grid out at the main road.

At the far end of this space was a bed, a work desk with a familiar old laptop, and a selection of bookshelves. Some of these were occupied by digital Betacam cassettes. *Yes, of course. The video from the cave. You made it, you put it out.* These days you could buy a transmitter on eBay, and they weren't big.

And all across the carpet, some in random piles and others in perfect neat lines and grids, were comic books, and a dozen chairs and cushions and tables to read at.

He even told me. 'Many floors underground in my secret volcano base. I drink brandy, wear a smoking jacket.'

The Sergeant took off his mask.

'Hello, Jack,' he said.

'Hello, Lester,' the boy replied.

It's not a monster at all. It's just the end of the world.

'Is she out there?' the Sergeant asked after they had stared at one another for a while. 'Sandrine?'

'No, of course not,' the boy said. 'She is back on the hillside. The town makes her crazy. Crazier. Everything is too big. Too loud. I sent the jeep, the woman. They sang to her and she went with them. It works sometimes.'

The Sergeant nodded. *Yes. I see.*

'She cannot,' the boy began, and choked. He tried again. 'She cannot be anywhere else. Do you understand? For her, this is the whole world. It is all she is. They cannot evacuate the island. She will still be here, even if we take her away. And in a camp, while they make forms and argue, she will die.' His voice harshened. 'And it is a lie! It is unnecessary. Worse, it is stupid. They say it will save the world but Inoue says it will not. I read her reports. All of them. It will not help and they will do it anyway because it is some stupid game! To make law and then hide from it and pretend that is good. And for this stupid game of law they will kill my mother. Throw her away like trash. Because they have no better answer than to explode her home.'

'So what did you need me for?'

A flash of shame. 'We were friends.'

'I thought so.'

'That is real! We were friends. But I needed magic. And you are magic.'

'I'm just some bloke!'

The boy shook his head. 'Not any more. Lester Ferris is a real hero.'

'Bollocks. You did it all. You made it happen.'

The boy shook his head. 'Some. I laid a path. But you were more, always. You made it real. The riots, the cave. And you saved my life. In Shola's.'

'And you finished the job.'

'Yes.' Not a hint of doubt. *Yes. I killed the men who would have killed me, who killed Shola.* 'I made it so that they would die. I let it be known that they were talking, and something must be done. That is how it is. Something must be done, and it is.' He sighed.

'I am Jack. Before, there was another Jack. I worked for that man, carried messages. I know everything because no one pays attention to me. I know how it works. Then he Left with his money and now there is me. I trade. I do business. No one can find Jack. I make silly voices down tubes. I am analogue. I am a shadow. Without Jack, nothing can happen. So they must deal with me. But someone did not want to. And they found me.'

'Someone?'

The boy shrugged. 'The Fleet. Someone. The photograph is me, not Shola. I am the target, the bullseye.'

348

'Do you know who?'

The boy nodded. 'Yes. It is the same, you see? Something had to be done, so it was done. I must die, so an attempt was made. That is the Fleet. There are no people. No one breaks the law! It is just what is necessary and very sad. Shola was collateral. Great shame. The island will burn and my mother will die. Very sad. Film at eleven, drinks and dips.

'But Jack is Jack. In Jack's world there are orders and people who give orders. It is personal. You want to know who? The Fleet. The Fleet killed Shola. And Jack does not forgive. So I will kill the Fleet. Shola was my friend and there was no reason . . .' He blew air through his teeth in a hiss, tried again. 'There was no reason for that! No reason at all, just stupid! Why would anyone—' He swallowed. 'You stopped it. You saved my life and I saw you and I knew. I knew everything then. I had another plan, before, but it was weak. Tigerman is full of win. Tigerman is everything.'

'Tigerman is a joke. Here today, gone tomorrow. A madman in a funny hat.'

'Not so. Tigerman is everyone. He fights crime! He walks through fire and saves the innocent. He burns up drugs. He stops riots.'

'Your riots.' Dog-killing, because it would upset the English in particular, and the BBC would have to cover it. And because Sandrine hated dogs, he realised, remembering the cobblestone and the mongrel. She was afraid of them, the way some people are afraid of spiders. Everything serves twice. Three times. Nothing is one thing. Everything is the story.

'Not mine. Mancreu's. You cannot make riots. Only make the possibility. You cannot control them. Real riots, real fire.' The boy stretched out his hand for a moment. 'Real Tigerman.' He left the hand there for a moment as if he hoped the Sergeant would take it, but it did not come within reach. Then he straightened and drew his hand back. 'And tonight he will expose the Fleet.

He will show the world. Live on TV! We interrupt this programme! It will be known: this is what is done here, under the cloak of law! Made possible by the nice countries, in the name of the good people. This place is a convenience for killers and torturers and tax evaders and drug bankers, for scum of the earth. But Tigerman will not stand for it! He will not back down! Because he knows what is right.'

'They'd blow my fucking head off!'

The boy nodded. 'Yes. They would. Lester Ferris, the hero of Beauville many times over, killed by his own side for being a good man. Close-up pictures. Scandal! He gave his life for a cause, for a people who had made him their own. You see? That is a story! And there is continuity. There is shape. First the cave, then the footrace, now this. And then I would say you gave me something for if this happened, and I would read Inoue's report. "Mancreu need not burn." Tigerman's last will and testament. "This mess was made to order. It is a lie from the beginning. The island need not burn, but if it *might* burn then it is an un-place and all the dirty deeds can be at home here." Two weeks ago, no one would care. Today, from Tigerman? It is the greatest show on Earth! Now tell me they would carry on! Tell me they would dare, after Tunisia and Egypt and Libya, after Khaled Saeed and Mohamed Bouazizi! No. No. People would march around the world. *Tigerman for ever! For Mancreu!* They would. It is a great story. Everyone wants to touch that kind of story.' He punched the air, then slumped. 'Already there are shirts. Shirts, and a band in Kentucky. By tomorrow there will be dolls. In six months, a movie. And it would have been an Oscar winner, too.

'I was going to buy my island with your death, you see. But now, not.'

The Sergeant dragged air into his lungs. He felt as if he was carrying the whole island on his chest. 'Why not?'

The boy threw his hands in the air. 'Because White Raoul tricked me! And then he tricked you! He is a wicked, deceitful old man who thinks he is wise, and now words have been spoken and it is impossible to unhear them!' And then his voice caught, with emotion or puberty or a little of both, the Sergeant could not be sure. '*Why couldn't you come before?*'

'I'm here now.'

'Too late.'

'It doesn't have to be.'

The boy nodded as if this was a perfect statement of despair. 'I am a leaf on the wind,' he intoned.

The Sergeant had no idea what this meant. He said so.

The boy looked at him as if he were a barbarian or an idiot. 'Stay here. I will show you.' He walked to the door through which the Sergeant had come in, and closed it behind him.

A few moments later the Sergeant realised he had locked it and taken the car.

His first reaction was a sort of weary resignation. He was, genuinely, not cut out to be a costumed hero. This proved it. You'd never see the pros in this situation. Batman would never have managed to get himself locked into a dilapidated hotel lobby while someone nicked his car, any more than Superman ever woke up and found that Lois Lane had sold naked pictures of his body to the tabloids. Not even the Blue Beetle had ever had to deal with that sort of crap. But here he was, and the person who had created him, the evil boy genius who was both his herodaddy and his nemesis, had turned the key and left him standing by a plastic fern like a pillock.

It occurred to him that he was upset about this because for as long as he concentrated on it his heart would not actually break into a thousand pieces and kill him.

And then it occurred to him to wonder where the boy was going with his vehicle. Away, obviously, although there was nowhere which was away enough for a moment like this, for discovery and revelation and the end of a friendship.

Some part of him objected that they had never truly been friends, they had been something else, and the distinction was important. But leave that aside for now, the car was worrying at him, and the locked door. Away, yes, was a fine place to go when you were in pain, but where away? The boy was escaping in possession of a car full of explosives and equipment. Well, so. A child driving a load of military gear was no more likely to crash than a child driving anything else.

Not friends. Something else.

And the boy was not fleeing with the nearest vehicle to hand. He was answering a question. The plan, after all, was still a good one. It lacked only a sacrifice, a lynchpin. Would 'child-criminal emperor slain by Fleet' clinch the deal? It would certainly create a story, hours and hours of coverage, endless debate. Dead children always lead, always require soul-searching by organisations which on most days cannot locate their soul, let alone interrogate it. But someone would still need to deliver the coup, to accuse and to interpret.

Say, a heroic non-commissioned officer, recently seen in action helping fleeing refugees. And if that NCO also happened to reveal that he was the mystery man who had quelled a riot, who fought crime on those outlaw streets . . .

He stared in horror at the nearest table, at the papers spread out upon it like a map drawn for an idiot. Stages of a media campaign. And documents, too, showing his adoption of the boy, needing only his signature.

Not friends. We were never friends.

And now he thought about it: of course not. 'Friends' with your kids was a modern invention, the stuff of daytime talk shows and quality time, of that craven insistence that children make their own decisions while you lurked in the shadows to penalise the ones you didn't like. It was all so much nonsense. 'Friends' did not mean what it meant between adults, a balance of selves and strengths. It meant setting standards your children could not maintain, because if they could you wouldn't need to set standards for them. It meant child-rearing by remote and by phone. It was an abdication, for parents who never wanted to admit they were grown-ups, who dressed from shops which were too young for them and listened to the new music to stay in the swim.

To do the job right was something else, older and different and patient and endlessly enduring, something which got stronger the more it was clawed and scratched, which bounded and uplifted and waited delightedly to be surpassed. Which knew and understood and did not shy away from the understanding that there would be pain. Which could accept shattering, could reassemble itself, could stand taller than before.

No, not friends at all.

He laughed, and knew exactly what to say.

Jack.

I am your father.

He used the sharkpunch on the door, and stepped through.

21. Win

When this was over, Lester Ferris promised himself, he would never run anywhere, ever again. He would walk. For the bus, for exercise, for fun. In battle, even, if it should ever come up. He would just walk. He would never gasp, never burn like this again, with the heavy suit weighing on his shoulders and the mask's tongue flopping back and forth across his chest. Never again.

He had considered calling for help, but there was no one he could really explain the situation to, not with the Tigerman outfit on, and no one he trusted anyway. A child with a consignment of ordnance was a present threat, and would be treated as such. They would take him down from a distance and worry about the blowback later. The apparat had a long experience of blurring the deaths of children. *Male insurgent, not yet a full adult, killed in action*. And that was that.

So he had no one to call, and he ran: out of the utility door and down the hill, through the shanty and down to the waterfront. Some of the houses were burned, some of them were pristine, and some had scaffolding up as if the people intended to rebuild them, as if the island was not in its last hours. He reached the water without seeing anyone: the streets were empty. The rain was coming down hard now, and there was nothing for the press pack to look at. The Fleet was just a distant collection of lights, even if they'd been disposed to look at it, and nothing was happening outdoors. He was just a man running.

He reached the Portmaster's office, and went in, water streaming from his clothes.

Beneseffe sat in front of his communications gear, listening and talking, his voice very tense. The storm was rising and it had come in fast, the ships were out of place. Was he working them? Had the boy reached out to him? Or was he doing his best?

'I need a boat,' the Sergeant said, and saw Beneseffe jump. 'Give me a boat. Now.' He wondered whether it would speed things up if he shouted or did something violent, broke something.

'You're here,' the Portmaster said.

'Yes.'

'He said you would not come.'

'He was mistaken.'

In ten seconds, the Sergeant was going to tear him apart. He wondered if he could afford to wait that long. What if he was three seconds too late? Would he come back and kill the man? Wring his neck, and tell himself that was somehow absolution? *'It wasn't my fault, guv'nor, he kept me hanging on.'*

The Portmaster handed him a set of keys. 'Red button, green button. Then it drives like a car.' And then, with something like shame: 'Do what you can.'

Lester Ferris ran through the back door of the office and onto the dock, went out onto the black water.

The speedboat was light and strong, but the waves were higher than he had realised and it was terrifying. Twice the boat nearly flipped over before he learned how to make ground through the troughs and peaks, when to change direction and when to slow or accelerate. Even so, he was pounded with spray, and salt built up on the eyeholes of the mask so that he had to keep wiping it. Without it, he thought, he would have been blind. His clothes were sodden and heavy. They wrapped around things and billowed in the wind, trying to take him overboard. If he did go over, he would die. He was simply wearing too much that was heavy and would drag him down.

He could see the Fleet about half the time, had no idea how the boy might be doing or where he might be, but Jack was experienced on this water, knew the shape of the land and the shallows, knew the ships of the Fleet and might even seek shelter aboard one if he needed it. That might even be his plan for boarding: simply ask and be admitted, as a gesture of friendship. Sailors held to their obligations, even secret ones.

Jack. He tried the name in his head, didn't like it. Too much came with it. The boy was the boy, and that was that, and if he needed another title then it should be 'son'.

Son.

A wave took him in the chest, warm water slamming him, wind chilling him instantly until he shivered. His hands were clenched on the wheel of the boat; releasing them was harder each time, and so was closing them. He was already exhausted.

Then he was between the ships, in the lee of a pitted metal cliff which must be the *Pride of Shanghai*, watching it roll over towards him until it was actually sheltering the speedboat from the rain. The ship was sucking water in along its sides, huge stabilisers churning, and he spun away, leaned on the throttle. The boat almost couldn't cope, chugged and sputtered as water washed into the exhaust, blasted back out again.

In his mind there was a map of the Fleet, but it was out of date now and nearly useless. He remembered how it had been. He had intended to sit down with Beneseffe – or with someone – and work out an understanding of where the ships should be in relation to one another, how to reach the *Elaine* in the chaos. Now he was staring into the murk as the water got rougher. He had to get on board something soon, anything, or he would simply vanish below the surface, a stupid footnote, and the boy's plan would come to nothing. Or, not nothing. Because surely he had taken out insurance against the possibility the Sergeant would not play ball. White Raoul, no doubt, knew it all. Perhaps he had even been Bad Jack himself once. Perhaps that was how it had come about, how it had begun.

The sky howled, a first great blast of thunder. Thunder on the water was different: unmitigated by hills and trees it was a stunning hand of pressure closing in a fist around him. Even over the storm he heard the *Pride of Shanghai* reverberate.

And the sea answered, in a great whooshing column of white fire. Thermite or phosphorus or maybe both, and all he could think was that it looked as if God was coming up out of the ocean to deliver some kind of appalling justice and: *That's a fuck's sight better than custard powder.*

The Fleet seemed to think so too, because abruptly the night was a blazing webwork of searchlights and incomprehensible demands blared from massive speakers. Circles of white picked out the boiling muddle where one of the Brighton House inflatables had been, combustion still going as the incendiary it contained fell down into the depths, then off towards other ships: *Was it you, was it you? Did you do this? Why? What does it achieve? What do you know that I do not? What is your operation, your gain?*

The Sergeant knew to look away, and, squinting into the penumbra at the very edge of his vision, off towards a black hulk which ran even in this catastrophe with barely any lights, he saw a speck which might have been a half-brilliant, half-mad teenager trying to save his mother.

The second bomb went off a moment later, over on the other side of the Fleet, and something bad must have happened because a ship started sounding its horn over and over, like a donkey screaming in a marsh. *Dear God, he must have holed it. He can't have done. There wasn't enough stuff.*

But perhaps there had been more from another source. No doubt Jack could lay his hands on the necessaries. And close on the heels of that: *He can't have meant to.* In this weather, people would die. Rescue would be all but impossible and the captain would be under orders not to beach the vessel, not to expose the secrets it contained.

That was a score in itself, to drag the Fleet out from behind the curtain. And they were on stage now, for sure: the white pillars of flame would see to that. Kathy Hasp and her friends would be staring out of their hotel windows and calling their network bosses, letting them know that the Mancreu theatre was good for another impossible scene before it finally gave up. The plan was working and the story was alive. All it lacked was the big finish.

The night went bright again and the Sergeant was in the middle of a searchlight beam and someone was shouting. He couldn't see but he recognised the tone, the demand for surrender. *Yes, you prick, I came out here in this weather just to turn myself in to a bunch of confused wankers in the spook trade.* He gunned the engine and lurched away. If they fired at him, they missed, and they couldn't keep the beam on him in the swell.

He vanished, following the boy.

Elaine was a shadow against a background of night. Picked out occasionally by the desperate lights of the main Fleet, it skulked at the edge of the safe channel. Lester Ferris wondered whether that was for operational reasons, or whether whoever chose the station had been secretly ashamed that Britain, diminished now and unreconciled to the fact, should participate for power's sake in the slow slaughter of a place it had claimed and cherished in its high imperial day. He wondered if it had been Africa herself, or if she had simply been handed the mess and told not to interfere; if *Elaine* looked the same in her office as it did tonight, a dark ghost rolling on dark water, Brighton House's own bitter twin.

The crewmen were lowering a ladder. Whatever tactic the boy had used to gull them was working. It was a telescoping metal ladder with a motor, built into the structure of the ship so that it wouldn't easily tear away. The upper reaches had a cage around them, a wide tunnel of metal, but the boy hadn't got to that part yet and the sea was throwing the inflatable all over the place. It could end here, the Sergeant realised, and the boy must know that, must know this was an insane way to carry on.

The boy lunged, knapsack on his back, and the inflatable yawed away. He got both hands on the ladder, but his feet were still on the little dinghy and it was unguided so he might as well be hanging by his arms, and then he was, shoes trailing in the water, but he hauled himself up and went on, fast, as if this was nothing, as if it was just what he did. The Sergeant grinned as a sort of mad pride bloomed in him. The boy was doing a great thing. It was terrible and it was all kinds of wrong-headed and dangerous, but he was making it work. He was near as dammit leading the world around by the nose, and he was a genius and an action hero and everything he wanted to be. If it wasn't going to cost him his life the Sergeant would be inclined to let him get on with it, but you had to draw a line in bringing up a young person, and this was definitely on the far side of it.

Then the small figure reached the deck and was hauled aboard. How long before he started doing whatever he proposed to do to create a death for himself that would resonate? And for that matter, how would he transmit it? In the end perhaps he didn't need to, he could just incriminate the Fleet and let those left behind do the talking. Perhaps it could work if he just went off somewhere, to France, say, or Thailand, and bought a house. The Fleet vanished bodies all the time. But no: the full impact, the vileness, required a body. Or better, live footage. There would be a plan for that, too. If the Sergeant had been quick enough, he might have tackled this from that end, stopped the signal on shore and used that to leverage retreat. A parental stand-off.

Well, next time, eh?

Lester Ferris took the boat close as fast as he could, not wanting that ladder to retract before he was ready, then waited for the right moment, feeling the rhythm of the waves. The *Elaine* rose over him, then twisted away until it looked as if he might shortly be able to walk up it and get on board that way, then back – and he jumped.

His right hand hit the rung hard and he clenched the greasy metal, feeling the crosshatching grate under the rubber grip of his glove. He got one foot on the bottom rung, too, and then a perverse, sideways wave came in and nearly ripped him off in one go. He slammed against the side of the *Elaine*, fingers protesting as they carried his full weight, wet, with all that extra gear on his belt.

He wrenched himself back around and began to climb, felt the ladder tug under him, grind upwards. They were drawing it in. He hoped like hell it didn't automatically stow itself in some sort of flatpack chest. He pumped with his legs, running from rung to rung. Up above, he heard the first flashbang go off and knew it had begun.

He reached the top and threw himself forward just as the ship lurched and he was flying again, always flying through the air in this outfit, always landing hard. This time there was no one underneath him and he rolled to save his ankles, slithered across a slick deck and kept moving, waiting each second for cries of alarm and the impact of shots. A man appeared in front of him and he used the taser, low and fast like a knife strike. He hadn't even been aware of taking it from his belt. He glimpsed the man's eyes, absurdly clear as they rolled up into his head, then pressed himself into an alcove in the metal supports of the bridge. There had been no gunfire since that first explosion. That might mean this was still containable. It might. He looked towards the prow.

And saw the boy.

The *Elaine*'s captain had turned on the main floods for the boy's boarding and these were now doing duty as TV lights. The boy had brought his own camera, and it was sitting on a tripod with some sort of magnetic clamp which locked it to the deck. A short stubby aerial suggested it was broadcasting live, though whether it could get through the storm the Sergeant was unsure. But the boy would have thought of that, prepared for it. This was his big scene.

He was wearing ordinary clothes which made him look even more like a child than he usually did. Water flowed from his head down over his face, which was contorted in a desperate plea. In his off-hand, he held a radio remote for the camera which looked like every filmmaker's standard prop for a terrorist, but his body hid it from the lens.

There were four crewmen on the deck, woozy from the flashbang, but that might or might not come across on grainy footage of a lightning storm. The boy was shouting at them, bending his knees like any angry child, compressing and then bouncing in his insistence: a school footballer disputing the ref's decision with all his might. The Sergeant couldn't hear what he was saying, and quite certainly nor could the crewmen in the aftermath of the flashbang, so the monologue must be for the camera. He said it again, and again, hand pointing, and finally the Sergeant saw his mouth full on and read the words on his lips:

'Give me back my mother!'

Had he lied, then, earlier? Was Sandrine on board? No: she couldn't be, because this would not retrieve her. If the boy had been genuinely trying to save his mother from this ship, he would have done things differently. Lester Ferris tried to wrap his head around the bigness of the plan.

They cannot give him what they do not have. They cannot produce her, ever.

But when the dust settles, it will be seen that she was the woman who was kidnapped.

The woman Tigerman had chased.

A victim of the Discharge Clouds whose body might yield secrets.

It would seem inevitable that they must have taken her.

If they found her on the island and produced her, it would simply be proof that they had had her all along. The accusation would persist for ever, the investigations would go on, and the cruelty of killing her son would seem exceptional.

And when the Sergeant, or Tigerman, or both of them, delivered Inoue's papers to the wider world, the story would compound, becoming the story of how the Fleet had stolen a child's mother and then slain him, how even Tigerman could not stop it, how the great powers of the world had conspired to murder a boy in furtherance of their wretched, meaningless agendas.

Game over.

If anything could save Mancreu, it would be that scandal at fever pitch, delivered with perfect visuals through the news organisations and the Internet, scouring the world. Leaving the island unburned would seem a meagre enough first act of contrition.

The stunned men were extras, there to absorb the boy's accusations. The real antagonists in his story must be seconds away, a fire team who would be armed and very frightened, riding the fear with long practice and established orders, and the boy would provoke them, he would die, and it would begin. The Sergeant couldn't think of any way to deal with that, couldn't see a path which would get them both out alive, let alone uncaptured.

He felt footsteps in the decking, the vibration of booted feet.

His first instinct was to give himself up, explain that the boy was no actual threat – or, not on a physical level – and let the whole thing crash down. He might be able to salvage something from it. The surrender of Tigerman on live TV – by now, he had no doubt, this was on every station – ought to be worth some good ratings, and his notoriety might protect them both.

But they would not hear him. Keyed up and afraid, in the blinding rain – even assuming that they didn't shoot him down – they would not credit his assurances regarding the remote. And why should they? Out there somewhere a Fleet ship was taking on water, and there had been columns of fire in the night, and now Tigerman was on their ship, and the boy with him, and the whole operation was fucked up at best.

Lester Ferris could not prevent the fight. But he could draw fire.

So when the men barrelled past him towards the bright lights of the foredeck, he waited, then stepped into the middle of them and did all he could to take them down. He fired the taser again, then stamped and used his fists. He dropped two of them and then the remainder swamped him and they fell forward in a seething pile onto the deck, in the midst of the lights.

He felt a fist rebound off his armour and heard a shriek. He drove his forehead up into a man's face, rolled away as one of them finally started shooting, threw a gas grenade back the way he'd come. It was useless in this wind but they had no way of knowing what it was. They scattered, and he got to his feet and charged. He lashed out with the sharkpunch and it went wide, struck metal and the cartridge went off, sending shot zinging everywhere. A piece of it pinged into his shoulder and lodged in the meat and he yelled. He saw a man go down clutching at his leg. Then the aluminium tube went spinning away, and he walked into a succession of sharp blows like a drum tattoo, powpowpowpowpowpow, that went on for ever against his sides. Someone was hitting him, and doing it right. He dropped to slip a scything punch and weaved away, breath rasping, making space.

His opponent skipped after him, whip-lean and fast, and he realised it was a woman with a fine, peaceful face and short brown hair. He tried to circle and her knee moved, faster than he would have imagined possible, shot like a piston into his liver. She snapped away, off-axis, guard up to deflect his counter. She moved with the ship, her back upright and supple as the deck shifted. Naval training, and a lot of it.

One counter. A single punch in the time she took to land five. She's better than me. She's so much better.

363

Away towards the front of the ship the boy was playing to the crowd. He was good at it. He kept his face well lit, his body filled with hope, tension and need. *Give me back my mother. She is nothing to you. She is my life. Why would you take her? Will you sell her? She is very sick. Sell her to me! I will give you everything. Or take me instead! I am young, I can work, she is sick. Please. Why would you do this thing? Please, please, please.*

Give me back my mother.

The Sergeant felt more blows on his body, his legs. The peaceful woman was trying to numb the muscles in his thighs. Already the left one was agony. It would freeze soon, but if she hit the sweet spot he would just fold, and that would be that.

He was old and clumsy. He just didn't have the training for this. She was far, far beyond him. He wanted to tell her so, to give due respect to her skill and to buy her a drink. In another place, he would have asked her to teach him, just whatever she would for however long they had. But he was here and now, and the boy needed him, and skill was never the end of it. You could always shoot somebody who outdrew you. You just had to be ready to get shot. And he could see it in her, the faintest hint of frustration. He was armoured, yes, but even so he should have gone down by now. No one could soak this up for ever. Why wouldn't he go down? He wanted to tell her to take it easy, just wait, she was doing fine.

Instead he put his hands up like a good boxer, then when she came in he shunted forward stupidly, rode out the punches. When he lunged on his good leg, she was just a little too close. Fumbling, he seized her body beneath her arms, lifted. She was slight. He felt her tense.

You silly sod, he thought, vaguely, *if I was really your enemy you'd be up the creek now.*

She knew it, too, hammered at him violently, elbows and fists coming down onto his neck and back, but nothing like hard enough, not when a sergeant has put his mind to something. He looked for something to smash her against.

She reared up.

Just as the deck did, too.

She got the strike exactly right, deep into the muscle of one arm.

A second wave, out of rhythm with the rest of the sea, smashed into the ship and threw her high in the air towards the prow. She twisted, landed hard and rolled, came to her feet in the midst of the boy's perfect tableau, arms spreading in an arc like a seabird as she caught her balance.

As she collided with the one thing between her and the abyss.

And that one thing – small and lighter even than she, still holding the camera remote – staggered backwards and over the edge, and was snatched away by the wind.

The moment lasted for ever, and after it, nothing else mattered; not when Lester Ferris fell down on his knees and tore the Tiger mask from his face and screamed and screamed; not when they surrounded him and took him into some approximation of custody, marvelling and bewildered at who he was, and what was he doing here, and was this an operation they had somehow not been briefed on? Not even when they realised sickly that the camera had never stopped running, that the boy's extinguishing and the Sergeant's revelation had been beamed across the water to the shore and streamed live to a YouTube channel and gone out around the world, the most unrecoverable of security breaches contrived on the boy's own terms, delivering the best possible iteration of the scenario he had set out to achieve.

None of it mattered, and the Sergeant doubted it ever would again, because what mattered was down there in the threshing sea, and gone for ever.

By morning the storm had blown itself out.

The Sergeant was transferred to the custody of Jed Kershaw, who said 'Fuck, Lester' a very great deal. They emptied one of the storage rooms in the old prison and it became his cell. There was still a coffee machine in the corner, but it had no plug.

*

Out in the Bay of the Cupped Hands, a line of orange lobster buoys marked the shortest route to the land, and each of them sported a small, kludged-together signal relay by which the Tigerfall signal – it already had a name – had been transmitted to the boy's computers and onwards to the wider web. The Internet took this technical knowledge as a sign that the boy had belonged to its citizenry, and caught fire.

People came to visit. There were things they needed to say. Marie, who had been Shola's girl and his someday-maybe wife, came and said thank you, because at least he had tried to find out something and no one else had. The Sergeant said, 'Jack did,' and then felt like a fool. She nodded without saying anything.

Beneseffe came and brought fruit.

Kathy Hasp came and talked about what was happening in the world. There was a lot of it, and mostly his fault. But there wasn't going to be a war with China, so that was good.

Kershaw came back with a man from the embassy in Sana'a and they said a lot of formal things about lawyers. The Sergeant didn't listen. Kershaw said 'Fuck, Lester' again.

Dirac came and said nothing at all. When he left, he kissed the Sergeant lightly on the crown, and his cheeks were wet.

'You are kind of the biggest asshole in the world,' Pechorin suggested.

'Not even close.'

'That's true.' Silence. 'You did kick the shit out of me. And you exploded my nose.'

'Sorry.'

'I get over it. You ever find out who killed your barman friend?'

'The Fleet.'

'Sure. Everything is the Fleet. But you know who?'

'No.'

'Was Belgians.'

'Why?'

'Fuck do I know why. Maybe politics. Maybe just being Belgian. Is closure. You feel better now?'

'No.'

'Me neither.'

The Sergeant slept and dreamed fitfully about Madame Duclos, sitting alone in her little house without her dog. He pestered the nursing staff to let her know what had happened, but they were evasive. They seemed to believe it must be some sort of code. Finally Arno's man, Guillaume, came and told him she had been evacuated during the rioting and the house was gone. He agreed that the Sergeant could write her a letter, so long as he, Guillaume, could read and photograph it before it was sealed.

'It won't be very interesting,' the Sergeant said.

Guillaume politely disagreed.

Arno visited him then, and asked him a series of quiet questions which the Sergeant answered quite frankly. Arno shook his head.

'I should have seen this,' he said.

'You saw me instead,' Lester told him.

Arno sighed and nodded.

The story all came out. Inoue's report was headline news. The island did not burn. Not that day, and not that week.

On the fourth day of the hiatus, a Discharge Cloud wreathed the island in mist, and when it was gone the plants were all in flower.

*

A week later the boy's YouTube channel was hacked, and a new slogan was added:

Tigerman Make Famous Victory, Full Of Win.

Because they had never recovered the body, a few people took this as a sign that the boy was alive somewhere.

The Sergeant was not one of them.

Some time later, Mancreu was reprieved.

The ships of the Black Fleet vanished. Even the names turned out never to have been registered in the places they were thought to have come from.

White Raoul never spoke to the Sergeant again. The Witch came once to see him in his hospital bed. She tried hard to make him smile, but her face was lined and fraught, and he thought he had exceeded the capacity of her compassion.

He was shipped home.

He had expected Africa to be cold and official in her anger. He had pictured her as an aloof sort of person, tight lips and steel-grey hair. Instead she shouted, her voice cracking and then descending into a hiss, as if he were an unfaithful husband caught in the sack with a girl from the post office.

'You bastard!' she began. 'You stupid bastard! I will ruin you! I will take everything you have, and I will cover it in shit.'

Beside her sat a man in a suit who had identified himself as being from the Press Office. He didn't say whose, as if there was only one, and perhaps there was. He seemed to be waiting for his moment, and to be in no doubt that it would come.

Africa was still talking. 'You're a traitor! You're an actual traitor to the Crown! I'd send you to a court martial but they can't have you shot any more and I can! I can make you go away for ever. I'll send you to Morocco and they can cut your tiny fucking balls off in a hole somewhere and make you crawl on your hands and knees across broken glass.' She ran down suddenly, because she couldn't actually hit him and that was almost the only thing she had left. 'Were you at least sleeping with him?' she demanded. 'Was that what this was about?'

'I wanted him to be my son,' Lester said.

Africa laughed sharply and turned away. He thought she might be hiding tears, because anyone so angry must surely have them ready. 'Well, no one will believe that, at least,' she said. 'You're going to prison and everyone will think you're a pervert.'

The man from the Press Office cleared his throat. 'They *will* believe it,' he said.

She stared at him.

'They will believe it,' the man clarified. 'They already do. And we will encourage that belief. This may be a pig but right now it's got lipstick on it and it's our pig. We will not be pointing out that it stinks. Nor that it is something of a surprise to us to find that we own a pig. We will march it in triumph through the streets of the town, we will detail the painstaking care required to raise such an exemplary animal, and if we're very lucky by the time it goes back to the wallow everyone will think this was something glorious we did on purpose.'

'What do you mean, "march it through town"? Which town?'

The mild man frowned. 'Any fucking town which will take us, Laura, and believe me, we are already fortunate that there is more than one. But specifically: tomorrow at three p.m. at the Royal Society in Carlton House Terrace. The Prime Minister will be attending a talk by a French lepidopterist to emphasise his devotion to science, and he will by complete chance encounter Lester Ferris, sergeant, newly retired and the man of the hour, who has a lifelong fondness for the insects of the British hedgerow. There will be a brief and quite spontaneous greeting, a handshake, and everyone will go home feeling good about themselves. Do I make myself clear, Lester, or do I need to get

369

someone in your chain of command in here with my hand up their arse to puppet some orders?'

'No,' Lester said.

'And you,' the man told Africa, 'don't piss about. I'm saving your job and the honour of your service, insofar as it still has any in the eyes of the general public at this time. Do not even think about screwing this up or I will fall upon you with great fury and the weight of mountains. I don't see that I can make myself any clearer.'

They glared at one another, and then for a wonder she nodded, and stalked out.

'Be there at two forty-five,' the man said. 'So we can do your hair. Don't extemporise.'

The Sergeant realised he was a hero.

He shook hands with the Prime Minister. The man had no calluses, and his eyes were perfectly empty.

The Sergeant went back to his father's house and sat in the ghastly chair. He read comic books and laughed when they were funny. Every so often he turned around, looking for someone at his side who would enjoy the joke. Then he would remember and, in a fury, screw up the comic and rip it apart, only to find himself again a few moments later on his knees, tears all over the floor and tape in his hands as he pieced it back together. He had a stack of them like that. He refused to throw any of them away.

He tried to get work. It turned out to be very hard. The jobs which would otherwise have been offered to a retired soldier-diplomat were closed to him. A proven track record of insane idealism was evidently not a positive for employment by large financial institutions. He wondered whether Africa had put the word out, but he didn't think she'd have had to. The Brevet-Consul would have been a safe pair of hands, a man experienced in not rocking the boat. There were a lot of positions in the world for someone who kept his mouth shut and filled a comfy chair. Far fewer for someone who actually did what the job suggested he should.

A local school briefly took him on as an assistant teacher, but after the first day the press arrived in vast numbers. *DANGEROUS! Tigerman Sergeant Entrusted With Vulnerable Teens!* The headmistress asked him to come to her study and he expected her to let him go. Instead she told him stoutly that she had spoken to the parents and the board and they wished to convey their absolute support. The school would keep him if this was what he wanted – the press would get bored after a few weeks. She was bristling with rage and ready for the fight, and he understood that here, finally, he'd found a decent officer. But he'd already realised he couldn't stay. Every admiring face in the throng of students became in the action of blinking the face of the boy; the whole playground was a mute accusation he could not answer. So he shook her hand and told her the truth, and she embraced him. He left with a promise that he could return whenever he wanted to.

He was too shy for television.

In the end he settled to a sort of ugly mirror of his first days in Mancreu. He rose early, ran, and worked in the garden. He grew tomatoes, but they were weak and sallow and they died. The sun wasn't bright enough for the exotic plants he wanted to try. His morning route took him through grey streets he vaguely remembered, and they seemed more modern but not more hopeful than they had thirty years ago. The same estates were sinks. The same factories were closed, the same shops had smashed windows. He concluded that governments were like wars: the reasons and the faces might change, but it was still the same dying over the same soil. When he allowed himself to see it with his sergeant's eyes, the city seemed bent in upon itself like an addict. He looked for the enemy in the sky, in the wind, and saw just endless weight.

He realised that he could live like this until he died, outside the world. He had not reached the end of himself, he just didn't know what else to do. So he ran, and read comics, and wept, and that was all.

On the first day of December, the postman arrived with a letter addressed in a very correct script. He opened it immediately, as he always did: he had acquired a hatred of delay. It contained a short card and an airline ticket, representing a significant expenditure, in the name of Lester Ferris.

> Lester —
>> It's time.
>> — Kaiko

He sat for a while, cradling the paper in his hand. Finally, the inner sergeant took him upstairs, and ordered him to pack.

Acknowledgments

Driving in an implausibly enormous Toyota Hilux out of Chiang Mai, my nephews Chris and Dan and I were talking nonsense to one another. I have no idea what we were saying, but between one breath and the next this book was born. Thanks, guys.

Clare is always my first reader and my first editor. She denies having a particular talent in this direction. She is wrong about that, though about remarkably little else.

Clemency and Tom are just magic.

Patrick is wise, and into his orbit at Conville & Walsh are drawn other wise people, which is how the world ought to work.

Jason Arthur and Edward Kastenmeier continue to rein in my worser impulses – like using "worser" in a modern novel – and are calm and accepting when I stick to my idiosyncracies. Like Patrick, they have superb people around them.

A small team of test readers got early sight of this book, and they performed wonderfully: they said they liked it, and then very gently they pointed out where it was broken. You know who you are. Thank you.

And to everyone who patiently waited while I ran around looking for a pen or dictated a note to my iPhone during a meeting or stared abstractedly into space and then shouted "tomatoes". . . This is what it was all about.

Cheers,

Nick Harkaway
London, January 2014

Nick Harkaway

The Gone-Away World

'Breathtakingly ambitious...written with such exuberant
imagination that you are left breathless by its sheer ingenuity.'
OBSERVER

The Jorgmund Pipe is the backbone of the world, and it's on fire. Gonzo
Lubitsch; professional hero and troubleshooter, is hired to put it out –
but there's more to the fire, and the Pipe itself, than meets the eye.

Equal parts raucous adventure and comic odyssey, *The Gone-Away World* is
a story of love and loss; of ninjas, pirates, politics; of curious heroism
in strange and dangerous places; and of a friendship stretched beyond
its limits.

Angelmaker

'An entertaining tour-de-force that demands to be adored.'
INDEPENDENT ON SUNDAY

Joe Spork, son of the infamous criminal Mathew 'Tommy Gun' Spork,
just wants a quiet life, repairing clockwork in a wet, unknown bit of
London. Edie Banister, former superspy, lives quietly and wishes she
didn't. She's nearly ninety and the things she fought to save don't seem
to exist anymore, and she's beginning to wonder if they ever did.

But, when Joe is asked to fix one particularly unusual device, his life
is suddenly upended. Joe's once-quiet world is now populated with
mad monks, psychopathic serial killers, scientific geniuses and threats
to the future of conscious life in the universe. The only way he can
survive, is to muster the courage to fight and help Edie complete a
mission she gave up years ago.